YOU BE MOTHER

MEG MASON

First published in Australia in 2017
A later edition published in Australia in 2020 by
HarperCollins*Publishers* Australia Pty Limited

First published in Great Britain in 2021 by Weidenfeld & Nicolson,
an imprint of The Orion Publishing Group Ltd
Carmelite House, 50 Victoria Embankment
London EC4Y 0DZ

An Hachette UK Company

3 5 7 9 10 8 6 4 2

ISBN (Mass Market Paperback) 978 1 4746 2502 9
ISBN (eBook) 978 1 4746 2503 6
ISBN (Audio) 978 1 4746 2504 3

Typeset by Born Group
Printed and bound in Great Britain by Clays Ltd, Elcograf S.p.A.

MIX
Paper from
responsible sources
FSC® C104740

www.weidenfeldandnicolson.co.uk
www.orionbooks.co.uk

'The kind of book you pick up . . . and never want down . . . You will fall in love with this book'

Lauren Sams, author of *Crazy Busy Guilty* and
She's Having Her Baby

'A domestic drama with humour, charm . . . A love letter to motherhood in all its complexity. An impressive debut novel that finds the biggest drama in the smallest of actions'

Better Reading

Praise for *Sorrow and Bliss*

'While I was reading it, I was making a list of all the people I wanted to send it to, until I realised that I wanted to send it to everyone I know'

Ann Patchett, author of *The Dutch House*

'Sharp yet humane, and jaw-droppingly funny, this is the kind of novel you will want to press into the hands of everyone you know'

Jessie Burton, author of *The Confession*

'A thing of beauty. Astute observations on marriage, motherhood, family and mental illness are threaded through a story that is by turns devastating and restorative. Every sentence rings true. I will be telling everyone I love to read this book'

Sara Collins, author of
The Confessions of Frannie Langton

Meg Mason began her journalism career at the *Financial Times* and *The Times*. Her work has since appeared in *Vogue*, *Grazia*, the *Sunday Times*, the *Sydney Morning Herald* and the *Sunday Telegraph*. She has written humour for the *New Yorker*, been a monthly columnist for *GQ*, a regular contributor to *Vogue* and *Marie Claire* and a contributing editor at *Elle*. She lives in Sydney with her husband and two daughters.

It has to be for you, Bebs.

Any idiot can face a crisis.
It's this day-to-day living that wears you out.

Anton Chekhov

PART I

PART I

1.

Good luck getting home

From behind, it looked as though the girl might be trembling, although it could have been the constant up and down movement of her jigging the baby strapped to her front.

Brigitta, next in line, watched as the girl removed one item at a time from the counter of an all-hours chemist. A packet of scented wipes and a Twix were first to go. Next, the travel-size deodorant and two-pack of blue plastic dummies. Each time, she asked the man to try her card again. 'What about now? Or now?'

As her baby's dry, reedy cries gathered force, the girl's rocking motion grew more frantic. Brigitta tried to be patient. Truly though, she only wanted to pay for her water and find some deserted corner of the airport to wait out the night.

She looked at her watch. It was still on Sydney time. She guessed it would be midday in London, and some non-existent hour here in Singapore. It had been more than forty minutes since they'd all been herded off the plane, after sitting for twice as long on the runway while rain pelted the fuselage and gave the inside of the cabin the quality of a tin shed.

The head steward had come over the intercom at ten minute intervals requesting patience until finally announcing, to jeers from the cabin, that there would be no flights out tonight and they would now begin *deplaning*. Nobody could exit the terminal, he warned, in case they were required to board again at short notice. 'Shouldn't that be called *replaning*?' Brigitta said to her rowmate. 74D and E. He shook his head, no English.

Now the terminal heaved with exhausted, grubby-looking travellers and the line forming behind Brigitta began to radiate a restless energy.

'What about just them?' the girl asked. A single packet of newborn nappies remained on the counter. She spoke with a strong Croydon accent, although to Brigitta's ears trained by drama school and a year and a half in a studio flat in Kentish Town, it sounded like she'd gone to some effort to knock the South London out of it. 'How much are those nappies on their own?'

Brigitta could tell she was on the verge of tears now and felt a twist of sympathy. Being stranded for hours on your own was bad enough, but with a tiny baby…

'Do you sell them in ones then?' the girl pleaded. 'Why are they so much?'

Brigitta shifted her weight from one foot to the other. When the girl's card was declined again, Brigitta leaned forward and tapped her shoulder. She turned, braced.

In normal circumstances or kinder lighting, her face might have been quite lovely. But her pale skin, unblemished except for a hair-thin scar on her forehead, was taut and drained, tinged lilac beneath her dark, sloe eyes. Tears quivered at their rims. Her copper hair was pulled back and tied with a rubber band; two strands escaping from the front had jagged ends, as though they'd been cut with school scissors. Brigitta glanced into the carrier and saw that the infant inside was so small, only the top of a dark, soft crown was visible below the padded rim.

'Could I just put all our things together on my card?' Brigitta whispered. 'Just so we can get out of here?'

'Oh no, I couldn't. Here, you go ahead of me. Sorry.'

She stepped aside as the man behind the counter picked up the nappies and tossed them into a plastic basket at his feet.

'Don't be silly,' Brigitta said, 'you obviously need all those things. Who knows how long we'll all be stuck. Truly.' Then turning to the man, she said crisply, 'We'll have all those things back thank you.' Brigitta handed over a black Visa card. Well, her mother's card, really, for emergencies only, although clearly this was one.

'If you write out your details, I could pay you back when I get to Australia,' the girl said, accepting the bag with a look of immense apology.

'Oh, funny. That's where I've just come from,' Brigitta replied. 'Don't worry, though. I quite like the idea of being the *bailer-outerer* instead of the *bailee* for once.' On impulse, Brigitta reached out and squeezed the girl's hand. 'Good luck getting home. If that's where you're going.'

'You too,' she said. They separated at the door and walked in opposite directions to their own flights that, when the weather finally broke, would carry them as far from home as it was possible to go.

2.

I just lie there, really

The gate would not open, but Abi could not turn back now. She pulled hard at the bolt on the other side of its low pickets until its rusty casing lifted a small crescent of flesh out of her thumb. The bolt shifted a promising half-inch, then held. With her other hand, Abi held the handle of Jude's heavy pram to stop it rolling further down the steep path that veered off the main walking track around Cremorne Point and led down to this fenced enclosure ringed by tall trees. She stood in their shade and worked the lock. Overhead, a mob of brightly coloured birds pecked at the hard, black nuts that clustered about the trunks, casting the empty shells down onto the paving. They made a ticking sound like rain all around her.

Abi's need to be in and on the other side rose into a sort of fury. It was so hot. Ferocious in the sun, humid in the shade and so relentlessly stifling in the flat that sweat found a continual course from her neck, through her bra, to the waist of her jean shorts.

* * *

Before arriving at the gate, Abi had found a small, grassy playground and gone in to feed Jude, feeling certain that although empty now and exposed to blazing sun, other mothers would begin to arrive at any moment. Almost immediately, a little girl greased with suncream had appeared out of nowhere and run towards the swings.

'Two minutes, that's all bubba, it's too hot. No. Emily! Hat stays on,' a woman's voice, high and broad, called after her. Abi straightened her back.

'Scorcher, hey?' the woman said, ambling in and noticing her there. She removed her sunglasses and began cleaning them with the hem of her T-shirt. 'Where's your other one?'

Abi smiled brightly. 'Oh, he's my only one.'

'God.' The woman sounded offended. 'Then why are you at a playground?'

Abi could not think how to reply so after a polite interval, she interrupted Jude's feed, returned him writhing and unhappy to the pram and continued along the path.

* * *

It was around the next broad curve that flashes of bright, gold light through trees appeared on her right, and Abi skittered down to where she now stood, peering over the gate at what lay on the other side. Even as Jude's crying swelled to suggest a state of near starvation, she could only survey it in silent awe.

A pool. A long, narrow rectangle of deep water, bordered on all four sides by a sun-bleached wooden boardwalk. The far side was cantilevered above the bright, surging water of the harbour, but its concrete edges were painted a municipal blue that somehow turned the water inside a pale, riverish green. Captivated, Abi tried to locate a suitable metaphor, but her tired mind could not think of anything better than Aquafresh toothpaste in the cool mint flavour. There was no one on the other side of the fence, a faint breeze ruffled the pool's surface. The thought of pushing the pram back up the hill, without first touching the water, feeling it wrap around her wrists and cool her blood, concentrated her energy. As Jude's crying reached a pitch, she tried forcing the bolt further into its barrel, in case that was the knack of it.

It wasn't.

'Fuck.'

The knot behind her breastbone tightened as Jude became frantic. Maybe you had to pay someone and they gave you a key? She hoped not, since she didn't have any Australian money yet.

When her next effort failed, a wave of intense fatigue passed through her body. It had been so hard to get here. Each leg, Croydon to Heathrow. Those eight lonely hours stranded in Singapore. To Australia and to a top-floor flat in this unknown suburb.

But her course had been set ever since a weary GP in the Student Medical Centre confirmed her pregnancy. By then Abi already knew but remained so deeply terrified by the prospect of motherhood that when she brought home a Boots own-brand test kit, she found herself unable to provide a single drop of the necessary fluid across three separate attempts. It was only when strangers started giving up their bus seats, and other students eyed her knowingly around campus despite the loose T-shirts and men's duffel coat she had started to wear, that Abi forced herself to make an appointment.

The doctor took out a pamphlet called 'The Three Trimesters', scored through the first two with a marker, and slid it across the desk towards her.

'How could you not know?' she asked, vexed.

'I just thought I was getting fat.' Abi could not meet the doctor's eye.

'But you're so tiny, you didn't notice when you began showing?'

'I didn't show for ages,' Abi said truthfully. 'And anyway I haven't got a mirror you can see your whole self in at home. You have to stand on the loo and then you only get to here.' She made a sawing motion just below her chest.

The doctor took a cardboard dial out of her desk drawer. Two layers turned on a split pin, and shaking her head, the doctor rotated the smaller, inner circle.

'Well, if the dates you've give me are right, you're due in ten weeks. January 13. You *really* didn't know?'

Abi stared into her lap.

'How long have you been sexually active?' the doctor asked, exhausted by the task of running interference between all the sperm and eggs on the Kingston University campus.

'Oh, I'm not,' Abi said, reddening. 'I just lie there, really.'

The doctor sighed and returned her dial to the top drawer. 'Well, if you know who the father is, I'd let him know quick-smart.'

3.

A saviour is born

Abi sat in the bus shelter outside the medical centre and tried to call Stu but her phone was out of credit. When she got back to Highside Circuit, she shut herself in her room, undid the complicated system of rubber bands that had been keeping her jeans together for some time, and sat down with her thick, ancient laptop. The task could not reasonably be put off any longer. And besides, Abi needed to begin formulating her means of escape. Her baby would not be raised in the ex-council where she had grown up, and still lived in with her mother Rae, who generally speaking, sat sixteen hours a day in her armchair wearing a parka and knit hat against the aching cold of the front room, a mug of Weight Watchers Cream of Veg skinning over on the card table in front of her.

She would liven up whenever Pat from next door came around with her *OK!* to trade for Rae's *Hello* and stay on to watch *Strictly Come Dancing* without ever letting her Parliament Blue lose its salivated purchase on her bottom lip.

Occasionally the pair applied themselves to collages, made from magazine pictures glued into cheap scrapbooks from Poundstretcher. Pat liked proper glamour shots, with hair and makeup and preferably taken in the star's own home. Rae preferred pictures that proved Celebs Are Just Like Us! So they rarely went after the same prize with their scissors.

'Which do you like better, the samba or the rhumba?' Rae would occasionally ask her daughter, one eye on her pasting, the other on the glittering stage.

Nestled into a sleeping bag on the facing sofa, Abi would say she didn't care. Then, guiltily, 'Probably the samba.'

'Ooh, listen to you. Aren't we posh?' Pat would say every time Abi spoke in an accent that wasn't uncut Croydon. Abi had adopted it as a matter of survival when she started at a girl's grammar on the other side of the river. You couldn't get by with a South London accent there, they would know instantly you were a scholarship girl.

'Sahm-ba. Saahm-ba,' Pat would repeat in imitation 'Hear that, Mum? Oooh, I do like to dah-nce the saahm-ba.'

'Leave her alone, eh Pat. They're about to say the scores.'

Now in the cold of her bedroom, Abi opened Instant Messenger. Stu's status was 'online' and Abi began to type.

Abi.Egan89   Are you there?
SRKellett   What's up.
Abi.Egan89   Sorry I couldn't ring. No credit. But ...
Abi.Egan89   ... turns out I'm a bit
Abi.Egan89   on the pregnant side

She considered adding a surprised face made of punctuation, but did not want to seem flippant. Then came a lengthy pause that Abi knew wasn't due, in this instance, to Stu's need to look down at his hands as he typed. He was a solid, confoundingly dyslexic student of architecture, considerably more able with pen and graph paper. When 'Stu is typing' appeared and disappeared twice more, Abi could no longer bear it.

Abi.Egan89	I just found out today.
SRKellett	I thorght you said u had stuff sorted???
Abi.Egan89	I did. I don't know what happened.
SRKellett	& yr sure? No chance it's a mix up?

Abi lifted her vest and looked down at her stomach as a small ripple passed below the surface. A tiny hand, possibly a foot.

Abi.Egan89	Nope.
SRKellett	Faaaaaaarg. Babe!!!
SRKellett	Can u ... u know .. (!)
Abi.Egan89	It's too late. Have missed cut off.
SRKellett	Okthen.
Abi.Egan89	Am really sorry.
SRKellett	Geuss we'll just have to figure it out.

After that, Stu moved through an accelerated cycle of anger, denial, grief, acceptance and logged off.

SRKellett	Hey. Congratualtoins
Abi.Egan89	Oh. thx.
Abi.Egan89	I miss you
SRKellett	Miss you aswell.

Over the coming weeks, they put together a plan. Stu would finish the academic year in Australia, earn his ticket working split shifts at the pub until Christmas, then fly to London two weeks before her due date. As soon as possible afterwards, they would go back to Sydney and, in Stu's words, make a go of shit.

'You won't be able to stay at mine, is all,' Abi said, during one of their rare phone calls. 'We've not got any room. I'll be packing and my Mum's not been specially well anyway. Do you think you can find anywhere else?'

'Will I ever see your house, do you reckon?' Stu replied. 'I'm worried you're cooking meth in the bath.'

Abi laughed. 'Of course you will. And the meth is for personal use.' They said goodbye and hung up. The plan was made.

* * *

Two days before Christmas, in the nail care aisle of Superdrug, a hot rush of liquid down the inside of Abi's leg announced Jude's early arrival. An hour later, in the general waiting area of St George's Hospital in Tooting, she gripped a hospital porter by his collar and bore down so hard it began to come away at the stitching. The midwife, crouching at her ankles, begged Abi to please step out of her knickers as the baby pressed headfirst into the soaking gusset.

At the moment Abi received her son's perfect, slippery body into her arms, the lights of a small, artificial Christmas tree beside them spontaneously flickered on. The porter straightened his collar. 'A saviour is born, eh?'

He laughed, but Abi knew in herself it was true. Five hours later, Jude was deemed three days and five ounces clear of official prematurity, and approved for early discharge. She phoned a mini-cab and that night, on her single bed, Abi taught them both to breast-feed.

On the other side of the room was her sister's bed, long since stripped and deputised for storage. Whenever Jude woke in the night, and Abi needed to keep herself awake while he fed, she whispered into the darkness as though Louise was lying opposite. The 4 a.m. feed was the loneliest, when all the lights were out in the tower block visible through the circle in the frost on the window, which Abi had rubbed with her hand.

When Jude was three weeks old, Abi got them both to
Heathrow – the District Line to Earl's Court and a change – with
a suitcase full of clothes that would turn out to be too warm and
a library copy of *First Year with Baby*. She had meant to return it
before they left but when she ran out of time, the only thing was
to make it hers by tearing out the fly-sheet stamped 'Property of
Wandsworth Borough Library'.

4.

I think he likes you
more than me

All the time, a force that felt entirely outside herself compelled Abi forwards, but now she was here finally, reunited with Stu, she was not sure what she was supposed to do. They had been apart for eight months, twice as long as they were together.

As she grew rounder and rounder, counting the days until she could take her baby to Australia, Abi had tried to imagine what it would be like. The flat his parents had offered, Stu as a father, and Sydney, which she knew then as a composite of nature documentaries, *Home and Away*, and a Christmas card of Bondi Beach that her mother had acquired somewhere and hung onto because the surfing Santa always gave her a laugh.

Sydney would not have any shit bits, that Abi was sure of. Sydney would be all new and clean, and richly populated with mum friends. Not the sort of pramface girls even younger than her, who hung around outside the Centrale Shopping Centre and let their four-year-olds talk around a dummy, smacked them on the legs until they cried and bribed them to stop with a sip of Fanta. Abi would meet nice, good mothers of the kind she planned to be. In Sydney, her bad habits would be shed like an old skin. Swearing, lying, Red Bull in lieu of breakfast. Biting her nails, sucking her hair. To be sure of that, before she left Highside Circuit for the final time, Abi stood on the lavatory in the tiny bathroom and bobbed her hair with nail scissors, wrapping the uneven ends in toilet paper and flushing them away.

* * *

Stu had been late to meet them. He arrived, flustered, and found her waiting off to one side, beside her suitcase and the folded pram.

'Wow, early again, babe! It's a bit of a theme,' he said, trying to hug her in a way that accommodated the carrier on her front. A second later, he stood back and rubbed his chin, as he'd only thought as far as the hug and was now at a loss.

'Would you like to see him?' Abi said, realising Stu was not about to ask, even though Arrivals Gate B adjacent to the Avis counter was now the hallowed ground of father and son's first meeting.

Stu stiffened as she lifted Jude out. 'Oh right, yep.'

He arranged his arms like a cradle and let the baby's head loll alarmingly before it settled into the crook of his elbow. The carrier, open and undone, hung from Abi's shoulders like an apron and she watched Stu attempt a series of tentative bounces, until Jude released a single, sharp cry.

Stu handed him back. 'I think he likes you more than me.'

'Don't be silly. He loves you,' Abi said, with the familiar fizz of a lie. But it was only to spare him, to make the plain facts of their situation happier, nearly normal. 'He's just not used to you yet.'

It was the first time she had let anyone else hold him, not counting a community visitor from the South London health authority. Her mother asked once if she could have 'a love of the babbie', offering her bony lap, but Abi heard herself explaining that the general thinking now was that no one except the mother should touch the newborn until it was one month old. When Rae did not question her, Abi wished she'd made it six months.

In the airless taxi that carried the small, sudden family towards Cremorne Point, Stu and Abi held hands, the heat creating a mist of condensation on the vinyl seat. Abi rested her free hand lightly on Jude's tummy, hoping that the taxi's furry baby capsule was not crawling with bubonic plague. Her tracksuit pants had hardened in places where patches of Jude's spit up had dried during the long journey. She could smell her own underarms, and the beef en croute and orange juice she'd consumed 40,000 feet over Tashkent were repeating on her.

Distinctly, from the window, Abi saw stretches of inner city streetscape that could have been the rubbish part of Croydon between Tesco Metro and the Ruskin Road. Her spirits sagged. She had imagined it all wrong.

Abi took a deep breath and turned to study Stu in profile. In their time apart, she had started to think of him as blond, but now he appeared decidedly ginger, with such a density of freckles in the same reddish tone he might have been all one colour. She remembered his broad back, thick arms, and short, stocky legs, neither of which were ever truly still, but jogging busily up and down.

Sensing her gaze, Stu turned towards her. 'Hey, I love you, eh?'

As she'd once noticed when Stu took her to the Overseas Students farewell, his accent also tended to waver in intensity depending on who he was talking to. With Abi, he'd mostly given up speaking in a slow drawl, laughing like a drain and garnishing his speech with impenetrable Australian slang. For taxi drivers on the other hand, the accent was dialled to its highest setting.

'Me too. Massively. I love you as well,' Abi replied, as she turned to look out the window and noticed with dismay that the Opera House was tiled like a men's toilet, not uniformly smooth and white like cake icing, the way it looked on TV.

5.

Basic meals and snacks

They had met at the Kingston University Student Services Office, where Abi worked part-time to subsidise her fees. It was a bleak Friday in January, and the thin ribbon of sky visible from the window near her desk was a flat, unshifting white. Shortly before closing time, her supervisor, a New Zealander called Tanya Teo who had a septum piercing and calves like Christmas hams, asked if she would be all right to wait on in case the missing student for the spring term showed up. They all wanted to go to the pub, Tanya said, and she knew Abi was always up for overtime.

She quickly agreed, for the extra £12 and the not having to go home. Also, Tanya had been acting funny around her ever since, two Friday-drinks ago, Abi downed three White Russians on an empty stomach and accidentally told Tanya she thought of them as best friends. 'My only friend, if I think about it. Shall we get another one of these nice drinks each?'

As the staff straggled out, buttoning coats, Abi switched off the lights and monitors at each station. She smoked a quick cigarette through a slit of open window in the kitchenette and returned to her desk to wait.

The last Orientation Pack sat in her Pending tray. She unclipped the attached student file and leafed through it out of boredom, absent-mindedly drawing a hank of hair to her mouth and brushing it over her lips. It had dried as hard as a paintbrush, from where she'd sucked it on and off all day.

Kellett, Stuart Roger. DOB 27.07.1990.
School of Architecture, University of Technology, Sydney.
B minus average.

Shortly before seven, the outer door rattled and through the glass Abi saw Kellett, Stuart Roger, oversized hiking pack on one shoulder, no coat. She led him back to her workstation, with added briskness to offset the fact of them being alone in lamplight.

He swung his pack off and arranged himself in a chair facing her desk. Abi waited, wondering whether her steepled fingers were a bridge too far, in terms of officialness.

'Right. Sorry. Hey, Stu Kellett,' he said, offering her one of his meaty hands which felt unexpectedly warm and rough in hers.

'Yes, I know.'

'Course, sorry. Hope you didn't wait around just for me?' he asked, realising apparently for the first time that they were alone.

'No, it's all right, I had loads to catch up on,' she said, sliding a campus map over the copy of *Jude the Obscure* open on her desk. 'Right then, well, we better get on with it.'

As Abi leafed through each page of his packet, turning it upside down so he could read along as she circled sections of particular importance with a Kingston University: Gateway to Knowledge ballpoint, Abi sensed that Stu's concentration had wandered off the documents. He kept leaning back in his chair, screwing his fists into each eye, yawning and saying, 'Man, that flight is a mother … I didn't know it would be so cold … So are you a student as well or what,' in a broad Australian accent which Abi could not help finding desperately exotic. She tried not to be distracted, but there was something about him, an energy that made her want to return his packet to Pending and be swept up in it. She drew a lock of hair to her mouth and silently spat it out, hoping he hadn't noticed.

All the time, Stu's foot bounced up and down, in a way that reverberated through the floor and up the column of Abi's swivel chair. 'This is our spring term,' she said and he laughed as though she'd made a brilliant joke.

Although privately elated, Abi pressed on. 'There's a map here. K-15, that's your hall of residence. Selwyn is one of the new ones so that's good.'

'That *is* good,' Stu said, reaching a hand up inside his T-shirt and lazily scratching his stomach. 'Hey I'm so starving. Are you done after this or what's the story?'

Abi felt a thrill. Had he just asked her out for dinner? Sort of? She cleared her throat. 'So then, just initial here to show you've read the rules of conduct and that's it.'

'Is there anything in there about not getting dinner with a girl from Student Services because I seriously need something to eat and I don't know where the fuck I am in relation to where the fuck anything else is.'

'We're at H-8.'

He accepted the map, and pushed it into a zippered section of his backpack without folding it. 'I got some supremely dodgy private taxi here and the guy just dropped me at the main entrance. He's probably busy printing copies of my parents' credit card by now for all his cousins.'

'Well I suppose I could help you find the Student Rec because it is on the way to my security bus. It's open until eleven o'clock and does basic meals and snacks.'

Stu stood so abruptly Abi thought he was about to storm out, insulted by the Rec's meagre offering.

'A basic meal and snack is *exactly* what I feel like,' he said. 'Get your stuff and I'll shout you whatever to say thanks for waiting.'

As it was, Abi was ravenous. She'd only had a snacksize Hula Hoops and two hot chocolates from the free machine all day. There would be nothing at home and her lower back was already aching with hunger.

'Okay then,' she said, glancing towards Tanya's deserted station. 'I'm sure it is okay, because I'm a student as well anyway. Part-time,' she added quickly. 'Mature.'

Stu laughed loudly, until they reached the doors. How could anyone, Abi wondered, be so nice and happy all the time.

'Here give us a go,' Stu said after watching her struggle with the outer lock for a minute. As he brushed past her, she felt the heat of his arm against hers. A second later, the door gave a loud click and, side by side, they walked through the orange sulphur light of the deserted campus towards the Rec. Abi crossed her arms and dipped her head against a sharp wind.

'What course are you on again? I forgot,' Stu said. His hands were deep in the front pockets of his jeans.

'I didn't say. Social work. But I sort of hate it.'

'Shame,' he said, as they reached the Rec.

His response, economical as it was, gave Abi an unexpected rush of relief. Delight almost. Because it was a shame to be nearing the end of a course you had hated from the start, that would get you a job you didn't want. It was a *huge* shame. Stu was the second person she'd told, after Tanya, who considered it emblematic of Abi's tendency to rush in. She gave an example from the week before, when Abi had gone to Clare's Accessories on her lunch break, and immediately regretted the two extra holes in her left ear. 'You should think about things before you do them,' Tanya said at the time, forgetting she'd been the one to suggest it as a way for Abi to look more edgy.

Inside the warm Rec hall, Stu picked up a plastic tray from the stack and shook the water off it. 'Whatever the lady wants,' he said, passing it to her and waving a hand the full length of the hot food station.

When Abi had finished her baked potato with butter and cheese, the cheapest thing on the board, she watched Stu work his way through a plate of curry and rice, buttered bread and two separate desserts in lidded plastic bowls. His appetite amazed her. She had never seen someone eat so much and so happily.

'So what's your story?' he said, mouth full. 'Hobbies, brothers and sisters, outstanding arrest warrants.'

'Oh,' Abi said, desperate to be interesting. 'Well, I was born in Southfields but I live in Croydon, and I used to have a sister who was a year older than me but she died when I was nine. And I've never been arrested, although I did once steal some tights from Debenhams but then I felt so guilty I snuck them back into the shop.'

'Far out. That's *terrible*,' Stu said. Abi readied herself for the condolences she knew to expect if ever she mentioned her sister.

Stu shook his head slowly. 'Tights, eh? I hope it wasn't a three-pack.' He reached across the table and gave her a single pat on her wrist. It was the best display of sympathy she'd ever had.

'Anyway, my turn. Last year I backed my mum's car into a skip and said I didn't. No brothers or sisters. My growing up was probably all right compared to yours but I guess we both know what it's like to be the only one, eh? I'm my mother's golden child, which now I think about it, is probably why I've come here.' He moved his tray to the side. 'So she can't spit on her hankie and try to wipe my face anymore.'

At that, he dug his documents from the pocket of his pack and ran his hands over the crumpled mess. 'Does your official orientation service extend to showing me to my dorm?' he asked.

Abi said it didn't.

'What about, service as a friend?'

'We're friends now, are we?' Abi hoped it came out flirtatious, although really, she just wanted to know.

'Well I did just drop two-twenty on your potato.' He flicked to the back page. 'But if we're not, then one Pra-Sharnt-Nai-Doo, School of Engineering, is about to become my main man.'

Abi checked the time on her phone. 'Okay then, but I cannot miss my bus.'

6.

Comprehensively inducted

Abi missed her bus. When they found Stu's dorm, there was no sign of a roommate and somehow, he convinced her to keep him company while he unpacked, which turned out to mean pulling handfuls of clothing out of his pack and stuffing them unfolded into a drawer. His back was turned to Abi who perched on the edge of a metal desk. She could not stop looking at the back of his neck, so freckled and brown, and the way his shoulder blades moved under his T-shirt. She bit her thumbnail and tried to think of interesting things to tell him about campus life, but he appeared not to be listening. So when she started to tell him about the student mixers she had never personally been to, and he stood up, took a step closer and kissed her until she couldn't breathe, she was caught quite off guard.

She would always wonder why he did it, why he broke away for a moment, laughed, wiped his mouth with the back of his hand, and started again. When it was over, he stretched his arms above his head, exposing an inch of stomach, and asked if anyone had ever drawn her before.

'What do you mean?'

'As in, drawn a picture of you.'

'I don't think so. No, probably not.'

From his half-empty pack, Stu pulled out a leather folio that opened to reveal two rows of expensive-looking pencils.

'Are you seriously going to draw me?' Abi laughed. 'Can you draw people?'

'I can do hands and everything,' Stu said, pointing her towards the bed and settling himself in a facing chair. 'Sit however.'

Abi hesitated.

'Serious.' Stu pulled out the finest lead. 'In my head, it's four o'clock in the morning. I'm not going to sleep any time soon and who knows if Prashant will want to pose for a tasteful nude.'

Stu looked at her open-faced, waiting. 'Just if you want, though. No pressure. I'm sure I can find a fruit bowl I can do instead.' He was the least self-conscious person she had ever met. Abi only ever thought of herself the way she imagined other people did. Tiny, a bit weird, always staring, but Stu was happy to sit, and stretch and draw and kiss people on the mouth whenever he felt like.

'All right then,' Abi said, first sitting then lying on the bed. 'Draw me like one of your Croydon girls.'

Stu looked at her quizzically.

'You know, from *Titanic* when he …'

'Haven't seen it,' Stu said.

Abi reddened. 'Never mind.'

'Maybe move that arm a bit,' he said, and Abi did as he asked, the colour in her cheeks lingering for some time.

* * *

The next morning when Abi arrived at Student Services for her half-day Saturday in the same outfit as the day before, Tanya stirred her Nescafé suspiciously and asked if the missing student had ever turned up. Abi was happy to confirm that yes, he had, and he'd been fully and comprehensively inducted. Carefully rolled in her bag were three pencil drawings, of a small, slender girl with dark eyes, hair that caught the light and elegant limbs, in advancing stages of undress.

When she left work that afternoon, darkness already falling, Stu was waiting for her on a low brick wall opposite the entrance. He sat with knees spread in a posture of total ease, as though needles of rain were not coming at him sideways. In his hand was a plastic bag from Boots, The Chemist. 'Got you a present,' he said, holding it out. A toothbrush, a pink pocket hair brush and a stick deodorant claiming a connection to summer orchids, instantly became the most romantic gift she had ever received.

'I thought we could have another evening in,' he said, draping a heavy arm around her shoulders. 'Prashant Naidoo appears to be a no show.'

* * *

A month later, on the top deck of a night bus propelling them noisily back to campus, Stu, happy and drunk, laid his head in Abi's lap. They had been to Chinatown for cheap noodles and walked back along the river from Charing Cross almost to Pimlico, taking turns drinking from a bottle of £9 vodka.

As Abi stroked his hair, Stu let out a soft groan. 'Do you reckon people can fall properly in love in not that long? Like, a few weeks?'

Yes, they could. 'Um, I don't know. Maybe.'

'I reckon I would have said no, but now I'm not so sure.'

Prashant, blissfully forgotten, arrived out of the blue the following day and drew to a close the best weeks of Abi's life. But Stu continued to seek her out between lectures, and after every shift at Student Services, she would find him waiting on the wall. Abi tried not to let herself expect him, but he was always there. 'Our man Prashant will be having a huge one at his first Maths

Olympiad this evening, and I have a bottle of finest no-label wine. Let's go.'

As the weeks wore on and the end of Stu's term abroad drew closer, Abi began to dread his departure. Stu talked more and more about home, with a degree of nostalgia that Abi felt, at times, was disproportionate to the length of his absence. His accent returned with gusto. 'Far out, I've missed it Abs. The heat, my mates. The harbour. You want to fly in over the Heads one time. Serious, babe, it's the best city in the world.'

'You sound like you're returning from the Western Front,' Abi said as they lay side by side in his bed.

'What?'

'Like you've been fighting Germans in a trench for three years.'

'Oh right. Yeah, nah. Reckon I'm just looking forward to being back on my own turf.'

Abi lifted her head onto his chest. 'What about us though?'

'I don't know,' he said slowly. 'We'll figure it out. When I'm back and I've had a chance to think, we can decide what we'll do.'

'Okay. That's okay, I guess.'

Too soon, the day came. Abi stood with her arms wrapped around Stu's waist and her cheek against his chest. A yellow crocus had pushed its way through a section of bare, black earth, and she wanted to stamp it back in again. She could not bear to let go, even as the airport bus drew up. It would be stupid, Stu had said, for her to come all the way to the airport and say goodbye when they could just do it here and save £16.50 on the round trip.

When he heaved his pack onto his shoulder, Abi made a sound, a sort of *gah*. Stu let her hug him once more. 'Hey Abi, I love you,' he said. 'You know I do.'

'Are we still together and everything?'

'Yes, of course we are,' Stu said, impatient. 'Babe, true, you've asked me that a thousand times.'

Abi let him go, and stared at her feet. It was more like only ten. Twenty at the most. 'Call me when you get there?'

'Yep. Will do.' Stu pulled her towards him and kissed the top of her head, before bounding up the bus steps. Abi waited for him to appear at the window and wave, but he must have sat on the other side.

She had never felt so alone. Even though, she thought as she turned back to Student Services, she'd been alone most of her life.

At home late that night, Abi ran the shower and sat beneath the needles of warm water, missing Stu with a physical longing. It felt like her chest had split open and all the air was hissing out of her lungs. But for three days already, something had been forming in the deepest, most hidden part of her that would one day mean she'd never be alone again.

7.

Briggy's Starving Artist Period

In one of the thick paper carrier bags was a plastic tray of sushi but Brigitta couldn't find it. Kneeling on the floor of the combined kitchen-living-sleeping area of her Kentish Town studio, she dug through bag after bag of new towels, crisp sheet sets and goose down pillows, until she turned it up beneath a pair of ready-made curtains for the room's only window.

She tore off the lid – gosh, had it really cost £12? – and bolted each oily segment while surveying the loot. It was a lot. But coming back to London and specifically to Kentish Town had been significantly more depressing than she'd anticipated.

Those weeks in Sydney, as intermittently tense and emotional and lovely and awful as they had been, were enough to alter her memory of what life in London was really like. Compared to the indignity of being told by her older sister that she was clearly emotional and needed an early night, living by herself in a fourth-floor walk-up, in a manageably gritty part of a foreign city, had come to seem quite romantic. Although it pissed her off to hear her mother and sister laugh between themselves about 'Briggy's Starving Artist Period', in a way it was true.

Then, as the weeks following her father's death, his funeral and memorial wore on, Kentish Town presented itself as a refuge from her family's various modes of grief. Her mother's long slumps followed by febrile bouts of *doing*; Polly's ordering everyone about as though domestic tasks were the only thing that would save them; Freddie being alternately frivolous or refusing to talk at all, hiding from all duty in his room.

Brigitta had longed to be alone, allowed to grieve like a grown-up, instead of the sulky middle child she unavoidably became after prolonged exposure to her family. But the allure of solitary living had evaporated the moment she opened the studio door.

The wicked delay in Singapore had forced her to take the first Tube from Heathrow direct to the Barbican to make the company's first full Saturday rehearsal. She stayed until the very end, becoming almost nauseous with fatigue during an hour of blocking on stage, under hot lighting, and causing the female lead to remark on how different some people look from their headshots. Her only reward for bearing up had been a moment of meaningful eye contact with the director, the other reason she'd been eager to get back to the life she had carved out for herself.

Finally, as she made it up four flights with a suitcase, shouldered open the door and flicked on the studio's only, bare bulb, the room lit up like the set of a very bleak stage play. The soiled dish cloth crisped into board where it had been left on the dish rack, a fresh peppering of mouse pellets across the stove, the sash window milky with grime. In desperate need of a shower, Brigitta dropped her bags by the door, took the three requisite steps to the bathroom and slid its concertina door off its runners.

The next day was Sunday. She woke at 3 a.m. and lay still, listening to the thickening traffic on the street below. As she contemplated the many empty hours before her bistro shift that evening, a sense of dread began to gather somewhere just beyond reach.

When it became impossible to stay in bed as she'd planned, she got up, took a taxi to Selfridges and spent the morning buying emergency homewares to assuage her misery. On her way out, Brigitta passed the gently illuminated entry to the Selfridges day spa, deciding it couldn't hurt to look in, in case there was a therapist sitting around doing nothing, who would be better occupied attending to Brigitta's complexion, as dry as a cracker from all that economy class air. Also, it would eat up the afternoon and there'd be a pleasant rush about getting to work.

Her mother would not mind. She should not mind, having raised Brigitta to be so pathetically dependent on comforts. The studio and the bistro job had been part of an effort to cure herself, but so far, they'd only made her slightly more susceptible.

Brigitta swallowed the last piece of sushi, dropped the empty tray in the sink and took a pair of scissors out of the kitchen drawer to score open her purchases. But as she turned back to the assortment of wares, it was instantly clear they were insufficient for the task of brightening the dreary room. It had all looked so luxurious under shop lighting.

Why had she bought so much? Without even thinking to check the prices, noticing only now that the sheets by themselves cost nearly £200.

Against rising shame, she began replacing each item in the stiff carrier bags, but when she came to a bottle of aftershave she couldn't bear the idea of returning it.

On her way out of the store, through Men's Accessories and Cologne, she saw it displayed on a glass counter and recognised the bottle as the one that always sat on her father's tall bedroom bureau. She spritzed the tester onto her wrist, and the woody musk that rose off her skin was so entirely her father that Brigitta wheeled around, half expecting to see him.

The counter girl had to offer her a tissue from her own pocket, as Brigitta tearfully explained that her father had passed away unexpectedly just before Christmas and this was his cologne. The girl accepted Brigitta's card and handed her the tissue-wrapped bottle, in a small carrier bag. He couldn't really be dead, Brigitta thought as she pushed out onto Oxford Street, at least not in a permanent sense.

After stowing all the bags in the broom cupboard, Brigitta returned to her unmade bed and saw her purse where she'd tossed it against the pillows. As soon as the idea came to her, she leapt up, removed the credit card and used the scissors to snip it into four jagged pieces. A rapturous sense of freedom came over her as she gathered the pieces up and dropped them, one by one, into the toilet. She yanked the chain and watched exhilarated as they eddied around the rust-streaked bowl. It was only when the water settled and pieces of unflushed credit card floated to the surface that Brigitta realised her error.

'Fuckfuckfuckfuck,' she said, rolling up her sleeve as she knelt in front of the toilet and, staring ceiling-ward, plunged her hand into the water. With some careful sellotaping, she could still make out the sixteen-digit number and while dialling the bank, Brigitta hoped to God her next emergency was the sort she could pay for over the phone.

8.

This ruddy latch

Brigitta tossed her apron into her locker and left the bistro for the long journey home, footsore and smelling faintly of kingfish carpaccio. At the same moment, halfway around the world, Abi stood in front of the gate, biting the inside of her cheek and trying to think above the relentless wail of her hungry baby. The sun seemed to be getting hotter by the minute and for the first time she considered turning back for home.

'Fuck it,' she said. The effort of dragging the pram backwards up the communal stairs, returning to the stale heat of the flat. 'Fuck it.'

Raising herself on tip toes, Abi lifted one leg and straddled the pickets, trying hard not to impale her private parts, having lately put them through so much. A stumble, a wobbling correction and the other leg followed. In. Easily then, she reached over for Jude and lifted her perfect, furious boy into the sheltered enclosure. Abi held his face to hers, smelling his clean, metallic breath as he howled with an open mouth. The weight of his head in her cupped hand still gave her a twinge in her knicks, it was so real and lovely. Her tiny human anchor; and ever so slightly cross-eyed. Abi kissed his soft forehead and sat down on a wooden bench warmed by sun to resume his feed. Immediately he fell into a fast, silent rhythm, a faint click attending every suck, and Abi allowed herself a minute of tearful relief. Her head dropped to her shoulder and she wished, in no order of preference, for a Twix, a fag, her mother, any mother, something to read, an engagement ring and different shorts.

All around her was the fragrance of leaf mould, rotting berries and the brine off the harbour. Jude fed on, eyes closed in milky concentration.

'Now that's better isn't it?'

Abi sat up, looking for who had spoken. An older woman was holding loosely to a rung of the ladder, doing a stationary sort of kick, only her head visible above the waterline. 'What an absolute dot. How old is she?'

'Oh. He. Jude. He'll be four weeks on Thursday. Unless it's Thursday already, I've sort of lost track of my days.'

The woman pushed off and floated on her back, working both arms gently underwater. 'Ah, well, I'm not the person to help you there. I haven't a clue either. Anyhow, aren't you doing well, out and about so soon? How *darling*.'

Abi felt queasy with pride and could not think how to answer. The woman returned to the ladder and climbed out. Her shoulders were strong and square, her legs long and well-shaped. Only her middle had developed a stoutness, and a heavy bust rested on top of it. Her neat, dark blue swimming costume was the kind cleverly designed to draw the eye away from areas of thickness. Abi guessed her to be in her late sixties although it was difficult to tell, her only measure of similar age being Rae, who had begun a preternatural decline in her late thirties and could have passed for seventy now.

The woman retrieved a thick terry robe from where it was slung over the fence, pressed it to her face a few times and, toting a French market basket, came over to where Abi sat.

Her hair, still dry except at the nape, was the soft grey-brown of finished embers, with a starburst of white at its parting. When she raised a hand to smooth it back, Abi saw that her ring finger was stacked to the knuckle with gold bands of different thicknesses, dull and mottled, the most prominent of which had a very large, clear blue stone at its centre.

'And then you will blink and he'll be quite grown,' she said.

While Abi plumbed her shallow well of maternal observations for any sort of reply, the woman threaded her arms into the robe and knotted it around her waist. 'I'm off then. Have a lovely day, whichever one it is.'

As the woman reached the gate, she turned back and called out, 'For next time, dear, this ruddy latch wants a push in, a little lift up and a good jigger.'

Abi waved her thanks and watched the woman disappear through the trees. She was so, so sorry to see her go. Like a wave it almost pushed her sideways. She wanted to tell her that she'd already taken him on a plane, how hard it was getting him to open his eyes for his passport photos and filling out two lots of forms, hers and his, in hardly any time and with no help. How, before him, she'd never held a baby and now she could change a nappy in the dark. Abi sat where she was, immobilised by the weight of longing. Jude, nearly asleep, took quick, urgent sucks each time she tried to take him off so she let him stay there, eyelids fluttering, tiny fists clenched.

Abi lifted her eyes to the harbour, as a ferry droned past on the far side of the bay. The word *Friendship* was painted squarely across its stern. Abi mouthed it, silently, and then against Jude's upturned cheek, whispered, 'If you walked around Croydon in a dressing gown you'd get locked up.' A faint breeze ruffled his duck-down hair and he opened his eyes.

'I love you so much, Jude,' Abi said, waiting for the sense of absence created by the woman's departure to pass, but it yawned open further and further until Abi felt she could fall in. 'Mummy loves you.' Dizzy, tired, thirsty, she got up and went home, without touching the water after all.

9.

A hundred and ten per cent ready

Jude slept all the way home and did not wake as Abi bumped the pram backwards up the dark stairs, or when she lifted him out and laid him in the centre of the double mattress that took up most of the bedroom floor. Stu had installed a cot against the wall on Abi's side and when he mentioned it had been his as a baby, she prayed the lemon paint was not throbbing with lead, and decided to use it only when necessary.

Still sweating from the walk home, Abi shed her jean shorts, top and bra and put on a T-shirt of Stu's that hung off her small frame like a dress. She covered Jude with a muslin and went back to the living room.

After two days, her eyes hadn't adjusted to the emptiness of it all. Its stretches of plain white wall and sparse furnishing still amazed her. Although Stu had promised that the flat would be 'a hundred and ten per cent ready' by the time she arrived, his acquisitions were meagre. In one corner sat a pull-out sofa covered in fabric that looked like rich brocade, but was in fact a highly flammable poly-blend gone shiny across the arms. Facing it, an oversized television sat on an arrangement of bricks and wooden planks and a small table had been pushed into one corner beside an empty Ikea bookcase, thrown forwards by the furred cream carpet that banked up beneath it. Where the bookshelf was missing a strip of veneer, it showed its mulchy wooden innards. There was nothing else. No magazines, no stacks of the *Croydon Advertiser*. No ornaments. No ashtrays, bulging cartons, saved Christmas paper, collected plush toys. No archived scrapbooks filled with pictures of Posh and Becks on their wedding day.

Hard sunlight poured in through the flat's large windows, only one of which boasted a functional set of blinds. And although the temperature inside could be unbearable by afternoon, to Abi the slanted rays of sun that moved across the carpet from morning to evening felt like the most glorious antiseptic.

She was hungry and ate half a yoghurt in front of the open fridge. When she jerked open the window above the sink, the collected heat of the kitchen was replaced with a gust of salt-sweet air, mingled with something tropical and the tang of two-stroke petrol from dinghies in the bay. The closest thing to it, Abi decided, was probably walking past the Body Shop at Putney station.

The tips of tree branches tapped against the glass and from further off, Abi could hear the bell-like clanging of yachts' rigging clattering against their masts. It would have been nice to phone someone and tell them what it was like.

'There's nothing in London the same blue as that water,' Abi said quietly, trying to summon the image of her sister. 'Except the Greggs sign. But not in nature, that blue's never occurred.'

But trying to see Louise here, breathing sultry, summer air, was beyond Abi's powers of imagination. It was hard enough in their room at Highside, where Louise's empty bed served as a placeholder.

Stu had left first thing and would not be home until evening. Abi's bag hung over the kitchen door and she fished out a half-eaten Twix and a packet of Marlboro Lights. Boosting herself onto the kitchen bench, she pulled her knees up inside the T-shirt and smoked what she promised herself would be her very last cigarette.

From her benchtop vantage, Abi could see down into the still, empty garden of the next-door house, appearing so vast under its slate roof she wondered if it ran the entire length of the flats. Well-kept lawn edged by enormous flowering shrubs sloped all the way down to the edge of the track.

From the living room, Abi had already seen the side of the house, shingled, with multiple recessed porches. If she looked at an angle, she could see a deep window seat, with faded squab cushions, built into a recess.

Further along, a side entrance gave onto a mossy green courtyard. The green painted door had a leadlight window, and pretty baskets dripping blowsy orange flowers hung on either side. Their trailing leaves were as round as lily pads. Abi's botanical knowledge was derived mostly from *Milly Molly Mandy's Summer* and on that basis, she thought they might be nasturtiums.

The street-side of the house, with its herringbone-brick area for a car and immense potted trees, was visible from the flat's bedroom. Every time she looked down, Abi wondered what sort of people got to live in a house like that.

She had seen no comings and goings, and the house sat motionless under the lid of afternoon heat. But as Abi leaned into the sink to thread her finished cigarette down the plughole, French doors which faced the harbour rattled, then opened from the inside. Out stepped the woman, dressed in a loose silk wrap. Abi pressed her forehead against the glass and stared down, disbelieving. The woman stood on the patio and looked across the water, her arms wrapped tightly around her chest.

Abi wished she could shout down, wave and call out, but a moment later the woman disappeared inside and the doors came together behind her. When it seemed that she would not come out again, Abi slid off the bench and looked in every cupboard for cleaning things.

Under the sink she found a damp sponge that smelt of meat and a single tin of Ajax that had rusted over and made a sound like a baby's rattle when she shook it. She wrote 'cleaning things' on a takeaway menu tacked to the fridge and left the room.

She thought about waking Jude for something to do, but sank onto the pull-out, feeling the hot, prickling fabric against her sagging shoulders. As the light in the room faded from white to gold, Abi felt like whatever energy she had summoned to get herself here had finally run out. Her chin dropped to her chest and she fell into a heavy sleep.

10.

Very English skin

She was woken by Stu gently shaking her forearm.

'Abi, babe,' he whispered. 'Mum and Dad are here. Do you want to pull your ... you're a bit all over the show.'

Her head snapped up. Someone had turned on all the lights.

'Well. Hello Abi,' said the woman, stepping out from behind Stu. 'I'm Elaine.' She emphasised the E, as though sadly accustomed to people making too short of that important first syllable. *E*-laine. She had a narrow frame, neat bosom and a coarse, ferociously brushed plume of hair. Its short sides and rounded top put Abi in mind of a toilet brush. 'And this is Roger, Stuart's father.'

As Elaine spoke, Abi tried to stretch Stu's T-shirt to cover her bare thighs. 'Wow, hello. Hi. So nice to meet you. Excuse my ... I forgot you were coming! Tonight, I mean. Still a bit jetlagged I think.'

'And where is the little Jude?' Elaine asked.

'He's in the bedroom, sleeping I hope. I can go and get him if you like.'

Elaine said nothing, before turning to address her son. 'Stuart, it would be good to get a cross-breeze in here. It's stifling. Haven't you noticed?'

'Mum, do you want to meet your grandson?' Stu pointed a thumb over his shoulder to the other room.

Elaine had nodded assent, causing the toilet brush hair to quiver. Roger brought over a dining chair so that Elaine could sit down. She smoothed her skirt in readiness to receive the child. Roger stood sentry behind her, jingling change in the pocket of his trousers and bouncing softly on the balls of his feet.

Abi's eyes prickled threateningly as she stayed pinned to the couch, stretching at the T-shirt's hem. It made a tent over her braless chest, and through its neck she could see all the way to the top of her underwear.

Stu returned with Jude who was asleep, swaddled tightly in muslin. Abi had taught herself how to do it by following the diagrams in the 'Troubleshooting Sleep' chapter of *First Year with Baby*. Elaine took the baby into her arms. 'Well, he's very nice, Stuart. Although I can't see any of you in him. No Kellett at all, is there Roger?' Elaine inclined her head, sorry to have to be the one to say it. Roger did not speak. He stayed as he was, looking over his wife's shoulder with an expression of all-consuming wonder.

Abi watched him watching. Every time Jude's eyelids fluttered or his mouth arranged itself into a perfect O, Roger's face would change. His woolly eyebrows would lift and crinkles form at the corners of his eyes and he would nod, just once each time, as though Jude's cleverness was a rare and surprising thing. It was difficult not to feel as though her own cleverness was being admired. Reluctantly Abi tore her eyes away as Elaine spoke again.

'And the name's absolutely set, is it?'

Abi flicked a helpless look at Stu who was leaning against the wall with his arms crossed. 'Um, I think so? I mean, that's what I put on all his forms.'

'Wherever did you come up with it? Did Stuart have any input?'

'I've always loved, um, Hardy and I was reading that one, *Jude the Obscure*, when I met Stu so—'

Elaine looked momentarily irritated, as though Abi was using made-up words that she shouldn't be expected to understand.

'Abi loves reading, Mum,' Stu said.

'Oh well,' Elaine sighed. 'We can only make the best of things now I suppose. Kelletts pride themselves on doing the right thing. It's our way. Hopefully he will start filling out soon, although I expect he'll always be small. Stu told us you were petite, Abi, but goodness me, you're tiny aren't you?'

It was coming so thick and fast, Abi didn't know what to apologise for first. In the end, she could only manage a low, breathy *ha*.

'You've got very English skin,' Elaine said, peering more closely. Abi raised her hands to her cheeks.

'I must ask, how did you get that scar?' Elaine gestured towards the cotton-thin seam running from Abi's left eyebrow nearly to her hairline.

Automatically, Abi touched her finger to its familiar ridge, the downward stroke of a letter 'P', put there by an enormous sixth-former who had held her down, knees pinning her chest, trying to write the word 'PIKEY' across Abi's forehead with a mathematical compass.

'I ran into the corner of a table when I was little,' Abi said.

Roger was still looking quietly on at Jude, who hiccoughed now, three times in a row. In between each small pop, like corks being tugged from a bottle, his heart-shaped belly puffed up, and each time, Roger raised his shoulders, involuntarily mimicking the movement. Slowly, he drew a hand out of his pocket and reached over Elaine's shoulder, intending to cup his grandson's head, but Elaine leaped up and handed him back to Stu.

Roger looked about to see if anyone had noticed, and nodded apologetically at Abi who had been watching. As he put his hands back in his pockets, he smiled at her. They agreed then. Jude was the best one.

'So what are your plans while you're out here?' Elaine said, brushing her skirt with a series of short, brisk strokes.

Abi thought for a moment. 'Well. I'm going to drink more water but um, after that my schedule is still quite on the open side.'

'Mum,' Stu cut in, 'Abi's not out here, she lives here.'

Elaine made a tsking sound. 'What sort of visa did you manage in the end?'

'Oh,' Abi began, her throat catching. 'Excuse me. I could only get Working Holiday, in the time, but I've got all the papers to transfer to ...'

'Student. Or Prospective Marriage,' Stu cut in.

Elaine looked at Abi with a gimlet eye. 'Well.'

'Well what, Mum?' Stu said.

Abi squirmed. The sofa fabric was starting to feel greasy beneath her bare legs.

'A Student visa would be more than adequate, I think, Stuart,' Elaine said. 'Presuming Abi plans to resume her course? Do you, Abi? Because the offer of minding Jude three days a week, which I have already made to Stuart, is still on the table, although of course you will have to get him on a bottle. I recommend doing it now so he won't learn to miss you. Remind me what you were studying?'

'Social work. I was part-time and I worked in the Student Services office.'

'She oriented me,' Stu said. 'Big time.'

Stu laughed, a sort of snort, and Abi refused to meet his eye.

'Yes. Stuart said something about that. Well, our system here could be very different so I'd get onto it. There will be a great deal of paperwork.'

'Give it a rest, Mum, she's only just got here,' Stu said. He lowered Jude into Abi's arms and stalked off to the kitchen. At that, Jude woke and turned his head towards his mother's chest, trying to latch on to her arm. Abi put her little finger in his mouth, to delay the horror of having to feed him in front of Elaine.

'Thank you for the flat,' Abi said. 'It's such a lovely spot. I went out this morning, and then I was just about to do some cleaning and whatnot but I couldn't find the things.'

'We had cleaners through when the tenants left.' Elaine looked offended. 'Didn't we Roger? I hope Stuart has told you the unit isn't forever, Abi. Only until he graduates, and then we'll require you to stand on your own feet. If indeed … that's where we find ourselves. Of course we can't know the future. I gather we can't expect any help from your side.'

'Elaine,' Roger whispered sharply. Abi looked at him again, realising then it was the first time he'd spoken.

'Unfortunately Rae isn't working. At this time.' Abi looked at both faces, embarrassed.

Elaine's blank expression demanded further explanation. 'Rae's my mum. I've just always called her by her name. Since I was little. I don't know why!'

'How unusual. I wouldn't have stood for it, personally, my own child using my Christian name, but each to their own, I suppose. Not everyone's cut out to be a mother.' Elaine touched a finger to the corner of her lips, in case coral lipstick had found its way into the deep creases, which Abi suspected had been formed by decades of tight pursing.

'No,' Abi looked into her own lap. 'You're probably right.'

'Either way I expect your mother would be very disappointed if you walked away from your studies altogether.'

The day Abi left for Heathrow, Rae had not felt able to make it as far as the front door. She had lower back pain and didn't want to catch a draught. They'd said their goodbyes in the sitting room, with the television muted appropriately. In deference to the moment, Pat shielded her face with an *OK!*, which made it look as though Jordan and Peter Andre were bearing witness to mother and daughter's farewell from their luxury villa on the Costa del Sol. Abi remembered the thin coil of Parliament smoke rising from behind its pages.

'Mum would be *very* disappointed, yes. She'd definitely be on my back about it.'

They fell silent again and all three cast about for somewhere to look, until all at once, they settled on Jude. Abi loosened the muslin so he could pedal his tiny feet in the air.

A minute later, Elaine cleared her throat. 'There's a sausage casserole in that cooler by the door, Abi.' Then to Roger, 'Five minutes, or we'll get traffic on the highway.'

Stu was leaving with them for the second part of a split shift, and wanted to be dropped off. Abi nestled Jude in the corner of the sofa and they congregated by the door for goodbyes. Elaine wondered out loud whether they should take the cooler now, or whether she could do without it until the Sunday lunch she had already arranged with her son. Knowing as little of Abi as they did, Elaine seemed to be thinking, there was no way of knowing if she was a reliable returner of coolers. In the end, she decided it would be safest to take it. She lifted the rectangular Pyrex dish, laminated with cling film, out of the bag and put it into Abi's hands. The rounded ends of naked-looking sausages sticking out of a dense, reddish gravy made Abi blush.

'Ignore all the crap. It's going to be amazing,' Stu whispered as he passed her.

Elaine coughed, as dry as a cat, and they turned to go. Only Roger stuck his head back around the door and said, 'Lovely boy. Lovely grandson.' Abi wanted so much to hug him before he backed out and closed the door. She was glad the heavy sausage casserole stopped her from doing something that would definitely have seemed a bit on the weird side.

11.

Southbound traffic

When Stu returned after midnight, Abi was lying awake on the mattress, the sheet shrugged off and a washer that had been wet and cold, now blood-temperature, spread out on her chest. Night had not brought relief from the heat. As he undressed, Abi propped herself up on her elbow, whispering so as not to wake Jude who was asleep in the crook of her elbow.

'Do you think your mum and dad think we should be getting married? I mean. I don't. Unless you do. Do they, though?' Abi could not make out Stu's expression in the darkness of the room.

'Babe, it's not the fifties.' He got in beside her and Jude. 'I think they're sweet with us getting our heads around the parenting first.'

'Me too. Yep. That's what I think.' It was only a half-lie.

Abi fell back against her pillow and listened to the ceiling fan that clicked with each slow rotation. 'I am going to need some money soon though.'

'What? From me?'

'Just for nappies and groceries and whatnot.'

'Yeah but I'm not exactly minted, babe. I've got six grand of fees to pay just for this semester. And books. And I've got a bit of a credit card situation to sort out from my study abroad stuff. No offence, but do you get how expensive architecture is?'

'No offence, but do you get how expensive a baby is?'

Stu turned to face her. 'Yeah, fine. But I'm working pretty much every day already. Do you reckon you'll start looking for a job soon?'

'Well, I can't really until Jude's a bit more on the independent side. And has stopped feeding practically every half an hour. Can your parents help us a bit maybe?'

'They're already helping us with the flat.' Stu let out a ragged breath. 'I think there's two tens in my wallet you can have. Then we'll have to work something out I guess. I can probably do maybe seventy bucks a week or something for groceries but you'll have to go to the discount one at the junction. Super food something, warehouse or barn, I can't remember. Either way, things are going to be pretty lean.'

'Fine. I'm going off truffles anyway, they're so oily.' Abi rolled away to face the cot, irritated. Did Stu for some reason think she had grown up in comfort? As though things being lean wasn't the only state she'd ever known? As though juggling grocery money and the gas bill, Rae's medications and her own school things hadn't been a source of constant anxiety ever since she took over the running of the household before her twelfth birthday?

Before she arrived with Jude, Stu had agreed to support them all until Abi could reasonably get a job. Although she hadn't noticed it in London, she was beginning to realise that Stu had a tendency to forget things they had decided on. And sometimes, Abi was starting to see, he could be a bit impractical. She wondered if Elaine's ready provision of Pyrex had delayed his full entry into adulthood.

As she lay on her side, nursing frustration, Stu turned again and fitted himself in around her, hand reaching towards her knickers.

Abi moved it away. 'We can't until six weeks. Sorry.'

'What? Oh right. Ignore that, it's just muscle memory.' Stu's breath was warm on the back of her neck.

Although she had been the one to put him off, Abi felt faintly offended. 'Well good, because the last time I checked, it still looked like there's been quite a violent murder in my pants.'

Stu yawned. 'Yeah, well considering the southbound traffic that's come out of you recently babe, I was hardly expecting much of the northbound variety.'

'Wow, Stu. That's a really powerful image. Very visual.'

'I am very visual,' Stu said without irony. 'Okay then. Anyway, I really need to go to sleep. Don't worry too much about the money, eh? It's early days and I can just ask Mum to bring us some more casseroles until we've figured things out.'

As Abi began to drift off, Stu muttered something about finally finding the old Nokia he'd been meaning to give her. 'But I reckon calling your Mum will cost a bomb, so maybe you can just text her instead,' he said, voice trailing off. It was the only privation for which Abi felt grateful. Rae found talking on the phone tiring anyway, she told herself against a stab of guilt, so texting every other day was probably best for both of them.

12.

I would hang on to those

The next day began when Abi decided it might as well. Stu was already gone when she woke up, and after she checked Jude and found him still sleeping, she ate a mug of Stu's Nutri-Grain with a teaspoon and realised she had nothing to do. Abi peered down at the big house, but no one came out. As she squared a pile of Stu's drawing blocks, the phone rang.

It was Elaine, whose voice on the other end of the line sounded like a recorder blowing a never-ending high C. Privately, Abi had begun to think of her as the Brush.

'I'm not sure what you have planned for today but you and the baby are going to need structure, especially once Stuart is not around as much.' Abi gripped the phone, feeling as though she was being surveilled from headquarters, the Kellett family home in Gordon. Stuart was hardly around *now*, but Abi decided not to interrupt Elaine's flow. 'You will need to try and meet other mothers. They're unlikely to be as young as you in such a nice area, but you take my point.'

'Yes, no, I know. I've already phoned up about mothers' groups, and got a load of hot leads.'

It was true that before setting out on her walk the previous day, Abi had looked up the number for the Cremorne Early Childhood Unit. Kim on Reception asked when she was due.

'I've already had him.' Abi told her. 'He's coming up for four weeks. I've just moved here.'

That was going to be a problem, Kim was sorry to say. All the groups were put together by the midwives prenatally.

'He shouldn't actually have been born until last week though so I could technically still be pregnant if you think about it. If he went over. Maybe we can count it from then?'

Kim said they could not, but welcomed Abi to try any one of the drop-in playgroups listed on the website under Community Groups. 'Mothers usually start when the little ones are one,' Kim said. Abi had hung up and made a mental note to call back in eleven and a bit months.

Elaine cleared her throat. 'Are you listening, Abi?'

'Yes, sorry. Also, I meant to say, I actually have met one other mother already. Down at the pool yesterday, so that's good. She's really nice.'

Elaine did not need to know that she was also probably seventy. 'Well, I'm pleased to hear that. I'd try very hard to make her a friend.'

'Definitely.'

'And you'll know there's a baby music group, Little Movers it's called, at the Uniting Church on Wycombe Road on weekday mornings.' Elaine's voice bristled with challenge. 'It starts in half an hour. I suppose you were just about to leave for it.'

'I was. You're right. I was just looking up how to get there.'

'Well good, because it's a very steep walk. There'll be a morning tea, but you won't have had time to make something I expect. We'll see you on Sunday. I have to go. I don't like calling mobiles.'

Abi added it to her mental list of Elaine's dislikes, just below losing track of coolers and babies being born out of wedlock. Reluctantly, she dressed, fed Jude for long enough to last him all the way up to the church and took a packet of Monte Carlos out of the cupboard above the fridge.

They arrived minutes before the music was due to start. A woman sat behind a trestle table set up with a money tin and a roll of sticky name labels. Hers was a more permanent variety of name tag, encased in hard plastic, attached with a safety pin, 'HELLO, MY NAME IS ROS', handwritten in capitals. She held out her hand for the suggested gold coin donation.

'Prams stay outside and nannies usually sit towards the back.'

'Oh. I'm not his nanny. I'm his mum.'

'Are you sure?' HELLO, MY NAME IS ROS looked sceptical. 'You don't look old enough.'

'I'm definitely sure. I remember him flying out of me Christmas just gone.' Abi took the biscuits out from under the pram. 'Do I give these to you?'

'Oh.' Ros's face was a picture of disappointment. 'I would hang on to those. This isn't really that sort of group. I'd bring fruit next time. Or sushi. All the littlies seem to like sushi.'

Abi entered the hall with Jude in her arms and made her way towards a tight circle of mothers sitting cross-legged on the floor, babies on their laps. Hello My Name is Someone Else was taking wooden instruments out of a tub and arranging them in an intricate formation. The few mothers who had not managed to secure a place in the ring milled around its periphery, talking to their babies in educational tones. Abi felt certain that should a place in the circle open up, their teaching moment would be happily abandoned.

As Abi made her way over, a woman whose bearing suggested she was, to all purposes, the head mother, turned towards her with an expansive smile already in place.

'Oh, I thought you were Katrina,' she said, face falling.

'Thank God it's not,' another one said. 'I really hope they've stopped coming. Not for our sakes, but for the children. You cannot tell me it's any fun for her anyway when Ethan has one of his meltdowns. You know he scratched a *newborn* last week and it bled. I seriously hope it'd had its tetanus.'

Abi waited for someone to point out that you couldn't really get tetanus from an angry toddler. No one did.

'She needs to get him assessed. He is so on the spectrum.'

'I wouldn't be surprised. I'd want to know, personally. If it was the other way around and it was mine. I'd want someone to say something.'

After a minute more, Abi knelt on the floor behind them and put Jude discreetly on her breast, imagining what it would be like to announce to a group of women that cashews were actually the most toxic nut according to a thing she'd just read. To declare with authority that nine months was the time to face the car seat the other way.

Husbands were referred to by their first names: 'Craig likes a lie-in.' 'Rod's in Japan.' 'I told Chris no more golf til everyone's at school, I'm sorry but there it is.'

Abi looked down at Jude, feeding intently in her arms, kissed his upturned cheek, and whispered, 'Stu is a student and earns fifty dollars a shift.'

A final rice shaker was added to the arrangement of children's instruments, now more elaborate than a Celtic Fertility Circle, and the talking ceased.

13.

Clayton's panicking

When the singing reached its merciful conclusion, Abi went over to look at the morning tea. A mass of children had already clustered around it and unable to break in, Abi carried Jude to a semi-circle of empty chairs. Hoping no one was watching, she drew the biscuits out of her bag and ate one behind her hand.

'You'll love a Monte Carlo when you're older, Jude,' she said, wiping a fallen crumb off his tummy.

'Can I sit here? Please?' said a woman who appeared in front of her. 'Before someone tries to put me on the tea roster?'

Abi looked up. A mother not much older than her was already shrugging off an oversized nappy bag, and with a single movement, she swung the toddler on her hip onto her lap as she sat down. The boy seemed enormous to Abi. He wore huge brown sandals with velcro straps and could pick up his own dummy from where it was clipped to his chest and manoeuvre it all the way into his mouth.

'I'm Tiffany. This is Nicholas. He's had a virus but he's fine now. Look at your little one! He's so titchy.'

'Are you English?' Abi asked, realising only then that the woman was speaking in the voice of home.

'Wolverhampton originally, but then Clapham. You are as well.'

'Croydon,' Abi said.

'Which bit, bab?'

'The less nice bit.'

Abi hesitated and offered her a biscuit.

'Thank fuck,' Tiffany said, taking three at once. 'I hate those stupid fruit kebabs. So how long have you been in Sydney, then?'

'Since Sunday.'

'Right, gosh. Okay. We're coming up five years. Hold on, look busy.' Tiffany released Nicholas from her lap and shunted him gently towards the free play area as an ox-like mother strode towards them, pushing a huge red stroller that had escaped redirection to the designated pram area.

'Well, that's perfect,' she said, braking the pram. 'I finally get here and she's asleep. We've missed the music and I've blown two dollars bringing her out. Hello Tiffany. And what's your name? I haven't seen you before.'

'I'm Abi. And this is Jude.'

'Well he can't be more than a week old. You're keen, I'll say that. Coming here with one that small.'

'He's older than he looks. He was a bit early.'

'Lydia, in there, is sixteen months. She's not walking yet. She doesn't need to. She's a bum shuffler. Gets around like nothing else. Clayton's panicking, but I'm not.'

Tiffany sighed and looked away.

'How have you been anyway, Tiffany? We all got your cold after last week, thanks very much. Lydia couldn't go to care but I got it the hardest.'

'How did you know it was *our* cold?'

'Because we saw you here in the morning and then Lydia was 37.9 by bedtime. Clayton wanted to take her to A&E but I knew it was just what you and Nicholas had.'

'Well, I'm very sorry. We will try and keep our germs to ourselves from now on.'

'I haven't been right since,' the woman sighed, dropping into a facing chair.

'No. I can see that,' Tiffany said, then leaned closer to Abi, 'Let's scoot, bab. A seniors dance class comes in next and although getting the ride-ons back in the cupboard before then is generally the most exciting bit of the Little Movers experience, I cannot be arsed to help pack away.'

'There's no way I'm doing it either.' As the woman rose again, she reached a hand behind her back and performed an intimate readjustment of her leggings. Abi, still seated, could tell they had also ridden up uncomfortably in the front. 'I was only here for five minutes but I'm going to get some morning tea at least. I hope they've got fruit kebabs. Nice to meet you, Abi. See you, Tiffany.'

Abi started gathering her things. 'Do you live near here?' Her voice rose as she mustered courage. 'Maybe we could meet up one day but only if you want to. If you're not busy. Don't worry though. I don't even have my diary here anyway, so I probably can't either.'

Tiffany looked at her sadly. 'I'd have loved to, but the truth is me and Nicholas's dad are splitting up and I'm going back to the UK next week … I don't know how long for.'

'I'm really sorry,' Abi said, as much for their marriage as her own empty diary.

'All right, well I better go and get Nicholas before he pulls that white board over on himself. It was lovely to meet you Abi. Good luck. It's lovely here, you'll like it. Once you're used to the heat and those fucking birds that sound like crying babies.'

Tiffany walked off to retrieve her son. At the door, she turned back and waved. Abi waved back and ate the last Monte Carlo.

* * *

Abi took a longer way home, winding slowly down the hill to where the main road curved past an entrance to the harbourside path. She bumped the pram down the wide stone steps, and after a series of bends, she came to the pool from the other direction.

The woman she had met the day before was standing in front of the gate in the same robe and sunhat, this time with a small dog that strained at its leash as she tried to knot it around a picket. Abi's heart leaped. As she approached, the dog started yapping. Jude startled and let out a sharp cry which made the woman turn.

'Ah, hello again.' She smiled broadly. 'Dear Jude, I *am* sorry. You must excuse this wretched animal.'

Hearing his name in the woman's rich, lilting tone gave Abi a little shiver – that she'd even remembered it.

'Domenica Regina, be quiet. *Sit!*'

'Is your dog really called Domenica Regina?' Abi bit her thumbnail.

'Well, she came to me as *Sophie*. But I simply refuse to be a woman of a certain age with a silly dog named like some longed-for child. And since the ridiculous animal is always trying to project a royal bearing, well – you can see.' She lifted the latch and held out her arm to usher Abi through with the pram. 'You can't imagine the indignity of having to use the words *bichon frise* in company.'

The woman chose a bench in the shade and took off her hat. Waves slopped noisily below the boardwalk. 'Will you sit?' she asked, sliding across to make room for Abi.

Abi parked Jude in deeper shade and sat down. 'The dog must be good company though? They say companions are good for ...'

'... the aged? I beg your pardon.' There was a note of teasing in the woman's voice. 'My eldest daughter got her for me after my husband passed away last year. Absolutely did not consult me but that is very typical Polly, do you see? She's also in London – a more salubrious part than her sister, I should say. I expect she felt guilty for going back so soon afterwards, as well she ought, so she foist an animal upon me in consolation.'

The woman spoke with an accent Abi could not identify. It was proper, but neither English nor Australian. 'You're not from the UK, are you?'

'No. I was raised in the east, before I married Frederick.'

'Oh, like the Emirates or whatnot?'

'The eastern suburbs, dear. Rose Bay. Now tell me, why have I never seen you until yesterday and now we've come across each other twice?' The woman smiled with bright, waiting eyes and Abi felt as if the knot in her stomach loosened for the first time in days, or weeks, or her entire life until that moment.

14.

The pastry will lose its crunch

Roger had offered to meet them at the station and drive them back to the house. It was Sunday, the day of Elaine's scheduled luncheon. 'There's a car seat for the wee tacker in there,' Roger said as he held the door open for Abi. 'Elaine thinks of everything. She's a marvel.'

As soon as Abi had mastered its complicated system of buckles, Roger nosed out of the carpark and waited for a break in the fast-moving traffic. The highway was banked by sparse trees, with no footpath on either side. It was leafy, Abi thought, without being in any way green. 'This is very ... foresty out here, isn't it?'

'Yes. We like it. So close to the national park,' Roger caught Abi's eye in the rear vision mirror. 'And the birds. We get all sorts up here. Galahs ...' the thought petered out and it was left a list of one.

'You could have gone then, Dad,' Stu said. 'Dad, go. Seriously, there's stacks of room.'

Finally Roger saw his chance and they drove for a while in silence. Abi took a photograph of Jude in the capsule on her phone and texted it to Rae with a short message. Although it must have been the middle of the night, her mother's sleeping pattern was unpredictable and an erratically spaced reply came back immediately, followed by another.

'Do u know whereabts of teh nail clipper??'

'Pat is havingfoot trouble.'

Hoping there was no connection between the two, Abi put her phone away and looked ahead. Above Roger's headrest, she noticed a circle of moony white scalp in the centre of his thinning hair, as soft and vulnerable as Jude's fontanel. Worried that she might reach and touch it, Abi leaned between the front seats and said, 'I love Australian birds I meant to say.'

'You don't love that one you said sounds like a lot of chavs having a go at each other,' Stu said.

'Now, I've heard that word, *chav*,' Roger said, eyes on the road. 'But you'll have to tell me what it is.'

Abi faltered. 'It's a girl who's a bit of a sla— a bit common? From the estates often. Some people call them pramfaces as well? They wear shell suits and have names like Chanel, spelt with extra letters and whatnot.'

Roger accepted her explanation with a single nod. Stu had started jumping between radio stations, making further conversation impossible.

Eventually they turned into a quiet residential street. The driveways leading up to wide, single-storey houses shimmered with heat. At a stop sign, Roger reached into the pocket of his trousers to retrieve his phone. 'Your mother wanted me to message her when we're ten minutes away so she can put the vegies on.'

He handed the phone to Stu but he shut it in the glovebox. 'Don't worry about it, Dad. Let's go crazy and just turn up, eh?'

It was clear when they pulled up in front of the Kellett homestead and saw Elaine peering through a gap in the vertical blinds, that she was not pleased. She appeared in the carport like a shot and stood with her hands on her hips. The brushed plume quivered as though independently furious. 'The vegies, Roger! Didn't I say?'

He looked stricken.

'Thought we'd give you a surprise,' Stu said as he lifted Jude out of the car and held him face down under his arm, like a football.

'You've given me enough surprises lately to last a lifetime thank you Stuart. We won't be able to eat until 12.15 now. Hello Abi. You look tired. Well, don't stand around out here. We'll all get cooked.'

Abi followed the others inside. The air in the hallway had the cool, stale quality of an unused guest room. Along both walls, glass-fronted cabinets displayed expensive-looking china figurines, apple-cheeked children kneeling in prayer, wistful mimes, very realistic forest animals. Abi could not imagine someone with Stu's energy growing up surrounded by so many breakable things, and such a volume of *potpourri*. The hallway led through to a tidy kitchen and conservatory dining area looking out to the back garden. Roger and Stu took a wicker loveseat that let out a startling crack as it received their weight. Jude's arms and legs shot out with fright and Stu let Abi take him.

She remained standing, unsure where to put herself, until Elaine motioned towards a peacock chair that Abi assumed was only for show due to its careful arrangement of cushions. They were embroidered with sayings she could not imagine coming from Elaine's own mouth. 'A mother holds your hand for a day and your heart forever.' 'Perfect mothers have dirty ovens and happy children.'

Elaine's oven turned out to be fairly spotless, she discovered, when Roger asked to hold Jude, and Abi wandered into the kitchen to make offers of help that were reluctantly given in to. Elaine allowed her to take a salmon quiche through to the table but yelped audibly when Abi missed the trivet by an inch and earthenware met glass.

'Well, don't wait. The pastry will lose its crunch,' Elaine said in lieu of grace as they all sat down.

Roger raised his glass of Appletiser towards Abi. 'Your first week in Australia, eh? Good on you, dear.'

With Jude back in her arms, Abi tried to reach her glass and knocked a tall pepper grinder into a bowl of shredded iceberg. 'Gosh, I'm so sorry.'

Elaine winced. 'Abi, give the baby to me so you can eat properly.' For the rest of the meal, she stood on Abi's periphery, rocking Jude. Every so often, Abi heard her sigh and say, 'Goodness me Jude. What are we going to do with you?' Abi felt like her throat was closing up and swallowing each mouthful of creamed salmon filling became an act of will.

When they finished eating and Elaine had reprimanded Roger in a whisper for scraping at the table, Stu was sent outside to help his father move a heavy pot. Elaine followed to supervise, taking Jude with her. Left alone in the conservatory, Abi felt like a cord connecting her to Jude had stretched to breaking. She could see him out the window, and longed to take him back.

Abi dared not start the dishes, so instead found the loo and after washing her hands, folded what looked like one of Elaine's good handtowels back into the shell-shape she'd found it in. Unable to think what to do next, she returned to the peacock chair and sat down, trying not to touch a scratchy bolster that said 'Home, where friends are family and family are friends.' Feeling distinctly that she belonged in neither group, Abi yawned and closed her eyes.

Somewhere between awake and asleep, her mind returned to the pool and the woman she'd met there. This time, Abi called out to her before diving confidently into the water. Snatches of their conversation replayed themselves, but Abi heard herself saying much cleverer things.

Sometime later, Abi woke to the sound of Roger carefully wiping his feet at the back door. 'Do you like Chinese chequers?'

Abi sat up straight. 'I love them. But I might need reminding of the rules.' She rubbed her eyes. 'I mean, if you want to play. Or were you just asking in general? Sorry. I think I might have nodded off just then.'

Roger found an old set from inside a lace-trimmed ottoman with a lift-up top and took the seat opposite Abi.

'I expect you're still feeling a bit upsy-down town, eh?' he said, opening the faded box.

'I suppose I am. I didn't think it would be this different. The food. The telly, your plastic money. I keep having to work things out in pounds so I know if they're expensive or not. Maybe that's why I'm so tired, from so much long division.'

'No doubt,' Roger said. 'I went to America for a conference in '92 and I was the same. Did you know that when you flush an American lavatory, the water comes right up to the top? You think it's about to overflow,' he paused, pensively, 'and then it doesn't. I was very glad to get home.'

'I bet. I do like it here though, the weather especially.'

'And you've got the ferry. Jude will love the ferry when he's bigger.'

'I saw one called *Friendship* yesterday. You'd not get a Hammersmith & City train called *Friendship*. More like *The Verbal Assault*. Or *The Fatal Stabbing*.'

'When Elaine and I lived where you are as newlyweds, I used to get the *Sirius* into town. It often ran late, and I'd say, you're not *Sirius*!' Roger paused again and his look became grave. 'Jude's lovely, Abi. A very good little boy and I think you're lovely with him.' At that, he fell back in his chair, as though he'd finally let go of a secret too enormous to contain.

Abi could say or do nothing. No one had said such a nice thing about her as a mother.

'Sometimes, I feel like I'm not good enough for him,' Abi said when Roger began to look worried, as though he'd been inappropriate. 'I almost expect someone to come and take him and give him back to a real mum. That probably sounds weird, it's like he's too good to be true.'

'No, no. I understand. I feel like that about Stuart, still now. And I probably shouldn't say this, dear, but I know how Elaine can be. She's always wanted a daughter, you see. And now here you are, but she sometimes takes a bit to warm up.'

Because she was beginning to love Roger so much, Abi smiled as though she really believed him.

As Roger finished setting up the board, Elaine returned, still holding Jude and followed by Stu. 'You ought to get going shortly if you want to avoid traffic coming back from the Coast.'

Roger poured the counters back into the box and went off to get the car keys.

At the door, Elaine gestured towards a stiff paper shopping bag, tucked behind the umbrella stand. 'It's baby clothes from the St Luke's Mother's Union. Pre-loved, but there's some very nice things in there, which you can return for bigger sizes when he grows out of them, so please keep them nice.'

'Thank you very much,' Abi said, taking it by one handle and hoping that whatever was inside would not make Jude look like an orphan who needed sponsoring for as little as a dollar a day.

'Hey, Mum said she'd babysit for us next Saturday night,' Stu said, on the train home. 'That'll be fun, eh?'

Abi gave a weak thumbs-up, and went back to kissing Jude's cheeks, which had absorbed the synthetic lilac scent of Elaine's perfume.

15.

Absolute steel

Her name was Phyllida. 'But no one's called me that since my games mistress,' she said, holding out her hand to be shaken. '*Phil*. Very nice to meet you, Abigail.'

They were sitting on a striped cotton towel that Phil had tossed over the slats of the bench. It was Monday again and as soon as Stu had left for work, Abi set off with the pram in the hope of finding her there.

Abi went to correct her, but decided it was better not to seem fussy about her name. They performed a funny half-shake, laughing at the formality of a proper introduction now, when they'd been chatting for nearly an hour and Abi was up to the getting pregnant part of why she'd moved here.

Phil found it all delightfully unconventional. As she listened, she glanced occasionally towards Jude, who was lying on a towel in the shade, turning circles with his fists and blinking up at the dappled green above him.

Abi tried to explain, as delicately as she could, how contraception-wise she probably believed on some level that she had credits owing, having managed not to get pregnant right up until she did. 'But it doesn't work like that, does it? It's like the Tesco ad, "every little bit counts" but with …' Abi stopped. 'I mean …'

'I know quite what you mean, thank you,' Phil said, amused. 'I never really mastered the precautionary arts either, dear. I found it easier simply to get married.'

'It probably would have been better if I could have told Stu, that's my, um, partner face to face, and a bit sooner as well, but he'd already come back here, so I just had to do it on the computer.'

Phil threw her head back and released a high, operatic laugh. 'Don't speak. How extraordinary.'

'There probably aren't that many people who've found out they're going to be a dad on Instant Messenger, I suppose.' Abi bit her lip, recalling the ribboning thread of message saved somewhere on her laptop.

As the sun began to creep across the bench, Phil shuffled closer and listened rapt, a hand to her cheek. Abi told her about Jude coming three weeks early so that Stu missed it, of giving birth in the foyer, the mini-cab home, and coming out here to have a go at things.

'Well, that really is tremendous, Abigail.' Again, Abi thought about correcting her, but Phil kept on. 'Nobody seems to do it the old way anymore, do they?'

At that, she stood and took off her robe, casting it over the pickets. Abi moved to sit beside Jude, who was pedalling his tiny purple feet in the air. She picked him up and felt the warmth of his back through his little vest.

'Are you coming in?' Phil called from the ladder. 'It's very fresh.'

'Oh probably not,' Abi answered quickly. 'I think I forgot my bathing suit.' Although it was true that she had rummaged one out of the off-season bin at the TK Maxx on Hammersmith King Street before leaving London, the price tag was yet to be removed.

'Surely your little shorts would suffice. There's not a soul around. Come on, slip off your sandals and have a paddle at least.'

Abi laid Jude over one shoulder and took a few nervous steps towards the edge. She peered into the depths.

'What about you cool your toes on the step there? Jude looks not long for this world, don't you think? You can sit and let him have a zizz in your arms.'

Phil motioned towards a platform running along one end of the pool, creating a long shallow strip of warmer water. Abi stepped down onto it and felt the water rush around her ankles.

'I must say,' Phil said, watching her progress, 'you do have the most fetching little figure, dear. I could feel like farm stock beside you.'

Abi looked down at her thin, white legs, knock-kneed and shivering like a child's. 'Oh my gosh. Fudge, it's really freezing, isn't it?'

'Yes, we must be brave. Although clearly you're made of absolute steel. Having a baby and emigrating all on your own. Really, truly Abigail, you're a wonder.'

'Not really. I mean it was all an accident really. A happy one, I hope. It's just all a bit mental at the minute.' She laughed awkwardly as she peeled Jude away from her shoulder and sitting, laid him along the length of her thighs.

He had, she thought, only today stopped looking so newborn. Where there'd been soft wrinkles in his skin, thick, creamy rolls were forming and a whole extra chin had appeared, needing to be wiped clean of milk and fluff that somehow collected there. No longer could she span his entire tummy with one hand. 'I didn't realise about the love. I really, really love him. Sorry, that's so soppy.' She glanced towards Phil, embarrassed.

'Well I'm not one for sop generally, but I rather accept your excuse.'

Phil waded over and with one brisk movement underwater, hoisted herself onto the platform so they were side by side. 'And of course you love him, my dear. Babies are never accidents. They're born when they jolly well feel like it and we mothers simply make a fist of whatever circumstances they find us in.'

Warmth, like hot blood, spread through Abi's chest, down her arms. *We mothers*. Is this what absolution felt like? Was this why people went and did religious confessions, for the exquisite release of being let off by someone so obviously good?

'I'm sorry about your husband,' Abi said. She wanted to return the kindness. 'You said he passed on?'

'Ah. An awful blow, yes. He hadn't been ill you see, so the children didn't know to come home. They did not get the moment of saying goodbye, only that dread phone call, and I really mind that for them. As for me, well I feel other people's sympathy might be the really deadliest bit of the whole business. And I'd rather not have got a dog out of it.'

She let out a sharp little laugh and began moving her hands back and forth beneath the water, sending ripples out from where they sat. 'I hear myself saying, *last year*. My husband passed away *last year*, but it was only November, do you see? Still I wake up most mornings having simply forgotten. Polly keeps telephoning to see if I've done his wardrobes and for a minute I can't think what on earth she means.'

She fell silent, still working her hands below the surface. Abi watched, mesmerised by the way the blue stone of her ring dissolved against the water. 'My dad died when I was little,' she said, without shifting her gaze. 'And my sister. Louise.'

It was a moment before Abi realised she had spoken. She rarely talked about it. Not even Stu had heard about it exactly. Now to Phil, she couldn't stop, as though she had coughed up the tip of a soggy silk scarf and had to pull it all the way out, colour after grubby colour. 'I was nine. We were only thirteen months apart. My mum and I went out to get me new trainers and Louise wanted to come but she changed her mind before the bus came and my mum let her run back. When we got home, it was freezing inside but the telly was on and Dad was lying face down, halfway up the stairs, like he'd tripped on his way up. Then I ran up and my sister was on the floor between our beds.'

Phil had turned to look at her, her face set in quiet horror.

'Her eyes were open,' Abi went on, putting herself close to tears. 'So I didn't click at first. I thought she was just being an idiot and I was like, "Louise, I can see your pants!" It turned out the gas fire in our front room had gone off and they said my dad had probably realised too late to save them. Sorry.' She wiped her nose with the back of her hand. Abi saw Louise on the floor with her arms above her head, as though she had fallen from a height. As always, she willed her sister to get up and be all right. To point her finger and say, 'Ha! I was only joking, innit!'

'I didn't mean to go on. I always used to hope it would make me a bit mysterious and tragic, you know like someone in a sad novel. But people get bored of feeling sorry for you and decide you're just a weirdo. Or probably that was just the girls at my school.'

She exhaled roughly, and tried to smile it off. 'In the end I'd just make up all sorts of different versions of what happened. Not lies, but you know … less full on.'

Abi lifted Jude off her lap. Phil said nothing. 'I just wish Mum had made her come with us. Sorry.'

Below the water, Phil placed a weightless hand on Abi's knee. 'No. You mustn't apologise, dear. Not to me anyhow. I also had my darling James, you see. My first boy. It was his last year of school and one day, he came off the rugby field and took himself to bed saying he felt off colour. I should have suspected.' Phil's eyes reddened at the rims. 'I thought I'd let him sleep until tea. He'd been up there for hours, you know, when I – he wasn't quite eighteen. I should never have let him play that awful game. And like you say, people almost become afraid of you afterwards.

They can't bear it for you, I suppose, so they all remember there's somewhere else they need to be, or spout some tosh about time being the great healer. Well, we are thirteen years on and frankly, it is fresh every morning.'

'Same. It's the same with me and Louise.'

'Although you know,' Phil went on. 'I listened to a radio programme the other week and there was an author on, whose name escapes me, but he said when a loved one dies, for the first few years you can still see them walking into the room, hear their voice and such like. But at some point you can't anymore and it makes them somehow … *deader*.'

Abi nodded. She had tried so hard to keep Louise alive in her mind but the real girl slipped further away as each year passed. 'And you can't really imagine having them around now. Like, if they did walk through the door, because their clothes start to be all wrong, and their hair. They'd look a bit old-fashioned, wouldn't they? Like they'd got trapped in their photos.'

Louise was not a real girl anymore. She was a long ago person, flat and unreal in her velvet newsboy cap and denim overalls with the bib pinned all over with badges. It wasn't the Louise who laughed and swore and talked too fast, who took money from Rae's purse without asking and tried on her bra whenever they were left home alone. She wasn't Abi's protector, her good, bossy mother, the divvier up of KitKats and holder of the bus money.

Phil heaved out a deep sigh and hauled herself back up on the platform. 'What about your mother, dear?'

'Oh,' Abi stuttered. How could she ever describe Rae to somebody as vivacious and full of life as Phil? Even in her mind, the contrast between them was overwhelming. 'No. I mean, unfortunately she … my Mum's no longer …'

Phil dropped her head to one side. 'Surely not!'

Abi could tell she had misunderstood.

'No, no ...' She cast about for a way to explain that after the accident, Rae had entered a tunnel of grief and never emerged.

But Phil fixed Abi with a look of such deep affection, Abi froze. 'You needn't say any more, Abigail. You suddenly look quite wrung out. So much loss, dear, too much loss for such a little thing as you.' She slid off the platform and began to tread water.

Abi had not meant to lie. And she hadn't, not on purpose. The only movement now was the slightest sealing of her lips.

'Good *Lord*,' Phil said a moment later, falling into a lazy backstroke. 'There must be two other mothers somewhere in the world who've not had a single whiff of tragedy thanks to us. We've had more than our share, haven't we? Anyhow, you won't have a plunge, just in what you're wearing, Abigail? Will I hold the dear boy while you do?'

'Oh, no thank you,' Abi said. 'I should get him back really. He'll be yelling in a minute.' She stood up and felt the water running down off her shins.

'Well then, I shall do a few desultory laps in that case,' Phil said, moving off towards the other end. 'No doubt we'll meet again, if you're now of the Point.'

As Abi carried Jude home, smelling his soft, downy head, she promised she would make it all straight next time. Explain properly. There was going to be a next time – Phil had just said so.

16.

There's no need to be vulgar

Phil felt oddly energised by her little talk with the girl at the pool, even if the conversation had been tragic in substance. To have lost your entire family by such a young age! Phil could hardly fathom it – and it was not as though she was a stranger to tragedy herself. With her basket over her arm and Domenica yanking at the leash, Phil took her time to walk home, after swimming ten rather good lengths. She sighed, thinking of Frederick. Then again, more absent-mindedly, remembering James.

The girl had introduced herself as Abi, although Phil did not enjoy the use of diminutives outside her immediate family and would certainly not have them foisted upon her. She would use Abigail.

She was a recent émigré and her eagerness for company was plain from their first meeting. Phil had spoken to her briefly and then again the next day when the plaintive looks in her direction became impossible to ignore. Although cautious of becoming obliged – the pool was Phil's own sanctuary and the last thing she wished to create for herself there was duty – when the chatter got up and going the girl turned out to be infinitely more interesting than one would expect from the look of her.

She was such a slip of a thing, with a skittish way of moving, like some poor animal that's been belted all its life, and bolts to the corner whenever anyone tries to give it a pat. But then, when it came, a husky smoker's voice and a charmingly dirty laugh that followed nearly everything she said, even the particulars of a really ghastly life story. Truly, it was no wonder those nails were bitten to the quick.

And her hair, although a lovely, almost Titian colour, looked for all the world as though it had been nibbled round by a mouse in the night. But then the glorious milk-white skin, so unlike the leather handbag variety so often seen here, Phil thought, as she covered her décolletage with her damp Turkish towel and walked on.

The jewel of a baby too. It was hard not to be smitten by something so new, and the cautious, tender way a new mother had was always lovely to watch. Abigail looked when she held him as though she'd been asked to mind the infant Messiah while Mary popped out to run errands.

Still, it was hard not to feel rather low about the child's prospects. Idly, Phil wondered if she ought to stand in the gap, as it were. A little motherly direction was clearly required and it was not, Phil noted with dismay, as though her own dance card was full at the present time.

She gave Domenica a sharp tug on the leash and opened her side gate. At the back door, she braced herself before entering the tomb-like silence of the kitchen. Oppressive, that's what it was, the silence was oppressive. It lay in wait and pounced the moment she walked in.

A less disciplined woman, Phil thought, as she felt out the key from inside the planter and stuck it in the lock, a less *disciplined* woman would stop going out just to avoid the horror of coming back in and finding everything exactly as it had been left. Newspaper untouched, tea cold in the cup and a dripping tap like a bloody jungle drum.

But anyway, there it was, she'd done it now. 'There you go, Poll,' she said out loud. 'Mother's had her outing, you'll be pleased to know.'

Since Frederick, Polly had developed a near obsession with how Phil was handling what she called 'the grief process'. Was she getting out? Was she keeping busy? Seeing friends, eating properly and – most galling to Phil – keeping up a standard of personal care?

Phil picked up a few bits of mail stacked by the phone, waiting to be dealt with in a stronger moment. All addressed to Frederick Woolnough QC and all now her problem even though, she realised with immense disappointment at the cliché of it, she had no idea how to go about it. Fred had taken care of all that side of things. Once or twice, when the children were small, he'd tried to get her interested. But sitting beside him and being made to stare at a lot of printed papers always gave rise to the most fearful bout of yawning. 'Never try to teach your mother anything, girls,' she heard Frederick saying in the teasing tone he had passed on to every one of his children.

As Phil hovered, mail in hand, she could see them all there again, together, in the pleasant chaos of the family kitchen. Polly, scowling over some schoolwork, chin only just higher than the table. Brigitta bathed, pyjama'ed and sulking about some imagined slight. The boys still outside, battering the kitchen door with a ball.

'If you do, my girls, she'll go out of her way not to learn it,' Frederick would say, bopping Phil on the behind with a rolled newspaper.

Phil's half-laugh became a sigh and then, looking down at his name on the envelopes, she realised it was too late. She was in for one now. She steadied herself against the kitchen bench and let it come – an enormous, juddering wave of agony that constricted the chest, swelled her tongue until she was gasping for air. It grabbed onto her, tossed her about, threatened to knock her to the floor. She held the edge of the benchtop with both hands and waited – it would move on as quickly as it had come. It was useless to fight against it, she knew. It had been the same with James.

A minute later she released her grip, wrists aching from the pressure. So many years ago, a midwife in a starched white apron and neat cap had stood beside her as she delivered one of the boys, and with every harrowing contraction, she had patted Phil's hand and said, 'There's another one you never have to have again.' As Phil pressed her face into a tea towel, she hoped the same rule might apply to this brutal business. *The grieving process.* Except, of course, the desperate moments of grief never did stop after James, only became fewer and further between.

After a lie down, a few chapters of a political memoir and a half-hearted attempt on Frederick's sock drawer, Phil picked up the cordless and dialled Brigitta.

She took forever picking up. Phil counted the rings and tried not to work out what time it would be in London. It was certainly on the early side, but if she was going to wake Brigitta she'd be truthfully able to claim she didn't know exactly how early.

Finally, Brigitta's groggy voice came on the line.

'Mum. Hello.'

'Briggy dear. How did you know it was I?'

'Because nobody would ever ring at this hour, unless the person happened to come out of them.'

'Darling, there's no need to be vulgar,' Phil said, regretting it immediately.

It was vital to get these chats off on the right foot. A bad phone call to a child overseas had a way of lingering until the next one and sometimes that wasn't for days. Generally, you could tell within seconds if it was going to go well or poorly. And although Brigitta seemed to share the same intuition, neither was game to hang up as soon as the conversation veered into tall grass. This one was yet to establish itself.

'Also because your number comes up on the screen,' Brigitta said.

'Well, I was only wondering, how is my darling girl,' Phil said, wishing she'd left out the *only*.

'I'm fine. But truly Mummers, I'm so zonked. Couldn't you wait until a bit later to call me? I didn't get in until one.'

Phil hated to think of Brigitta slaving away at that bistro, and had offered her an allowance that would let her concentrate on her acting – the entire point apparently of her being in London when Phil could so have done with her at home.

The logic of continuing the evening job – and one that left her on the cusp of exhaustion – quite escaped Phil, who could hear, even now, the fatigue in her daughter's lovely voice.

Still, Phil arranged herself more comfortably on the window seat, propping a cushion behind her back, in the expectation of this becoming a nice lengthy talk. 'Really, Briggy, couldn't you take a little *loan* from your mother so you could put the waitressing business away? Then you could give the acting a good go if that's what you truly want. I wonder anyway if twenty-seven isn't a touch on the mature side for the service industries.'

'Say what you think, Philly, why don't you?' Brigitta laughed. 'Since I'm awake now, will I make a cup of tea and we can go over my life choices one by one?'

'There's no need to be facetious, darling.' Phil felt the lurch again. 'I only know Daddy never liked the idea of his only daughter doing something so backbreaking.'

'His only daughter apart from Polly, you mean.'

'Well. Quite. But we all know he rather numbered Polly as one of the boys. Certainly after James.'

His name was Phil's trump card. It had been for as long as Brigitta could remember. She was forced to change tack. 'Mum, you can be so hopeless,' she said. 'I'm front of house for God's sake. Taking people's coats is hardly backbreaking. Honestly, I'm not as fragile as you all think.'

'You know Polly would happily have you live with them. They've got room, and then at least you could give up the *o-vel*.'

It was a joke between them from when Phil had visited Brigitta in London a year prior and been shocked by her astonishingly basic living arrangements. If she had to live in a hovel, Phil had declared after refusing a cup of tea owing to the look of the cupboard it came out of, at least they might pronounce the word in h-less French. At the time, Phil had given Brigitta another three months to last in such dismal surrounds, but her daughter continued to be uncharacteristically stoic in the face of its privations, and the unceasing grind of being a jobbing actress in London.

When Brigitta first decided on drama school, Phil considered it a passing fad, like the ceramics jag that had come after an unfinished journalism degree, which itself began after two disastrous semesters of law. Yet two years after graduating with really quite good marks, Brigitta was still at it, no sign of fading interest. If pressed, Phil would not have been able to say what sort of career she considered her daughter best suited to. She had never given it concentrated thought. Perhaps, it came to her now as she adjusted the cushion again, something to do with interiors. Or a very smart shop. Phil heard Brigitta yawn, and then from somewhere in the background came a low, mannish cough.

'Is there someone with you, darling?'

'Mum, I need to hang up. I'm as fat as butter and I want to go running before rehearsal. I love you. I don't want to live with my sister. I don't need any money. Please go and find something to do or else I'll tell on you to Polly. I love you, goodbye. I'll ring you soon, I absolutely promise.'

'All right. But please remember, we've got plays here as well, you know. It mightn't be Shakespeare's Globe but –'

'Thank you, Mum. I need to be here. I'm doing well, you know. You should be proud of me.' A moment of silence passed between them before Brigitta spoke again. 'You're all right, aren't you? You're just missing Dad.'

'Oh darling, please.' Phil had no intention of weeping into the cordless, no matter how strong the impulse at that moment. 'Let's not be feeble. And I am proud of you, I'm just not one to be vocal about these things.'

'Okay, Mummers. Loves, honestly. I'll ring you later.' Brigitta gave a kiss into the phone. It went dead against Phil's ear and she remained for a time with it on her lap, thinking the call could have gone worse. Eventually, she forced herself up and to the kitchen, to prepare an early supper for which she had no appetite.

In the end, the setting of a single place at the kitchen table unleashed the tears that had threatened since Brigitta's well-meaning inquiry, and Phil took a dish of buttered Digestives up to bed.

* * *

Brigitta dropped the phone on the floor and, turning over, wrapped herself around Guy, the cougher. Pushing one leg between his, she closed her eyes and hoped she'd delivered her little soliloquy about not needing money with sufficient feeling. 'Make me believe you,' Guy was always saying. 'I want to see your motivation.' He was her director and he really was teaching her all sorts.

17.

Baby corn was very big in Gordon in the nineties

Abi was asleep on the sofa with Jude passed out on her chest, milk-drunk, onesie flaps undone, missing one tiny sock. She woke to the sound of Stu at the front door, struggling to get his key in the lock. On the television, the menu of the DVD that had put her to sleep continued to loop and her water glass lay on its side in a patch of wet carpet. After another moment of effort, Stu got the door open and took two staggering steps into the room. 'Hey babe. Looks like you two had a big night!'

'What time is it?' Abi whispered.

'No idea. One-ish? I had a few beers while we cleaned up and I feel like the last one's only hitting me now. Is there anything in the fridge?'

Stu disappeared into the kitchen and returned a moment later with a bowl of stir-fry, which Abi had made the day before with two-minute noodles and a can of peas she turned up in the Reduced for a Quick Sale! barrel in the back corner of Supa FoodBarn. A layer of dust on the tin suggested that the barrel's object had not been realised.

She longed to go to bed properly, but Stu's energy pulled her back to wakefulness.

'Hey, have you ever noticed that every family has its own stir-fry taste?' Stu said, mouth full. 'You go to anyone's house and their stir-fry is trademark to that family? I could pick Mum's stir-fry out of a line up. Baby corn would give it away in a flash. Baby corn was very big in Gordon in the nineties.'

Since Abi arrived, Stu had developed a habit of reminiscing about his childhood and asking for the details of hers. Already she had run out of stories to exchange for all his memories of Kellett family holidays, kelpie crosses with amazing natures and injuries that had required stitches.

'Rae was not really a mega cook.' Abi's voice was still croaky with sleep. 'Well, she didn't cook ever once it was just me.' Jude whimpered and she adjusted her hold.

'Yeah, sorry, of course.'

'Do you think we have our stir-fry taste?'

'Definitely,' Stu said. 'Shame if this is it though. Still it's good to get that sort of stuff locked in. The rest will fall into place now.'

'I hope so.'

He scraped his fork into the corners of the container. 'So, what did you two get up to today?'

For a moment Abi couldn't think. She was not sure if she was imagining the note of accusation in his voice. Did he presume she did nothing, instead of the endless three-hour circle of critical activity, broken only occasionally by trips to the pool or walking the pram up to the junction for remaindered foodstuffs?

'Well apart from all the normal stuff, we went to the pool in the morning and I ran into that nice lady again. Remember I told you about her? It's weird, she's really interesting even though she's old. She's got one of those yappy dogs, but it's called Domenica Regina. Isn't that the funniest dog name you've ever heard? We chatted for ages today, about all sorts.'

'But she's old? Like Mum's age?' Stu asked, fork aloft.

'A bit older. Maybe seventy or something? No, probably not that old, I don't know. She's got grown-up kids but they all live overseas I think. The daughters definitely do, and there's a son but I don't know where he is. Anyway, her husband just died a month before Christmas, so I think she's a bit hard up for company as well. Which suits me. I mean, not to be mean.'

'Yeah. Don't you think it's weird hanging out with some old lady you're not related to? Especially when you've got my mum right here. She's been trying to arrange a visit and she says you never answer your phone.'

'She phoned once and anyway, I'm creating structure like she said. She keeps telling me to make friends but did you realise that every mum around here is forty-five? And rich.'

Stu's interest had passed and he got up, leaving his bowl on a sofa cushion where Abi knew she would find it in the morning.

She got up and carried the sleeping baby to the window. She could hear Stu gargling loudly from the bathroom. As she peered through the darkness at the big house, the window seat lit up as a perfect rectangle of yellow. Abi could make out the precise shape of Phil in a nightie, holding a glass of something. As she watched, Domenica leapt onto the squab beside her and Phil scratched under the animal's neck.

'Abi! Earth to Abi? I just said I'm going to bed?' Stu was at her elbow.

'Okay,' Abi said without turning. After a time, Phil got up and wandered out of view. The light went off, returning the window seat to darkness. Abi slid into bed beside Stu, already asleep, and savoured the knowledge that Phil was both friend and neighbour.

18.

A night off the Jude talk

The week passed slowly. When Saturday came, Elaine arrived at the flat at 5.59 p.m. and some seconds and let herself in with a key that Abi had not realised she had.

'Thanks for this, Mum,' she heard Stu say. He'd showered and dressed and was looking after Jude on the sofa. He would be bouncing him too vigorously, Abi was sure, but she remained cross-legged on the mattress, with her dress off one shoulder and one breast squashed into a pump that sucked like a feeble dust-buster.

After forty minutes, she had managed to extract somewhere between 7 and 8 ml of thin, bluish milk. There was no way to tell for sure because the measuring lines didn't start until ten. Maybe she was meant to do it before she fed him? But then, wouldn't he need it straight away? How did it work, going out and not taking your baby? *First Year with Baby* had been uncharacteristically opaque on the subject.

As she reached the 15 ml line, hand cramping, nipple like sandpaper, Stu came in to suggest they get a move on. Elaine wanted them back by 9.30 p.m. at the latest and soon it wouldn't be worth going. Abi uncoupled herself from the apparatus, capped the bottle and went through to where Elaine was perched on the sofa with a basket of knitting things on the floor beside her. Jude squirmed unhappily in her arms.

'I couldn't really do much,' Abi said, holding up the bottle which, under Elaine's scrutiny, felt like an embarrassing pathology sample. 'Maybe I'll just, I'll pop it in the kitchen. You won't need to heat it or anything if you use it before ten apparently.'

'We won't be needing it,' Elaine said. 'Will we, baby? Will we?'

'Well, we definitely won't be later than 9.30 anyway. Or earlier even.'

'Good. I don't like driving in the dark,' Elaine said.

'Abs, let's go babe.' Stu was waiting by the door.

'Call if he gets upset? I don't really let him cry, yet, that much? I'm happy to come home if he needs me.'

Elaine didn't look up. 'Goodness. Who's got his mother wrapped around his little finger?'

'Abi, come on,' Stu said from the hallway. She wanted to kiss Jude goodbye but it would mean leaning uncomfortably close to Elaine's chest, so instead she squeezed his bare foot and hoped he knew that was code for *I love you*.

There was a restaurant at the back of Stu's pub and if they went there, he explained on the way to the bus stop, they'd only have to pay staff rates.

When they arrived, Stu introduced Abi to the three boys behind the bar. They were all close in age, with names that sounded like in-jokes. Stu leaned on the bar and carried on a loud conversation as they moved away and back, to serve customers. As Abi listened, Stu's accent became broader with every word. His laugh got louder, he swore more, and finally he punched a passing workmate hard in the arm. At one point, to Abi's horror, he laid a heavy arm around her shoulders and let his hand dangle in the exact vicinity of her nipple.

When someone who Stu had introduced as Luggage winked at her and asked what a girl like her saw in a dickhead like Stu, Abi suggested they should probably go and sit down.

'Righto babe,' Stu said, carrying two large beers he let slop onto the carpet.

'Well this is all very Australian, isn't it?' Abi said as they sat down. 'You sounded like Steve Irwin before. The crocodile person.'

'Don't know what you're talking about,' Stu said, clasping his hands behind his head and leaning back on his chair until the front legs lifted off the floor. Abi tried not to laugh.

'Finally, just you and me, eh?' Stu said.

'Mm, finally,' Abi said. 'I miss Jude though. I just love him so much. He was so sweet today. When we ...'

Stu sucked foam off his beer without lifting the glass. 'Maybe we should have a night off the Jude talk? Since we're doing something fun.'

'Yes. Of course.' Abi rolled her eyes. 'Sorry. I just hope he's all right, that's all. I've never left him before. Not counting last week when your Mum took him out to the garden while you moved that pot.'

Stu seemed not to remember. 'Babe, he'll be fine. Mum knows what she's doing. Anyway, what do you think, nachos? Or will I go a burger? You look hot by the way. You suit skirts.'

It was a dress, but Abi said, 'Thanks. You too. Not the skirts but –'

'Hang on,' Stu said. 'Hey, Slowmo. Get over here, you bastard.' A lanky figure sloped over to their table. He had fried-looking white-blond hair tucked behind his ears and his forehead was peeling from sunburn. 'Slowmo, this is the missus. Abi, this is Slowmo. Worst fucking waiter on the North Shore.'

'Stewed,' the waiter said in a drawl, 'you are on the wrong side of your apron this evening, my friend.' He whomped Stu on the back, shook Abi's hand with a series of slow tugs, then dragged a chair over from the empty table next to them. 'Nice to meet you, Abi. Think I speak for everyone here when I say we're glad to see you're real and that this prick has not been making you up. We'd started to wonder?'

Stu picked a damp cardboard coaster off the table and frisbeed it at him.

'Are you two kicking on with us tonight? Logan's putting on a little open house after we've finished here. Should be good. We've already started laying down a good alcohol baseline out the back.' Slowmo winked at Abi, who was growing accustomed to the gesture now.

Stu paused, glanced at Abi. 'Nah. Another time. Me and Abs are after a quiet one.'

Fighting the sense of being the third wheel on her own night out, Abi looked from Slowmo to Stu and shrugged. 'You could go and I could –'

'Would you mind?' Stu's excitement was palpable. 'Logan's a mate, that's all, and I could really use some downtime before uni goes back. We'll still have dinner and everything.'

Abi tried to look grateful, although the beginning of the semester was still a month away and it seemed like there would be other opportunities to have downtime with Logan.

'Ooh, mate,' said Slowmo, palms raised. 'Might leave you to it. Looks like I've started something here.'

'Wait up, mate,' Stu called after him. 'Where's your little waitress pad? Take our order, that's a boy.'

Slowmo took his time writing 'one large nacho to share' on his pad, and wandered off after calling Stu a massive tool. Stu reached out a hand and took hers under the table. 'Thanks, babe. You're such a legend.'

'All your friends seem really nice,' she said. 'Fun I mean.'

'They're all right, yeah. Mostly students though, except Luggage, who surfs all day and sleeps in his van. No other commitments to speak of, eh.'

'Why do they call you Stewed?' Abi asked.

'As in drunk, I spose.'

'Oh yeah, of course. That's funny.'

'Better than what I used to get, anyway,' Stu said with a touch of nostalgia. 'Before I settled down.'

'What did they call you before?'

'Helen Kellett.'

Abi bit her thumbnail and thought for a moment. 'Oh like, because of being blind?'

'You got it.' Abruptly, Stu pulled his hand out of hers and stood up. 'Back in a sec, I need another one. You right with that?'

Abi nodded and took a series of small sips to catch up. When Stu returned his mood had shifted. His foot tapped furiously under the table as he finished his beer in three enormous slugs.

'Thanks for taking me out,' Abi said.

'Yeah, no problem. It's just, it's weird being here with you. I mean, it's great but I sort of feel like this weird old dad.'

Abi did not mind that his workmates kept coming over to chat as they ate. It gave her a chance to check her phone in case Elaine had tried her – no new messages – and although she hadn't expected it, she was fine to get the bus home by herself as soon as they finished eating. Stu wanted to crack on and there was no point them both going back, he said, kissing her goodbye at the curb. It was all so fine. She'd had a great time, she told herself, leaving Jude for the first time so she could eat nachos with the crocodile hunter.

19.

A complete milk food

Abi could hear Jude crying as she climbed up the dark stairs. She took the last flight in bounds, arms folded across her chest against the sharp tingling of a sudden letdown.

As she tried to force the key in the door, she pictured Elaine on the other side, pacing with him, screaming and rigid in her arms. But when she entered, Elaine was sitting perfectly still on the pull-out, knitting, while Jude howled from behind the closed bedroom door.

'Hello there,' she said, without breaking the rhythm of her stitches.

Abi ignored Elaine's look of censure as she rushed past her to the bedroom and found Jude in his cot, struggling against a too-tight swaddle with all the force in his small body. His face was the colour of a deep bruise and his mouth open to expose the wave-like ridges of his palate and a tiny epiglottis quivering with every fresh bellow.

'It's all right, Mummy's here, Mummy's here,' Abi said, over and over, self-consciously once Elaine began calling out from the next room.

'Abi, really. He's perfectly fine. If you pick him up every time he cries, he'll only learn to manipulate you.'

The idea that a baby who could startle himself with his own hand was already putting together elaborate cause and effect scenarios based on Abi's picking him up or not seemed ridiculous, although she still flushed a deep red. 'Yeah, no, I know,' she said, forcing herself back out into the living room.

Elaine raised a finger to signal quiet while she counted stitches.

'I've never left him,' Abi said. It came out as a growl and Elaine looked at her sharply. 'I've never been away from him.'

'I doubt he noticed. He's got a full tummy and a clean nappy so I really don't think he needs to be babied.'

Abi stared, mute, sure Elaine's face would show that she was joking, in her way. It did not. As Jude's pained screeching dropped to intermittent gasps, Abi moved towards the door, hoping to induce Elaine's departure.

'So did you have to use what I expressed?'

'It would have been nowhere near enough,' she said matter-of-factly. 'Fortunately, I thought to bring reinforcements.' From under a neatly folded cardigan, Elaine withdrew a barrel-like can with a rubber lid and a picture of a baby wearing feathered angel wings. 'I might as well leave this here.'

She looked around for somewhere to put it. *PediBest20: A complete milk food for infants 0–6 months*. The realisation that Elaine had given it to Jude swept through Abi like a fever.

Since she had taught herself to feed him, alone at Highside, holding her breath against the pain, it had been the one thing she could do for him – the one perfect thing. If she could not dress him in new clothes, if she could not put him to sleep in a nice nursery with a jungle motif and stimulating mobile above a pretty cot, if she could not be married to his father, she could do this. And she would do it perfectly, following every stern injunction from *First Year with Baby*.

Although breastfeeding may be painful at first, mothers are
encouraged to persevere … Studies show breastfeeding protects baby

from asthma, eczema as well as common colds … The World
Health Organization recommends continuing for 12–24 months.

Elaine was still holding the can top and bottom like a saleswoman. 'He gobbled it down,' she said. 'It did make me wonder about your *supply*.'

Abi wanted to grab it out of her hands and hurl it at the wall, but stood where she was, gripping Jude. As Elaine continued to speculate on Abi's milk production, the book's imperious narrator sounded on in Abi's mind and she pressed one ear to her shoulder against the noise. *Be careful to preserve your supply by resisting the temptation to supplement with formula … Some less expensive formulas have been found to contain harmful …*

Finally, Elaine exhausted her line of thought and carried the tin through to the kitchen. Abi heard the opening and closing of a cupboard.

'Where is Stuart anyway?' Elaine said, reappearing. 'Did you lose him?' Her laugh was a silly titter.

'He decided to stay on with some friends.' Abi opened the front door and held her arm out, grinning so furiously that Elaine appeared to shrink back as she passed into the hall.

'Oh well, boys will be boys,' she said. 'It's good for him to have some time off, to be young and footloose. He's got a lot of pressure on him and every year matters in architecture. He'll need his down time.'

She paused, waiting to be thanked.

'Drive safely,' was all Abi could manage after sucking in a huge breath and expelling it through her nostrils.

As soon as she heard the high whine of the Daihatsu pulling out of the driveway, Abi climbed into bed with Jude, and peeled off his clothes, then hers. She fed him, with his legs folded up against her stomach and her palm pressing him gently to her skin. His shoulders rose and fell with every suck and slowly he extended his arm and twisted his fingers in her hair. Abi stroked the soft space between his shoulder blades with the side of her thumb. 'I am so sorry, Jude. I'm so sorry. I won't do that again. Your dad and I can go out when you're grown up. I love you. I'm home now and I will never leave you with the Brush as long as I live.'

Stu came home just as it was getting light. He fell face-first onto the mattress, narrowly missing Jude, who had spent the night nestled against his mother. The tang of alcohol and stale smoke rose sharply from Stu's clothes.

Abi snatched up the baby and sprang out of bed. 'Your mother gave Jude formula!' When Stu didn't respond, she gave the mattress a sharp kick, which failed to rouse him. 'Stu. Did you hear?'

'Babe, I'm a bit dusty just at the moment,' he said into his pillow. 'Can I just sleep? I just need to lie really still for five minutes.'

'No. Stu, sit up. Listen to me! She gave him formula without asking me!'

'So?'

'So, I wasn't going to give him formula. I was going to do it myself, properly. I was going to follow World Health Organization guidelines ...'

Stu rolled onto an elbow and looked at her skeptically. 'What does the World Health Organization say about the mum's diet being ninety per cent Twix? Not to mention the odd ...' he mimed a few fast pulls on a cigarette.

Abi winced. She thought he didn't know. 'I have basically quit and anyway, it can't be that much worse than what's in formula. Some less expensive formulas have been found to contain ...' She couldn't remember exactly. '... talcum powder. And bits of ... other stuff.'

'I had formula and I turned out all right, didn't I?'

Abi felt unable to agree at this particular moment. 'Well, just don't blame me if he's covered in eczema on his *wedding day*!'

Stu rolled his eyes. He was finished with the subject. Abi stormed to the bathroom with the baby in her arms. 'And breastmilk's free! You should be pleased about that bit at least,' she called, then slammed the door behind her.

A minute later, as she tried to break off a length of toilet paper with one hand, she heard Stu on the phone to Elaine, thanking her for a great night out. Abi wiped her eyes and dropped the wet wad of paper into the basin.

'Might be nice if you texted Mum to say thanks at some point,' he said when she emerged, her face still streaked with tears. 'Smooth things over. She sounded pretty miffed. And asked for the can back at some point so she can give it away. Cos she hates –'

'Yes, I know! She hates waste.' Abi sighed. Her rage was spent, replaced only by grinding fatigue. 'Can you please call in sick?' She did not want to be alone again today. Families invaded the point on weekends, picnicking in large groups, taking over the shallow end of the pool, fathers piggybacking their children in the water. She didn't want to sit and watch that, alone with Jude.

'Love to, babe,' Stu said. 'But it's Sunday. Time and a half. I'll be back in eleven hours anyway. You'll find something to do. Go to the pool. It's going to be another scorcher.'

20.

A first-rate interferer

Jude slept much later than usual owing, Abi decided, to the slurry of harmful additives in his stomach. When he woke up, she changed his nappy and found it greenish, and different smelling, and resolved to feed him twice as much for the next few days, to flush out his pipes.

Abi wasn't sure if Phil would be at the pool on a Sunday, but late in the morning, unable to think of another way to pass the time, she carried Jude down while eating both halves of a Bounty Bar. 'Coconut is fruit,' she said to Jude, who stared back at her solemnly.

She peered over the gate and, after a moment, saw Phil set up at the other end from usual, exiled by a group of noisy teenagers. Abi unlatched the gate with an easy in-out-up and went over to join her. Phil had the Sunday magazine on her lap, and the rest of the paper pinned under her heel. Another striped towel, salmon pink and white this time, was draped around her shoulders like a shawl, and her usual hat cast a wide circle of shade over her face.

'Ah, good morning. I bought you one of these,' Phil said, plucking a takeaway coffee from a tray on her other side. 'Rather on faith since I thought perhaps today was a family day. I expect it's fairly tepid by now.'

Abi could not think how to respond to the untold kindness and, after settling Jude in her lap, took a sip of its warmish contents. Revived, she looked at Phil square on and said, 'Tell me if you think this is weird.'

Phil cast her magazine aside and rubbed her hands together. 'Go on.'

'Jude's only had breast milk so far, right? Then last night Stu and I went out and his mother minded him and she gave him a huge bottle of formula. Without asking or anything. I got quite upset, because I wasn't going to do bottles really and I don't even know if it was a decent kind.'

Phil clutched Abi's wrist. 'Don't *speak*. Who is this woman? That's appalling, Abigail. Utterly appalling.'

Abi's entire body relaxed as Phil worked herself into a lather. 'I would *never* wade in on the business of feeding and I'm a really first-rate interferer according to Polly. It's a sacred thing, the arrangement between mother and babe. Truly, Abigail, I'd say she was having a dig. She ought to know better.' Phil's voice softened. 'Admittedly, I did learn that the hard way. I once gave Polly's older boy a glass of, what's it called? *Ribena*, and you'd have thought I fed him a vodka tonic. Polly practically did his mouth out with a pot scourer. No, you're right to mind.'

'And studies show,' Abi began, but Phil cut her off.

'Studies be damned, Abigail. It's simply that you can no longer look at these lovely rolls,' she prodded the dense white of Jude's thigh, 'and say it was all you.'

'No,' Abi said with fresh sadness. She hadn't thought of that. 'Now it's a bit of Elaine as well.' Abi dipped her chin and kissed Jude on the head. Phil took a tissue out of her basket and tucked it into Abi's hand.

'Thank you,' Abi said. 'You've made me feel so much better. Stupid Brush.'

Phil looked at her quizzically.

'Oh, it's what I sometimes call her. Just in my head. Because of her bristly hair that looks like the sort of brush you have in the lav.'

Phil laughed and Abi felt doubly consoled. Against the prospect of Phil's leaving suddenly, she ventured further conversation. 'Polly's your oldest, and she lives in London, is that right?'

'Quite right,' Phil said, crossing one leg elegantly over the other. 'Married to another lawyer, Mark. Well, he was a lawyer, I should say. Now does something in finance that requires him to bellow into a fistful of phones when we're trying to dine. Very nice, but you know, intensely conventional. They've got two boys, six and eight, both as smart as paint. Then Brigitta, she's also in London, a working girl.' Phil leaned over and gave Abi a nudge. 'Not in that sense, I should say. An actress, although whether that's more gainful … No chap. As far as I know. Then James of course, was between the girls, and Freddie. My last little treat of a baby. Although he's gone rather wildly off course, I'm sorry to tell you. Was somewhere in Asia, last we all heard.'

Phil's face drooped into sadness, and she held out a finger so Jude could wrap his plump hand around it.

'Is he … as in … is he missing?' Abi asked earnestly.

'No, dear.' Phil laughed. 'He contacts me whenever he's near a bank.'

'Oh right. Four kids though, gosh.'

'Well, I always thought three had an air of indecision to it,' Phil said, withdrawing her finger before Jude could get it all the way to his mouth. 'Yet this is where we find ourselves.'

'It's a shame none of them live around here,' Abi said, feeling the opposite.

'Yes, I do wonder why I went to the trouble of having quite so many if they were all going to desert me in one way or another. The best I get now is a lot of these blasted text messages.'

Leaning into her basket, she took out her phone and held it at arm's length. 'Briggy this morning, "Having dinner with Pol and boys, driving all mad but say hello granny, missing you. Call soon x." Tell me, Abigail, quite what the point is of a message like that?'

The word *granny* lodged itself in Abi's hearing. As she shifted Jude in her lap, her mind was invaded by the image of Rae sitting alone in her front room, snipping carefully around the head of Kate Winslet spotted in Waitrose. She was yet to reply to her mother's text from earlier that morning, about a controversy involving two *Strictly* contestants ... '... who are abit that way,. It's an abscess Pat's got. on the foot.'

'I suppose texts can be handy if you're not able to ring up,' Abi said.

'Why can't you ring up, though?' Phil insisted.

'I don't have international ...' Abi stopped herself, realising in time that Phil meant it rhetorically. She was asking about daughters in general.

Still, just then, Abi considered putting her right about Rae. She would not have to tell her everything – the staying in, the scrapbooks, Pat – but she could clear up their misunderstanding by explaining that it really felt like Rae was dead. Grief had turned her into a shadow, a sort of half person, leaving Abi with the bones of a mother, but not the flesh. It might earn her another ration of Phil's glorious sympathy, her easy, warm understanding. Abi opened her mouth to speak. 'So, did you work before you had kids?'

21.

The *longueurs*

'Yes, I did,' Phil said, re-angling her hat. 'Well, after a fashion. I was married at twenty-four, but we were nine years before children, which in those days was an age and I think everyone had written Frederick and I off as breeders. I was a painter. Trained, I should say, not a dreaded dabbler. But just as my career was reaching a low peak, we found out Polly was on her way and the whole business was put away. Lost under a pile of cloth nappies, Frederick used to say. Although to be perfectly frank, I had a girl who helped me with that side of things. But of course in those days, we didn't have such a mania for working as your lot. Truly, Polly works like a woman possessed while whatever Polish girl she's got stuck up in the loft-room minds the babies she paid thousands to conceive. I shouldn't be disloyal.' Phil held up her hands in surrender. 'I only mean to say, I couldn't have done it. But then Frederick always said I was a terrific rester. An eleven o'clock peaker, in his words. Any bursts of endeavour are really only to support more resting.'

'Do you paint anymore? For fun or anything? Stu does. Well, he draws. He did a sketch of Jude the other day but apparently babies are really hard because their heads are so giant compared to their bodies. I thought it was good though. It's just his thing on the side.'

A small bank of clouds was gathering behind the city towers that glinted on the other side of the harbour and Phil stretched, but seemed in no hurry to go. 'Likewise, I suppose. I get my things out and then I put them back immediately. Since Frederick, I haven't any will. It feels too much like make-work, which at my age you acquire a particular dread for. Perhaps it would help break up the *longueurs*, but when I see a woman of my age setting her easel at the Point, it's everything I can do not to kick the legs out on my way past. What about you? What was your line, before the advent of little Jude?'

'Oh, I was doing social work at uni. But it wasn't really for me, so when I had him I didn't mind giving it up.'

'Why did you choose it in the first place then, dear?'

'I thought you had to do something you already knew how to do. And I've always done a lot of care work.' Helping her mother out of the bath, bringing a milky Horlicks up to her room, removing it untouched in the morning. 'And I'm probably naturally quite good at it. Not to brag, I mean.'

'I don't think you're in any danger there.'

'Plus, I could get in with just GCSEs and not hang about for A Levels.'

'Oh.' Phil looked surprised. 'Did you not finish school?'

'Not quite, no.'

Phil rewrapped the towel around her shoulders against a stiffening breeze and motioned for Abi to continue.

'I was in at a posh academy. Well, not posh but you know, a school for clever girls in another bit of London. My dad had always wanted me to go there so I sat the test, for him really, but then they all turned out to be posh.' Abi touched her finger to the place above her eyebrow. 'They said my fees would be covered but it turned out there's more to it than that. Trips and whatnot. The blazer was eighty pound, just on its own. And you *had* to have the exact right one. You couldn't make do with similar. I got an after-school job on the till at Greggs – that's a not-very-nice bakery? – but I still couldn't cover it and then I didn't have time for all the homework. I don't think the other girls had jobs, generally speaking.'

Phil listened with her index figure curled against her chin like a question mark.

'So once I'd done my GCSEs, I just stopped turning up. I was in the top set for everything. Before I, you know ... stopped going.'

'Hmm,' Phil said. 'There's something to being a finisher though, isn't there? Perhaps you'll take up a little something here when the time is right. When Freddie started to flounder, I remember his father saying that an arts degree is one thing but half an arts degree is precisely nothing.'

She removed her hat as the clouds moved in front of the sun. 'Well, that turned out to be rather portentous. Not to return to Woolnough woes but I do blame myself, Abigail. I let him off too much, but we mothers aren't as good at being really, really tough with them, are we? Perhaps I should have been harder on him, but then Frederick could be formidable and of course you find yourself seeking to be the balance.'

Abi moved to say something placatory but Phil would not brook interruption. 'No, I did, I went wrong with him. He adored his brother and it was such a blow to him. He took it the hardest of the children I think, but at the time of course you don't notice, or you can't notice. All your energy goes on simply trying to get yourself up every morning and simply not drowning in it. And my prize is a lot of ruddy text messages. Anyway, enough of my dread regrets. If you don't mind my asking, what is it you and Stuart do for funds? Are his parents rather helpful, when they're not interfering?'

'Stu does loads of shifts at the pub he works at, and that covers us for groceries and whatnot, but it is his parents' flat we live in. Actually, I think I might live next door to you. I think I saw you down below, if you're that pinkish house with the big windows on the side?'

'The Arts and Crafts, yes. Really?' Phil said, standing up with an *oof* sound. 'I've often wondered how much those flats overlook me. I'll be careful not to do anything illicit on my window seat from now on. But you were saying?'

'Oh yes,' Abi got up. 'And then on top of all that I'm still getting my child benefit from the UK, because I haven't told them I've moved here.' To impress Phil with her frugality, she said, 'I'm trying to save that for Jude when he's older. So mostly, I'm just being as careful as I can and using my student tricks, Weetabix for dinner and whatnot.'

'Abigail,' Phil said sharply. 'You *must* let the authorities know you've left, immediately. You could get yourself in all kinds of difficulty. Tell me you will, please, girl. That's beyond a fib. It's simply not worth the trouble of a continued falsehood. Perhaps that's forty-four years married to a barrister, but I cannot *bear* any kind of lie.'

Something acid flooded Abi's mouth and she swallowed hard against it. As they made to leave, she avoided Phil's eye.

'Lord, look at those clouds,' Phil said at the gate. 'We'll get a buster tonight if we're very lucky.'

'What's a buster?' Abi asked.

Phil clapped her hands together. 'Perhaps I won't say, and we'll let you have a lovely surprise. Give me a wave from above when it comes. And in the meantime,' Phil took out her phone again and held it out, 'why don't you pop yourself in here. I haven't got my glasses but it might be useful for the odd communiqué. Although I expect we could make do with two tins on a string between yours to mine.'

She laughed in her high trill. Abi took the phone and did as Phil asked, without the excitement that such a grand invitation deserved.

* * *

That night, Abi fed Jude to sleep on the mattress, turning over her conversation with Phil. She could not bear a lie. *You could get yourself in all kinds of difficulty.*

But Abi needed the money. The twenties and tens that Stu was still giving her every few days could be eked out to a point, but the fortnightly payments ticking up at home were her safety net. She extracted her arm from beneath Jude and left the room. The sultry heat of the day hung in the dark flat. In the kitchen, Abi leaned against the fridge and drank from a TetraPak of vanilla custard. She would wait a bit longer, then cancel the payment when Stu announced the permanent solution to their money situation that had been promised a fortnight ago. As she stood thinking, the trees outside the kitchen window began to toss their branches about messily. She turned to the window and watched as wind tore across the harbour, enveloping the building with a loud rush as it reached her.

The window flew off its latch and a gulf of cold air filled the kitchen.

'Oh my gosh, oh my gosh,' Abi said out loud, hair whipping around her face as she leaned over to close the latch. The wind in the narrow passage between the flats and Phil's house rose like a roar, and Abi ran through to the living room, slid the window open and watched Phil's door fly open against its hinges. Abi squinted against the swirling grit and saw Phil step out and wave, shielding her eyes and trying to keep Domenica from escaping.

She waved back, exultant, and shouted, 'A buster! It's a buster.' Her voice was carried away by the gale. Phil turned, tugging Domenica by the collar, and shut herself back inside. Abi stayed where she was, watching the trees bending at their trunks, the harbour whipped to a frenzy, until she heard Stu's distinctive footfall up the stairs.

'Yes!' he said, throwing the door open. 'I was hoping you'd think to open everything up. Feel that, babe.'

'It's a buster!'

Stu sat on the sofa and patted the space beside him. Abi sat down. 'Hey, sorry about this morning. I was so wrecked, that's all. And you're doing well with Jude and everything. I'm the one who's struggling. So just … don't worry what people say.'

Which people, Abi wanted to ask. What do they say? But instead she rested her head against his broad shoulder, glad for company and relieved by the cool air whistling through the room.

'It's all right,' she said, 'don't worry about it.'

'And now you've nailed the cross-breeze, so that's another thing.'

* * *

Somewhere below, Phil was locking the kitchen door that rattled against its bolt. After wedging it shut with a rolled newspaper, she dialled Brigitta, not bothering to check the time. There was no answer. Polly's phone went to the funny American voice that meant it was turned off. She gave up and took herself heavily up to her room, listening to the howl outside as she tried to fall asleep and feeling for all the world as though she were lost at sea.

22.

Their train is stuck at Potters Bar

The phone was in her hand, but when Brigitta saw the number she slipped it, still ringing, into the pocket of the enormous Max Mara camel hair coat she had found in her mother's wardrobe before leaving Sydney. It is so wasted in the Southern Hemisphere, she had thought at the time, slipping it off the wooden hanger and carting it off to her room.

She knotted the belt more tightly around herself and pressed on along City Road towards the Barbican, for a last-minute Sunday call. She needed to be on form when she arrived and hearing her mother's voice immediately beforehand would make her woolly and distracted. What no one in her family, and least of all Phil, seemed to understand was that any part in a new piece by the current Playwright Laureate was a huge thing – no matter how many actual lines you had. Her agent, a six-foot New Yorker with a man's voice and unwavering fidelity to plum-coloured lipsticks, had called it a *coup* for someone who was so new on the circuit.

Brigitta found out that the part was hers a fortnight before her father's stroke. As she trudged towards the theatre, she tried not to think that in a computer somewhere would be the two business class flights he booked immediately in the name of Woolnough, departure date not yet elapsed. 'Get us two for opening night, will you darling? Philly and I wouldn't miss it.'

Brigitta loved her father desperately, even though Polly was, if not his favourite, then his closest ally. It was an open secret, but it didn't matter anymore. She missed him more and more with each passing hour. Phil had found him on the bathroom floor, when she'd gone in to join him in evening ablutions. As ambulance men took away the body, a police officer had helped her phone Polly, who had taxied over to Kentish Town in her pyjamas and overcoat at four o'clock in the morning to tell Brigitta. He had hit his head on the edge of the bath on the way down, Polly said through choking sobs, but would have been dead already. The sisters stood in the mail-strewn stairwell of Brigitta's building, holding each other and crying until the ground floor lady came out to ask if they needed 999. They flew back to Sydney together as soon as they could to arrange the funeral. It took place on the last day of November, and the cemetery had been carpeted with jacaranda flowers, lilac and brown.

The day after the service, Brigitta had called London to tell her agent there'd been a death in the family and she would have to withdraw from the production – her agent understood, she said, but felt obliged to point out that Brigitta would be closing a door not easily reopened.

Torn, Brigitta had made a plan to fly back to London in the middle of January. The production didn't start rehearsals until the fifteenth, which would give her the best part of two months with her mother, and a day or so in London to prepare. Still, Phil had been awful about it when Brigitta told her after the quietest Christmas they'd ever had. Her mother had cried and howled and blown her nose into a paper cocktail napkin left over from the wake, the running dye staining the underside of her nose. Red had been the only colour the caterer had to offer but Phil had gone berserk about it as guests poured into the house, shouting that Frederick Woolnough was not the sort of man you commemorated with a bowling club serviette in your hand and to hell with it, why not put out sausage rolls as well. 'Cut on the bloody diagonal,' Phil had called after the caterer as she fled to her van. 'And a plastic bottle of sauce, why not, and people can do their own!' The memory of her mother's many outbursts during that time still made Brigitta quake.

Although, more recently, she had remembered those weeks with a rising sense of indignation. No one had raised an eyebrow when Freddie took off two days after the funeral, duty to family apparently done and the job of managing some divey beach bar in Indonesia by then more pressing. Polly could do as she pleased, exempted by a proper job, a husband and the start of a new school term. Only Brigitta's plans were picked over by the family corporate. It was all so unjust.

Fuck! Brigitta thought, beginning to cry. This is why she was right not to answer her phone. She wiped both cheeks on the cuff of the Max Mara and hoped she didn't look like a dog's breakfast, as she punched in the stage door code and let herself in.

Guy was on stage, seated with the main players in a circle of high stools. They had scripts in hand, open to the final scene. All were wearing versions of the same actory uniform Brigitta had on beneath the coat – leggings, a sweater that fell off one shoulder, thin scarf wrapped twice around her neck. Brigitta's hair was twisted into a loose knot on top of her head. Polly called it her Thesp in Training look.

The sight of Guy, so tall and slender with his precise, studied way of moving, gave Brigitta a thrill somewhere enjoyably deep. Unnoticed, she watched as he felt his chin with one of his long elegant hands, which Brigitta knew from experience were also unusually dexterous. She decided to let him see her first, and slipped out of her coat, taking a seat in the front row.

For the time being, Guy thought it best to keep their little thing, whatever it was, between themselves. It wouldn't be good for the rest of the company to know their relationship had moved beyond the professional only days after they'd met for the first time on a quiet Friday night at the bistro, and again at a cursory audition held very late one evening in his office.

Jealousy, Guy said, was an industry hazard, and since he sensed that Brigitta had a rare and very particular talent, more experienced actors were likely to find her sufficiently threatening already. How he could tell – she only came on at the beginning of Act One to say, 'Their train is stuck at Potters Bar,' and again at the end of Act Two to take away a tray – Brigitta wasn't sure, but she readily agreed to all of it since he was a director of such experience and standing. Early in their relationship, he had made a call from her bed to someone he kept calling 'Ken darling'. Although he seemed a touch eager for Brigitta to figure out that it was Kenneth Branagh, she could not help being impressed.

There was something addictive about Guy's attentions. Although she resented the cliché, there was no other way to describe it – he made her feel like she was the only woman on earth.

She was yet to tell Polly about him, unusual for her, but then nothing was usual anymore and might never be again. First James, now her father, her mother in pieces and Polly being so tough about it all. At least Freddie was a constant. He was rubbish but very consistent about it. Such a mess. It is all such an awful mess, Brigitta thought as she crossed her legs and arched her back expansively, in case Guy happened to turn at that moment.

Also to be dealt with was his soon-to-be ex-wife Sylvie, who was a bloody nightmare in real life apparently – as in properly mental even though she always looked amazing in the papers. Whenever her picture appeared, the accompanying caption would be sure to point out she had a face wasted for radio. Brigitta listened to her programme once, a snoozy late-night drama discussion thing on Radio 4, but found the whole thing stupidly luvvie and Sylvie's tinkling laugh incredibly grating.

None of that was her problem at this particular moment, she decided, as Guy finally swivelled on his stool. 'Hello Birj, darling,' he said, smiling as he gave her a furtive once-over.

'Oh, hello Guy. I didn't see you there.'

23.

Jude, get your wallet

For the first time since Abi arrived, the sky outside the bedroom window was not its usual hard blue when she opened her eyes. Rain fell in heavy bursts and poured down the glass in twisting silver cords.

Stu had left for work in the dark and would return in the dark. As the start of the semester drew closer, he became more and more agitated about money, complaining about a night of bad tips, starting and abandoning household budgets when the numbers couldn't be reconciled and focusing instead on how much Abi was spending on Supa FoodBarn's loss leaders. Even though he came home too exhausted to talk or lug a load of wet washing up from the communal laundry or show any interest in Jude, Abi missed him, almost as much as she had during the eight months of their separation. At least there had been Instant Messenger, the possibility then promise of a reunion. His long daily absences and unhappiness when home were a new norm.

For the entire week that followed, a week of a million hours, it rained. Water poured from the sky, bending the thinnest branches of the trees and pouring from the guttering.

Abi tried to keep Jude occupied, but could think of little to amuse someone whose range of vision didn't extend beyond his own hands. In *First Year with Baby*, she flipped to a chapter on 'Infant Toys and Games for Mothers on a Budget' in case there was anything for Jude's age. The nearest was an onion bag filled with screwed-up paper, supposedly both aural and tactile. It was an idea more economical than Abi could bear. Cabin fever set in. Even Jude seemed to resent the contraction of his already tiny world.

When he slept, Abi chipped the black bits off the inside of the oven with a butter knife or sopped up the water that leaked through the living room windows, creating semi-circles of darkness on the carpet. When she couldn't hold out any longer, she smoked a Marlboro out the window, letting herself be soaked to the shoulder. She texted Rae a picture of Jude in his bath, to which she replied with a message about her other-side neighbours sneaking rubbish into her bins. '... of course I Cant fill it on my own. Pat tryin gto get off the Parliaments.'

Only once did she look down and see Phil, sitting with her back to the window with a steaming cup of something that made a circle on the glass.

Abi longed to call down, to share Phil's window seat and let her hold Jude. Most of all, Abi longed for a conversation of two sides. As the rain continued, Abi began speaking both parts out loud, as though she was there with Phil. 'Oh thank you, I feel like Jude's my teacher really. He makes it all worth it.' 'Thank you, I would love to stay for lunch.' 'I love what you have done here.' 'Just water for me, thank you.'

When Jude was happy to be put down, lying on his back and staring cross-eyed into the near distance, Abi let her mind embroider the scene in such detail, she came to believe she really knew what sort of sofa Phil would have, how the guest lavatory would be prettily wallpapered, that there would be cut flowers in every room.

By Thursday, when she woke up worrying that she had gone mad, she bundled Jude into the pram and set out to find the library.

Before they reached the bus shelter at the top of Milson Road, the sky released a downpour that soaked Abi through and pooled in the hood of the pram.

Then, Friday. Abi stood at the sink eating a sandwich made with loaf-ends and tomato sauce. All at once, the rain stopped like a switch had been thrown.

'Oh my gosh!' she said, tearing to the living room where Jude had fallen asleep on a towel. 'It's stopped, Jude! Get your wallet, we're going out.'

Downstairs, the pavement steamed, and trees shook heavy droplets from their leaves. Abi breathed in lungfuls of the humid air, and jogged the whole way to the pool, ballet flats squelching

She dried a bench with her sleeve and waited. The water looked uninviting, the murky green of an aquarium. She could not imagine getting in and as she sat, her hope of Phil appearing began to fade. Eventually, she stood and began a slow walk home but as the flats hove into view, the image of an onion bag filled with scrunched paper compelled her onwards. They could go as far as the ferry, and sit and watch the boats.

As she made her way down the slippery ramp to the enclosed pontoon that served as the terminal, she noticed for the first time a hole-in-the-wall café tucked into a protected corner. Upturned milk-crates that had been fitted with square cushions served as chairs. The day's newspapers hung folded on a rack. Abi had change enough for a small coffee so she steered the pram onto the floating dock. It lifted and fell with each sloppy wave.

'Abigail! Thank heavens.'

Abi almost slipped as she spun around to see Phil tucked in a corner. She had a coffee in front of her and a thick novel open face down on her lap. Immediately, she drew another crate towards her and waved Abi over. She wore a soft white linen shirt, fitted trousers, many strands of amber beads and a dash of rouge. To

Abi, better used to Phil in a robe and swimsuit, she looked quite breathtaking.

'Hello dear, hello Jude. Good to know you weren't swept out to sea. What a fearful week. How did you bear up?' As she spoke, Phil made a little signal to the man behind the coffee machine and pointed to Abi. He nodded and discharged the steamer.

'I was starting to go a bit crackers, truth be told. It's actually *so* nice to see you.' She reached over to lift Jude out of the pram and Phil held her arms out for a turn.

'I do think you've grown in a week, young man. Really, he's getting so bonny, Abigail.'

Soon the man set Abi's coffee down in front of her. Unsure, she took coins out of her purse and held them towards Phil in her flat hand.

Phil stared at the coins quizzically, as though failing to recognise the small objects she was being offered.

'Oh why don't you keep those, dear,' she said after a moment, 'I've got a sort of arrangement with the chap here.'

'If you're sure, thank you,' Abi said, feeling Phil's eagerness to have the tedious business of money behind them. 'What are you reading?' Abi tilted her head to read the title upside down.

'Ah, this ruddy Booker. Although I think I've finished with him. I gave him fifty pages to turn me around but he's not done it. It's like a school writing project allowed to get out of hand. All this jolly sex when he couldn't think of anything else to put.'

'I heard it was heavy going in places, but I liked the first one.'

Phil pressed her hands together, prayer-like. 'Have I uncovered a passion? Are we both readers?'

Abi nodded. 'My dad was an English teacher. I mean, just at the comprehensive near us but he probably would have been head of department if – some times I think I got it from him anyway. He was always reading more than one thing at a time, same as me.

Well, not at the moment because I couldn't fit anything in my suitcase, so right now I'm only really reading *First Year with Baby*. You probably haven't heard of it. Anyway, he used to take me and my sister to the library on Saturday mornings and we were allowed to get anything we wanted.'

As she spoke, Abi glimpsed her father in his corduroy coat, standing at the high circulation desk, smiling as she struggled to fit so much loot into her homemade library bag. 'Sometimes I'd choose hard things to try and impress him. He probably knew I wouldn't finish them,' Abi said, realising it only as she spoke. 'But he still let me get them. He did make me carry them though. I tried to get up to the library this week but it was too wet.'

'I must confess I've never been much of a one for the *bibliothèque*,' Phil said. 'As a girl, more so, but you see Frederick felt having library books in the marital bed was unsavoury. But of course if I can't have a thing in bed, it simply won't get read.' Jude had begun to squawk and Phil handed him back.

Abi let Phil's chatter wash all over her, a salve after those days of speaking only to Jude. '*First Year with Baby* sounds a bit dire, I must say,' Phil added.

'I know the whole introduction off by heart. Do you want to hear it?' Abi continued in a high pitch. 'Baby's first year is a magical journey of discovery for mother and child ...'

'For Lord's sake, what a lot of rot. First year with baby is a bloody shock.' Phil snapped her book closed and held it out. 'You really must take this then. I was about to biff it into the harbour, so do.'

'If you're sure? You don't have to,' Abi said. But she had already taken it in both hands and stowed it under the pram.

'I would consider it a favour. I think I'm finished with anything that centres on a mango tree that turns out to have *powers*. Goodness though, it's feeling distinctly tropical today, isn't it?' Phil reached for a folded newspaper and fanned herself with it.

'I took Jude down and had a look at the pool but it's gone a greenish sort of brown.'

'Ah yes, it'll be vase-water after so much rain, but the council will put a sieve through it over the weekend and we'll swim again on Monday.'

* * *

Abi waited until Jude was asleep later in the afternoon to open Phil's book. She pressed her nose deep into the middle crease, inhaling the scent of lemon and powder. On the second page, Abi saw Phil had written her name in a large, looping hand and underneath, 'Milson Road, Dec '10. Poll etc. just got back.'

Abi ran her finger over the inscription feeling the indent Phil's pen had made, and then borrowing one of Stu's markers, wrote below it, 'Abi Egan, Milson Road, 2011, just come to Australia.' She put it beside the mattress under *First Year with Baby*. Stu wouldn't notice or worry that she'd spent money on it, but it was better to be safe.

Late that night, a lengthy text message arrived on her phone.

Are you a Mitford reader, dear? Plucked one off shelf just now and thought you wld like: "Housework is far more tiring and frightening than hunting is … yet after hunting we had eggs for tea & were made to rest for hours, but after housework people expect one to go on just as if NOTHING special had happened." Love in Cld Climate, emphasis mine.

She signed off *Regards Phil* as though it was a letter, and Abi made a note to find the library the very next day and check out its entire stock of Mitfords.

24.

Cohabiting's a bit louche

'Oh my God, Mother, the sun isn't even up,' Brigitta said by way of a greeting.

'It's London darling. It may never come up.'

'Really, though, it's not a madly good time.'

'Ought that to surprise me? I suppose not.'

Brigitta heard her mother sigh into the phone 'How are you, Mum? Are you all right?'

'Yes, I suppose – gross tedium of late middle age to one side.'

'Poor you, Philly,' Brigitta made a gesture of shushing Guy, who had woken up and was moving towards the bathroom covering his best bits with her copy of *An Actor Prepares*.

'Why don't you go for a late swim?' Brigitta suppressed laugher.

'It's gone five, darling. But anyhow we've had rain and it's made me maudlin.'

'Why don't you take a book down to the kiosk?' Brigitta said, feeling just then like a mother trying to think of holiday occupations. 'Only boring children get bored, remember? Or so you used to tell me on a weekly basis.'

'I've already done that, thank you,' Phil said crisply. 'In fact, I met my rather sweet little friend – well, I don't know what you'd call her really – but there's a young girl who's moved in next door.

She turns out to be quite diverting and has the dearest baby. She put me in mind of that lovely bit of Wharton. Wait a minute, I wrote it down.'

Brigitta waited, listening to a rustle of papers at the other end.

Phil came back on the line. 'Here we are. "She was one of the episodical persons who form the padding of life. It was impossible to believe that she had herself ever been a focus of activities." Isn't that glorious? Anyway, I thought you'd be pleased to know your aged mother has an episodical person at least.'

Brigitta bristled. Sometimes she couldn't tell what Phil was driving at. Was she supposed to feel pleased, or was her mother trying to stir up a measure of jealousy?

'No family of her own apart from frightful in-laws,' Phil went on. 'Although actually, she and the child's father aren't married. They're both extremely young as I said, him even younger than her.'

'Oh well, I expect you'll have them up the aisle in no time if that's your new project.'

Guy was now in the kitchenette, four paces from the end of the bed, still unclad and making coffee. Brigitta watched him, with half an ear to the phone. The excitement of having a proper, grown-up man and a known director to boot rooting around in her top cupboard had lost none of its allure.

'Darling, I'm not quite as old-fashioned as you like to think,' Phil was saying. 'I'm quite aware your generation prefers to keep their options perpetually open. Heaven forbid anyone should have to pick a horse and stay on it.'

With a teasing look at Guy, Brigitta said, 'So you won't mind when I tell you I've shacked up with a much older man?' He wheeled around and cocked an eyebrow at her.

'Well, I didn't mean for *our* sort,' Phil replied. 'Cohabiting's a bit louche, don't you think, darling?'

'You are such a snob, mother! Honestly!'

'Do you have company, dear? It sounds like a camp kitchen from my end.'

'No, but I've just seen the time. I'd better go, I'm sorry. Really, Mum, I think you're doing brilliantly, and I'm glad you've got a bit of company even if it is with a louche cohabiter.'

'Yes well, it makes a change from Noel *et al.*'

'Oh how *is* Cremorne Point's foremost coffee klatch?'

'More tedious than you could possibly imagine, darling. I've been avoiding the lot of them. Perhaps you'll phone again in a day or so?'

'Definitely, Mum. Loves. Bye.'

* * *

'What is it with women and their mothers?' Guy asked as he slid back into bed with two drinking glasses a quarter full of strong espresso. 'Wouldn't you find it odd if I telephoned my mother from our post-coital bed to see how she's getting on?' He held a hand to his ear. 'Hello Mummy, it's Guy. Yes I know I'm forty-four ...'

Brigitta batted his imaginary telephone away. 'She called *me*. And it's completely different anyway. You know we've just lost Dad. I'm trying to be a good daughter.'

'You're right. I'm sorry. You're a splendid daughter.' He rolled towards her and kissed the expanse of bare skin below her neck. 'And a beautiful woman. Really, Birj, I think I might be in real danger.'

Brigitta swelled with delight but said nothing.

'I suppose we ought to be getting up if we're going to make convincing separate entrances this morning, don't you?' Guy said.

Brigitta yawned. 'Will you come back here tonight?'

'Birj, you know there's nothing I'd rather do but Sylvie's out of town and I'm under orders to take Ludo to whatever it is, karate or something.'

Do you have to use their names? Brigitta thought with irritation. 'I could come over after he's gone to bed.'

'Unwise, dearest. But the minute I'm moved out, officially and properly, things will be infinitely easier. I know it's all so tedious, but being in the public eye means these things have to be managed very precisely. I beg patience.'

After he kissed her again, Brigitta gave up and watched him get out of bed and pull on his trousers. Imagine, she thought after he'd collected his things and closed the door behind him, a man with a son and his soon-to-be ex-wife. What would Philly make of all that?

25.

Dear as he is

The rain did not return and the summer re-exerted itself with force. It was a hot, bright morning and Abi managed to get dressed while alternating bites of a hard-boiled egg with quick puffs on a cigarette out the window before Jude began his burbling chorus.

When he woke and Abi leaned into the cot to get him, Jude's dark eyes found focus on her face and then after a moment of consideration, the corner of his mouth hitched into a smile.

'Hello!' Abi said, surprised almost to tears. 'Are you smiling? Are you smiling at me?' she cooed, and then as though to prove it wasn't wind, Jude smiled again, revealing his rosy gums.

'Hello little boy, hello!' she said over and over, as though they were meeting properly for the first time. Stu didn't answer his phone, so Abi jogged straight to the pool, bursting to show someone.

'Guess what!' Abi called out as soon as she saw Phil toeing the water that was back to its usual colour. The moment was perfect. A baby who knew his mother and Phil who was always around. Phil always interested, Phil in her same robe, with basket and dog. Reliable reactor to news, filler of empty mornings, giver of advice, sayer in low tones of terrible, hilarious things about her own children, always so *sure*.

'Jude smiled! Just now.' Abi was panting as she sat down and held Jude so that he faced them both. 'I'll see if I can get him to do it again.'

'Ah! Isn't that wonderful,' Phil said when he obliged. 'As though you needed another trick, Jude!'

They watched for a while longer, poking and prodding at him in the hope of a reaction. Phil blew gently on his tummy, which worked twice, and Abi, desperate to prolong the moment, sang a made-up song and only felt self-conscious towards the end when he didn't smile again, and she couldn't think of anything to rhyme with 'Cremorne' except for forlorn, which wasn't right.

'Will I hold him for you while you have a whiz up and down?' Phil asked, standing and removing her robe. 'I promise I won't make off with him, dear as he is. I realised just this morning I'm yet to see you have a proper plunge.'

'That's fine, thank you though,' Abi demurred. 'I'm a bit of a cat when it comes to water, actually. It has to be really boiling for me to go in properly.'

Phil looked at her quizzically. 'How much hotter can it get, really dear, before things start melting? It must be thirty degrees and it's not gone ten.'

'Well, to be honest.' The impulse to lie rose sharply and she spoke slowly, struggling against it. There was already too much held in balance, facts to be glanced over and careful sidesteps to be made. 'I don't really like having my face under. It's probably an English thing. We're not massive swimmers like antipodeans.'

Abi tried to reach a section of hair into her mouth. Phil narrowed her eyes as she batted Abi's hand away from her mouth, as though she'd told her a thousand times to stop sucking her hair. 'Abigail, *do* you swim?'

'There's not really any pools like this in Croydon so …'

'Of course not, but *can* you swim or am I getting a load of flannel? I suddenly realise I'm yet to see that costume wet above the waist.'

With her hand still tingling where Phil had batted it away, Abi said, 'Um, not really. Not as such. No.'

'Well then, let's not have any more fibs. Although –' Phil laid a hand on her chest '– I've been insensitive. There's been no one to teach you.'

Abi longed to tell Phil the whole truth but again the words did not come.

'Well then, yes.' Phil was resolute. 'You shall have to learn, if you're to become a proper Australian.'

'No, really. I don't think I can.'

'Abigail. I have taught four children to swim in this pool and I don't expect this'll be any different. And we shan't wait. You'll need to teach Jude tricks by next summer so you'd better be ahead of him. And Lord knows I need a project, lest Polly threaten me with another *bichon*. It is pointless to resist.'

'I suppose I haven't got anything else to do, much.'

'Well then, this will be our work.' It was decided.

'Okay then. Thank you. I suppose. As long as Jude won't end up an orphan.' Abi said with a weak smile. 'Oh also, I meant to say, I got that book you told me about, *Love in a Cold Climate*?'

'What do you think?'

'I love it. Aunt Sadie, and that Uncle Matthew, how he's always raging at them and chasing after them with farm equipment.'

'Ah yes. Perhaps I'll bring an entrenching tool tomorrow so I can prod you along. Now excuse me will you, I ought to drag myself up and back a few times.'

With that, Phil eased herself into the water and began her elegant breast-stroke. Abi sat and watched her smooth progress towards the other end, wondering how on earth a person could ever learn to do a thing like that.

26.
Are you on drugs?

Brigitta had been waiting outside a nondescript Vietnamese in Camden for nearly an hour by the time Guy finally called and explained in a whisper that something had cropped up and he wasn't going to make it. There was an odd echo on the line that made his voice sound tinny and far-off.

Starving and blue with cold despite the Max Mara, Brigitta said, 'Are you in the toilet, Guy? It honestly sounds like you're calling me from a nasty men's room.'

'Birj, don't be tedious. I said I'm sorry, I'll come to the bedsit tomorrow night. But this evening's buggered. I forgot about a thing, so you'll just have to be a good girl and wait until tomorrow. We'll have fun, as long as you're not boring, please, darling. Can you be lovely?'

Brigitta sighed and stamped her feet against the cold. 'Fine.'

They hung up and Brigitta looked at the time on her phone. 8.40 p.m. Already out and not madly keen on going back to her room, she hailed a taxi and gave Polly's address in Ladbroke Grove, hoping her sister would be home and, just as much, that she'd have cash for the fare. It was well after nine by the time he stopped in front of a tall white terrace house. The driver had refused to take the Westway and wound confusingly through the back streets of Kilburn instead, until Brigitta became convinced she would be murdered in a laneway behind a Carpet One. He waited while Brigitta bounded up the steps and rang the bell. Mark opened the door, wearing an embarrassing pair of loose drawstring trousers.

The fourteen years between Mark and Polly was the sort of age difference that Phil had once said will make a man 'vulnerable to fashion … they feel a pressure to keep current, do you see, which only gets worse if they're the kind who eventually runs to fat.'

Brigitta would have remarked on this latest experiment except he had already lifted his wallet out of the big bowl on the hall table and started down towards the taxi.

'I swear the bell rings differently when it's you,' Polly said when Brigitta found her in the reception room, sitting on one of the vast sofas with a thick file open on her lap and a blanket tucked around her. Heavy drapes were drawn across the tall windows to the street, puddling on the carpet at the bottom and giving the room, at least twice the size of Brigitta's studio, a pleasant cocooned quality. It was the nearest thing, Brigitta always felt, to being at home. Polly closed the file and held the blanket open. Brigitta shed her coat and shoes and nestled in beside her.

'Ugh, your feet are freezing,' Polly said as Brigitta forced them under her sister's bottom.

Polly had their father's square jaw and Phil's ash-coloured hair, expensively picked out with blonde. Brigitta felt that the seven miles Polly ran each morning, supposedly for stress relief, was making her unattractively thin, although she could not help feeling simultaneously jealous. Her only compensation, according to Phil, was that Brigitta had got both their allowances of bust.

No one ever guessed they were sisters by appearance or manner; Brigitta languid to the point of draping, Polly with the quick, darting manner of a pigeon, which became the basis of her hated childhood nickname thought up by Freddie.

'Give me a sip, Pidge,' Brigitta said, gesturing towards the bulb-like wine glass Polly had beside her. As she finished it in a single go, Brigitta watched her sister's gaze move beyond her to the mountain of coat abandoned by the door.

'Is that Mum's? Did she give that to you?'

'Sort of.' Brigitta wiped her mouth on her sleeve.

'I bet. Well, stolen goods suit you is all I can say.'

'Are the boys awake? Can I go and smell them?'

'Yes, and no you can't. You'll get Max completely wound up and Toby's already been down four times. Why is it you're here, darling? I'm guessing the lipstick wasn't applied with Mark and me in mind?'

'I had a thing cancelled and I was nearby.'

As she spoke, Mark put his head around the door. 'I wouldn't call fifty-two pounds nearby, Briggy. We'll put it on the tab, will we? Anyway, excuse me. Hong Kong's about to wake up.'

A phone buzzed somewhere inside his pocket and he rummaged it out.

'Mark Crouch. Shoot,' he said loudly as he disappeared.

Polly waited until he was out of range. 'Go on, then.'

'What?'

'Brigitta. There's clearly something going on, so just tell me.'

'Okay,' Brigitta took a deep breath, knowing to go carefully on subjects liable to touch off Polly's hyperactive sense of responsibility. She had been like that – well always really, when Brigitta thought about it – but in a concentrated way since James died and their mother went into a fog that lingered until Brigitta had almost finished school. Polly had been the one to get her through exams. Polly had taken her to David Jones for her formal dress and driven to collect her from an address in Point Piper that Brigitta had gone to afterwards and thrown up a pepperminty streak of crème de menthe in the indoor spa. Polly had helped her with money and drama school and flats, and although Brigitta was grateful for all of it, she sometimes wished they could just be sisters.

'Well as long as you literally do not say a single thing to anyone, not even Mark … I've sort of started seeing my director. Guy. Can you believe it? It was just stupid fun at the beginning, Pidge, but he's so lovely, and he thinks I'm –'

'Guy –' Polly stopped her. 'As in Guy Kidd, of Guy Kidd and Sylvie Allen Kidd?'

'They're split up, Poll. They're getting divorced but it takes forever, because of having to work out custody and all that. And being in the public eye, it's got to be managed a certain way. He has to stay living there for the time being so Sylvie doesn't get the house. She's a total nightmare apparently. Real scissors to the trouser legs sort.'

'Brilliant.' Polly flung the blanket off both of them and got up. 'Brigitta, are you on drugs?'

Polly would not be taking the news in a spirit of sisterly confidence then.

'A man who is technically still married and not just technically but *actually* living with his wife is going to chuck all that and a child as well for a girl he's just met on a play? Is that what you honestly think Brigitta? Are you really that woman?'

Brigitta was twisting a blanket tassel into a tight coil.

'Look at me! Is this a delayed rebellion or your form of grieving? Genuinely. I want to know.'

'They were broken up before I even met him,' Brigitta said, sulking. 'He sleeps in their media room.'

Polly let out a caustic laugh. 'My God, he sounds like a complete invertebrate. Besides which, it's just as tacky as fuck.'

'Apart from the *fuck*, you sound exactly like Mum at the moment I hope you know. Are you worried I'm being common?'

'How can you say that, Brigitta? I'm worried you're going to get your heart broken! Again. I'm worried you're going to get yourself in trouble. And fine, yes, I am worried you're going to upset Mum.' Polly's eyes narrowed. 'Although why do I feel like she doesn't know?'

Brigitta's voice dropped to a whisper. 'Can you not tell her, please?'

'Believe me! Sorry, can you imagine? Oh, hello Mum, remember how Daddy just died? Well guess what, Brigitta's a mistress!'

'Polly, don't be so mean. Fuck. I wish I hadn't said anything now.'

'Me too, don't worry.'

Sarcastic Polly always made Brigitta quail and she said nothing.

'I'm going to bed,' Polly said, gathering up her files. 'I've got a call first thing. You can sleep there if you want.'

Wounded, Brigitta would have loved to refuse but the sofa was so soft, and home was two Tubes and a lengthy walk away. 'Okay. Fine. I will.'

'Good,' said Polly. 'We can't afford another one of your cab rides anyway.'

Brigitta drew her feet up onto the sofa and lay down. At the doorway, Polly paused and looked back at her sister. Her entire being seemed to deflate.

'Briggy, I'm sorry. I'm sorry.'

'It's all right. Don't worry.' Brigitta could bear Polly's anger but not her sadness. 'Can I have an over-the-top cuddle?'

Polly smiled. She'd forgotten. As children, Polly's room was the nearest to her sister's. Whenever Brigitta cried out in the night, it was Polly who would go in and, finding her curled up in a ball, arrange her entire self over her sister, enveloping her in a warm darkness until the whimpering stopped. Phil had admitted much later, after two champagnes, that the rooming arrangement was by design and frequently saved her a job of getting up.

Polly sat on the edge of the sofa and cocooned Brigitta as she so often had.

'I can't bear to see you get hurt. These things do only end one way. With a total buggering, and not of him.'

'Do you miss him?' Brigitta was no longer thinking of Guy. 'Do you miss Dad all the time?'

'Every minute. I went to ring him tonight and got halfway through his number before I remembered. Whenever I worked late and was by myself in the office, I'd call him on his way to Chambers. He'd ask me what I was working on and tell me what I should do.'

'How are we supposed to know what to do now?'

'I don't know.' Polly got up and Brigitta saw that her face was damp with tears. 'I'll figure it out. Go to sleep.'

She kissed Brigitta on the forehead and turned off the light as she left the room.

When Brigitta went down to the kitchen the next morning to greet Max and Toby, Polly had already left for work. The boys were eating a grim-looking health cereal while a sullen Eastern Bloc nanny, a different one from last time, leaned against the bench, texting. The morning paper was laid out on the table. A Post-it had been stuck next to the picture of a tuxedoed man above the mast-head, escorting his soon-to-be ex-wife up a length of red carpet. 'This Guy?' it said, in Polly's handwriting. It would have seemed unkind, had Polly not given him an elaborate moustache and blacked out one of his wife's perfect teeth. 'Let's talk tonight xxx.'

27.

It doesn't even hurt

Abi arrived at the pool exhausted and rattling with apprehension. All night, she'd dreamed busily of drowning, dark green water closing over her head, sinking to a silty concrete bottom.

She could not eat breakfast except for a single finger of KitKat, which she ate looking down at Phil passing back and forth in front of her bay window, first in a nightie, then her swim robe. When finally she saw Phil swing the basket onto her shoulder, Abi knew she had run out of time to think up a reason why she could not go, and made her way downstairs with the pram.

They met at Phil's gate, and Abi noticed a foam kickboard sticking out her basket, with Polly Woolnough written on the side in faded marker.

'Ready, then?' Phil asked gaily as they arrived at the pool.

'I suppose so. I've heard it's quite peaceful at the end.'

Phil laughed, as though Abi was joking. Jude had fallen asleep with a tiny hand holding a corner of his muslin. Abi parked him a way away from the pool. 'So he doesn't have to watch his mum drown.'

But it turned out the only thing Phil expected her to do was wade into chest-deep water holding one end of the board and put her chin under. It did not seem enough to warrant a night of turmoil.

Phil held the other side of the board. 'Nice and steady. Righto, go.'

'Just my chin?' Abi asked. 'Not my mouth as well?'

'We're only interested in chins today.'

Abi obliged, feeling the warm water wash over her shoulders.

'Very good.'

'Should I try and lift my feet off or something?'

'There's plenty of time for that. Little by little's the way,' Phil said. 'I don't want to frighten you off in our first session.'

As she spoke, the gate clattered behind them and they turned to see a tall, elderly man in sagging Speedos and boat shoes let himself in. He had a thick pelt of white hair on his chest and back and a towel hung over one shoulder.

'Ah, hello Noel,' Phil called crisply.

'Morning, Mrs Woolnough! Up to something, by the looks.'

Phil lowered her voice. 'I think we'll stop there for today, Abigail. This is a private project and we don't need all Rabbit's friends and relations looking on.'

'Who is he?' Abi asked as she submerged her chin without thinking about it. 'Is he your *special someone?* Have you got a secret man-friend?'

'Oh please, you beastly girl. He's one of the dispossessed of Cremorne Point. A group of them sit for hours down at the kiosk every morning. Awaiting death, I should imagine.'

Abi began to laugh, accidentally taking in a mouthful of water. She spluttered and coughed until her eyes streamed.

'Serves you right,' Phil said. 'All right, out we get.'

As they made for the ladder, Noel swam past, smiling at them every time he turned to breathe.

'Look, I join in from time to time, but the conversation's terribly uphill,' Phil said as they wandered home. Jude had woken up but was making dove noises in the pram. 'When a group of my age peers gets together, things are wont to become unpleasantly medical. I'm sure you'll meet them soon enough and be brought up to speed on the state of Noel's prostate.'

Abi gave Phil what she hoped was a knowing look, but privately the idea of sitting in on a coffee morning excited her, no matter how old the others were and how prostate-focused the conversation was likely to be.

'Well, a good day's graft, I think Abigail,' Phil said as they parted at the gate. 'Tomorrow, we'll put that mouth of yours in on purpose.'

And every day after that, they met at the same time. And every day, another measure of progress was made. Stu began his semester, and for Abi and Phil too it seemed, the lessons became a chief occupation.

Abi forgot to be embarrassed when she splashed too hard while dog-paddling towards the edge, with Phil's hand holding her lightly under her stomach. The feeling of it, being supported from below, sometimes made Abi forget to move her hands, and she would drift into a kind of meditation. Jude, increasingly alert, could be raised up in his pram seat, and would sit watching the movement of the water, while gnawing wetly on his hands that had unfurled from fists like poppy heads. And somehow, in the midst of it all, Abi was able to put away the fact that she should have cleared up the lingering misunderstanding about her mother already.

By now, summer was fading towards autumn. Leaves from the overhead trees began dropping into the water, collecting as dark triangles in each corner of the pool. Phil's singular interest was finishing the job before the water got too cold.

Sometimes in the afternoons, Abi would return to the pool and try to practise what she had learned that morning, but without Phil there to stand beside her, dispensing instructions and praising good work, the sessions felt formless. Mornings were the thing, and Abi's days found shape around their standing appointment.

When Phil decided the water was too fresh for her, she began instructing Abi from the side, plucking Jude out of the pram whenever he grizzled. He was instantly calmed by the proprietary way Phil had with him, laying him along her forearm, tummy down, and patting his nappied bottom firmly with her other hand. More than once, Abi looked up at them and let herself believe Phil was really his grandmother.

On the first day of April, a morning that dawned clear and fresh, Phil announced it was the day to join up everything Abi had learned.

'Everything at once? Arms, kicking, and face totally in?'

'Precisely. You're amply ready and the only way to do it, is to *do it*. And best with eyes open so you don't knock your head on the edge.'

'Oh. I don't think I can open my eyes,' Abi pleaded. 'I think it might be bad for my retinas. I've got really sensitive ones. What about if I do all the other things and we could do eyes another day? Or not. I could be more of a closed-eye swimmer. We could train Domenica to be my swimming-eye dog.'

'Abigail, don't be tiresome. I'd like this to be done before we've got to crack ice off the pool. Just open the ruddy things and we'll all be relieved to find they don't explode out of their sockets.'

Abi dithered until she sensed Phil becoming genuinely cross. Inhaling deeply, she pushed off on her stomach and let herself drop below the surface. Her eyes prickled when she opened them, but as they came into focus, she saw in front of her an endless green behind a mess of bubbles like liquid silver. The world was silent, except for the faint clicking of her breath reaching the surface. When there was no more air in her lungs Abi burst out of the water. 'You can see everything down there!'

Phil only smiled as Abi wiped curtains of wet hair out of her eyes and dived under a second time, beginning the one long lap that had been their object for so many weeks. As she pushed herself through the dense green towards the deep end, she saw Phil's hand reach into the water. Abi took it and let herself be helped out.

'It doesn't even hurt! Oh my gosh, Phil! Oh my gosh!'

'Surprise, surprise,' Phil said, but her pleasure was plain. 'I think we've got a real swimmer on our hands, Abigail.'

28.

Dust in my flutes

All the way back from the pool, Abi kept up a stream of chatter. 'Imagine!' she said, steering the pram with one hand, trying to keep her towel around her with the other. 'Me, a swimmer! I never even thought of trying to learn, if I'm honest. But that's because I'd have to have done it at Waddon Lido, in Croydon? And I always felt like being in a public pool in London's a bit the same as being on the Tube with a lot of grubby strangers, except you're all floating around together with your kit off.'

Phil looked suitably revolted.

'But down there,' Abi went on, 'it was like the Maldives or something! Thank you so much, Phil. Honestly, thank you.'

'Really, you can stop saying thank you, Abigail. You've done all the work. I was simply the prodder.'

Soon they arrived at Phil's house. She paused, her hand on the gate's latch. 'What about a spot of lunch, Abigail? I think we deserve a little celebration, don't you?'

'Really? Okay! Yes, thank you. Okay!' Abi said, unable to hide her ecstasy at being invited inside.

She followed Phil through the gate and parked the pram in the courtyard, watching as Phil reached into the hanging planter and used a single key to unlock the door to her dim, cool kitchen. With

Jude in her arms, Abi followed her in. As her eyes adjusted to the light, the scene developed like a photograph.

Here it was. Here was what she wanted. Here was everything that reading Malory Towers to yourself on a twin bed and eating Müller caramel rice with a bent fork was not. Here was life lived in thick layers. A scrubbed pine table, big enough for ten, stood in the middle of the flagstone floor. It was scattered with mail, *New Yorkers*, notes to self scribbled on backs of envelopes. A fruit bowl in the centre contained lemons, garlic and a pair of reading glasses.

Phil flicked on a small radio, which emitted the low purr of a classical music presenter, saying something about the third movement of something by the Polish philharmonic something, and began bustling about, opening cupboards and leaning into the fridge. Its surface was cluttered with handwritten lists and children's drawings and newspaper cartoons that fluttered every time she closed or opened the door.

While Phil's back was turned, Abi let her eyes range further, unable to fix on any one part of it. It was not a mess, of the kind Abi so hated. It was comforting, homely. From the threshold, Abi could see past the window seat, through to a large front room washed in sunlight pouring through French doors that looked out onto the harbour. The furniture was gently worn but plump and heavy-looking, not the sort that sank in the middle or slid across the floor as you went to sit down. Oriental rugs overlapped at their corners, occasional tables held dishes, bowls, large blue and white china vases, and tall potted orchids. Every wall was hung with framed pictures in oils so thick her fingers twitched to feel the ridges. She had never seen a house filled with so many things that were there only to be pretty. How, she wondered, could one person have all that beauty to themself?

Abi turned back to the kitchen as Phil took a bottle of champagne out of the fridge. 'Frederick used to say if you don't keep a bottle of fizz cold, it says a great deal about your outlook. You can't be expecting good news, do you see? Well, come in, sit.'

Abi realised then that she wasn't dressed or even dry, and hesitated beside one of the rush chairs. 'I'm still quite drippy though.'

'I'd be more worried about what the chair might get on you. I've never been a scrubber, do you see? The Woolnough detritus, Fred used to call it. Anyway, what was I saying? Oh yes, I'm afraid I'm rarely braced for good news anymore but I suspected we might have cause for celebration today, so I put this in this morning. I'm gasping, I don't know about you. Another great tragedy of widowhood – one doesn't open anything one can't finish on one's own.'

Phil put the bottle of champagne down on the table, shoving aside a pile of mail and quartered newspapers, their half-done crosswords facing outwards. 'Goodness, do excuse all this,' Phil said, pushing it aside. 'Frederick used to rib me dreadfully about my piles.' The bottle began to bead in the still, warm air of the kitchen. 'Why don't you put the babe in the corner of the window seat there, make a little whelping box of it with a few of those pillows.'

Abi did as Phil said, digging her clothes out from underneath the pram and pulling them on as she returned inside. She sat down and watched Phil take two tall champagne glasses out of a cupboard and inspect them, displeased. 'Oh marvellous, dust in my flutes. Doesn't that say it all? I'm in the dusty flute stage of life.'

'Good name for your memoir though. *Dust in My Flutes,*' Abi said, silently savouring the fact that here she was, at Phil's table, having a lovely chat and a special drink. And the promise of lunch to come. She glanced over at Jude, who had fallen asleep in a patch of mild sunlight. His knees had dropped out to each side, and the soles of his feet were pressed together, plump legs making a perfect diamond.

'Ha, indeed. *Life, Loss and Grubby Christofle* by Phyllida Woolnough.'

Phil rinsed and dried the glasses and set them down, opened the bottle expertly and poured.

'Now, you did say you had time for lunch? Nowhere you need to be?'

A bubble caught in Abi's throat and she coughed. 'That could be the name of my memoir. *Nowhere I Need to Be: The Life of Abi Egan.*'

'Well pip-pip, dear then,' Phil said, raising her glass. 'To new tricks.'

29.

Lettuce can tolerate a setback

Lunch turned out to be a lot of posh sandwich fillings without the bread. Chopped up tomatoes mixed with basil and oil, cheese out of waxy paper, olives, and lettuce from a pot by the back door that Abi was sent out to pick.

'If you've got a leaf, you've got a meal,' Phil said, pointing towards the back door with the vegetable knife held in her wet hand.

'I feel like that about a Twix,' Abi said and then smiled when Phil laughed, as though again she was joking.

Outside, Abi carefully plucked a few tips of buttery green lettuce from a planter, trying not to uproot the whole flimsy tangle.

Phil glanced down at the offering Abi brought in and put beside the sink.

'No no, dear. You've got to give it a real seeing to. Lettuce can tolerate a setback. Rather like us, don't you think? Have another go, would you?'

The second harvest was accepted, and while Phil whizzed up a dressing in a jar and chatted on, Abi stood sipping her champagne. How did Phil manage it without having to tip her head all the way back? Gradually, she edged nearer to the farmhouse dresser against one wall. Besides a lot of blue and white dishes, Domenica's lead and a pile of prescriptions held together with a clothes peg, it held dozens of family photographs in heavy silver frames, beginning to tarnish. Abi edged closer and inspected them one by one.

'Ah, yes.' Phil said, turning to lay two lots of everything on the table. 'That's Polly there, at her graduation. She read law like her father, a surprise to no one. That's Briggy on the pony.'

Abi gasped, and covered her mouth. Phil was still talking and did not seem to notice, even as Abi leaned in and stared aghast at the girl in the photograph. She could not have been more than thirteen when it was taken, but it was undoubtedly her, smiling out from beneath her riding helmet.

'Briggy had the most endless-seeming horse phase,' Phil continued. 'And that's dear James there. He really was the most charming boy. Kind, desperately amusing. Such an all-rounder at school.'

There were three photos of James to every one of the others, in rugby clothes, or rowing, on the side of a mountain with ski goggles pushed up his forehead. Always laughing at the camera, not knowing that his garish ski jacket would one day give him the extra measure of *deadness* Phil had heard about on the radio.

Sighing, Phil picked up the final photograph of a boy of about fourteen in school blazer and tie. He had smooth, olive skin unscathed by puberty, a head of thick russet-coloured hair, and the most brazen grin. 'This, of course, is the wicked Freddie.'

Abi looked over at it and wondered what such a magnetic child would be like as a man.

'I wouldn't get too close,' Phil said, as though reading her mind. 'Brigitta tells me he's apparently lethal to girls, although it's not a mother's business of course. Right, I think we're about ready. Why don't you put yourself there, and you'll be able to see Jude, although he looks to be sleeping the sleep of the righteous.'

Abi sat down and, for a moment, panicked at the lack of a sliced white. The salmon did not looked cooked, but then she wasn't sure it was definitely salmon. 'This looks amazing.'

'You do eat trout, I hope. It's smoked. Lord, how nice it is to set two places, Abigail. There's really nothing more drear than cooking for one. After the children moved out and it was just Fred and I, it took me an age to stop cooking for six, and now I'm reduced to these dire spinster teas.'

'I don't cook either,' Abi said, accepting whatever Phil put onto her plate. 'We had more of your ready-meals and whatnot, growing up.' She felt herself lurch onto hazardous ground, a reference to childhood that could invite further question. She fell silent and focused on knifing the translucent layers of trout into smaller and smaller flakes that she hoped would be easier to swallow.

Phil did not take Abi up on her recollection. In the quiet of her own kitchen, where it seemed as though the world outside the back door had ceased all doings, Phil became reflective. 'Fred used to call my particular school of cooking "survival fare". He'd often ask how I could turn out another lot of leftovers, without ever seeming to produce the meal they must have come from. But you lose any gourmet pretensions when you've got boys roaring in from training. Your only aim is to fill. It could be terribly snug in here, Frederick was rarely home at that time, but they would all sit up, even as teenagers they would eat at the table. I'd come around behind, you know, serving whatever it was. That's it, Mum, slop it out.' Phil glanced around the room, as though watching a different self go around the table with pot and spoon. 'Freddie was such a tease, of course. Come on Mum! James will take a second blob.'

Phil looked down at her plate. 'Good Lord, I seem to have fallen into a brown study.' She pressed a linen napkin briefly to her nose. 'It's simply, Abigail, that I've known this house at its fullest, do you see, and this luncheon is the first time since they all left after the funeral, that it isn't me and my dreaded tray. I feel as though I'm living out an ending,' she said morosely. 'The fag-end to be sure. Lately, I've come to think it's entirely my fault. I wonder, did I force them all away?'

'I'm sure you didn't.' Abi could not believe anyone would ever want to get away from Phil. 'I'm sure you were a lovely mum. Are, I should say.' Abi blushed and tried to spear an olive with her fork.

'I *was* lovely – when they were out. Truthfully, they exhausted me. I spent years wishing they'd go and slam someone else's doors.'

She paused, and then put an olive in her mouth with her fingers. Abi set down her fork. 'Well,' Phil said, 'I seem to have got my wish. Do you know, Abigail, I've never told a soul this but I insisted they all went to school in town for a proper education but if you pressed me, it was so they wouldn't be home until half five. Ha! What I'd give for a slamming door now.'

Phil stood and made her way slowly to the kettle. 'Shall we share a pot? Lapsang's all I've got loose, I'm afraid.'

When the tea had brewed, Phil set the pot and two teacups on the table. 'Will I be mother?'

Abi looked at her, bewildered.

'It means, will I pour, dear,' Phil said. 'Now, I've been meaning to ask, tomorrow I thought I'd do a recce into David Jones and if you and Jude have no plans you might like to accompany me. I'm in the market for a whizzier heater for in here, before the weather really turns, but once we've done that, I thought we'd have a bite of something in the food hall.'

Phil was half asking and half telling. Abi shifted in her seat, being for once unavailable.

'Oh. It's only that Stu has a whole day off tomorrow and I thought I would show him my swimming. I haven't told him about the lessons so it could be a surprise.'

'Of course. Tomorrow's Saturday. I forget.' Phil covered a small yawn with the tips of her fingers. 'Well, I've certainly had my last swim of the season so I suppose there'll be no more mornings at the pool for me.' She smiled impassively and picked up a teaspoon.

Abi put a ragged cuticle between her teeth. It felt as though a small punishment had been meted out. Until that moment, she had never considered summer would end.

'Well, thank you for the lovely lunch.' She did not want to cry in front of Phil and hurried to collect Jude, asleep on the window seat, and take him home.

'You don't need me to see you out,' Phil said, rising. 'But very well done today, Abigail. Goodbye, dear.'

When Abi got upstairs, the flat seemed emptier than it had before. The stark white of the walls, the windows staring at her like gormless, unlidded eyes. The pull-out with its worn fabric and shredding armrests mortified her. She felt overpowered by the familiar homesickness that, after so many years attached to nothing, had suddenly found its object. She laid Jude carefully in his cot, and realised then that the only thing was to kick the wall until her stupid toe bled all over the fucking carpet.

30.

One up from dead

Stu had forgotten. When he emerged from the bedroom on Saturday morning shortly before ten, naked except for a pair of football shorts, Abi was kneeling on the living room floor, taking Jude's things out of the bag she'd packed the night before. Beside her, Jude lay on his tummy lifting his head for seconds at a time, then resting back on a cheek when the effort became too much.

Stu gave her a vague nod. 'I'm a bit dusty this morning. It got huge last night after we closed. Some of the uni boys turned up. Have we got any Gatorade?'

As Abi looked up at him, the plastic rattle in her hand began vibrating with its own desire to be flung at him. 'Our budget doesn't really run to hangover aids.'

Stu went to step over a zip pouch of spare nappies, then paused. 'Where have you guys been? Do something fun?'

'We've been here, waiting. We were supposed to have a family day, remember?'

'Oh right.' Stu rubbed his stubbled chin. 'I thought you'd already gone out. I didn't hear him.'

'That's because when you woke us both up coming in at 5 a.m. you asked me to move out to the sofa with him so you could have a sleep-in, which I did. By letting him feed, non-stop all morning.'

'Simmer down, babe. I don't even remember saying that. But then I have just worked ten days straight, and I've got a massive set of drawings I've got to finish for Monday.'

'I've just done ten days straight too, though, if you think about it. With him. I am so tired, Stu. Yesterday I had to look up bone cancer on the computer. I took my pulse and it was one up from dead. I hardly ever ask you to do stuff for us but I just had something I wanted to show you.' With that, she burst into tears.

Stu looked briefly sympathetic, before appearing to remember his own, worse predicament. 'You knew I wouldn't be around much because of uni. I was totally upfront about that. I'm freaking out, babe. You have no idea how much pressure I'm under. I'm twenty for fuck's sake and I'm a dad and a breadwinner. Full time at school and every spare minute pulling beers for people my age who have zero responsibilities.'

'But you said we'd have a day all together,' she said, adding with a self-destructive flourish, 'I suppose if you don't want to, there's nothing I can do about it. I just wish you'd said so is all, so I could have gone into town with Phil.'

Stu's face took on a hardness she had not seen before as he opened his mouth to speak and then closed it again.

Abi's stomach flopped. 'What were you going to say?'

'Nothing. I need some food.'

'No, you were going to say something.'

'I didn't realise you were still hanging out with the fake granny, that's all. I guess that explains why Mum can't get a look-in. I should let her know. Explains everything.' He walked into the kitchen with a pace of defiant leisure and stayed there.

Abi swept everything back into the bag, picked up Jude and left without closing the front door. She dragged the folded buggy behind her, letting it bounce off each stair.

It had looked fine all morning, but now as Abi stamped towards the pool a bank of white cloud drew over like a hood and the heat of the watery sun disappeared. She thought about knocking on Phil's door, but could tell that no one was home from Domenica, exiled to the garden and yapping at her through the crack beneath the gate. Slowly, she walked on, willing the temperature not to drop any further.

The pool was empty. There was no shade or sun, only a flat grey pall hanging over the entire area. She left Jude in the pram, and after sitting for so long on the edge that her buttocks began to ache, Abi slipped into the water and let herself drop down and down and down, staying under for as long as she could. When she burst up, she laughed a mean bark of a thing, realising of course Stu wouldn't care about seeing her swim. She'd never told him that she didn't know how.

Shivering even before she was out, and worried at the bluish tips of Jude's toes and fingers and a pale purple shadow around his mouth, she tucked her towel in around him and ran all the way home. Babies feel the cold more than you, whispered the imperious voice of *First Year with Baby*. Always be prepared with a variety of warmer layers.

Stu had scrawled a note on the back of an unfinished sketch. *Couldn't find you. Gone up to Mum and Dads. Will prob stay over. Sorry about everything.* She brushed it into the sink and ran the tap over it, watching the paper soften and dissolve, and wondering how far back his *everything* went.

To get warm, she climbed into bed with Jude and they dozed, until sometime later she woke with a heaviness pressing on her chest like a sack of sand. With effort, she fed Jude, who kneaded her with his hand, pulled off, grizzled to go back on only to pull off again.

Her loneliness was total. Abi began to feel that if she did not speak to someone, anyone, at this moment, she might never speak again. As though so much isolation could leave her mute. There was nothing but to call her mother.

But reaching for her phone, she saw a message waiting. 'Couldn't be faffed with DJs. Noel holding court at kiosk, w.suspected basal cell,' it read. 'Pop down when finished with fam. duties.'

Abi tore around the flat collecting her things, deciding there wasn't time to shower. She pulled on leggings and a jumper and skeltered down the stairs, Jude in her arms and dragging the pram behind her with one hand.

31.

Quite the motley crew

Minutes later, Abi came down the ramp and saw the group sitting around on the milk crates. Phil waved her over and shuffled back to make room. Abi left Jude against her chest and sat down, still panting.

'Goodness, you're looking a touch peaky, Abigail. Have you got something coming on?'

'No, I'm fine. Busy morning, that's all.'

Phil turned to Noel, who was explaining to the others exactly what they could expect to see under the square of gauze he was about to peel off his mottled shin. 'Hush for a moment would you. All, this is Abigail. Abigail, Valentina,' Phil said, gesturing towards a coffee-skinned older lady with a deep cleavage, into which a diamond-studded crucifix had become sacrilegiously wedged. 'Finally you come to our little club.'

'And Barb. And her good friend Sandy.'

Barb smiled to reveal a row of child-size teeth and a glistening strip of upper gum. Sandy nodded and continued to stroke Domenica, who was lying at her feet. Sandy wore a sort of PE teacher's outfit, only missing the whistle. The pair had similarly close-cropped salt and pepper hair, asexual in style, which suggested a possible two-for-one at a reasonably priced salon.

'And Noel, you'll remember from our brief encounter at the pool.' Phil sucked in her cheeks. 'He was just telling us about a recent biopsy.' Phil shot Abi a wicked look.

'Well,' he said, revealing the fishtail of black stitches below the gauze. 'You can see the size of the bugger. They've done my bloods so now we wait.'

The group gave knowing assent. 'Entire life in the sun,' he went on. 'You watch the little fella won't you, Abi. The Australian sun is a silent killer.'

'We found something very similar on my back last Christmas,' Barb said, 'Didn't we Sandy? It came back clear.' Then, sensing the lack of drama in her contribution, she added, 'But you *never know*.'

Everyone stared gravely into their coffees.

'How old the baby?' Valentina said, breaking the silence.

'He'll be fifteen weeks on Thursday? I suppose I should probably stop counting in weeks, shouldn't I?' Carefully, Abi turned him around so he sat facing outwards.

'They're like campfires, aren't they?' Barb said, gazing at him wistfully. 'You can just sit and stare.'

Sandy lifted Domenica into her lap. The dog gave her a lick on the mouth and Phil looked away, mildly repulsed.

'I have one child, Abigail. My son,' Valentina said. 'And I tell you, he suck my blood. He twenty now. He still live at home. I ask, why he at home? Why he there all day, no working? I give him education, I give him everythings.' Valentina circled her arms outwards in a violent gesture of constant giving. 'I come home, my apartment, issa pig sty. I say, "Alejandro, why so many tissues?"'

Barb listened with an expression of intense sympathy, then looked back at Abi. Her face sprang into the gummy smile. 'Don't listen to any of it, Abi! All children are lovely. I've got two grown-up daughters. They've both moved away, unfortunately. One to *Wollongong*.'

'How are you liking Point life, Abi?' Noel asked. 'It's a good spot we've got here, isn't it?'

'I love it. Especially the pool, and the walk.' Abi meant it, although the memory of her argument with Stu lingered like a bad dream.

'Speaking of,' Phil interrupted. 'I ought to be getting back. Wander back with me, will you, Abigail? I've got a small something for you.'

As Abi clipped Jude into the pram, Phil scooped Domenica off Sandy's lap and released her to the ground a fraction early, causing the dog to squeal and Sandy to flinch.

'Right, goodbye all.'

Abi followed her, waving back as Noel farewelled them with a mock salute, Valentina gave a deep bow, and Sandy sat with her hands folded into the Domenica-less lap of her teacher shorts.

'See you again, Abi,' Barb called. 'Lovely to meet you finally. Having a young person around, so nice for a change, isn't it, Sandy?'

'Well. There you've had them,' Phil said as they fell into step along the path. 'Quite the motley crew.'

'They're all so nice, aren't they?'

'They suffice. I shouldn't say that. I simply mean they're not kindreds, per se.'

'I wonder how long Barb and Sandy have been together.'

'I beg your pardon,' Phil looked at her sharply.

'Oh, well, you know, in terms of – I thought they lived together?'

'They do. Barb has adult children, as you heard.'

'Right, it's just that –'

'And Sandy is a very useful tennis player,' Phil said as though to settle it. Abi said nothing and a minute later, Phil spoke again in clipped tones. 'Abigail. I know what you're thinking and I'm hardly an innocent. I simply doubt we've homosexuals on the Point.'

She went on considering, then burst out laughing. 'Goodness, *are* they, do you think? Lord, I suppose they must be. What a thought. Barb and Sandy, *you-know-what-bians* as our dear Mitfords would say. How terribly cosmopolitan for the Shore. Our own little Bloomsbury group.'

'But with more sensible shorts.'

'Sandy loves a short! Year round!' Phil said, as though fitting the final piece together. 'She's always loved a short.' It was decided as they came to Phil's gate. 'Ah, now, here we are. Wait here will you and I'll just fetch you out my little offering.'

When Abi got upstairs with the parcel Phil hadn't wanted her to open on the doorstep – 'too mortifying, you'll see' – and peeled off the brown paper without tearing it, she found a small unframed canvas. Thick oils made a jar of orange and yellow flowers, their papery petals beginning to drop. A glint of light on the jar made it look so real, although when Abi examined it more closely, the paint used to do it was actually green and grey. Daubed messily in one corner, 'P. Woolnough, '86'. There was no point to it at all, except for being beautiful, and it was. Riveting, extraordinary, and the first time, Abi thought, an Egan had owned something truly beautiful. Its only job to be looked at. She lay on her bed, with her face turned towards it and only stopped staring at it late that night, after Jude had fed to sleep and it was too dark to make it out anymore. The plain white card that had been stuck to the back, 'For the swimmer. Much love, P,' was still in her hand as she drifted off beside him.

32.

Artisanal condiment

Phil had never called Abi's phone before, only texted choice bits of whatever she was reading and spottily capitalised lists of things she might need if Abi *was* passing what Phil called the Milson Road Inconvenience, because it sold very little at a fiendish mark-up, during opening hours that varied capriciously. 'I think the owner may have a depression,' Phil had said, by way of explanation.

Occasionally, she would chime in first thing to find out if Abi was expecting to walk past a post box, and if so, perhaps she would come and collect a thing that really needed to go out today. They were always pale blue envelopes, addressed to Freddie Woolnough, at a constantly changing *poste restante* office somewhere in Asia. They felt so thin Abi couldn't believe there was really a letter inside but held up to the sun, she thought she could make out the slim rectangle of a cheque.

It was odd, then, when Phil's name flashed up on the screen the following day, a slow, grey Sunday that was dragging itself along like a child tired of walking. Abi was lying on the living room carpet, presiding over a period of tummy time as mandated by *First Year with Baby*, and wondering if the fried rice she had made three days earlier with a packet of instant basmati and a can of diced veg would be safe-ish to eat, provided she blasted it for ten whole minutes on high. Stu had not come back from staying overnight at Gordon.

'Hello?' Abi said, lunging for her phone.

'Ah. Abigail. Thank heavens.' Phil's voice sounded weak on the line. 'I'm terribly sorry to interrupt you.'

'No, no, it's fine. I'm not busy.'

'I've gone over in a puddle of something in the ruddy DJs food hall and done something rather bleak to my foot. They brought me to St Vincent's – the hospital – and now they won't release me without anyone to shepherd me into a taxi. I'm suitably insulted, never you mind. I was about to try Noel but no doubt he'd consider it a proposal of marriage, do you see?'

'Of course.' Abi leaped up. 'Jude and I can come get you. Stu's out so it's no bother. I'll look up buses and ring you when we're nearly there. Where is that hospital roughly?'

'Actually dear, I took a liberty and there should be a taxi outside yours shortly. I'll fix it when you get here. You're a lamb, really Abigail, a lamb. I'm tempted to phone Polly but I wonder how pleased she'd be with a ringing phone at three in the morning.'

'Yes, she might panic,' Abi said, elated by the thought of being the only one on the ground. Deciding it would be easier to manage without the pram, she strapped Jude into the carrier.

Phil looked disconcertingly smaller when Abi found her in a corner of Accident and Emergency. One foot was on the floor, pigeoned inwards inside her leather driving shoe, the injured one propped up on another chair, bare toes sticking out beyond messy plaster, a tight, boiling purple. That she was still dressed smartly for town, in a soft linen blazer with a large abstract brooch of the sort Abi had seen in art gallery gift shops, made her feel teary for a minute. Abi crinkled her nose and sniffed, careful not to show sympathy to someone who had more than once described herself as a 'hater of soppiness'.

'Nice pedicure,' Abi said. She bounced up and down and patted Jude in the pack.

Phil looked relieved. 'Yes, I went with purple as you can see. Rather a lurid shade though,' she continued wryly, 'and it seems they've gone over the lines. I shan't be coming here again.'

Once the paperwork was dealt with – 'Cause of injury. Abigail, will I write artisanal condiment/puddle of?' – and Phil finally agreed to take a geriatric-looking crutch the doctor pressed on her, Abi offered an elbow for the steps at the exit.

'Thank you, Abigail, but you needn't treat me like I'm decrepit. I'm quite capable of walking unaided.'

A middle-aged couple were making their way up the stairs and looked sympathetically at Abi, standing with her unwanted arm still outstretched. An aged mother and a little one too, their faces seemed to say.

Abi forced her arm under Phil's. 'All right Mrs Woolnough? Mind these stairs.'

'That's right. One at a time. Can you tell me where we are? We'll get you a nice cup of tea in a minute.'

'Abigail, stop it,' Phil hissed.

'Lovely to get out, isn't it Mrs Woolnough? There we are, careful as you go.' When the couple disappeared inside, Abi broke into giggles that did not abate until they were in the back of the taxi that Phil had told Abi to have wait for them outside, since the ones with baby-seats could be so hard to snag.

As the got in, Abi saw the meter tick up by another 20 cents to $64.90, and prayed Phil would remember what she'd said about fixing it up.

Abi buckled Jude in and although Phil refused to look at her, her reflection in the window showed a smile at the corners of her mouth.

'Now, Abigail, if you can stop being so beastly, shall we hunker down and watch a film this evening? I'm feeling rather useless, suddenly. And you're husbandless, aren't you? Partnerless, I should say.'

'I am. Although I did tell them I'd have you back at the home for your tea by four. It's fish pie on Sundays.'

'*Awful* girl,' Phil muttered as she leaned back and they watched the streets of Darlinghurst slip by the windows.

33.

A toothbrush for Kentish Town

'Thank you actors,' Guy shouted from his seat in the empty front row. He dismissed the company with a brisk clap. 'Lovely work everyone. And thanks again for your Sunday. Understudies off book by our next meeting please.'

As the company waited to walk single file down the rolling staircase drawn up to the edge of the stage, he called over at Brigitta. 'Could you hang back for a moment, please?'

To her disappointment, none of the others seemed to have heard and they continued noisily down the hollow stairs. Brigitta left the line and took up a spot on the edge of the stage, letting her legs dangle like she was sitting on a jetty. After the rabble had collected their satchels and duffel coats and straggled out the stage door, Guy came over and slotted himself between her knees. Her thighs filled the space under his arms, and he clutched her bottom with both hands. Brigitta shivered.

'So *Birj*,' he said in a purr. 'Sylvie has decided to take Ludo with her next week after all, so I find myself quite, quite alone. We obviously can't leave town, what with the little production of ours, but I thought we might go to ground, if you felt so inclined.'

'At yours?' Brigitta asked hopefully.

'No, darling. Best not. But I'm thinking quite seriously of splashing out on a toothbrush for Kentish Town. I know it's not a weekend in Venice, but what do you think?'

'All right then, why don't you?' she said. 'I'm sure Venice is horrible anyway.'

Although privately she was disappointed that she was yet to see the inside of his house, she knew better than to let Guy see her sulk. His affection had a way of cooling when she showed displeasure.

'Right, well, that's sorted then. Unless that's you trembling in my presence, I think you've a phone call so I'll leave you to it, Birj. Be sweet will you and kill those lights off before you punch out.'

She could have done with a kiss but he was already sauntering towards the exit.

'Pol, hi,' she said, tucking the phone under her hair and making no mention of her sister's twelve missed calls.

'Brigitta, bloody hell. Did you see I've been trying to ring?' Polly gave one of her expansive sighs, which in Brigitta's experience could mean anything from Freddie's written off another rental car, to Toby's suddenly refusing to eat anything that isn't white. 'Mum called. She did something to her foot. Broken it, possibly, although it could be a greenstick sort of thing. I really think one of us should go over. I'll pay for your flights of course.'

'My flights? Polly, I can't go. How on earth could I go? Did you hear I'm in a play?'

'There's no need to be chippy, Brigitta. I obviously can't go. I've already used up every kind of leave there is, and did you hear I've got two children?'

'Did she actually say she needs one of us to go and see her?'

'No, but it's our duty. She sounded so pitiful on the phone, Briggy. You'd have wept.'

'Why can't Freddie go? He's nearest. I assume.'

'Don't be stupid, Briggy. He'd have her bringing him breakfast in bed. Can you not just sneak off for a week? It's not like you're the lead. Or is there another reason you can't be away?'

'Gosh, do you need to be so bossy, Polly?' Brigitta asked. 'Really, unattractively mannish. I'm not going. Sorry. I can't. Philly will just have to tough this one out.'

Polly hung up without saying goodbye, which gave Brigitta a start.

'Fuck,' she said, into the empty theatre. And then three times more, louder and louder each time, until she felt sure she'd reached the back row. Our target should always be the pensioner who's paid twelve pounds for a spot against the wall, Guy was always saying.

Brigitta held her resolve as she let herself out of the theatre, but when an image of her mother hobbling around the big house by herself, trying to manage the stairs with a stick, invaded her thoughts in the Australian pinots section of Majestic Wine Warehouse, she texted Polly. 'Fine, book it. A week max. Premium economy or better. I honestly think I might hate you.'

'Good girl. Be ready for a Tuesday a.m.' Polly immediately wrote back, which made Brigitta want to hurl her phone under a passing bus.

She phoned Guy next and told him she was going to have to fly home, an emergency, and miss most of next week's rehearsals.

'Domestic drama isn't my genre, Birj,' he said, cutting her off. 'Sorry, but you knew that. I'll see you if and when you come back. Goodbye, lovely.'

'I will be back,' she said, 'Of course I will. In time for dress!' But he had already hung up.

34.

You must go

Phil chose a French thing with subtitles and decided they could do with the fire lit. Somehow she knelt to set it while calling instructions through to Abi as to the making of tea and English muffins and where to find the tray, which she loaded and carried back to the front room.

Jude had been fed the moment they walked in and was now in a faded bouncy chair that had appeared since Abi's last visit, eyelids already drooping. Phil telephoned Polly, then arranged herself at one end of the deep, velvet sofa with her foot propped on a cushion, and Abi took the other end, shuffling backwards until her feet did not touch the ground. She folded them under her bottom, and tried to focus on the film, although there was so much to look at in the large room, which she'd only seen from the kitchen, that she struggled to keep her eyes on the screen. The low coffee table was piled with hard-covered books about art and copies of *The Times Literary Supplement*. On top of it all was a large hand of bleached white coral. More family photographs decorated the piano and a large bowl of mustard-coloured roses were shedding cupped petals onto the keys. Abi tried to memorise it all, but as the warmth spread across the room and the wind picked up outside, her eyes began to ache. The murmuring French dialogue felt like a lullaby and eventually, she closed one gravelly eye, then the other, just for a minute. Soon she was tugged backwards into a thick sleep.

When she woke again, darkness had fallen outside the French doors and ashes smouldered in the grate. A blanket had been put over her, another tucked in around Jude, who was still asleep in the bouncer, breathing softly. Phil was not in the room. Abi had no idea of the time, but her bladder was pounding and two coin-size circles of wetness were forming on her T-shirt. An hour, longer.

As she stood in the quiet room, listening to the tick of the mantel clock and deciding whether to let herself out or establish first that Phil had managed to get upstairs and into bed, a sense of trespass began to gather. But she was a carer who had lost her charge, Abi told herself, and leaving Jude where he was, she took the passage to the stairs and crept up in bare feet.

Three doors off each side of the landing, all closed. The only light came from downstairs, and Abi ran her hand along the wall until she reached the first door, opening it to find an airing cupboard. For an instant, she pressed her face into a pile of folded towels. Lavender, powder, dust. Abi longed to take one, but closed the door and moved on. The next room was a small lavatory and the sight of it sent it pulse through her bladder. With no choice, she slipped in, leaving the light off and the door ajar in case of Jude.

As soon as she let go, Phil's voice, sharp with panic, came from further down the hall.

'Fred?' she called. 'Who's there? Frederick? Is that you?'

Abi stood up too fast. A hot stream ran down the inside of her legs, and as she tried to tug up her underwear against wet skin, Phil appeared in the gap in the door, leaning on the crutch.

'Frederick?'

'It's just me. It's Abi. I fell asleep and I was just coming to see where you were.' As the door opened further, the light from downstairs revealed Phil's face, bare and creased with sleep, and Abi saw her awful confusion. 'I was downstairs, Phil. I just woke up.' She hurried to get her jeans up, but her fingers would only mash at buttons. 'We were watching a film, remember?'

Phil let out a cry, pure in its agony, and took a heavy step back, trying to close the door on Abi with the crutch. 'Frederick!'

Abi heard her move off. She emerged and as she slipped silently down the stairs, she heard Phil call out, 'Go. You must go please.'

A closing door, then a muffled howl from the other side. 'Fred, my darling. Frederick.'

The sound of Phil's wailing, 'my darling, my darling,' followed Abi to the last step, which she skidded over, losing her footing. She pulled Jude out of the bouncer, catching up the blanket, and ran out the back door, still in her socks.

It was not until she got upstairs to the flat that she realised her house keys were sitting on Phil's piano, beside the dying roses and a photo of wicked Freddie on a white sand beach with a T-shirt wrapped around his head like a silly turban.

35.

Fresh-ish

Abi was sitting against the flat door, feeding Jude, when Stu came up the stairs an hour or so later. The baby's nappy was heavy and sharp-smelling but there had been no question of going back to retrieve her key. After trying to kick then scratch then paw the door open, she had sat miserably on the communal carpet, waiting and thinking and seeing over and over the moment in Phil's hallway. Her lined face, her bare feet, the cry of horror that turned to sobbing as Abi ran away. The thought raised gooseflesh on her arms.

'Just hanging out?' Stu asked, seeing her first. 'Should I ask what happened?'

After twenty-four hours away, it seemed he'd moved on from their unhappy Saturday morning. Or forgotten, Abi wasn't sure. 'Jude and I just fancied some fresh air. Well, fresh-ish. Not fully fresh, but you know, hallway fresh.'

Then, as simple as that, Stu unlocked the door and stood to the side so Abi could carry Jude in ahead. 'You look a bit over it, babe. Shall I put him to bed?'

'Yes please. Thank you. That would be so nice. He needs a change and new clothes. Sorry, I'm so tired.'

Abi handed him over, and retreated to the bathroom where she ran the shower until the walls were slick with moisture. After peeling off her clothes, she got in, remembering just in time that sitting down in the shower and letting the water run forwards over her bowed head, screaming without making a sound, was only for Highside Circuit. She stood with her back against the tiles and tried to think. If she went back to Phil's tomorrow, she could apologise for the intrusion then, explain that she was only trying to be helpful, but had accidently nodded off. It would be all right, Abi could somehow make Phil understand. And either way, Phil would need someone to help her for the next little while. There was no one else, Abi thought, apart from her.

When she got out and walked into the living room in her towel, Stu seemed to be waiting for her. Phil's blanket had found its way to the sofa and was caught behind his back. 'Feel better?'

'Much. Thanks. I'm so sorry.'

'Hey, listen though.' Stu pummelled the tops of his legs with his fists, like a drum roll.

'You don't have to say sorry about the fight. I was just tired.' Abi looked at her hands. 'It's just that I've been practising swimming and I wanted to show you. That's all.'

'Good one,' he continued. 'Anyway, what I was going to say was, I got heaps of work done up at Mum and Dad's today. I was thinking about it on the train back and I think I should stay up there during the week and come back here on the weekend.'

Abi tightened the towel and tried to follow what he was saying.

'It's a massive year and I can't afford to stuff it up. Abi, I'm so rubbish during the week anyway, so I may as well. I doubt you'll even notice.'

'Do you mean, this weekend? Or, *on weekends.*'

He exhaled heavily, as though her need for specifics had quickly become exhausting. 'I haven't really thought about it. Mum and Dad are for it though.'

'But if you were only thinking about it on the train, how do you know they're for it?'

Stu tugged the blanket out from behind him and tossed it on the floor. 'Well, it was their idea. Originally. At the start of my semester.'

'Does your dad think that?' Abi could not bear the idea that Roger would be involved in a conspiracy against her.

'Well, more Mum, I guess. It's nothing against you. She just knows how much work I've got on, it's probably easier on everyone if I just – Mum can do all my cooking and washing and stuff. I'll smash it Monday to Friday, see a mate or two, whatever, and then be way better with Jude when I *am* here. I think it would be good for us, as in long term, because you'd probably see more of me, ultimately.'

Abi reeled. Did he mean they were breaking up? She made to ask, but stopped herself. Because what if he said yes, and here she was, standing only in a towel?

'But you do love me and everything though?' she said after a lengthy silence.

Stu took a fraction too long to reply. 'Yeah, of course I do. It's not about that. It's just what's best for me at the moment. I mean, us obviously. Going forward. And I'll still flick you money and everything. I'll set it up properly even. Have it go straight into your bank. And actually, you'll probably be better off, because I'll be eating all Mum and Dad's food.'

'Okay,' Abi said flatly. 'Sure. If that's what you need. It's totally fine.' She walked slowly back to the bathroom. The prospect of so many hours alone, all day and all night by herself with Jude, filled her with dread but she would not let herself turn back and beg Stu to change his mind.

'Thanks babe, I knew you'd understand,' he called after her. Again, she wrenched the shower on, sitting under it until it ran cold.

36.

One of my foremost traits

There was no reason to get up the next day when Stu left for university with a week's worth of things crammed into his hiking pack. Abi lay face down listening to him dress and open and close drawers, zip a thousand zips and tear noisily at Velcro. Softly, he kissed the top of her head but she did not move until she heard the door click shut. Eventually she rolled over and stared at the dusty ceiling fan. Falling and falling and falling. Pushed from a high building into nothingness.

There was nothing. Nothing. Except for the perfect, unknowing baby slowly waking up in the cot beside her. She lifted a hand – it felt heavy, as though filled with lead or too much blood – and slid it through the slats, running her bent finger along the curved sole of Jude's foot.

A thought, the pushing back of the thought, and then *Fuck it, what else is there?* Phil and Stu had been kicked out from under her, like chair legs. She couldn't stand on her own. She picked up her phone and dialled. Who cared what time it would be? How much it would cost.

'Hello?' She heard her mother's rasping voice, the sound of the telly in the background. 'Who's this please? Who's phoning me?'

Abi jerked the phone away from her ear and stabbed at the off button. When it wouldn't hang up, she pulled the back off, tore out the batteries and threw all of it onto the floor. She picked up Jude, held him tightly against her chest. He dug around, nuzzling at her neck. She sat up and let him feed, feeling her hands shaking against his tiny back. When she looked down at him, the side of his face was wet with tears. 'Oh little boy,' she said, 'I'm sorry. I'm so sorry. I've snotted all over you, and you don't even mind. We'll get up after this, Jude. We will. We'll get up.' After a day, then another, she did.

* * *

Soup. The solution was soup and once she'd come to it, it was only a matter of making herself do each bit, one at a time. Getting up on legs that felt wobbly and wasted, combing the matted bits out of her hair, collecting all the balled-up nappies on the floor into a single rubbish bag, and pushing the pram up to Supa FoodBarn to buy ingredients.

There wasn't much on offer by way of fresh. Potatoes, a leek and another green vegetable Abi thought was definitely courgette, sat in a cardboard carton near a rack of bread marked 'Day Old', its original price scored through. Stock cubes, a tall squeezy thing of table salt (they didn't have the posh kind she knew Phil used), a Crunchie for the way home and a pack of Marlboro Lights. Outside, Abi emptied all but three cigarettes into the bin and hid the packet under the pram. As though someone, anyone, was watching.

When she returned to the flat, it smelt stale from the previous days of incarceration. She slid open the kitchen windows and put her big laptop on the bench so she could find a recipe, and chop the vegetables and talk gaily to Jude who lay on his tummy on a towel, headed raised, and followed her movements around the kitchen with his dark gaze.

The soup didn't look like the picture when it was finished – most likely, Abi decided, because she had had to mash hers with a slotted spoon, noticing too late that the final step in the process involved an electric food processor. She tipped it into two takeaway containers, grimacing at the foul plopping sound as it fell in, and pressed on the lids. Although she'd meant to return Phil's blanket at the same time, she decided against it at the last minute, realising it needed a wash after being worn around her shoulders as she'd lain in bed or dashed madly around the flat to bring food and drink back to the mattress.

When Abi arrived at Phil's back door, she saw that it was open. She hovered on the threshold before calling out in her cheeriest voice, 'Hello?'

Abi waited, patted Jude in the carrier, and adjusted the soup bag on her shoulder. 'Hello? Phil?'

Just as she turned to leave, Phil appeared in the doorway, leaning on the crutch, which now had a silk scarf in a botanical print wound up its shaft and knotted underneath the handle. 'I thought I heard a voice. Hello Abigail.' Phil looked flustered, as though she'd been interrupted. 'Well come in then. Don't hover there like Prufrock,' she said, before abruptly turning back inside.

Abi followed and as she backed herself into a position beside the kitchen door, a youngish woman wandered in from the living room. She had light brown wavy hair that came to her shoulders and caught the light whenever she turned her head. She was barefoot and wearing one of Phil's long cardigans over a thin white singlet. The bottom few buttons were done up in a way that made it impossible to tell if she had shorts, or anything, on above the long expanse of bare thigh.

Abi stood, frozen, watching as she came up behind Phil and rested her chin on her mother's shoulders. Phil's whole person seemed to relax. The girl smiled expectantly in Abi's direction.

'Abigail, this is my daughter Brigitta. She came in very late last night from London. All very spontaneous.'

'Hello,' Abi said, in a strangled half-whisper.

'I was hardly not going to come, was I mother?' Brigitta said. She shot Abi a look, drawing her into some sort of joke at her mother's expense. 'Once we found out about your run-in with the puddle of pesto. Abi, can you believe I came all this way for a bad sprain? My sister made it seem like the whole leg was going to have to come off. Anyway, Mummy loves surprises.' She jutted her chin forward and rested it on the top of Phil's shoulder. 'Don't you, Philly?'

Phil shrugged her off. 'Yes, I'm an enormous fan of surprises. It's one of my foremost traits.'

Abi did not know where to look as the mother–daughter pantomime played itself out. Was she meant to insinuate herself into it, join in the fun? How, when they didn't leave any gaps? Instead, she dropped her eyes to the carrier and pretended to adjust Jude's sock. Phil crutched awkwardly over to the kettle and Brigitta's gaze returned to Abi. 'You look *so* familiar. We haven't met though, have we? I can't think.'

'No, I don't think so. No.' Abi willed her not to remember. 'I've seen you in those photos, but you definitely won't have seen me anywhere.'

'Oh, do you mean the shrine?' Brigitta spun around to the dresser, diverted for now. 'We've begged her to put a few away, haven't we Mummers? Makes you look a bit desperate. Could you at least rotate them? You could have child of the week, or just devote the entire thing to James.'

'Thank you Brigitta for your kind input.'

Brigitta appeared to have touched a nerve, and tried to smooth it over with a lot of loud, trilling laughter that sounded exactly like Phil's.

'Abigail lives in the flats up here,' Phil said as Brigitta settled down.

'Oh brilliant. And who's this little person?'

'This is Jude,' Abi said, stepping nearer so Brigitta could get a glimpse of him, asleep now in the carrier. 'He's nearly four months. The time has really flown. He's a Capricorn, so he'll probably be quite loyal.'

'Gorgeous. What a pudding.'

A moment passed before Abi realised Phil and Brigitta were waiting for her to explain her reason for coming. 'Well, I just thought I should pop, um, over and see how you were going, Phil. With your foot and everything. But I should get going really.'

'Have you made us something?' Brigitta asked. 'Your bag looks quite heavy there.'

'Oh, I tried to just make soup but I don't have one of those processors. You don't have to eat it or anything.'

'You are so sweet. Isn't that so sweet, Mum?' Abi could not tell if Brigitta was teasing.

'Yes, very kind,' Phil said, as the kettle reached its high note. In a single movement, Brigitta went from standing to sitting on the table with her legs crossed.

'It *is* sweet. Poll'll be glad to know you've got someone looking after you, Mum, if we're having *falls* now.' Brigitta extended her leg, long like Phil's, and prodded her mother on the bottom.

'Don't let us detain you, Abi, if you need to be getting on,' Phil said, crutching back to the table with one cup and then another. 'You're ever so kind to inquire after me.'

'I'll probably see you again while I'm here if you're just next door,' Brigitta said. 'I'm barely staying and I only want a bit of Sydney autumn sun and a zizz. Although I expect Mum'll have me on bedpans and rolling over duty, won't you?'

'I'll be sure to telephone, Abi, if I need to be rescued from my daughter's ceaseless tongue-lashing.'

'Learned at my mother's breast. Were you meaning to leave that here, Abi?' Brigitta gestured towards the soup bag.

Reluctantly, Abi let the bag slide off her shoulder and tried to push it back against the wall with her foot, hoping it might be forgotten. 'I'll just leave it there.'

'All right then,' Phil said.

'Okay well, I'm glad you're all right and everything, Phil. Nice to meet you, Brig-Brigitta. Okay then … off I go.' She backed out of the kitchen, cheeks burning. As she hesitated at the back door – close it, or leave it as it was? – she heard Phil say, 'That's the girl who's become a sort of chum. I've mentioned her to you before. I wasn't rude, was I? Only we had a rather vexing moment the other day and I find myself rather abashed.'

'Oh right, of course! Was that the *cohabiter*?' Brigitta asked. 'You were a bit brisk, Mother, but I expect she's used to you. She seems very sweet. I do feel like I know her from somewhere though …'

'The point is, I have moments of grief for Daddy that send me quite mad. So I can't always be on my best behaviour.'

Abi listened on, willing Jude not to let out a cry that would give her away.

'And you were mad already,' Brigitta went on. 'Truly though Mum, we all think you're bearing up pretty well, all things considered. Don't you remember one night after James, you tore out every rosebush in the garden till your hands were ribbons?'

'Ah, did I? Yes, how shaming. Lord, Brigitta, do you forget nothing?'

The conversation dropped below Abi's hearing after that, and she turned to leave. But as she reached the gate, Brigitta shrieked, 'I've just figured out where I've seen her before! Or I think. No, I have! We were both stranded in Singapore that time, when I flew back after Dad. She had the wrong money and needed baby things. I knew it, I *knew* I'd seen her.'

'How extraordinary, are you sure? It seems fairly unlikely to me.'

'No, definitely it was. Poor thing. No money and a tiny baby.'

Abi turned and dashed out. If they discovered her there now, they could ask to be repaid and Abi knew that all she had in her purse was her change from Supa FoodBarn. It was all right, she told herself on the walk home. It was all right. Until Brigitta left and she had a chance to apologise to Phil for coming upstairs, she could try to be invisible.

37.

A stitch of harm

Later that night, Jude settled in his cot, Abi peered down at the big house and saw Phil and Brigitta sitting on the window seat, holding glasses of wine. She wrapped her arms around herself, and alone in the darkness of her living room, she watched Brigitta stretch out and lay with her bare feet in her mother's lap. At one point, Phil said something so funny that Brigitta had to sit up and hold her wine away from herself, to stop it spilling all over the squab. Abi knew they would be talking about her. The soup had been such a stupid idea. Who would even try to make something when they didn't even have all the right things? She tried to cry but nothing came. She was too tired. After a few moments more, she broke away from the window and went to bed.

Too soon, Friday morning came, disappointingly bright and clear. She wanted the miserable grey of Croydon. With effort, she got up and then, realising Phil wouldn't be walking to the kiosk, decided it was safe to push the pram to the end of the point and back.

All the way, she made up stories for him about things that lived in the trees and under the water. He gurgled and held his feet. Then, as she came down the ramp, she saw, too late, Phil and Brigitta sitting side by side on a pair of crates, talking intently. Phil was leaning against the glass, with her foot stuck up on another crate, and the crutch tucked in behind.

Abi took a short step backwards and began to reverse, but Brigitta leaned back in laughter and saw her. She waved. Abi waved back and forced herself to continue down.

'Hello again,' Brigitta said. 'I've brought mother out for her constitutional. It only took us forty minutes to get here. Do you want to join us? We're only gossiping.'

Abi shifted her weight from one foot to the other, jigging the pram in a rapid back and forth. Phil turned away from her without expression. 'I can't,' Abi said. 'I am, I was just off to baby music. Yes. Little Movers. Jude loves it. His favourite day of the week. So I'm just here for a takeaway.' Abi had not returned since the first session, but faintly remembered it being on Mondays and Fridays. Either way, the walk to the church and back would pass an hour.

'Gosh, you're such a *doer*.' Brigitta patted Phil on the knee. 'Did you take us lot to baby classes, Mother, or did you have one of your heads?' She began to laugh. 'Solidly, for a decade.'

Brigitta smiled back at Abi, inviting her into the joke. 'Mum was more about sending us out to roam the streets of Cremorne until nightfall, that sort of thing.'

Phil folded her arms. 'That is rubbish. I played with you constantly.'

'Any game that let you be prone. Poll and I had to do a lot of doctors and dentists, Abi.'

'If letting you fossick around in my mouth with a cake fork wasn't adequate maternal sacrifice, I apologise, Briggy. It certainly felt like it from where I was ... lying.'

Brigitta let out a fresh gale of laughter. Abi wished she could make the warm, teasing reminiscences stop, although she tried to look as though she was enjoying it as much as they were. When it got so hilarious Abi felt like weeping, she knelt down to find something under the pram.

'Has Mum told you about the time I had a sleepover in the car?' Brigitta said, forcing Abi to reappear.

'Oh Briggy, please. Abigail doesn't need all the family secrets.'

'Mum and Dad had been to someone's for dinner and taken the four of us in our pyjamas. I was only a baby.'

Phil rolled her eyes elaborately. 'You were two. Freddie was the baby.'

'Either way, Mother. When we got back, Mum and Dad carried us in one at a time but they both thought the other had got me. They didn't realise until the morning when Mum came into my room and my cot was perfectly made.' Brigitta folded her long hands in her lap, vindicated.

'And it didn't do you a stitch of harm. In fact I'd say you've rather prospered from it, since you jolly well bring it up every time you need a bit of sympathy.'

'I used to love being carried inside!' Brigitta said, appearing overcome. 'I used to pretend to be asleep just so Daddy would.'

Phil's eyes welled up and she reached for a paper napkin. 'I must apologise, Abigail,' she said, pressing it to each eye in turn, 'we seem to be in the throes, again.' Turning to Brigitta then, she said, 'Darling, are you going up to Mosman to get lunch things because if so I'd like to start hobbling back now.'

Brigitta stood up and brushed out her lap. 'Gosh, you must think we're such disasters Abi! Oh, but guess what, I figured out where I –'

'I should get cracking for Little Movers!' Abi said, backing away as quickly as she could, knocking the pram into abandoned crates in her haste. 'All the other mums will be wondering where I am. Nice to see you again!'

38.

There is no Monique

Little Movers was nearly finished by the time she arrived. Abi paid anyway, and carried Jude past the milling mothers to the morning tea table. They would not have talked to her anyway. She leaned across a platter of fruit kebabs and thought briefly of Tiffany.

'Excuse me,' said a mother. 'I was here. I'm trying to get at the mini-muffins.'

Abi turned to apologise, and the woman's face lit up.

'Oh you. Hiya. I haven't seen you here in ages. I thought you must have moved. I've gone and forgotten your name. I'm a shocker with names.' The woman squinted at her. 'I never forget a face though.'

'Abi.'

'That's it. And this is?' She looked at Jude, twisting a hand through Abi's hair.

'Jude.'

'That's right. I knew it was a girl's name. That I do remember. He's grown, hasn't he? You remember Lydia? She does her wees on the potty now, don't you Lydia?' The little girl appeared from behind her mother's hefty legs and lifted her skirt above her head. 'That's right. Those are your big girl undies. So, have you been back at work or what?'

'No, I've just been really busy,' Abi said. 'You know how it is.'

Without meaning to, Abi found herself following the woman to a chair and sitting beside her.

'Oh, I *do* know. Believe me.' The woman massaged her lumbar. 'I'm hardly ever here either, now that I've upped my hours at – do you know Beauty by Monique? Near Supa FoodBarn. You know, right there.'

She whirled one of her thick fingers over an imaginary street corner. 'I do three days now, including Saturdays because it's like, the richest day in terms of hourly rate. But to be honest, I do it for myself.'

'Brilliant,' Abi said, trying to concentrate as an image of Phil and Brigitta sitting down to a lunch of posh sandwich fillings formed in her mind's eye.

'Guess what?' The woman straightened up in her chair. 'There is no Monique.'

'Pardon?'

'Beauty by Monique? There *is* no Monique. The owner just came up with that. Her name's really Dawn.'

'Oh, right. How funny.'

'Do you want to have lunch after this or what?'

The woman closed her mouth around an entire mini-muffin. 'I'm so fat. Lydia's just given up her sleep.' With the other hand, she put two fingers to her temple like a gun. 'I still make her go in her room for two hours for what I call *downtime*. But to be totally honest, that's for me. I can't have her on at me all day. We could come to you for lunch. I'd have you to mine but it's a tip at the moment. We're painting. Off white, nothing crazy. You're down at Cremorne aren't you? I drove.'

The woman's prattle had become infuriating, interrupting Abi's concentration on Phil and Brigitta.

'That's right. I am. But we can't though, unfortunately.'

'What've you got on?'

The woman held her gaze, Abi held it back. 'I've got to get some things. From Mosman.' A charge went through her as she continued. 'For my mother.'

The woman looked doubtful. 'I thought all your family was overseas.'

'No. My mother lives next door to me now,' Abi said, as her eyes filled with tears that soon began cascading down each cheek. 'In a big, huge house. Arts and Crafts if you know what that is. She had a fall the other week, so I've been on bedpan and rolling-over duty. But luckily my sister has just arrived to help me out.'

She spoke faster and faster, feeling as if she had left her body and was watching herself from above. 'She's an actress, in plays. My sister. You'd know her if I told you her name. So anyway they gave me a list, all the expensive things we eat. Olives and whatnot. And trout. We don't even eat bread in my family.'

'Yeah, all right,' the woman said, getting up to leave.

As quickly as she could, Abi took Jude out to the pram and let it drag her down the steep hill home. She would not let herself stop until all the morning's misery had been burned away.

39.

Bed of peace

There was really no need to feel quite so guilty about Abigail, Phil told herself, as she performed her nightly ablutions and then, with some difficulty, got into bed. Why she couldn't budge the feeling was quite beyond her, especially with Brigitta in the house to enjoy. Their awful encounter in the hallway though. It was still mortifying to recall. As she fossicked around in her bedside drawer for the television remote control, Phil wondered if a certain amount of boundary setting was now required. Frederick was always leery of so-called 'entanglements' and although Abigail was terrifically useful for company, Phil worried she would never touch the bottom of her fairly obvious reservoir of need. And it was hardly fair to rely on Abigail always being so lively and diverting, when Phil was in no position to be relied upon herself. It was only that Abigail's funny ways, her peculiar expressions and lusty laughter were always such a tonic, and not to mention the darling baby.

Phil turned on the small television which sat on a dresser some distance from the bed, and flicked back and forth for something to put her to sleep. She was usually strict about night-time aids of any kind, having become too dependent for her own liking on a finger of Frederick's whisky and one of the Valium tablets a hospital doctor prescribed her for the dreadful first days following Fred's death. When they eventually ran out, Phil made an appointment to get more, only to lose her nerve when the moment came. In panic, she asked for a breast examination, the violation of which made her weep all the way home.

By comparison, a little bit of television with Briggy next door was simply luxury.

There was an arts programme on SBS and Phil lay back into her pillows to watch a man talking about a play. He wore a fine knit V-neck without a shirt underneath it and sat in a high-backed leather chair, with one foot laid rakishly over the other knee. It appeared he wasn't wearing socks with his leather loafers either.

'Briggy!' she trilled after a moment's watching. 'Are you awake, darling? Come in here. There's a man on and I think he's talking about your jobby, your play.'

Brigitta appeared in the doorway, in an eye-catching pair of knickers and a large T-shirt. Phil waved the remote control at the screen. 'Isn't this your man?'

'What?' Brigitta asked, caught visibly off guard.

'Isn't this your director, Guy something?'

Casually, Brigitta drew her hair back into a low pigtail and released it, although to Phil's eye she looked oddly pale. 'Oh yes, it might be. I can't really tell.'

She held back the bedclothes, and after a brief hesitation, Brigitta got in beside her. Phil put the sound up a few notches and settled in, enjoying the loveliness of the moment. 'He seems very charismatic. Is this like him, from what you know? I expect there's not much interaction, is there, with the *downstairs* players.'

Phil felt Brigitta turn rigid beside her. 'Darling? Briggy?' Phil bonked her on the shoulder with the remote control. 'He is your fellow, isn't he?'

Instantly, Brigitta threw back the covers and marched towards the television, wrenching the plug out of the socket. 'So Polly's told you everything, then. You could have said, Mother. This whole time! There was no need to string me along, that's really quite vicious. Is that why I was dragged out here in the first place? For a telling off? Twenty-four hours in economy class!' Brigitta put her hands on her hips but Phil could see they were shaking.

'Well I know from Polly it was premium, so you can drop the act. Anyhow, I haven't the faintest idea what you're saying but it sounds like I ought to. I will thank you to sit down and be out with it.'

Brigitta slumped against the dresser, eyes averted.

'In your own time.' Phil folded her hands above the sheets.

Finally Brigitta came to the edge of the bed and sank face-first into the covers, mumbling something out of Phil's hearing.

'Darling, you'll have to sit up. I can't hear you. Up, up.' Phil's foot found Brigitta's side and gave it a forceful nudge. 'And you needn't be so theatrical.'

Slowly Brigitta levered herself up. 'I *said*, Guy and I are seeing each other. Even though, technically, he's not quite divorced. Yet.'

Phil let out a short yelp and lunged for the box of tissues on the night table.

'This is exactly why I didn't say anything! Because I knew you'd go completely fucking Mrs Bennet about it.'

'Bed of peace! Bed of peace!' Phil wrenched tissue after tissue from the box until they ran out. 'Need it make you so coarse? Oh, but a married man darling, really truly.'

'They've been separated forever. He's been trying to move out.'

'What, so that you can move in?'

'I might,' Brigitta said with a flash of defiance. 'What if I did?'

'Darling, I'm sorry but it's simply not the way things are done. Your father would have been horrified, and as for me –'

'You don't mind when other people cohabit.'

'That's totally different and you jolly well know it. Abigail is from a totally different – this is all beside the point. The point is, Brigitta, this affair or whatever it is will not end well.'

'It's not an affair. He doesn't love her. He loves –'

'Don't say it! Even if it were the case Brigitta, and I'm sorry to say that I doubt it, but whichever – a man who's been married to someone else will never be yours entirely. Surely you know that, darling. You'll quite simply always be second violin.'

'No change there then.'

Phil looked arch. 'Meaning what, precisely?'

'Meaning, I should be used to it. In fact, second violin would be a step up from where I usually sit in this family.'

'Oh not this again Briggy, really,' Phil looked away, exhausted. 'I'm really not sure how, at your age, you can still carry such a chip about being *overlooked*, as you call it. Your father and I loved you all the same and there isn't any more to say about any of it.'

The air crackled between them.

'Well it's probably over now anyway,' Brigitta said, getting up and stomping into the hallway. 'Because I'm *here* again,' she called. 'And the others are all somewhere else!'

* * *

Phil slept badly and woke much later than usual the next day, feeling nauseated. She sat up and sipped the glass of stale water beside her bed. The memory of their argument lingered like a hangover and she longed to sink back into sleep. But no, she must get up and sort things out now. Clear the air before Brigitta left the following day, and with any luck she would weaken, Phil could set her on a path towards flicking the chap, and still have the prospect of a pleasant last day together.

Phil put her good foot down first – Lord, she was beginning to sound like Noel – and hobbled off on the crutch. Thinking how she might start things off, Phil made her way slowly down the hall and tapped on Brigitta's door. It was ajar, and after a moment she gave it a little push open. A rester like her mother, Brigitta would still be sleeping off last night's stoush.

Her bed was empty, unmade, with a soft impression in its centre. Phil looked around the dim little room – never the best in the house, wrong side for morning sun. A wastepaper basket in one corner overflowed with Brigitta's detritus and a pile of sour-smelling towels had built up in one corner. Phil backed out and softly closed the door, realising, of course, that she was gone.

40.

Sniffer of nighties

Abi stayed upstairs, out of the way, for as long as she could, not knowing when Brigitta was supposed to be leaving. Eventually, Jude's rising discontent forced them out and as she set off on the path, she saw Barb and Sandy ducking out of their low bungalow. Sheepishly, she fell in behind them hoping they were setting off to the kiosk. Abi's need for company finally overpowered her instinct to stay out of the Woolnoughs' orbit. She followed behind at a distance but before the ramp down to the ferries, Barb and Sandy peeled off towards the buses. Abi pressed on. Noel. Noel might be there. He would do, even by himself.

But as she came down the ramp searching for Noel, she saw Phil sitting alone, watching the water. The sky behind her was leaden and the near part of the harbour moved in multiple, messy currents. As a gull stalked across the wooden floor of the café, Phil tore off a corner of toast and tossed it in the bird's direction, before turning listlessly towards the ramp.

Abi watched her expression change from gloom to surprise.

'Pull up a crate!' Phil signalled straight away to the man behind the coffee machine. 'Well,' Phil said, folding her hands in her lap as Abi sat down with the pram drawn up to her side. 'She's gone. She had to go a day early in the end, so now of course I'm in slough of despond.'

'Well that's fair enough, definitely,' Abi said with dissolving anxiety. The coming and going of Brigitta seemed to have supplanted any thought of the horrible hallway stoush. Abi hoped against hope. 'Brigitta seems so nice. She looks loads like you.'

Something seemed to occur to Phil then and she looked at Abi soberly, causing her to blanch. 'Dear, I feel an apology is needed.'

Abi knew she was wrong about the hallway, and rallied herself to apologise.

'I worry –' Phil cut in, '– I worry I was rather brisk with you when Briggy was here. We've got a nice little friendship, don't we, so I do hope you didn't feel thrown over. It's only that grief makes one act in all sorts of terrible ways. But I expect, you of all people know that too well.'

'Mmmm,' Abi said, the catalogue of her crimes born of grief now too long to consider. 'I do, yes, definitely.'

'Anyhow, the less said on it the better, Frederick always used to say.'

'It was nice she came out for you,' Abi said, as eager as Phil to move the conversation on. 'Even though she's got loads on I bet. How amazing, being an actress.'

'Indeed. I am always thrilled when they come home. But then of course, they're only to leave again. And these goodbyes, Abigail, they simply never get better. In the sense of easier. Briggy left a nightie behind in her bathroom and you'll think I'm mad, but this morning, I couldn't help giving it a little sniff.'

Abi thought of Phil's throw rug, currently folded under her pillow. 'I don't think you're mad. I'm always smelling ... things of Jude's. If I'm ever feeling a bit lonely. I hardly ever am though, obviously. What with him actually always being around. And Stu being so ...' Abi swallowed '... hands on.'

'I suppose I'd never have anticipated that life would become this exasperating sort of cycle. The countdown to them coming and the looking forward to it. And then whatever it turns out to be. The visit, whether it's good or one that doesn't gel, so that we part on poor terms that can't be set right over distance. You would think that losing their father would bring my children, my *surviving* children, together. Well a mother can hope, but instead they're all behaving like brutes. And in the meantime, I'm reduced to a sniffer of nighties. Waiting for ruddy Godot, aged widow's edition.'

In spite of herself, Abi giggled. Phil looked at her crossly for a second, before deciding it might as well be funny. 'I see I've made myself the object of scorn.'

'I'm so sorry, it's not funny at all,' Abi said as they both dissolved into laughter. 'It's not funny, I don't know why I'm laughing.'

'No neither do I, with such rotten children. Goodness we must look a pair,' Phil said, wiping her eyes. 'Now. Abigail. Serious for a moment, what else did I have to tell you? Oh yes, the good news, this wretched thing can come off tomorrow.' Phil lifted her ankle an inch. 'I'm ready for a ghastly little brace apparently, but at least I'll be able to turn over in bed. I wondered if you'd think about coming along. More for company than anything else.'

'Of course. I'd love to.'

'Oh and thank you for the soup.'

Abi cringed. 'That's all right. I hope you didn't eat it or anything.'

'We gave it our best try, although I wasn't sure you'd really meant to put cucumber in it. Or did you? It made me wonder if we ought to have a little run of cooking lessons. There'll be bless all else to do once winter really sets in.'

41.

You've made everything worse

Brigitta forced her way through the crowds at King's Cross, dragging her suitcase behind her. When she emerged from the Underground, she turned her face up to a heatless sun and tried to slow her breathing.

Once again, Brigitta had intended to go straight from the airport to Barbican to make rehearsal on time, but as she'd got off to switch lines, a pressing need for air, daylight and coffee sent her surging towards the exit.

She found a Starbucks and switched on her phone, expecting a torrent of voice messages from her mother. There was only one. Polly. Brigitta waited until she was outside again and cradled the phone between her ear and shoulder so she could listen on the walk back to the Tube.

'Brigitta, it's me.' The barely suppressed rage in Polly's voice caused Brigitta to flinch. 'Mum is really, really upset. We spoke for an hour. What were you thinking? Really, Brigitta, this is *madness*. Going all the way over to look after her then leaving in a strop. You've made everything worse. I'm really struggling. Am I meant to be worried about you? Please call her when it's the right time there, and sort it out, would you? I have to go, ring me as well please. Although I'm in back to back meetings until six.' There was a pause. 'We are all grieving you know, Brigitta, just the same as you. But some of us are able to control the tantrums.'

Letting go of her case, Brigitta stabbed at the buttons until the message was erased.

'Fuck,' she said out loud. 'Fuck.' The accusation, the ganging up, the unfairness of her dropping everything to fly out and still ending up in the wrong.

In her other hand, hot coffee was leaking down the sides of the takeaway cup she had been holding too tightly. She let herself drop it. It hit the pavement and the coffee washed out in a steaming puddle. Commuters walking behind her cleaved around the spill and closed in again, like a river running around a rock. Miserably, Brigitta took up the suitcase and decided to walk the rest of the way to the Barbican. She needed to get her thoughts in order before she arrived but as she started towards the theatre, her mind couldn't begin to triage so many injustices.

* * *

The stage door wouldn't open. After retrying the code, she called Guy's mobile and mercifully he picked up.

'Hello Birj, darling, I wasn't expecting to hear from you. Where are you?'

'I'm outside. The fucking door won't open.'

'Oh right. Yah, they've changed the codes. Wait there, I'll be round in a jiff.'

Brigitta drew a tiny mirror out of her bag while she waited and moved it unhappily from side to side. Her skin was ashen, with dark smudges of mascara under both eyes. There was nothing that could be done.

'Good God,' Guy said as he stepped outside and let the stage door suck closed behind him. 'What have you come as?'

'I came straight from the airport. Sorry I'm late,' Brigitta said without expression when she realised he wasn't going to kiss her.

'Well, I wish you hadn't,' Guy said. 'You should have called, Birj. I wasn't sure you were coming back so I've had to flick your part to one of the studies. You understand, don't you? The industry. An unforgiving mistress.'

'I only missed four rehearsals!'

'Mmm. Anyway, I ought to jump back in. We'll get a drink or something when you've had a chance to recover. Truly, get some rest, Birj, you look like you've been dug up.'

With that he turned, punched in the code and disappeared through the door, which gave a dull click as it locked from the inside.

42.

No lectures please

The insistent buzzing of the doorbell woke Brigitta the next morning. She opened one eye. It twitched horribly from the two bottles of shiraz she had bought on the way home from the theatre and finished on her own before falling asleep in the early afternoon. When she lifted her head, her brain seemed to lag behind, then smash into the front of her skull. Half nine. It wouldn't be Guy and even if it was, she wasn't going to let him up while her tongue was adhered to the roof of her mouth. She pulled the covers up to her chin and felt the reassuring weight of the Max Mara laid over the top. The heating, controlled by downstairs, had flicked off in the night and at some point she had woken up shivering. Whoever it was could go away, Brigitta decided, nestling down further.

After a minute the caller abandoned their staccato ringing in favour of a continual buzz. Polly.

Brigitta got up and staggered to the decrepit entry phone to let her sister up. As she crossed the room, her fingertips subconsciously found her temple, as though checking there wasn't a very small axe lodged there.

In nothing but the underwear she'd put on forty-eight hours before in the bathroom at Milson Road, Brigitta opened the door. Polly stood outside, stern-faced but holding a takeaway coffee and a brown paper bag with grease soaking up from the bottom, which Brigitta acutely hoped meant bacon or pastry. 'No lectures please,' she said, accepting her sister's offering. The sound of her own voice made one side of her face explode with hot, white pain. She got back into bed and watched as Polly removed her coat and, after washing her hands in the kitchen sink, sat down on the edge of the bed.

'How did you know I'd need this?' Brigitta asked, taking a tentative sip of the coffee.

'Experience. Brigitta, what are we doing?' Brigitta had been expecting the voice Polly used when the boys put a soccer ball through the window, but instead Polly spoke in the soft and measured tone of someone trying not to upset a mental patient. 'I'm trying to understand what's going on. Are you all right, or not? Mark and I are actually starting to get quite worried.'

Brigitta looked inside the paper bag, where some sort of toasted panini shone in its own oil. She felt bilious, but after picking out the bits of green, managed two bites of bread and prosciutto. 'I am fine, thank you for asking. I'm just finished with being told what to do, and ordered around by you and Mum and sent to do your bidding. Her foot wasn't even broken. I flew all that way for a mild sprain. And then I get home and all I get from you is an incredibly nasty voice message. Just before I got sacked that is. No "Thanks for going, Brigitta." No "Sorry you just lost your job." Seriously, Polly, you need a pill or something.' It came out more harshly than she meant. 'You weren't always so tough, is all I'm saying.'

'There's no need to lash out at me, just because you're not coping.' Polly looked pointedly at the empty bottles on the floor beside a Styrofoam dish of chips Brigitta had only the vaguest recollection of purchasing from a kebab van. The sight of them, cold and skinned with sauce, turned Brigitta's stomach.

'Do you know, I would be coping a lot better if I was allowed to get on with my own life instead of being on constant call for you and Mum. Did you even hear me? I lost my job!'

'Look, I'm sorry about that but you'll get another one.'

If this was Polly's attempt to be kind, it was not working.

'We've both got to dig deep at this point and be there for Mum. She's lost her husband, Brigitta, and you know how useless she can be. It's a massive time for her, but I just feel like it's become all about you. This mad drama that you seem to create wherever you go.'

It was true, the bit about their mother anyway, but Brigitta still seethed. The impulse to kick her sister made her leg twitch. 'You're the one who turned it into a drama by making me jump on a plane. She didn't even need me there. She's got her little neighbour running around after her anyway.'

Polly's brow furrowed. 'What? Who?'

'Just a girl from those flats. Mum's apparently talked her into bringing her food and doing errands and that sort of thing.'

'How bizarre.' Wearily she laid hand across her forehead. 'She hasn't mentioned a helper. Anyway, I came to talk about you, Brigitta. You're the one I'm most concerned about at this point, since you're actually giving Mum more to worry about. But if you actually *want* to live like this, I suppose there's nothing I can do about it.' Again Polly cast her eye around the sorry roomscape and Brigitta felt her anger muddle with shame. Polly stood up to leave, but paused with her arms folded as though the seconds were counting down on Brigitta's chance to surrender.

'Could you stop being so mean please? I am trying, Polly. That's what you never seem to see. I *am* trying.'

'Then why do you need me to rescue you all the time!'

Polly rarely cried but it seemed as if she might now. Her voice cracked in a way that sent a bolt of alarm through Brigitta's core. She was the crier, Polly the shouter.

'I don't need you to rescue me, Polly. I really don't. You do it because you want to. You think it's your job, and I know it used to be but we are all grown up and your services are no longer required.'

Polly lit up with a fury that propelled her towards the door, where she began struggling into her coat. 'Why don't you act like a grown-up then! If you, or Freddie, or Mum, any of you, looked after yourselves for even one day, I'd quit in a second! I'd love to. Really, I would Brigitta. If a single one of you would just grow up!'

'Well I'm sorry if I don't have a nice rich husband and help and a perfect house,' Brigitta leaped off the bed, narrowly avoiding the styrofoam tray. 'And don't say it! I'm not jealous. I don't want your life. I just want *my* life.'

'Why now? Why now? That's what I'm struggling to understand. Why must this rebellion of yours happen now?'

'When would be a better time? When Freddie sorts himself out? When James magically comes back to life? Tell me when, Polly! When will it be my turn?'

'So it *is* all for attention then, is it? At least you've admitted it.'

'Fuck!' Brigitta said as she realised with forehead prickling and mouth suddenly streaming that she was about to vomit. As she lunged for the toilet, a great river of dark red liquid poured out of her mouth, splashing up the sides of the bowl. She clutched the seat with both hands as her stomach heaved in one vicious spasm after another.

'God, it's like being in Year 12 all over again,' Polly said from somewhere behind her. Next, a bouquet of tissues was handed through the broken concertina door. Brigitta accepted them, still unable to speak. When she re-emerged, jelly-legged and faint, Polly had put an outfit and toiletries into a Sainsbury's bag and was holding the door open. 'I've got the car downstairs. Come home with me. We can sort this out later when you've had a rest. Natalia is making pirozhki, and the boys are watching *X Factor* all day.'

After dressing, Brigitta accepted her coat, stepped sockless into a pair of boots by the door and began following her sister out. She felt exhausted. 'I thought her name was Nadia.'

'That was a different one.'

It was only when Polly stepped into the hallway to wait and was briefly distracted by her phone that Brigitta realised she wasn't going. 'Sorry, actually Polly, I'm going to stay here.'

Her sister glanced up, freshly irritated. Still inside, it was easy for Brigitta to close the door against her sister's protest. 'I'll call you later. Thanks so much for the visit. Okay, drive safely. Bye.' She slid the bolt across, and didn't wait to hear Polly retreat downstairs. The thrill of escape lasted until, a minute or so later, it was replaced by another powerful wave of nausea.

43.

Death by toxic towelette

Abi took the lid off the biscuit tin and passed it to Noel who was sitting beside her, blowing into cupped hands. May had been colder than usual, and a strong wind was whipping up the harbour, finding its way in through the cracks in the decking. Phil held Jude, cocooned in a thick baby blanket. The sight of him always bare-headed had compelled her to get an easy Aran hat on the needles and he was wearing it now. Perhaps she'd do him a little matching cardigan to grow into. Each fresh gust compelled the six crate-sitters to shuffle another inch inward until their knees nearly met.

'Like penguins on the ice,' Phil said. 'Noel, I expect you'll be on my lap in a minute.'

'What are these, Abi love?' he asked, blushing.

'Her first batch of ginger biscuits,' Phil cut in. 'A triumph I might say.'

Abi offered her the tin. 'I won't, thank you Abigail. I'm up to dolly's wax.'

'They've got a real crunch, Abi,' Barb said, covering her mouth as her gums became coated with crumb. 'I prefer a crunch biscuit to a cookie.'

'Do you now, Barb? How intriguing.' Phil, now always on

the lookout for evidence of Barb's alternative lifestyle, let her eyes widen imperceptibly to all but Abi.

'I shouldn't have another one,' Noel said, taking another one. 'A lot of diabetes on my side.'

'Indeed,' Barb nodded soberly. 'Sandy had to go to A&E over Easter and I thought it might be diabetes because she was very tired and had an excessive thirst. But it was only dehydration from doing the Spit to Manly walk without cream on.' Sandy confirmed the fact with a nod.

'What are you making next, Abi?' Barb went on. 'I have a crustless quiche recipe that's very good for visitors. And it keeps, so it's a real cut-and-come-again.'

'A *crustless* quiche,' Phil said, marvelling. 'How unconventional. But we're actually on a poultry jag. In fact, we've got a bird in as we speak.'

'At nine in the morning?'

'Barb, if we're going to get to braises by the end of the week as planned, we do what we must. Abigail, we ought to be going if we don't want to walk in to ashes. Besides which, Jude is about to turn blue.'

The timer was going when Phil let them in her back door, and with the whizzy heater left on, the kitchen had warmed up to a pleasant fug. With Stu gone, Phil's kitchen was Abi's best refuge against the ringing emptiness of the flat. She put Jude down on a soft, folded quilt that had become a fixture in the kitchen, now that his primary occupation was trying to roll over until the effort laid him out. 'Although he'll only do it when there's something really worth rolling for, like some carpet fluff,' Abi said at the time.

'Well I expect there'll be plenty to tempt him on my floors, dear.'

The oven light was on and, knotting her apron, Abi went over to look through the glass at the chicken, glorious and golden, sizzling in its own fat and looking exactly like the one on the cover of Phil's *Cordon Bleu Meat and Game*. She opened the door expectantly, and a plume of acrid smoke spilled out and billowed to the ceiling, hovering there in a dark mass, reeking of melted plastic. She covered her face with the apron and looked desperately at Phil, who was striding around the table with a tea towel pressed to her nose.

'Good Lord, what on *earth*?' Phil shoved past her, grasped the scalding pan with more tea towels, and dropped it into the sink. 'Something's melted, Abigail. Heavens, take Jude out. Put him through to the front room and shut the door, out of this air.'

At the same moment, the phone rang and Phil snatched it up.

'Briggy, is that you? Darling, I can't talk. Fighting fires.' Without waiting for a reply, she tossed the cordless into the fruit bowl and threw open a window above the sink. A gust of cold air thinned the worst of the trapped smoke, and Phil peered into the tray.

'It looks absolutely fine,' Phil said, prodding it with a long fork as Abi returned after installing Jude in a circle of cushions. 'I can't think what the dreadful odour is.'

Abi stood beside her, inspecting the carcass. 'I did everything you said.'

They wiped streaming eyes in unison and Abi tried to think. Before they left for the kiosk an hour earlier, Phil had nipped off to spritz her cymbidiums and left her in the kitchen with rattled-off instructions for getting the fowl into the oven. Abi followed them absolutely.

'Unless,' she hesitated. Phil was trying to flip the whole lot over but it was bonded to the tray. 'Unless, was I supposed to take out that funny pad thing from underneath?'

'Ah.'

At that moment, the chicken came away from the pan, exposing the remnants of an absorbent packaging pad, swollen with cooked blood.

'I wasn't sure. I didn't want to interrupt you,' Abi said. 'I thought you must be supposed to leave it, to soak up the juice or something. I'm so sorry.'

'The thing that looks a bit like a sort of a ... surgical dressing?'

'Yes,' Abi said, downcast.

'We've cooked that, have we? Then I'd say it's unfit for human consumption,' Phil said before breaking into hearty laughter. 'We won't risk death by toxic towelette. But we ought to eat something I suppose, so I'll see what's in the fridge and send a bit home for Stu besides. Is that Jude I hear?'

Bored with his own company, Jude was beginning to squawk and Abi went off to retrieve him. When she returned, Phil had open a new copy of *Hons and Rebels*. 'Fancy, I'd just read this line yesterday,' she said. 'Listen. "Darling, you know I don't know how to take things out of ovens, one's poor hands ... Besides, I do so hate getting up early."'

'Is that Aunt Sadie?'

'No dear, that's the real Nancy, so you're in good company at least. And it was too early to eat a roast anyway, but I will see what I've got.'

44.

The eternal hairshirt

It was over a plate of cheese and oatcakes that Abi confessed that Stu wasn't one hundred per cent around at the moment, dinner-wise. Abi had set Jude down on the folded quilt, where he lay contentedly blowing milky bubbles.

Phil cocked her head. 'What do you mean, not around?'

'I mean, he's staying at his mum and dad's during the week, and he comes back here on weekends. Well, he's supposed to, but so far he's had too much on, generally speaking.'

'I beg your pardon?'

'It's better in terms of him getting his work done. He's really under the pump with his course. Jude's still up loads in the night and Stu needs to concentrate. We need to have a proper chat really. It's not forever. I mean, I assume it's not.'

'You *assume*. And quite how long has this been going on?'

'Um, roughly, I would say … since Brigitta was here?' Abi said, admitting, when Phil probed her, that the days actually could feel quite long, and the evenings even longer, especially with it getting dark so early and there being no promise of company at the end. Even if he came home late and tired, or drunkish and overexcited, any time with him was the prize for patting Jude to sleep through the bars of his cot for fifty minutes every night and singing 'You Are My Sunshine' until her throat ached.

Now, the only time Abi didn't feel lonely was standing in this kitchen with Phil beside her, explaining that you always roll pastry away from the body, and when it says ten minutes for the onions it means ten minutes or else your gravy will turn out a fearful orange.

'It's funny really,' Abi continued. 'I'm used to being on my own a lot but it's a different sort of alone when it's with a baby, isn't it? It's a bit worse, to be honest, because you can't even go out when you want to.'

But it was clear Phil had stopped listening. 'Since *Brigitta* was here?' she said finally. 'He's been gone since then? Abigail, that's what, six weeks? I'm shocked. Really I am. And his parents haven't driven down and hiffed him out at the top of Milson Road?'

'It was partly their idea,' Abi said, embarrassed.

'Well that makes it worse not better, to my mind.'

'I think they're worried about him failing his course because of all the distractions here. Perhaps he'll come back after his exams.'

Phil rolled her eyes extravagantly. 'Abigail, I beg your pardon. Wouldn't it be lovely if we could all hive off when parenthood got all too distracting? I'm sorry but this is unacceptable. Truly. I have half a mind to go up there myself and drag him back by the scruff of his neck.'

Phil got up and for an instant, Abi feared she was going to drive her Volvo straight to Gordon and have it out with Elaine in the carport. But she only unlatched another window and threw it open.

'It's my fault really, I'm the one who bollocksed up the birth control and everything.' Jude was tiring of his place on the floor, and Abi lifted him onto her lap.

'But you're not *teenagers*, Abigail.' Phil leaned against the bench and folded her arms. 'Even if parenthood was not, in a sense, deliberate, you clearly believe you've got to wear the eternal hair shirt, but you're actually both adults. If you coming here was the arrangement you made together, he can bloody well rise to the trot. Certainly it's short rations at the moment and it will be for some time I expect, but you've got the makings of a very pleasant little family life if he would only hold up his end.'

'I'd hate him to fail his course because of us though. I know he misses his mates as well.'

'Oh Lord. Please.' Phil had had enough. She turned and lifted the scorched pan out of the sink then dropped the whole lot in the bin. 'I can't hear any more. Frederick got the Bar from revising almost entirely in the car with baby Polly conked out in the back. It was the only way to get any quiet, driving her to sleep, then watching the sun come up over Middle Head with his jurisprudence on the steering wheel. It's the spirit of the Blitz for the first five years at least. This Stuart of yours needs to toughen up. Although I suppose it means I can stop sending up his bloody tea.'

'I'm so sorry,' Abi said.

'Oh do stop apologising, dear. You're the last one to blame. We're all entitled to one or two disasters in this life, don't you agree? Now before I forget –' Phil wiped her hands on a dishcloth, returned to the table and started shuffling through the pile of papers. 'Ah yes, here we are.'

From underneath an American Express statement, Phil turned up an envelope with a university crest in one corner. She extracted a thick course brochure and set it in front of Abi. 'Since you've conquered the culinary arts, poultry notwithstanding, I wondered if it's time to give that brain of yours a little go. I put in a call to a friend of mine, the mother of one of Pol's school friends, who's nice and high up in the English department over at Sydney, and she's dispensed this rather delightful booklet about their short courses. Have a look, why don't you? Here, give me the boy.'

Abi passed him over and read the front page: 'The University of Sydney, Department of English Winter Programmes.'

'Of course, you'd choose whichever modules took your fancy but I did think the Literature of the 1930s looked very good, although I doubt beloved Aunt Sadie gets a look-in. And then that Fictive Self looks quite thrilling.'

Phil had circled the course description in fountain pen. 'The Fictive Self: Self Invention and Imagining Identity in Women's Writing.'

Abi read it, then glanced at Phil, searching her face for any sign that she suspected Abi was already expert in the area of inventing and imagining. But Phil only looked like someone waiting for their gift to be unwrapped at the party, knowing full well it would be the best one. She patted Jude, laying contently over her shoulder.

'In fact, it made me look out my old copy of *Dalloway*,' Phil said. It too was retrieved from the pile and she opened it to a page with the corner turned down. 'Have you read it?'

'Um.' Abi did not want to admit that she hadn't. 'I think I got stuck on the first chapter.'

'It doesn't have chapters, Abigail,' Phil said wryly. 'Anyhow, listen to this.'

Immediately her voice dropped to the sonorous purr of someone reading for radio. 'As we are a doomed race, chained to a sinking ship ... as the whole thing is a bad joke, let us, at any rate, do our part; mitigate the sufferings of our fellow-prisoners ... decorate the dungeon with flowers and air-cushions; be as decent as we possibly can.' Phil closed the book and held it against her bust. 'Isn't that glorious? Decorate the dungeon with flowers.'

Abi longed for the reading to continue but lifted herself out of the reverie. 'I love it. I do. I love that.'

'Well then, wouldn't it be lovely to pick two of these and give that quick little mind of yours something to gnaw on. Boredom is a housewife's ruin as we all know. Well that and gin, and of course Jude's all-consuming now but he won't always be.' She moved him higher onto her shoulder and continued the slow, rhythmic patting.

'And if it's not a degree course, it probably wouldn't matter for my visa,' Abi said, to sustain the fantasy for a moment longer. 'Oh, but what would I do with this one?' Jude snuffled, as though aware he was being talked about.

Phil slid the paperback in her direction. 'In life, dear, when one wants something, one simply does it and waits for the practicalities to arrange themselves. Perhaps the dear old *Brush* will turn out to be useful after all.'

A ripple of disappointment came and went as Abi realised Phil wasn't going to volunteer. Still, it wasn't possible. Abi pushed the envelope back towards Phil. 'It's such a nice idea, and thanks for getting all that and everything but it's probably, really, that I can't afford it just at the minute.'

'You've quite missed my meaning, dear. The bill will come here. I've arranged a little tab, in case you want to go on to something more formal afterwards. You only have to do the work. I know you haven't got a bean, you mad girl.'

There was nothing Abi could do then except laugh out loud at the thought that soon, there would be something else beyond wiping things and feeding and walking and waiting. And nothing to do with at-risk youth, which prolonged her outburst until Phil crossed her arms and became stern.

'All right. Hush, would you. I should say, Abigail, you'll work like a bugger, won't you? I expect to see finishing, please.' Phil handed the baby back. 'And if you do, we can see about lighting another one off it.'

'I promise,' Abi insisted. 'I definitely promise.'

They got up and, without thinking, Abi stepped in and hugged her, sandwiching Jude between them. 'Lord, dear, you smell like sump oil,' Phil said, obliging for a moment then releasing her with a firm movement. 'Go home and wash your hair, would you? And take this lot.' Phil handed her *Mrs Dalloway* and the course guide, and opened the back door while Abi put her jacket on and wrapped Jude warmly against the cold outside.

'Thank you so much,' Abi said, and again from the courtyard, and again from the other side of the gate. As she walked home, she sent her mother a picture she had taken of Jude on the quilt in Phil's kitchen, pausing in front of the flats to read and delete Rae's short reply. 'Pats abcess is back–its started weeping.'

45.

I'm having a personal
crisis, Lawrence

Brigitta sat in the back of a taxi, seething. Ordinarily she tried to take the Tube back to Kentish Town after a shift, but she'd missed the last one and decided Phil could shout her a car service. It was not an emergency so much as compensation for her mother being unavailable during the emergency earlier that night.

The restaurant had been overbooked, as it often was on Friday nights, but two no-shows by floor staff had forced Brigitta to swap her usual position behind the desk for a pad and apron. She was put on the private dining room, preferable at least to the open floor – until the party started to arrive at 8 p.m. It was a large family group, three adult siblings, their partners and many offspring, and handsome, silver-haired parents. The impeccable pair sat at the head of the large table, ordered lavishly, received grandchildren onto their laps and would, Brigitta knew, quietly attend to the thousand-pound bill at the close of the evening.

All evening, Brigitta closed her ears to the conversation, resenting her forced proximity to an excessively merry family. She tolerated their constant trading of places, even as it complicated the task of putting down their orders, and bore the offence of being beckoned over by adolescent members of the party who required more ice and some chips and a different spoon.

After dessert, the youngest children began to fall asleep under the table and Brigitta stepped around them as she reset for coffee. Unnoticed, she watched as one of the married daughters got up and moved to sit beside her father. They whispered to each other in confidence, the woman rested her forehead, for an instant, on her father's shoulder. He said something in her ear, which made her laugh, and then as Brigitta looked on, he gave her cheek a fleeting pat. The gesture, something about his large, lovely hand resting so gently against her face, made Brigitta drop both the plates she had just picked up to clear.

The entire table turned at the sound of shattering china. One of the older children began a slow clap and was reprimanded by the matriarch. Brigitta got down on her hands and knees to gather up the larger pieces into her apron.

'Might I call for reinforcements?' The father appeared beside her and crouched down. 'What a bugger.'

'I'm so sorry, I'll go and fetch a cleaner,' Brigitta said, folding the corners of her apron around the shards. 'I'm not actually a servant, you see. Or waitress, I should say. I'm an actress.' From the adolescents' end of the table, she heard a snicker, but the father looked sympathetic.

Passing through the kitchen, Brigitta dumped the pieces into a breakages bin and continued to the small rear office where she kicked the door shut and gave in to sobs.

It was not fair. It was not fair! How could a family be so arrogant in its good fortune? All of them together and happy and having pretend tiffs over the bread basket, while her family had been decimated, the survivors scattered.

The pain of it was overwhelming. Brigitta needed her mother. Wiping her face with her apron, she reached for the desk phone, dialled the long home number and waited. After a moment, she heard her mother's voice.

Brigitta released a single cry that came out like a cough.

'Briggy, is that you? Darling, I can't talk. Fighting fires.'

'Mum, I'm –' Brigitta said. The line went dead. Brigitta listened to three dull beeps, then hung up and tried again. The engaged signal came back.

'Fuck,' she said. 'Fuckfuck.' What kind of fire her mother could possibly be fighting on a Saturday morning, in the perfect sanctuary of the big house, she could not begin to imagine. If it was a moment of grief, Brigitta would have been recruited to it already, as she always was, no matter the hour, or what else she might be doing. Ever since James died, she'd been a servant to her mother's emotions. It would have to be a Freddie fire, or a small incident involving Domenica and a silk rug. They had barely spoken since Brigitta fled, so it was just as likely nothing was wrong and she was just being punished. The depths of pettiness to which her mother could sink!

Brigitta tossed the phone on the desk and brought her feet up onto the chair.

'Ah, scuse us, why are you in here?'

Her manager, a very tall and briefly successful male model with a self-conscious East End accent, stood in the doorway, both hands on his snake-like hips.

'I'm having a personal crisis, Lawrence. Sorry. Do you mind?' She smiled as politely as she could and waited for him to leave. If not motherly succour, she could have privacy at least.

'Ah, we'd all love a personal crisis, darling, but it's still chaos out there. Fucking Armageddon. So either get back on the floor or go home.'

'Right then.' Brigitta got up and began tugging at her apron strings. As she passed Lawrence in the narrow passage, she pressed the damp, dirty ball of her apron against his chest and stormed out via the service doors.

'Rochester Road, in Kentish Town please,' Brigitta said as she climbed into a taxi. 'But actually can you take us past that 24 hour Tesco and I'll run in and grab a few things. They've got a wine bit, don't they?'

'I'll have to keep the meter going, love.'

'Yes, that's fine. That's fine.' Brigitta sat back and before returning her mind to this fresh injustice, remembered to say to the driver, 'You take cards, don't you?'

46.

Changi Best Value Pharmacy

Phil had expected the warm glow of altruism to last a good deal longer that it did. As soon as she heard the gate close, her spirits drooped. All that phoning up the department and arranging the bills, and for that moment anyway, it felt like a damp squib.

Some hours passed, Phil could not have said how, and as it approached 4 p.m. she wandered back to the kitchen, still reeking of poison chook, and noticed the Amex statement on top of the mail pile, the table's permanent centrepiece. Too restless to do anything pleasant, Phil thumbed it open. She should get the paper knife from Frederick's desk and do the whole thing properly, the festival programme, investor notices, an invitation requesting the presence of Mr and Mrs Frederick Woolnough at a charity function. But her hips ached from a morning at the sink, and her legs were as heavy as lead.

Glancing down the first of many printed pages, Phil's eye fell on SELFRIDGE & CO. PLC, £180. AUD CURRENCY CHARGE 2.5%. Another, the same day, for SELFRIDGE & CO. PLC, £420.15. Waitrose Supermarkets, Jane Packer Flowers, somewhere called The Providores on Marylebone High Street, nearly £300 at a shop called Whistles. Majestic Wine Warehouse cropped up every few lines, between taxi fares, cash advances, three and four pound charges, daily, at Starbucks. Phil read through charge after charge. They ran in reverse chronological order to January, each attracting their own ruinous conversion fee. The final line was $67.23 Singaporean dollars at somewhere called CHANGI BEST VALUE PHARMACY PTE. At the very bottom of the final page, the statement requested a minimum payment of nine hundred and something, against the current balance of $17,433AUD. As she dialled Brigitta and waited, Phil forced a series of measured breaths, feeling alternatively furious and disappointed that this would be their first conversation since her daughter's dreadful departure.

She'd longed to speak properly this morning when Brigitta had phoned during the poultry crisis, but it could not have been a worse moment. They must pick up from here and there would be no easy détente now that the true extent of Brigitta's recklessness had been revealed.

'Hello?'

'Hello Brigitta. It's your mother.'

'Hello.'

Phil did not let herself be put off by the touch of coldness in her daughter's voice, and cleared her throat. 'Well.'

'Well.'

'Where are you?'

'It's seven o'clock in the morning, so in bed. Oh and by the way, I just got sacked.'

Phil gripped the phone, unpleasantly aware that this was a job much better suited to Frederick, who'd only needed to summon a child as far as the study door to have them keeling over with remorse. 'Well, if you're wondering where I am, or indeed how I've been since your untimely departure, the answer is at home, also. And you know I was just sitting here going through some post.'

'Was that your emergency?' Brigitta said archly. 'Sorting the mail?'

'Actually, I've found some really quite surprising charges on the Amex. Really, quite staggering. Shall I read them out?'

There was silence, before she heard a cough and then Brigitta's voice, drained of all provocation. 'Oh.'

'*Oh* indeed,' Phil said before she knew exactly where she was leading. 'I think this shows it's time to draw a line under this experiment of yours. Polly has told me that you lost the Barbican role as well, which I only assume means things are over between you and the married man. That and now this, Brigitta. I think you've had your go. It hasn't worked. Time to just rule off and write tomorrow's date, don't you think?' Phil softened her tone, waiting for Brigitta to collapse under the weight of maternal grace. As a child, she'd always been the first breaker after any group misdemeanour; Phil only had to wait her out.

But when she spoke, Brigitta sounded hard. 'No.'

'Say again?'

'No,' Brigitta said. 'I'm not coming home. I haven't failed. I only lost my part because I came to see you. And when I tried to call you tonight you were too busy for me, so why would I come home? You're not actually there for me.'

'Oh darling, don't be wet.' It came out much too strong. She heard Brigitta gasp, as though in pain. Things were getting out of hand and Phil scrabbled around for a *coup de grâce*. Briefly she considered fainting, but felt restrained by the medium. If Brigitta couldn't see her, there was no point casting herself onto the flagstones.

'I'm just stating facts, mother. You have been too busy for me most of your life.'

'Well then, if you choose to stay, and particularly if you continue your adulterous dalliance, there will be no more support of a fiscal nature.' Phil was furious. 'I've offered you a loan that many times, Brigitta, and you refused it like a true martyr, and now I find I've been subsidising you all along, and at such a rate. Well. I'm sorry, but that ends today. I will be calling the bank and cancelling this card. I won't insist you repay what you've already rung up, but I do hope you understand how genuinely disappointed I am. I think your father would feel the same.'

Phil stopped and waited for a sign of contrition but still Brigitta sounded more angry than sorry. 'All right, fine. And I assume you'll be stopping all Freddie's cheques too, will you? How many fuck-ups are on his tab?'

Phil put a hand to her neck, aghast. 'That is an entirely different matter.'

'The only difference that I can see, Mother, is that it's me this time. And I'm not allowed to be a complete disaster like Freddie or perfect like Polly, or bloody well sainted like James. You always needed me just to get on and be all right. And you were happy to pay for it, as long as I didn't make any work for you. I'm sorry I didn't realise that arrangement was over.'

Then, having already been so cruel, Brigitta hung up without saying goodbye.

Phil swept up the entire pile of paper and dropped it into the bin, on top of the chicken pan. A few of the loose pages sagged into the puddled oil. She was so deathly tired of her daughter's singular grievance. Brigitta had levelled it against her for years.

While it was perhaps true that a share of the focus had gone off her immediately after James's death, could Phil be blamed? She had lost a child! In her mourning, one or two of Brigitta's key moments had certainly been missed, but they ought to have been got over by now. Instead, the wound opened again and again, even though this time, mourning Frederick, Phil was trying so hard to include Brigitta in her grief.

Desperate to be out of the stifling kitchen, Phil went through to the front room and poured a generous measure of Frederick's whisky. She carried it to the French doors and looked at the sky over the city.

It would be dark soon, Phil realised, and she felt depressed by the thought. When the whisky was gone in a couple of bitter mouthfuls, she realised she couldn't stay in the awful, silent house a moment longer.

In the fridge, she found a half wheel of brie and a bottle of rosé, unseasonal but the only thing that was cold, and feeling unpleasantly self-conscious – a middle-aged woman marching around the kitchen in a fit of temper, shoving things into a basket like some silly film actress – she left by the kitchen door. At this moment, there was only one person she felt she could really talk to.

47.

One in four's a dry one

There was no security on the ground floor, and after locating the stairway in the rear corner of the dark, brown-tiled foyer, Phil climbed to the top floor and knocked on what was, by her best guess, the correct door.

She heard a rustle, then the voice, soft and hoarse. 'Who is it?'

'It's me. Phyllida Woolnough!' More shuffling, then the door opened an inch and Abi peered out. She was wearing a large woollen jersey as a dress, and her hair was wet. The fragrance of apple shampoo met Phil in the hall.

'Gosh,' Abi said, opening the door fully. 'Hello. Are you all right?'

Phil was annoyed by the look of pure shock on Abi's face, calling attention as it did to the irregular nature of the visit. But emboldened by the whisky she said, 'Quite, thank you.' She waited until Abi seemed to realise she wanted to come in and took a step back.

Phil found herself immediately in a tiny living room, which had an even smaller kitchen through a sort of arch, and a closed door on the opposite wall that presumably led to the bedroom where she could hear Jude making a weak protest against sleep. The only decorations were a quite good line drawing of the Opera House sails sellotaped to the wall beside her own little study of nasturtiums, hung too high to Phil's eye and both overshadowed by the most enormous television. Abi had been watching her inspect the room, holding down the hem of her knit to cover as much as it would of her thin legs.

'How did you know where I lived?' Abi asked. 'I mean, what door was mine?'

'It wasn't difficult, dear. There's only a dozen in the block and they can't all look at me.'

Phil strode over to the window with the basket on her shoulder and peered down at her own house from above. Her window seat was perfectly recognisable through the fading light. 'Goodness, I'll have to give a little shimmy to the binocs next time I'm there, won't I?'

She turned, hoping to find Abi enjoying the joke, but the girl still stood in the same spot, apparently petrified. One of her legs seemed to have developed the faintest tremor. 'Well, do shut the door, Abigail. Where shall I sit? I thought we'd have a drink. I brought some cheese.'

Phil glanced towards the only seating, and was pleased at least to see the course brochure open on a cushion with an uncapped highlighter resting in its centre fold. A faintly familiar-looking throw rug, boiled to felt in a hot wash, was crumpled beside it, as though it had been shrugged off Abi's lap when she got up to answer the door.

'Oh very good,' Phil said, taking in the tableau. 'Lots there you like the look of?'

Abi's eyes darted to the brochure and back to Phil, who was starting to feel genuinely aggrieved by the lack of welcome. 'You might pop that on a platter and put a few crackers with it,' she said, handing over the cheese.

Abi disappeared and came back a short time later, with the unwrapped brie on a plastic chopping board. She set it down on the seat of a dining chair that was to serve as the coffee table. 'I've only got Jatz, sorry. They are two-for-one this week so that's good,' she said apologetically, lowering herself onto the carpet and sitting with legs crossed like a schoolgirl. 'I hope that's okay. I love cheese.'

'Lovely platter, wedding present was it?' Phil said, meaning to make a little joke, but Abi's face told her she'd been unkind. 'Ignore me dear, I've had the most unpleasant phone call with Brigitta and a fairly decent helping of Scotch.' She cut herself a large wedge of cheese and smeared it onto one of the orange crackers. 'But never mind all that. I thought we could put our heads together and come up with a plan for getting this chap of yours back. What do you think?'

'Oh, okay.' Abi sounded uncertain.

'But would you be a lamb, please, and open that before we get to work.' With the cheese knife, Phil pointed towards the bottle in her basket and Abi disappeared to the kitchen again.

'Will these be all right?' she asked, returning this time with a beer schooner with German-looking lettering in gold around its rim, and a large jar that, judging by its shape, had once contained an inexpensive passata. 'I can't find the wine glasses just at the minute.'

She held one in each hand, waiting for Phil to make her selection. After a moment of consideration, Phil nodded towards the schooner and received it, half full of rosé.

'Dear, you should have told me your dungeon was rather in need of decorating. Mine is frankly *over decc'ed* and I'd be delighted to start fobbing a lot of it off, since I can't foresee a time when I'll need a range of serving options and glassware for forty, can you? Cheers anyway.' Phil tilted her schooner towards Abi's jar and drank for much longer than she thought she could.

'Now. Abigail.' The rosé was delicious, she realised, taking another sip and smearing another orange round with cheese. As she chewed, Phil tried to order the parts of a new project that had presented itself to her in the flats' common stairwell. She would help get this boyfriend back. 'You do, I'm right in thinking, want to make a go of things with Stuart? You love him and he loves you, can we agree on that?'

Abi was holding a cracker with both hands and crumbling tiny mouse portions off one side. 'I'm not really sure. I thought so. I mean I do,' she replied in a way that sounded like a question. 'We've had hardly any time together since Jude and I got here. Stu was so funny and so nice and always really happy in London, but he hasn't been anything like that here, except for about ten minutes. Maybe it's because of the baby, but I really thought he'd be a good dad once he got used to it. I suppose I was being quite romantic ...'

'What do you want then, Abigail? Let's start there instead. Tell me what you would like to happen.'

Abi dipped her finger in her wine, then sucked it. 'All I want,' she said, with a curious lack of emotion, 'all I have ever wanted is a family. That is the only thing, Phil, the one and only thing.'

Phil had never heard her speak quite so directly, without her usual darting eyes, wringing of hands and sucking of hair. She raised her glass in *salut*. 'Well, by dint of having had his child, Stuart *is* your family. So, excellent. That puts us well ahead.'

Abi relaxed, and began to look amused as Phil topped up her schooner with the last of the rosé.

'You know Abi, I really don't think he's a bad egg. Having never laid eyes on him of course. I get the distinct sense he's just a confused young man, scared witless no doubt, taking his time to get his ducks in the proverbial row. Don't mind my probing, but how have things been in the bedroom, as it were? Or how *were* they before he skived off? It's always a fairly good barometer in my experience.'

Abi blushed a ferocious crimson.

'Don't be childish Abigail, it's a genuine question,' Phil said. Unable to face another '*jat*', she skewered the last triangle of cheese and ate it directly from the knife, washing the lot down with another tremendous lug from the schooner.

'We hadn't actually, fully *you know*. I was still a bit ... on the tender side ... down there ... and so well we hadn't done anything ... *major*. And then he moved out.'

'Ah. I see. Well that won't do. Men are simple creatures, Abigail, and I'm afraid you're going to have to jolly up and get on with it. Your grace period is over. It'll be awful until you get going, but lie back and think of England.'

Abi looked very sincere. 'I think that would put me off.'

Phil erupted and, helplessly, Abi joined in.

'Have you got anything else?' Phil asked a moment later. She tapped the bottle with a knife. 'This one's as dead as a dodo.'

Over some kind of red that didn't look fit for gravy but was all Abi could find in the kitchen, they worked on a plan that relied in equal measure on sex, more many-layered lasagnes, the sweetness of Jude, acquisition of furniture and Abi resuming her studies to develop a wider range of conversation starters. 'And if required at a later point' – Phil said with a discreet burp – 'the most blistering ultimatum.'

Phil wanted Abi to write it all down, but the highlighter was being uncooperative and at some point, towards the end of the red, Abi started drawing all over her leg. Phil was slumped to one side, finding the display uproarious. It felt so good to laugh, harder and harder, until tears were streaming down her face, and Abi was lying on her back, smoking the highlighter like a fifties ingénue.

Shortly after, Abi seemed to remember something and crawled to the kitchen on hands and knees, coming back with a bottle of Baileys Irish Cream, which had been intended as a gift from Stu to his mother and never given. The plastic bow was still on the top and Abi was sticking it to her hair when a phone rang.

After a dozen rings, Phil realised it was hers and fished it out of the basket.

'Hello,' she said, with deliberate steadiness. Abi began modelling the bow as a corsage, then a single earring, then a sort of fascinator, and Phil pressed her fingertips to her lips to stifle more giggling.

'Hello Polly dear. Yes, I'm fine thank you. And h-how are you? Keeping. Well? I hope.' Abi tried the bow as an eye-patch and Phil turned sharply away from her towards the window, shoulders drawn in against a further outbreak. 'Having your breakfast?'

'What darling? I'm very fine. No I'm not. That's between Brid-ja and I. Don't wade in Polly. You're such a fearful wader, darling, honestly. Can I go please now? I'm terribly fatigued. Goodbye.' She mashed the keyboard with the flat of her hand, hoping she'd shut the thing off. 'Whoop! We're in trouble now. Poll's onto us. Truly though.' Phil tried to be serious. 'What do you have by way of sweets? I've got such a hankering.'

'Oh.' Abi planted the bow, finally, as a tasteful brooch and said, 'I have got Grandma Jenny's Microwaveable Self-Saucing Puddings, Flavour Selection, but there's only date left, sorry. They do have their own sauce, although to be honest, I've found that one in four will be a dry one.' She and Stu had discussed it once, and he agreed it was the case. 'And I can't remember if I've had the dry one from this packet yet.'

'Oh,' said Phil, sobbing with laughter. 'Oh, I don't like those odds at all, Abigail.' Phil rose very unsteadily to her feet and reached out for her basket, missing the handle the first time. 'I suppose I ought to go home. What time is it? Oh look, it's on here.' She was surprised to find the phone still in her other hand. 'Not even eight! All right well look, lean out your window and if you don't see me in five minutes I've been accosted and you'll need to be the one to tell Noel. Go gently, dear, he'll be utterly destroyed.'

She paused with her hand on the doorframe and refused Abi's offer of escort on the grounds of Jude and something about the blind leading the blind, and gave her a farewell peck on the cheek.

Abi staggered over to the window and a few minutes later saw Phil attempting to wave up to her, before teetering over the brickwork and disappearing inside. Leaving the chopping board and cups where they were, Abi lay on the pull-out with her feet up on the opposite arm and tried to memorise the plan for winning Stu back, because if she showered in the morning, it was all going to wash off her leg.

48.

Horrible, horrible

Brigitta lay with her face to the mattress and a pillow over her head. It had been a long, tedious Saturday since the phone call early that morning, which had left her unable to settle to any sort of activity. Fits of cleaning that had no visible result, leafing through an old *Vogue* and finding nothing that could sustain her interest, a run that she aborted after seven minutes, breathless and unhappy. And now too early to bed to sleep, her mother's accusations still playing in her mind as they had all day. 'Your father would feel the same … you've tried … it didn't work.'

Over the course of the day, her embarrassment and rage had settled into a low, throbbing panic, attached mostly to the question of money, and there being no more of it from her mother. If she hadn't stormed out of the restaurant last night, she would be there right now, with an apron pocket full of tips. As menial as the job could be, she felt the loss of it keenly.

After an hour more of tossing and turning, Brigitta fell asleep. She woke again too early the next morning, rolled onto her side and stared into the middle distance. Outside the window, clouds passed in front of a weak sun, making it seem as though a light inside was being flicked on and off with a switch.

Some time later, Brigitta got up and as she pulled an old cashmere jumper of her father's on over leggings, she began to think of walking down Marylebone High Street, having a look at the shops and picking up breakfast, until a painful stab of reality erased the picture.

Another day alone in the studio would send her mad and she considered decamping to Polly's for the day, but ever since she had refused her sister's offer of the *X Factor* and Polish savouries, relations had felt fragile. After the twenty-four hours she had just endured, another instalment of her sister's ongoing Be Kinder To Mum lecture would be the absolute end.

In the heat of the moment, she'd forgotten to ask Phil not to tell Polly about the spending and of course she would have by now. Brigitta tipped out her purse and realised she was set for a long walk and whatever you could get by way of breakfast for £3.12.

Setting out for Regent's Park, she hastened through less inviting sections of Malden Road, littered with takeaway boxes and stripped chicken bones, weaving through families doing Sunday market shopping and slowing once she crossed Haverstock Hill Road.

By the time she reached the northern tip of Primrose Hill, Brigitta had finished a processed egg sandwich and established the fact that acting was a poor job for meeting anyone, friends or lovers, vis-à-vis the temporary nature of the work; that her sister and mother were probably talking about her at this exact moment, picking over every embarrassing charge on the statement; that she needed to ring Lawrence and beg for her job back; and that life would be vastly improved if she were taller, and married to Guy.

Guy. The thought came to her suddenly, and wonderfully, like a boathook thrust towards a drowning soul. Although they hadn't seen each other again after her stage door sacking, soon afterwards he had started dispatching flirtatious text messages, requesting drinks, a visit after midnight one evening, and only yesterday, offering details of a director friend who was looking for someone of her 'precise physical form' for an experimental thing at the National. Against her strongest impulse, Brigitta had replied to none of them, wanting to simultaneously punish him for booting her off his production and further arouse his appetite for Kentish Town. Realising that she must be somewhere near his house by now, Brigitta sent him a short, enticing message and his reply came back immediately. He could meet her in half an hour. Anywhere she wanted. He was longing to see her, he said. It had been the most tedious six weeks of his life.

With a thrill, Brigitta replied to say she was actually quite nearby and why didn't she just come to him? After a pause, he suggested the European deli they both knew by sight on Fitzroy Road.

Brigitta ducked into a small Boots on her way and sampled a volumising mascara and dry shampoo, arriving with minutes to spare. She opened the tinkling door to a small room hung with salamis and onions and smelling pleasantly of espresso. A large family of tourists were seated around a table in the window, taking each other's photograph with expensive-looking cameras and speaking in loud, rapid Italian.

Taking a booth at the back, she sat facing the door. As she ordered coffee for both of them, Guy entered. She watched him edging between tables and checking each booth. He was wearing cords, an ancient cricket jumper and, uncharacteristically to Brigitta's mind, a plain baseball cap.

'Darling,' he said, with a smile that carried the full force of his charisma. '*There* you are.' It felt exactly the same as walking on stage with a tray and feeling the follow spot hit her face, hot and bright and for that moment, all hers. He slipped into the booth beside her, pressed her against the wall and kissed her with an intensity unsuited to a public dining room. Unnoticed, a waiter set down two espressos and backed away.

'God, I've missed you,' he said, breaking away and examining her thoroughly. 'Although this is bloody dangerous you know, Birj, I'm really shitting in my own kennel meeting you here.' He removed the cap and his hair fell about his face.

'Why dangerous?' Brigitta wiped the corner of her lips.

'Well you know, Primrose Hill is a bloody village. It's not that I can't be seen with you, it's just because I'm so recognisable.'

The notion that Guy could not be seen with her hadn't exactly occurred to Brigitta until then and she found it galling now.

'Anyway, darling, tell me everything.' He gathered her hands up in his. 'Where have you been, doing what and with whom, and why wasn't it me?'

'Oh you know, nothing.' Brigitta hoped her reply sounded mysterious, rather than factual. 'But I want to know about you, or us actually, Guy. The last time I saw you was horrible.'

'Oh, darling, I know. Horrible, horrible. Work is a beast, the pressure Birj. But listen, you must just hang on. Can you? Sylvie's days away from moving to the country, so it's only a question of time, darling.' As he spoke, still holding her hands, another round of flashes from the direction of the tourists lit up the room.

Brigitta kissed him. 'All right.'

'And is everyone well? The sundry Woolnoughs?'

Guy had never asked after her family before and his thoughtfulness was touching, especially after the conversation she'd had with her mother.

'Actually, they've all ganged up on me a bit,' Brigitta said. 'My mother's cut me off, would you believe?'

'Oh darling, how boring.' He found a wallet in his back pocket and drew out what to Brigitta's eye looked like at least five hundred pounds in twenty-pound notes. 'Take this and do something reckless with it, would you? Your poor thing.'

'Does this make me a kept woman?' she asked, half joking but strongly inclined to accept it.

'Only if you'd like it to. I actually ought to dash though, lovely.' Below the table, he slid both hands up her jumper and held her bare waist. 'It's been bliss to see you. Can I drop in tomorrow night? I feel an overwhelming nostalgia for the bedsit.'

'Of course.' Brigitta smiled as he shuffled out of the booth, bathed in another flash of white from the front of the restaurant.

As soon as he'd gone, Brigitta ordered a proper breakfast and nabbed a luscious-looking newspaper supplement from an empty table. Intensely satisfied, she opened the magazine in search of the Arts bit. There, grinning out of the social pages, was Guy Kidd. Of Guy Kidd and Sylvie Allen Kidd, who was wearing some sort of draped gown that clung to a rounded belly, then cascaded to the floor, pooling on the red carpet. She was leaning in so that her forehead pressed against Guy's temple. His arm was curved around her back, fingers appearing at the other side of her waist. They were frozen in the middle of a private joke. In a flare of paranoia, Brigitta thought they were laughing about her.

Burning, she got up to leave and found herself blocked by a waiter coming the other way with her breakfast. Already regretting the extravagance, she dropped one of Guy's twenties on the table and, pushing past him, headed to the exit where she vaguely sensed a final flash of the tourists' camera as she stepped into the street.

Looking up and down Fitzroy Road, she chose what she thought would take her in the direction of Guy's house, and as she began walking, a figure in a silly baseball cap emerged from the newsagent fifty yards up, holding a thick stack of newspapers under one arm.

She kept her distance, following him around the corner and all the way to a pretty mews, then hid behind a delivery van, watching him forage for his door key, then tap on the door with a knuckle.

A child in pyjamas wrapped himself around Guy's leg as he leaned inside, kissing someone out of view.

Brigitta had no plan as she strode towards the house. Instead, she only heard a voice, some version of her own, inside her head. It spoke as though testifying to an imaginary jury. No, I didn't think about what I was doing. No, I didn't plan it, it just happened. I expected Guy to answer the door, so when it was his wife … No, I didn't realise she was pregnant. I did throw money at her, yes. I don't remember exactly what I was shouting, only that the money belonged to her husband so she should have it back. That's when I saw the flash again, yes, and that's when Guy came to the door and saw the photographer, and that's when I ran off and got into a taxi. Yes, he followed me. The photographer, not Guy.

49.

Deadly Predators or Arsenal

Polly lay listening to rain tick against the sash windows of her bedroom and the rapid chatter of morning cartoons coming from downstairs. It was a wet bank holiday Monday. An hour of animated rubbish would be allowed, if it meant a lie-in. She wondered why Mark was taking so long with her tea and hoped to God he hadn't let the boys talk him into pancakes, which would mean every dish in the kitchen pressed into service and a precipitous drop in mood and behaviour when the sugar wore off mid-morning.

She occupied herself by starting a mental to-do list for the day until she heard Mark bounding up the stairs in such a way he couldn't possibly be carrying a cup and saucer. He flung open the bedroom door and stood there, holding the *Daily Mail*, which he took as a cheap weekday pleasure, and Polly took as a recurring moral and aesthetic affront. Mark dragged a hand over his bald scalp and looked decidedly queasy. 'Briggy's in the paper.'

'What?'

'She's been snapped having a stoush on the doorstep of some theatre person. Never heard of him, but there's another lot of them together in a caff. Being fairly amorous. Really nasty stuff. Who knows how they get it.'

Polly leaped out of bed and snatched the paper Mark was holding between two fingers like a dirty rag. 'Give it here.'

The grainy image on the front page showed her sister standing on a doorstep, throwing what looked like pieces of screwed up paper at Sylvie Allen Kidd, whose too-lovely-for-radio face was frozen in terror. Her hands were shielding her stomach, and in a smaller inset, a little boy had joined the fray.

Across the bottom of the page a blurry time-lapse sequence showed Brigitta running along the footpath with her jumper pulled up to hide her face. Polly's hands began to shake as she turned to pages four and five, which a cover splash promised would contain 'Bonus Pics!' There, Polly saw her pressed up against Guy in a seedy-looking café booth, and an overblown close-up, circled in red, captured what could only be Guy's hand under the table disappearing into the darkness of Brigitta's leggings.

Polly flung the paper at the wall, with a surge of protectiveness so strong it curled her hands into fists. 'Oh Briggy,' she said, out loud. 'Oh no.'

Mark strode over to his wardrobe. 'I'll go and get her.'

'No, I'll go. Call whoever you can think of who'll be useful, and get Natalia to take the boys out,' said Polly, pulling a trenchcoat over her pyjamas and noting her own commanding tone with approval. She was not sure she could do it, but she had to. She must.

Downstairs, she found the car keys, intending to drive all the way to Kentish Town and retrieve her sister. But as she opened the door, a taxi stopped at the curb and Brigitta struggled out. With a stricken expression, she mimed the signing of a bill.

Polly made her way down and paid the driver while her sister hovered behind her, wiping rivers of mascara off both cheeks. As the car rumbled away, Polly turned and faced her sister, who immediately collapsed against her chest.

'I'm sorry, I'm sorry, I'm sorry,' she said, as Polly folded her arms around her and sighed from her core.

'It's all right, we'll fix it. Mark will think of something, don't worry.'

As Polly steered them back to the house, Brigitta wiped her nose on her sleeve, leaving behind a glistening trail of clear mucus on the fabric. 'I'm so sorry. Really, I'm so sorry.'

* * *

Brigitta went straight down to the kitchen, while Polly paused by the door to shed the coat and shake rain out of her hair. 'Right,' she said, catching her reflection in the hall and trying to rally the exhausted-looking figure staring back at her. 'Right, then.'

Brigitta, still in her coat, was perched on a stool at the kitchen island, holding Polly's preferred teacup and letting Mark spoon in quantities of sugar.

'Okay, let's think.'

'I'm so sorry.'

'We're past that now, darling.' With Brigitta safely inside, Polly felt no further need of kindness, only pragmatism. 'Mark, who have you spoken to so far?'

'I've left a message for Mike Ross.'

'Bloody hard to get onto everyone today, of course.' He glanced at Brigitta. 'Libel chap. Damien is going to handle the PR side of things.' Mark pinched the bridge of his nose, thinking for a second. 'Hells bells, Briggy. Did you know he had a wife?'

'Mark. It doesn't matter now. Let's stay on point.'

Brigitta sipped her tea pathetically and avoided her sister's eye. Mark and Polly stood on opposite sides of the island, toggling through their phones, examining the papers, and speaking in legal jargon until the kitchen assumed the atmosphere of a war room.

'I think the best thing would be for you to go upstairs and change,' Polly said, when she noticed her sister's rising panic. 'I'm sure there's something of mine that will fit you. Then lie down in the spare room and I'll come and get you when we've decided on a plan. Go on.' Polly's tone was firm. 'Off you go.'

Brigitta slipped off the stool and left without a word.

* * *

By the time she reached the end of one of Mark's crime thrillers, which Polly wouldn't have on the downstairs bookcases because of the garish lettering on the spines, there was a soft knock, low down on the other side of the door. The handle turned and Toby, the younger of Polly's sons, struggled in carrying a large tray. He stood by the bed with an air of extreme importance. 'Natalia made you something to eat. It's toast with marmite on it.'

Toby was six and Brigitta's private favourite. He had a head of russet brown hair like his Uncle Freddie, and spoke with a lisp he'd once referred to as his thistle, as they all now did.

'Hello Toby,' Brigitta said, overwhelmed by the sight of him. He was a kind child and he was looking at her with concern.

'Are you sick, Aunty Briggy?'

'No. I'm just sad.'

'Do you want to play Top Trumps?' Toby asked, visibly buoyed by his own idea. 'I've got Deadly Predators or Arsenal. Mum says I'm not allowed to stay up here but we could just be quiet.' The effort to speak in a whisper had made him talk louder, and he stopped to look around the room for a moment. 'Me and Max aren't allowed to eat in rooms that have carpet in them.' One of his skinny legs starting twitching from the effort of holding the tray, and Brigitta sat up.

'Oh gosh. Put it down there, Toby. Sorry. What is Mummy doing, do you know?

'She's on the phone. Doing her cross voice.'

'Do you know who she's talking to?'

Toby shook his head.

'I'll give you 50p to go down and find out.'

He dashed out of the room and reappeared moments later, out of breath. 'She's talking to Granny. I wasn't allowed to have a turn because they are talking about grown up things.'

Brigitta didn't respond. She could only imagine the conversation taking place below.

'I think you actually are a small bit sick, Aunty Briggy. Your face looks all funny.'

'Come and give me a hug, Toby, and then you can go.'

Toby came to the edge of the bed and let Brigitta bury her face into his neck. 'Thank you Toby. You're such a lovely boy.'

'Can I have my 50p now?' he asked, before running off to find his brother.

The rest of the afternoon passed in slow motion. When the sky outside the bedroom window turned a pale violet and the feeling of incarceration became unbearable, Brigitta walked tentatively downstairs carrying her untouched tray. As sorry as she was about all of it, it was hard not to wish the scandal might induce a measure of incidental weight loss.

The kitchen was immaculate. All traces of the day's turmoil, including the papers, had been removed. Natalia stood at the sink rinsing plates in a way that broadcast her desire not to be spoken to. For something to do, Brigitta took a bottle of wine from the fridge, regretting it the moment Polly appeared from the family room and saw the huge glass she had poured herself. 'Sorry, Polly, I wasn't –'

'My first instinct was to send you straight back to Sydney,' Polly cut in. 'But all advice is to stay here with us and wait it out. Mark's people feel that doing a runner is only going to give the thing legs. They'll be waiting for you at the airport already, now they've dug up your bio. He's gone over to yours to pack you up. They've also worked out where you live apparently, so I've been in touch with your landlord. There will be a fee to break the lease but that's the least of our worries. My real concern now is Mum. Thank God she won't get the scale of it without seeing our papers but of course she is shaken.' Polly folded her arms and leaned against the benchtop. She looked exhausted.

'Do you want to know the worst part?' Brigitta offered feebly.

'What?'

'The worst part is, Guy and I hadn't seen each other since I got back. It was basically off. That was just a chance meeting which went completely wrong.'

Polly threw her head back and laughed sharply. 'My God, Brigitta. That is so not the worst part.' She stalked out of the kitchen, leaving her sister alone with her wine and a sullen Slavic au pair.

50.

Brigitta's got herself in the papers

At first, Phil had assumed she was sickening for something the morning she awoke after her visit to Abi's, until a fierce appetite for bacon brought the realisation that she was merely hungover for the first time in forty years. The evening had got somewhat out of hand, she had remembered as she snipped four rashers into a small skillet with paring scissors, and ate them out of it with a fork when suitably crisped. Perhaps, at some point, she would mention to Abigail that it was a momentary lapse in judgment that would not be spoken of again.

Two fairly dull days involving quantities of soluble aspirin and back-to-back *Poirot* from an ancient VHS omnibus passed before Phil began to feel on the up. The conversation with Brigitta still rankled and whenever she stood waiting for the kettle, peeling an orange at the sink or idling in the bath, Phil found herself returning to the many accusations that had been hurled at her to see if they still hurt. They did.

Sleep seemed like the only respite from the subject and Phil turned in early again on Monday evening, sitting up with the hardback le Carré that had been gathering dusk on Frederick's bedside table since November. She still couldn't bear to reshelve it, removing yet another trace of him, and instead found herself a third of the way through. But still with a slight head, she couldn't at that moment remember who anybody was, so she put it aside and folded her hands above the sheets. As the weight of loneliness began to settle, the phone rang and she lunged for the bedside telephone.

'Mum,' said Polly's voice. 'It's me. Now, stay calm but –'

Phil sat up. She loathed conversations that began this way, the order to be calm exciting precisely the opposite feeling. It was like a friend telling you about a new acquaintance they were certain you'd love, the surest way in Phil's mind to kill off the prospect altogether. 'What, darling? What is it?'

'Brigitta's got herself in the papers. They caught her having a meltdown on that disgusting man's doorstep and the pictures are everywhere. His wife's in them too. And their little boy. Also, it's pretty obvious she's pregnant.'

Phil shrieked.

'No, Mum! The wife, not Brigitta. Calm down. Everything's fine. She's here with us now. It's just got to get worse before it can get better. Mark's calling in favours and it seems like the best thing is for her to go to ground.'

'Oh Polly, oh no.' Phil caught sight of herself in the mirror on her dressing table, a beleaguered widow receiving more bad news. 'Oh darling. Can you put her on?'

'She's in her room and I'd prefer she stays there at the moment. She's got nothing sensible to say, but I promise she's fine.'

'We warned her, Poll. We both tried to put her off him. Why, why on *earth* did she pursue it? I feel I simply don't know her at the moment. She's usually so easily talked around.'

Polly agreed, and they spoke for ten minutes more until Phil heard one of the boys in the background, asking for a turn on the phone. Polly said she would call again when she knew more and begged her not to fret in the meantime. 'Try and keep busy, would you please?'

Sleep now impossible, Phil got up and made tea, carrying it through to Frederick's study, where she tried to bring up the British papers on his computer. Unsuccessful, she couldn't bear to linger in the room where so many of his things still sat where he'd last touched them. His spare glasses in a tortoiseshell dish, a tin of his mints, a club tie coiled in his top drawer. 'Lucky you, darling. Missing all this. Bloody lucky you.'

Much later, she fell asleep with the light on. Her final thought as she drifted off was that surely this sort of horrible mischief was more Freddie's bag and why was Brigitta suddenly so intent on cutting his grass? Or had the gods simply taken aim at the Woolnoughs again for their sport?

51.

The Cremorne Point
Benevolent Society

Abi did not see Phil again until Tuesday morning, when she was summoned to the kiosk via text message. When she arrived, Phil was explaining to the group how she'd spent two days in bed with a wog. She did not look her best, in comfortable trousers and a large sort of cardigan with pockets that sagged. Abi parked the pram and sat down.

'You've had your flu shot, have you Phil?' Noel asked. 'They've already had one death in Canberra.'

'Actually, I am certain it was not the flu. I suspect it was only dehydration.' Phil closed the matter. 'Now, Abigail. I find myself rather in need of a neat little project, and as it would happen, the crew here and I have just realised that between us, we've a vast surplus of household *accoutrement*.'

'That's right Abigail. I have all the chairs in the world.' Valentina threw her arms out to encompass an entire universe of seating options. 'How many you need?'

'We've got two lots of everything in our kitchen,' Barb said. 'Don't we Sandy? Now that we've decided two can live as cheaply as one.'

Phil coughed into a serviette.

'Write me a list and Sandy will pack it up,' Barb said. 'Sandy's a whiz at packing, aren't you?'

Silently, Sandy conceded that she was.

'I don't suppose you need garden tools,' Noel said, already defeated when his turn came. 'But I'd be glad to help you get all this lot up your stairs. Any day except Thursdays when I golf.'

'Anyone with a small desk? Abigail's got work to do.' Phil asked and Noel's hand shot up.

'Very good. The Cremorne Point Benevolent Society has come up trumps.' She turned towards Abi, to see if she'd enjoyed the little joke, but found her wide-eyed, speechless. Barb reached across to give Abi a reassuring pat on the knee, and the conversation moved on.

* * *

From then on, Abi's afternoons at home were punctuated by Noel staggering up four flights with assorted *accoutrement*, despite a persistent twinge in his left hip. One of everything from Barb and Sandy's kitchen arrived wrapped as tight as Christmas presents, in stiff butchers' paper. Valentina sent up a single sofa chair, which in the end was the only one she felt able to part with, and in a last herculean effort, Noel made it up the stairs with a small pine desk. Abi put it beneath the living room window, arranged the desk with a mug of pens, her course applications and a jar of hellebores from Phil's garden. The flowers had come with a hamper of towels, sheets, a ratted rug for the kitchen and one or two cushions from the big house. Phil had been mostly absent during the week of deliveries, but late on Friday afternoon, she popped up to appraise the new arrangements.

'The only thing we're really lacking is a window treatment and a base for that bed, although I feel that's beyond my remit. But I do hope you'll do something about the mattress, Abigail. It's so lowering. In all senses.'

* * *

Early the following morning, Stu texted to say he was actually probably going to hang around at Gordon because Elaine needed help with some stuff. In accordance with Phil's guidelines, Abi tapped out a reply, 'Sorry. That isn't the arrangement. Also I've made spinach and feta triangles, so will see you soon,' pressed send and cleaned the flat until she heard Stu let himself in at 1 p.m. Jude was sitting in a high chair that Barb no longer needed for visiting grandchildren, chasing two cold broccoli florets around the tray, as suggested by the baby-led weaning section of *First Year with Baby*.

'Whoa. Where did all this come from?'

'The Cremorne Point Benevolent Society,' Abi handed him a pile of folded singlets that needed putting away. 'Want to go for a walk?'

Abi wrapped up four spinach triangles and Stu put them in his hoodie pocket with a full-size bottle of ketchup. They wandered the track, Stu wearing Jude in the carrier and squeezing individual dots of sauce onto each bite. Abi wanted to tell him about her course, but hadn't thought up a way of doing it that would sidestep the question of funding. She wasn't sure that Stu would believe that scholarships were available for holiday programmes.

Stu brushed flakes of pastry off his chest. 'This is nice. Me and you and the boy. I don't think I can really stay over though,' he added. 'I've got tonnes to do for Monday, so it's probably better that I shoot up to Mum and Dad's. It's been good, hasn't it, little guy?' He let Jude take the last corner of pastry out of his hand and soothed him when he immediately dropped it.

'That's fine,' Abi said. 'I've got loads to do as well. Probably as much as you. Or a bit more.'

52.

Advanced Night Repair
for tired skin

The week had been an absolute bugger. But for the merciful distraction of the furnishing project, Phil had been existing in a state of permanent agitation, stoked by constant visits to Frederick's study to look up the British papers. Against her better instincts, she felt the need to follow every new and dreadful hashing-out of the event. No matter how foolish Brigitta had been, plighting her troth to a married man, how stubborn in keeping the thing going against all advice, it was torture to think of her being mauled by the gutter press. Phil felt so desperately far away, unable to protect her own darling daughter from the muck and beastliness.

Late into her teenage years, whenever Brigitta had a wobble of some kind, she would drape herself across her mother's lap without invitation and demand comfort – never mind those long legs or the certainty of an elbow to the bosom. Phil would always shoo her off or swat her with a book, it was part of the game, but she would have done anything at this moment to have Brigitta all but crush her to death on an occasional chair.

She'd seen Brigitta referred to as 'Guy Kidd's favourite extra', the 'North London nymph' and 'Barbican Barbie', which seemed both unimaginative and a plain reach since Brigitta was not even remotely blonde. They commented on her physique, hypothesised cruelly as to her virtue. One particularly rodent-like columnist, whose name Phil had noted down to mention to Mark, had speculated as to why money was even changing hands. Sitting uselessly in front of Frederick's computer, Phil swung between fits of weeping for Brigitta and moments of murderous rage towards the world.

Public sympathy was unsurprisingly falling to the wife. Guy himself, who'd issued a contrite public statement and promised a period of concentrated personal reflection, had been punished with record-breaking advance sales for his summer production.

Polly and Phil spoke daily, sometimes many times although Phil dissolved into tears within five minutes of picking up and it fell to Polly to steer the conversation back to practical matters.

Finally, towards the end of May, failing the acquisition of any new photographs and the unrelated sighting of a junior MP arriving at a private house party in black face, the coverage died down. Under sororal orders, Brigitta did not leave the Ladbroke Grove house, and although Phil had begged, cajoled, insisted and finally demanded that she be shipped home, Polly remained adamant it was the wrong move and gradually it became accepted that Brigitta was staying on. But against all inducement, she would still not pick up the phone to her mother.

Natalia, as it turned out, did not care to work in a house where her employer's sister moped around in her pyjamas all day, picking at the children's leftovers and keeping the television on so they were continually distracted from their homework. She gave in her notice on Friday afternoon of that first ghastly week. With no time to vet another Slavic arrivée, Polly turned the job of minding the boys before and after school over to Brigitta in exchange for her room and board.

Choosing to forget the position she had recently taken on fiscal support, Phil offered Brigitta a small allowance until she was back on her feet. Because she was still refusing to come to the phone, it was accepted through a perfectly infuriating set of Chinese whispers.

When she couldn't distract herself with bits of reading or television, Phil refined what would need to be a very cut and dry response to any inquiries that came her way regarding Brigitta. That the Woolnough name had been publicly besmirched mattered not. Well, mattered little, Phil thought. But it was vital to present the right front, since it would not do to weep in front of the kiosk lot. Mercifully, the scandal did not make it as far as the *Mosman Daily* and was never brought up on the crates.

Thank God, Phil thought each night, as she began her solitary lavations. Thank God Frederick isn't here to see this. Although he was just the sort of man everyone looked to in times like these. 'I wish you hadn't buggered off,' she said as her tears mingled with a thick coating of Advanced Night Repair for tired skin. 'I bloody wish you hadn't, Fred.'

53.

Lessons in Saltwater

When Mark delivered the boxes of Brigitta's things from Kentish Town to the spare room at Ladbroke Grove, her laptop was not inside. There hadn't been much time, he explained, what with the horde of tabloid muckers gunning for him downstairs. But Brigitta knew her computer had been weeded out by her sister, before the boxes made it upstairs. Mysteriously, the daily papers had stopped arriving at the house shortly after she moved in. Evidently it had been decided she was to be kept away from every source of news.

The atmosphere remained tense. Polly was in permanent command mode, rarely speaking to her sister except to issue domestic orders before work, and afterwards to see if she had yet managed to call their mother.

Brigitta had not. Because late each night when she was sure the house was sleeping, she snuck downstairs, opened her sister's laptop and typed her name into Google. The first time she'd done it, her cheeks began to burn and her mouth ran with saliva, forcing her to swallow again and again as the search results came up. It was a habit ecstatic in its agony, a simultaneous relief of pressure and a painful punishment. Almost, she thought, like self-harm.

As the days wore on, the coverage had broadened beyond hysterical reportage, to think pieces analysing the mindset of the other woman and the pathology of cheaters. After Brigitta read each one, she returned to the original photos that still ranked in the *Daily Mail*'s Most Shared! section.

That she looked quite slender in the running series was cold comfort. In the others, especially the money-throwing ones where Guy's little son could be seen in the background covering his ears, she was unmistakably the mad woman. The blurry restaurant pictures she lingered over the longest, always trying to reconcile the pleasant intimacy of that meeting with how it looked in grainy pap shots. Louche, her mother's word. Tacky as fuck, Polly would say. She finished, always, by reading Guy's statement to the press, looking for a coded message within its lines and phrases: 'I deeply regret the pain I have caused ... my wife's forgiveness ... privacy as our family heals.' It was never there.

Very late one Sunday night, a fortnight after the story first ran, Brigitta typed in her name and a raft of new images appeared as the first result. The photographs were not of her, but it didn't matter. Her name was now inextricably linked to 'Director Guy Kidd and his wife, the stunning radio presenter Sylvie Allen Kidd.' She scrolled down.

Spotted at Gatwick. The once beleaguered theatre personality and his wife, who is five months pregnant, will spend a brief vacation in Umbria before Kidd returns to helm the debut production of Lessons in Saltwater, *by last year's Olivier winner.*

Guy was carrying his son and clutching Sylvie's hand as he led her through the terminal. Brigitta studied each frame, noting the monogram on Sylvie's rolling case, the plastic figurine clutched in the son's hand identical to one Toby had, and Guy's pale grey V-neck, which Brigitta had often worn in bed.

Afterwards, as every night, she slipped back up to the spare room feeling hollowed out, grubby, and unable by then to pick up the phone and speak to her mother.

54.

Pantry staples

'Well this is very nice,' Elaine said with tangible disappointment. She cut another small square of foolproof lasagne and swallowed it gannet-like. Although she did not know it, the cutlery came courtesy of Sandy, part of a plastic-handled set that hung on a stand and had got her through her flatting days.

'It's very nice, very nice,' Roger said. Between each mouthful he looked over his shoulder to Jude, who was gumming on a set of plastic measuring spoons. He was surrounded on all sides by Phil's hand-me-down cushions, sitting now but liable to keel over without warning. Abi had arranged the Sunday lunch to celebrate the end of Stu's exams, and the solid run of Bs he had received.

'It relies heavily on pantry staples,' Abi said. 'You know, things you'd already have in the –'

'Thank you, yes, I know what a pantry staple is,' Elaine replied with an astringent smile. 'So, to what do we owe this pleasure, Abi?'

All three looked at her, expectantly.

'Oh well, apart from celebrating and whatnot, I wanted to ask you, Elaine, how you would feel about minding Jude a few days a week, because I'm going to do some study these holidays at Sydney University. The course is called "The Fictive Self".'

It was the first Stu had heard of it and Abi saw him open his mouth to raise the issue of fees. 'Fortunately, it's free. Your first one,' she said, picking a cuticle. 'Yes. The first one's free.'

Stu seemed satisfied and carved his lasagne into large squares.

'Now, what is that, Abi, the fictive self?' Roger asked. 'Is that a mental problem you see in social work?'

'Oh no, sorry. It's English. I've decided that what I really want to do, ultimately, is English. If I can swing it, I might even try and keep going after this one.'

Elaine could barely contain her pleasure at the prospect of having sole charge of the baby. She dabbed her lips with an olive-printed napkin Phil had purchased from an open-air market in Positano in the late nineties. 'I did offer some months back. So yes. That could work.'

'I've actually got my introductory half-day tomorrow so Stu, you can have him, since you're on holidays now.'

'In either case, what about the business of feeding?' Elaine asked pointedly.

'Well, he obviously eats food now. But I've also got more milk frozen than you'd believe. So you won't need to supply your own.'

Elaine sucked in her cheeks, as behind her, Jude grabbed his ankles and listed to one side, remaining in a perfect sitting position until he was horizontal.

Roger chuckled. 'Timber!'

* * *

'That was good, babe. Well done,' Stu said later, as he and Abi stood side by side at the sink, washing and drying the melamine lunch plates that had come in a ruffled picnic basket, which Barb and Sandy had found too heavy for regular use, once all its speciality inserts were actually filled. Elaine and Roger had decided to take a turn around the Point and let the highway clear before driving back up to Gordon.

'Thanks,' Abi said. It had felt like a form of torture, asking Elaine to take the baby, but it had to be done.

Time and again, Phil had stressed how vital it was to get her onside. 'And I'm afraid dangling the babe is the quickest way about it,' she'd said, closing the subject.

Stu continued, 'And I'm happy to help out a bit as well, but I think it's still probably the best thing for me to stay where I am.'

'But you're on holidays. Your work's nearer to here.'

'It's just not worth rocking the boat, don't you reckon?'

'Yip, fine,' Abi said. Her hands were hidden by the thick detergent bubbles and unseen, she clenched the scourer and scrubbed too hard at an Arcoroc lasagne dish that Barb received as a wedding present in 1982. 'Sure. That's fine. As long as you definitely come back on weekends, because you said you would.'

'Mum looked psyched about getting Jude. And I'm definitely good for tomorrow. You must be excited to get back to it. And not even social work.' Stu looked at her with sudden fondness.

Because he was so often forgetful, whenever Stu did recall a detail about her life, something she had said or done, Abi felt grateful out of all proportion. She pulled out the plug and wiped her hands on the front of her jeans. 'We can leave all this to dry on its own.' Turning, she boosted herself up onto the kitchen bench. 'Fancy a quick shag?'

Stu dropped a set of Sandy's tongs, which clattered to the floor. 'What?'

'We'll have to hurry in case your parents get back.'

'What? Okay. Yes. Yes I do. But Jude's asleep in the bedroom.'

'It'll have to be here then,' Abi said.

'Oh man,' was all Stu managed to say, again and again. 'Oh man. Abi. Babe.'

And Phil was right, it was awful until they got going. Although, still, Abi refused to think of England.

55.

The tectonics of structural systems

Stu was woken by Elaine rapping on his bedroom door, eight minutes before he was due at Cremorne Point. He clambered out of bed, covering himself with the nautically themed doona of his childhood as she stepped in and stood at the end of his bed, silently transmitting her displeasure at the day's arrangements.

Over an early tea of crumbed cutlets and three-bean mix the night before, Elaine had been more vocal about it. 'You've barely ever had Jude on your own Stuart, even for a morning. The task is more onerous than Abi has probably led you to believe, since she likes to look very self-sufficient.'

Apparently it was the impromptu nature of the set-up that Elaine claimed to find most demanding – and surely Abi ought to be working towards something more vocational, instead of indulging in story-writing or whatever it was. 'Although I suppose it's all right if it's free,' she said in the end, trimming the fat off her cutlet.

* * *

Stu fidgeted unhappily in his seat for the duration of the train ride from Gordon, chewing morosely on the muesli bar Elaine had plied him with at the front door. According to his phone, he was going to be forty minutes late at least. With that realisation came the familiar guilt of letting Abi down. Another cock-up.

Abi rarely complained but somehow that made him feel worse, not better. Lately he'd started to wish that, just once, she'd actually let him have it. Refuse to accept his sporadic provision of twenties, tens and tip money, demand he pull his weight with the baby and move the fuck back down to Cremorne. When Stu slunk back to his parents' house that first weekend, he'd expected Abi to beg him to come back straight away. The weekend turned into a week, and then another and another, until the temporary became the permanent, and in the pit of his stomach, Stu knew it was wounded pride that kept him from returning. Because you are a fucking dickhead, he thought, as the train finally stopped at North Sydney and he pushed his way through commuters to make a connecting bus.

But it was so hard to tell what she was thinking! Did she even still love him? She said she did and Stu felt that their recent shag was the best evidence in that direction. It just didn't feel like she needed him especially. The flat was always neat, Jude always as happy as anything. Abi said he'd started to act up a lot more, getting to sleep or if she tried to put him down to go and do something, but Stu had never personally witnessed it. Abi was all over it. She did look pretty tired a lot of the time though, Stu had started to notice, and she and Jude looked like they could do with some stuff. All his little legging things stopped halfway up his calves, and Abi's favourite jumper had a spider-web of loose stitching under one arm.

A proper boyfriend would send her off to the hairdressers, let her sleep all Sunday or hand over a loaded Westfield voucher and be like, 'All yours babe.' The knowledge that he couldn't take care of everything stopped him from trying at all. It was so embarrassing.

Stu jogged all the way from the junction to Milson Road and took the stairs in twos to rally his energies. The door was ajar and he could see Abi standing in the middle of the room, Jude on her hip, rucksack on her back, just waiting. She was wearing the jumper with faded jeans and Jude had on a pair of denim overalls that Elaine had found in the camphor chest that held her special collection of Stu's baby clothes. 'One thing that reminds me of you at every age.' Ideally, a father wouldn't have to dress his baby in his own hand-me-downs, Stu thought as he entered with a display of forced gusto. 'Sorry, sorry, sorry babe!'

Abi looked at him blankly. 'I thought you said you'd be here at eight-thirty.'

'I know, I know babe. You must be so mad. Mum was meant to wake me up and she must have forgotten. Not like her. You look nice. Anyway, you can head now.'

'But I've got things I need to tell you. His routine.'

'I'll figure it out. How hard can it be! Hey mate,' he said, lifting Jude out of her arms.

'There's two containers in the fridge …'

Stu placed a hand on her shoulder and steered her towards the door, ignoring the torrent of instructions, about dummies and milk and other obvious stuff. 'Yep, yep, yep, no sweat. I've brought a stack of uni reading to do anyway, so we'll probably just hang here.'

'You're not going to be able to do any uni …'

Stu gave her a gentle shove into the hallway and missed the last bit of what she said.

Jude seemed fairly happy sitting on the carpet, so Stu pulled out his textbook.

'All right, you all set, Jude?' He lay on the pull-out, tapping a pen against his teeth as he started reading.

Jude grizzled.

'Shh, there's a boy.' Stu tossed a squeezy toy towards him. It landed beyond Jude's range and he cried for it. 'Mate, come on.'

Stu read two lines of introduction and glanced up at the precise moment Jude reached for the toy and, overbalancing, fell forward. The audible crack of his head hitting the leg of a chair was followed by a second of menacing silence, an almighty shriek, then high continual crying as he lay stranded face down on the carpet. Stu picked him up and brushed away fluff that had adhered to the dribble running out of his mouth.

'It's all right mate. Sssh. You'll be all right.' A welt rose on Jude's forehead and Stu hoped rubbing it gently with his thumb would encourage it to go back down.

* * *

Abi hovered in the driveway, turning back to the flats, then to the road. She had not been away from Jude since the miserable date night. This morning was only the hour-long introductory session, but with the bus there and back she could be gone for three hours or more. She could not let herself think ahead to his days with Elaine, hostage in the back of a two-door Daihatsu. When she heard a bus approaching from the ferry terminal, she forced herself on, despite the certain sense that Jude would grow up to resent her for being such an absent mother.

* * *

'You're all right.' Stu sat the baby on his lap and held the textbook like a bedtime story. Jude had not settled down and writhed unhappily in Stu's lap, tugging his own ears.

In a soothing, singsong voice, Stu said, 'The tectonics of structural systems ...'

For a moment, Jude was quiet. Stu kept reading and when he got to a part about interpreting vernacular technologies, Jude reached out for a page and tore off a corner as he pulled it towards his mouth.

'Jude. No,' Stu said. He yanked Jude's arm away. 'This is a library book.' Feeling suddenly ridiculous as Jude began wailing again, Stu got up and carried him to the kitchen. 'What about a drink? That always helps your dad. Shh. Okay. Milk.' He glanced around the kitchen. 'How about we give Mum a ring?' He looked at his phone. It had been six minutes since Abi left.

In the fridge, he found three bottles lined up on the top shelf. He threw one in the microwave, bunging it on for five minutes. Abi didn't pick up and after two rings, Stu stuffed the phone back in his pocket, realising if she did answer he'd seem like an idiot.

He sat Jude on the kitchen bench, shuffling him back a bit towards the corner, and pawed through his hair a few times. Shit, he thought, right.

Jude tried to grab the tap, and Stu nudged him back further towards the windows to stop him tumbling head-first into the sink.

The microwave dinged. Stu reached in to retrieve the bottle, pegging it across the kitchen when it turned out the plastic was now molten.

'Five minutes might have been a touch long, Jude. We might not use that one.' The bottle lay on its side on the lino, boiled milk leaking out of the melted teat. Stu kicked it behind the bin. 'Right' he said, as Jude got hold of the plastic cutlery tree and sent it to the floor.

'Maybe we'll have milk later. Let's try Mum again just in case.' Stu held on this time, but it went through to voicemail. 'Or let's try Granny Elaine. See if she wants to come over.'

Elaine did not pick up, and neither did Roger. Somewhere around the twelve-minute mark, when Stu was trying to interest him in a piece of browning banana, Jude turned bright red and his eyes watered as he assumed a look of intense concentration. 'Oh right,' Stu said, 'okay. Where does Mum keep the changing stuff?'

* * *

Abi sat on the bus watching each call come in, forbidding herself to pick up. Phil had felt that no intervention, no assistance of any kind, was very much the order of the day. It was always useful, she felt, for men to have a clear sense of what life would be like without a helpmate, 'which is why I once spent four days at the Hydro Majestic in Medlow Bath when Freddie was still in nappies. It was something of a walk-out, Abigail, and when I returned Frederick's gratitude erred towards the pathetic.'

She only hoped that Stu had found the two pages of written instructions she'd left on the table, beside the nappies, rusks, a change of clothes and the only dummy that would get him to sleep in the daytime. Abi let her head rest against the bus window, feeling the vibration against her forehead. Her eyelids drooped and she could not have said how long she stayed like that before the driver announced her stop, and she walked in the front gates of the university.

56.

Mate, can babies eat toast?

Stu lay Jude down on the mattress and tried to tug the overalls off. Jude kept trying to twist away from him, forcing Stu to lay over his top half to pin him flat, feeling around blindly for the buckles.

'Oh mate,' Stu said, when he eventually got the nappy open. He'd changed him before. Loads of times. But not for a while, and not since he'd started eating eggs and oranges and meat. Stu breathed through his mouth and looked around for the wipes, noticing them on top of the drawers. In the second it took to reach them, Jude managed a series of seal-like rolls across the bed, leaving a set of perfectly spaced imprints behind him – half a dozen small brown butterflies floating diagonally across the doona, wings spread.

'Oh come *on*.' Stu picked Jude up under the arms. His bare bottom half, below his little shirt, seemed especially naked and vulnerable – like a fat kid who'd been pantsed. With his foot, Stu dragged the doona off the bed and kicked it behind the door to be dealt with later. He held Jude away from him, suspended from the armpits, and as he made to carry him towards the bathroom a bright yellow stream of warm liquid arced out of Jude's penis, leaving a rainbow of wetness across Stu's T-shirt. 'You're actually joking me.'

In the bathroom, he tried to fit Jude's bottom half under the tap and give it a quick rinse off. After jamming a nappy on him, Stu strapped him pants-less into the pram and parked it in front of the television. He clicked through the channels until he found live golf.

'Ladies, but still. You watch that while Dad has a little break. Actually, let's give Mum another try and see what's happening at her end.'

Abi's phone went through to voicemail again and this time, Stu left a message. 'Hey babe. Just seeing how you're going. Jude and I are just hanging. Okay, well, give us a call when you get this and also does he have lunch or – yeah, well maybe just call me back.' He hung up. The time on his phone said 9.42 a.m.

Stu rubbed his chin. His fingers smelt like shit and fragranced wipes. 'Shall we go for one of those walks your mum likes? We've got a bit of time to kill before she gets back.' He looked at his phone again. Still 9.42.

Unable to thread the overalls back on without the hassle of taking Jude back out of the pram, Stu decided a bath towel over his legs would achieve the same end. As they made their way down the stairs, Jude made a sort of er-er-er noise with each bump, and Stu made a mental note to tell Abi how much fun Jude had had.

It seemed colder outside than it had been on the way over, and Stu leaned over and tucked the towel in tighter, wishing he'd gone the pants option after all. Jude tried to sit up, straining against the straps because Stu had successfully dropped his seat back in case Jude wanted to sleep, and now he couldn't make it go back up. Jude's bottom lip began to quiver as they approached the Point and Stu decided to duck into the kiosk and get him a biscuit or something.

It was deserted except for a brigade of old people sitting in one corner, who waved as though they recognised Jude. Stu scanned the menu board.

'Mate, can babies eat toast?' he asked the man behind the counter.

'Sorry, I don't know.'

'That's fine. No worries. We'll take our chances. Just one piece probably and two macchiatos for me.'

Stu downed his coffees like shots and noticed as he pegged the paper cups into the bin that the older group was still watching him. When the toast came, he passed it whole to Jude, who pushed it straight into his face, anointing his own forehead with Vegemite. The group whispered amongst themselves and Stu turned his back before using the edge of his T-shirt to wipe Jude's face, remembering too late that it would contain traces of Jude's own wee. 10.14 a.m.

He left three more messages for Abi and spent the rest of the morning on the cusp of an unfamiliar panic. Jude refused to go in his cot, refused to sleep in the pram even when Stu rolled it back and forth across the same square foot of living room for half an hour. He refused to take the bottle, cold or warm, and filled another two nappies despite sucked-on toast being his only nourishment since breakfast.

As Stu knelt on the floor and tried to hook a wad of soggy tissue out of Jude's mouth that he hadn't seen going in, he couldn't shirk the realisation that Abi worked this hard, all day. Every day. No help, no other mums, no boyfriend coming home with a Prawn Pad Thai and a bunch of whatever the best flowers were. She did it all by herself, made the best job of it and never complained. After dredging the last bit of tissue out of Jude's cheek, Stu picked his son up and held him at eye level. 'Jude, your dad is going to get his shi … get himself sorted. A hundred and ten per cent, from now on.'

Many hours later or so it felt, Stu heard Abi's key in the door.

'Thank God,' he said, punting Jude into her arms. 'Where have you been?'

* * *

Abi took Jude and let his hot, sticky head, rest against her shoulder. His shirt was damp. His nappy was on backwards. He wasn't wearing pants and there was a raised red oval the size of a quail's egg on the left side of his forehead.

Abi held her lips to it as she surveyed the room. Balled-up nappies strewn across the carpet, the pull-out missing both its seat cushions, the television turned up, and Jude's favourite dummy perfectly sterile in a Ziploc bag precisely where she'd left it. Abi hated mess. It made her feel ill, the way it could creep across a room, spread up stairs. She spent more hours of her childhood hauling bags of rubbish out to the bins and scrubbing the bath than threading beads and drawing horses like other girls, and her rising impulse was to shove Stu aside and set the room to rights as fast as she could. But with Phil's voice in her head, she turned back to Stu and gave him a loving smile. 'So, what did you two get up to today?'

'What? Nothing. This. I wiped stuff all day. He hasn't really eaten anything and I reckon he slept for three minutes, altogether. I think he might like ladies golf though. Abi, I cannot believe that you do this every day.' Stu picked up his abandoned textbook and put it in his bag.

'All day though,' Abi said, feeling momentarily cheered. She could clean up as soon as he left. It would only take her a minute.

'What time is it now?'

'One-thirty. Well, almost.'

57.

Currants in the cake

A cold, drizzly fortnight passed, during which their only contact was the exchange of literary titbits via text message. Phil dispatched choice lines of Mitford and Abi wondered if she was reading them over again. In the pinch of crisis, Phil had once told her, she always did 'the complete Nancy', and Abi hoped it was only the miserable weather that had compelled her to begin at *Christmas Pudding* and go all the way through to *Don't Tell Alfred*. In exchange, Abi sent lines from her assigned reading. *The Yellow Wallpaper*, *An Angel at My Table* and *The Bell Jar*, until Phil asked if they might have a little break from female lunacy. 'But what about this from Pursuit of Lv. *Life is sometimes sad and dull but there are currants in the cake.* Isn't that lovely? Our dear Sadie.'

Now, at the kiosk, Phil seemed as hungry for actual conversation as Abi felt. 'Tell me, is young Stuart nibbling at our bait?' She leaned back so the chap could set down the two coffees she had ordered with her usual gesture.

'I think it's going quite well. He minded Jude on my first day of university. Although he had to leave straight away, because he said he needed a shower and a sleep. Stu did, I mean, not Jude.' She looked over at Jude who was asleep in the pram, his two tight little fists at ear height.

'Ah, yes, perfect. Perfect.' To Abi's eye, Phil looked tired and a bit flat.

'The second time he's had him was better, insofar as everyone was cleaner and had no head injuries when I got home. And now Elaine's taken over, which I'm just being strong about.'

'I am so glad to hear it, Abigail. An eye to the main chance. Has he made any noises about returning to the perch?'

'Not so far. But we've had some really nice walks and whatnot. Oh and I've done the moussaka, that curried beef thing twice and a roast chicken.'

Phil sucked her cheeks in. 'Towelette in or out this time?'

'I opted for out.'

'Best, I think. And studies?'

'Oh, yes. Apparently my essay demonstrated keen insight and a measure of original thought, marred only by its lack of obvious structure.' Abi had read the teacher's remark until she knew it by heart. It was so nice and specific and nine lines long. Social work was only ever graded on a pass or fail.

'Ah well, you'd better set about picking your next subject and then we shall see about shifting you over to a little BA perhaps.'

Abi beamed, and felt she ought to shift the conversation on from her now glorious future. 'What about you though, Phil, how have you been and everything?'

'Ah.' Phil found an earlobe and massaged it slowly. 'Also marred by a lack of obvious structure, I'd say, but otherwise well. Very little to report. Briggy seems to be over the acting bug, thank heavens. She's actually nannying for the boys and living with Polly after giving up that dire flat. But of course they're warring so I imagine Briggy will pack it all in soon and come home for good.'

Abi had just taken a mouthful of coffee and found herself now unable to swallow it. 'Really?' she tried to say without opening her mouth, while scorching liquid pooled under her tongue.

'Well, I can't think what would keep her there now.'

When Abi finally managed to get the mouthful down and spoke again, the sides of her tongue felt like they'd been coarsely grated. 'Right, no, I suppose not. And it is much nicer here.' They turned in unison to watch a ferry pass, cutting through the swell and leaving a froth of white water behind it.

'Well,' Phil said, turning back, 'she hasn't said she's coming. Not outright. But a mother can wish. It would certainly be a currant in the cake.'

'It would be.' Abi kept watching the ferry until it passed the peninsula. 'Such a big currant. In your cake. Wouldn't it be?'

58.

The Siege of Ladbroke Grove

Polly toed off one pinching heel, then the other, and rubbed her stockinged feet against the soft carpet under her desk. The fifteenth floor had emptied out and the motion lights above the bullpen outside her glassed office were ticking off, one by one.

She opened the Pret A Manger salad that had been sitting on her desk since lunchtime, took a bite of wilted greens and set it aside. She was never hungry anymore. The vast bank of windows behind her looked out to Canary Wharf. Polly swivelled her chair to face the glass and gazed out. The clocks had gone forward some weeks ago and the sky behind the towers was deep violet and crisscrossed with the chalk-trails of distant aircraft passing over London.

Strictly speaking, there was no need to work late this evening, but ever since Brigitta had moved in, the office after-hours had become Polly's only place of retreat. More and more, she found herself inventing reasons to stay back, only to sit numbly in her chair for an hour or more – at least until she could be sure Max and Toby would be in bed by the time she got home. She felt guilty. Of course she did. That went without saying.

But if she got in before Mark, the job of unravelling the boys, starting them on homework and dealing with the aftermath of her sister's overly creative dinners would fall to her. Schoolbags would be untouched by the front door and a coloured wash she had put on before work would be sour in the machine, a wet, tangled wad smelling powerfully of mould.

And between all that, it was up to her to rebuild relations between her mother and sister. Brigitta was still refusing to ring, insisting that she felt bad enough already so really didn't need to drink a cup of Phil's wrath. Over and over, Polly told her Phil had ceased to be angry some time ago and only wanted to talk. The raft of text messages Phil sent daily to both of them confirmed it to be true, but Brigitta held out.

Polly turned back to her desk and reached into a filing drawer for the very small bottle her father's preferred brand of whisky. No one ever thanked her for being the go-between, the peacemaker, tough old Pidge, always so strong.

She poured a generous finger into a Law Society mug. The taste was vile, but the burning feeling as it slid down her throat was deeply comforting. When it was gone, she poured another, picturing her father in his high-backed chair in the study at Milson Road, steepled fingers, crystal tumbler set to one side, listening seriously to whatever school-related problem had arisen for her that day. If only she could tell him about all this, she thought. That was the other convenient aspect of late nights in the office. Nobody had to see her cry.

According to the therapist that not even Mark knew she had seen, the week she'd returned from the funeral, journeying through the five stages of grief could take many months, even years. The silly woman, who'd been dressed in some sort of burlap sack, told her 'just to go easy on herself' and 'let it take as long as it takes', pieces of advice that infuriated Polly so intensely she declined a second session and gave herself six weeks to get all the way from Denial to Bargaining. She did not have time for grief to be a journey.

Her mother would be waiting, Polly realised, glancing at her watch. It would be 8 a.m. at home, and Polly could see her mother sitting up in bed, drinking English Breakfast with the phone beside her. She swept the salad into the wastepaper basket and pressed the one-touch dial on her desk phone. 'Hello?' Phil's voice rang out over the speaker and filled the quiet office. Polly heard the familiar call of a mynah bird in the background, and for an instant, longed to be home. Sitting on the terrace, face to the sun, preferably alone.

'Hi Mum. How are you?'

'Oh, Polly, hello darling. Well, much the same really. I was thinking about getting up for a walk but the weather's been bleak. I realised this morning I loathe June. You've still got July to go, and August is always so patchy. The garden's a tip from all the wind, but I haven't the will to get out there.'

'Why don't you start on Dad's things? It's got to be done sooner or later.' Polly berated herself immediately for sounding like a task master when she meant to be kind, suggesting a project.

'Darling, I would. You know I would, but I'm simply not ready to see a no-hoper traipsing through the IGA in your father's Burberry. It'll have to wait. I simply don't share your urgency, I'm sorry.'

Polly pushed her thumb deep into the muscle of her jaw, which gave off a pleasing pain, like pressing a bruise.

'What about your end though, darling? Tell me peace is restored. I hate the idea of you and Briggy still at loggerheads.'

'We're not. We're fine, just staying out of each other's way really. I'm sorry she hasn't called you. I've been trying but you know how stubborn she can be.'

'Of course, Pidge. But truly, she can't last much longer dear. The nannying, I'm sorry, but it's not her bag. Just keep doing what you're doing and you'll bore her out sooner or later. The Siege of Ladbroke Grove.' Phil sighed. 'I will be glad of the company when she comes home. And perhaps some help.'

A fragment of something her sister had said in passing rose in Polly's mind. She cast about for a moment and then said, 'Brigitta said you've had a neighbour helping you. A girl who brings you meals or something? I've been meaning to ask.'

'Oh no, that's nothing. She moved in next door at the beginning of the year with a very dear baby and we struck up a friendship of sorts. But there's no paid arrangement.'

'That's a bit unusual.'

'I don't see why.'

'Why does she want to help you?'

'Well, I like to think we help each other, darling. In fact, I put her on a regime of study, a short course, but she is already hooked I can tell, and I've no doubt she'll keep going with another now that the mother-in-law or whatever you'd call her is lined up for the childcare. We've also done a small amount of scheming to get the doltish boyfriend back, you see. It seems to be going rather well. Although of course, I've been hoist by my own petard, because now she's somewhat less available than she was previously.'

Polly frowned hard as she listened, confused by the sudden outpouring of new information. It was like being told the plot of a soap opera she'd never seen.

'All right. Well I suppose that's all right.' It wasn't all right at all but she was too tired to wade into it now. She drained the rest of her whisky and turned back to the window. The sky over the city was dark now and the awareness, suddenly, of still being in the office, the effort it would take to get her mother off the line, pack up, leave and get home was overwhelming. It would be easier just to curl up and sleep beneath her desk. 'Be careful though Mum, please. You don't need anyone depending on you and you're a magnet for strays. Dad always said that, remember?'

'Yes, thank you, I quite remember. You sound dreadfully tired, Pidge. You're not in the office I hope?'

'I am, but I'm leaving now. I should get home.' Slowly, she stood up and felt around with a foot for her heels.

'Oh darling. Your generation, honestly. You'll die in the harness. You ought to do more for yourself. Anyway, you'll call tomorrow, won't you?'

'Of course.'

When Polly arrived home, Brigitta was on the sofa watching television and eating pungent takeaway from a bowl balanced on a shot-silk cushion. Polly imagined a ring of oil settling into the fibres.

'You forgot to put out money for the cleaners,' she said without looking away from the screen. 'I told them you'd leave double next week.'

PART II

59.

September can be full
of false promise

'What's that amazing smell?' Abi asked, setting her teacup down on the grass.

The morning had been crisp but now, spring sun streamed into Phil's garden. Clouds of soft, yellow dust filled the air with a sweet, honey scent.

'It is wattle, dear. And it means we have made it. Or near enough.'

Abi thought Phil was looking much better than she had in weeks. Still, she'd declined a visit to the pool, claiming she never swam before Labour Day and rarely before the Melbourne Cup. Instead, she offered a little sit in *le jardin*, where they had been for an hour now, Phil in her chair, Jude practising his crawling on a blanket. So far, he could only go backwards and Abi sat behind him, giving him little helps forward. Grass stains on pudgy knees were her new best thing, she decided then and there.

'The winter of our discontent, finally done with,' Phil said, watching on.

In Abi's experience, it was generally better not to contradict Phil, but winter had been in many ways the happiest, most purposeful time of her life. There had been books and furniture, a baby who could sit in his highchair and make mumming noises while mashing banana into his jumper, a boyfriend who seemed to be slowly but surely coming around. Half a packet of Marlboros sat unsmoked in their packet on top of the high cupboard, and although her hair had grown out to chin-length it only found its way into her mouth when she watched very late reruns of *Masterchef* or got stuck on a bit of essay.

Winter had been a friend. 'I haven't really minded it, to be honest.'

'Ah well, no, quite. I suppose it's only that this time last year, Fred and I were in the Dordogne, with all of Polly's lot. How quickly things can change. Perhaps that's what I mean.' Phil rested her cup on the arm of her wicker chair, and got up to deadhead a large flowering shrub.

'And you, Abigail. Where were you a year ago?' Phil tossed the dead blooms into a dark patch of garden.

Standing on the loo in the Highside bathroom, halfway through her pregnancy and trying to shovel swelling breasts into a sports bra she'd been forced to shoplift from Debenhams, although she was careful to pick the cheapest one they stocked. There would be no way it could be returned later, but in compensation she'd committed to choosing Debenhams over John Lewis when she was able to shop as a regular customer.

'All the normal things. Working mostly. Bit of shopping. Anyway! I should probably get going.' Abi stood up and brushed grass off the seat of her rolled-up jeans. It was hotter now than she'd realised, and she felt momentarily light-headed. 'Stu is coming over this afternoon, before work. He says he's going to start teaching Jude to swim. He got a DVD from the library on how to do it.'

'There's a good sign if ever I saw one,' Phil said. 'Although do be careful, the water will be Baltic until we've had a real run of sun. September can be full of false promise. Goodbye now dear. I suddenly need a little zizz.'

* * *

'Are you sure about this?' Abi asked, wrestling Jude into a pair of too-big swimming shorts Stu had bought somewhere. A stiff wind blew straight off the harbour and the afternoon air was chill.

Stu waded in to his waist, and huffed into cupped hands. 'All right. Here I go.' He dived under and came up again, shaking off the water like a labrador.

'Are you sure it isn't too cold for him?' Abi said, feeling deeply uncertain.

'It's fine. It's good for him. Toughen him up.'

'I don't know if nine-month-old babies need to be toughened up that much. I think they're allowed to stay quite soft.'

Stu returned to the edge. Reluctantly, Abi lowered Jude into his father's outstretched arms. The moment his little feet touched the water, he let out an ear-splitting wail.

'It's too cold for him, Stu.' Abi stood as near as she could to the edge, flapping her hands and hopping from foot to foot. 'Give him back. We can do this later on, when it's properly summer.'

'He'll get used to it.' Stu carried him to the deep end and lowered him to his tummy. Jude's feet pedalled furiously under the water, as though he was trying to climb back up his father's torso.

'This doesn't feel right, Stu. Did the video say anything about how warm the water should be?'

'I can't remember. Watch this though.' He counted to three and blew in Jude's face. Jude took an automatic breath in as Stu took them both under, face to face with his son. A second later, Stu emerged looking triumphant. Jude, slippery, shiny, hair plastered to his head, came up already screaming.

'That's enough. Stu, that's enough.' Abi stepped down onto the platform, soaking her jeans to the knees, and held out a towel.

'He's like the Nirvana baby,' Stu said, giving him to her. 'Although maybe I will wait till it warms up a bit more before we have another go. It probably is a bit fresh.'

Abi rubbed Jude vigorously with a towel then swaddled him like the Christ child.

'All right if I come upstairs and change?' Stu asked, boosting himself out. 'Then I'll head.' He looked at Jude, only his round face visible from inside the towel.

'Sorry mate,' he said. With purple lips and tears still wet on his cheeks, Jude drew his mouth into a half-smile. 'See, babe, he's already forgiven me.'

60.

Crying, Excessive

Jude whimpered miserably in Abi's arms while Stu banged around the flat, showering, changing, packing his bag. The more she patted him, bounced him, rocked him, the unhappier he became. By the time Stu left, Jude was crying in dry, angry yelps. Abi kicked the front door shut and began pacing in tight circles around the room.

Jude's face became a furious pink as he arched his back, throwing his entire weight away from her.

'What's wrong, Jude?' Abi asked, switching him from one side to the other, trying to hold his rigid little body against her chest. 'What's wrong, little boy? Mummy's here.'

She took him to the kitchen and ran the tap, usually his favourite entertainment. Still, he cried. She felt his forehead, ran a finger around his gums in the hope of finding a tooth. Saliva ran out of his open mouth and down his chin as he lurched away from her again.

She tried the television, then the window, speaking all the time in a soothing singsong.

'Look Jude, can you see Phil's garden? What can you see? Birds? Can you see the birds?'

Phil's garden was quiet under the gathering dusk. Her saucerless teacup remained on the arm of her empty chair. Abi longed to be down there now in the perfect calm. Phil would know how to soothe an upset baby, most likely without breaking her stream of chatter. In her day, Phil once told her, it was perfectly all right to leave an infant outside in the pram, and for the briefest moment Abi wished that was still the case.

She could feel the tiny bird beats of Jude's racing heart against her chest. With one hand, she stroked his hair, now damp and curling with sweat, as his pitch continued to rise. 'Stop it, Jude, stop it,' Abi pleaded. 'Stop crying. It's all right.' She put him to the breast but he turned his face away and redoubled his cries. With panic rising, she carried him around the flat offering a banana, a wet flannel, house keys. Nothing worked.

In the index of *First Year with Baby*, she found 'Crying, Excessive' and opened to the short chapter, only to discover she had already tried every one of its suggestions. In her desperation, she texted Rae to ask what to do but her mother's reply offered nothing: 'not much of a one w babbies, me. it looks like Pat will be having the leg off.'

Jude cried on and on as evening came. Abi's T-shirt was soaked with his tears and her own. Her arms burned with the weight of him. From below came the machine-gun rap of a neighbour banging on their ceiling with a broom handle.

Abi looked again at Phil's, wondering if it was too late to go down for help. All the lights were off. Jude roared. The broom handle came again and Abi felt her grip around Jude's body tighten. Then, the impulse to shake him. Just once. Just to make him stop. Terrified, she dashed into the bedroom and lowered his hot, damp, writhing form into the cot, releasing him too soon so that he bounced an inch as he landed. Without looking back, she ran and shut herself in the bathroom, running every tap. But still, through coursing water, came the sound of Jude's cry. Abi curled up on the floor and covered her ears. 'Stop,' she cried. 'Stop it, Jude, stop it. Please stop. I can't do it. I can't do this.' When he did not stop, and she started to worry he was dying, she forced herself out, snatched him up and flew down the stairs towards the road.

The crying did not cease when she climbed with him into a taxi. It did not have a baby-seat but Abi could not wait for another. She held him on her lap, her breathing shallow. The radio played feverish Middle Eastern string music she knew from every mini mart in Croydon. The driver was murmuring into a headset and did not break his patter when Abi begged him to go faster. Every nerve in her body had been shredded and she squeezed Jude so tight that he could not struggle against her. It was too tight, she knew. 'Be quiet,' she said, again and again. 'Stop it. Stop crying. Please.'

When they reached the pub, Abi tossed all the money she had onto the front seat and dashed inside, pressing Jude's writhing body to her chest. As she forced her way through the crowded bar, shoulder first, she tried to ignore drinkers turning to stare at a wild-eyed girl and her screaming red-faced baby. It was only then she realised she had not stopped to put shoes on before she left and she felt their burning gaze move to her bare feet. Jude wore nothing but a white vest and nappy, and his curls were matted with sweat.

She bounded up the stairs to the bistro, relieved to find it mostly empty, just as Stu appeared from the kitchen, wiping his hands on his apron. 'Babe, what's happening? What's going on?' He hurried over and wrapped his arms around both of them.

'He won't stop crying. He's been crying since you left and I didn't know what else to do. I got really scared. I tried everything in the book, but I'll be fine, sorry. I shouldn't have come while you're working.'

'It's all right. Don't worry.' He lifted Jude carefully out of her arms so she could collapse into a nearby chair.

'There you go. You're all right mate. There you go,' Stu said softly as he carried him away to the kitchen. Abi put her head into her hands, listening to the ringing in her ears.

After a time, Stu reappeared with Jude asleep over his shoulder and a large glass of lemonade in his other hand. 'It may have a small amount of gin in it,' he said, handing it to her. 'I can't be sure. Hey, I just asked and I can finish now because it's so quiet.'

The lemonade had a strongly medicinal flavour and Abi drank it quickly, finishing with a tiny burp.

'Right,' Stu said. 'Let's go then, babe.'

Jude slept the entire way home on the bus.

'Hey, what do you say about me staying over?' Stu said as Abi's head lolled against the back of the seat. 'You know, going forward.'

'You don't have to just because of this. I'll be fine. This was probably just a one-off. I promise I can manage.'

'It's not just because of this. I've been thinking about it for a while. I was going to ask you tomorrow anyway, when I took you out.'

Abi heard Phil's voice in her head. 'When he does finally relent, for Lord's sake don't be soppy about it. A firm yes will suffice.'

'Well. All right then. That would probably be okay. Why are you taking me out though?'

'Um, because it's your birthday?'

'Oh, so it is.'

'Twenty-three, eh? Getting on a bit.'

61.

Something with explosions

They slept, a tangle of three in the bed, Jude starfished between them, until late the next morning. Abi did not want to get up, but as soon as he woke up Stu's energy began to fill the flat like so many bees in a jar, and the day developed a momentum she was unable to halt. He made eggs, burned toast, decided suddenly to move the sofa to the other side of the room. He sang 'Happy Birthday' on continuous loop as the television boomed and Jude lobbed enormous fingers of jam toast out of the highchair. When Abi eventually came out for a glass of water, she stepped in a clot of jam on her way to close the fridge, wide open for no reason.

Abi did not want the day. She did not want to go out that night. She wanted to take Jude for a long walk and a look at the pool, then go to bed as early as she could so the day would be over sooner. If there had to be a celebration, it would involve a king size KitKat and being left alone to smoke half a packet of Marlboros in bed, instead of out the window.

But plans for the evening were already made. Elaine would fetch Jude and take him back to Gordon for the night, because Stu said for sure they'd be out way past her Pacific Highway curfew. Early the next morning, they would train up to Gordon and collect him since Elaine had an early start on Sundays, indispensable as she was to the soprano section of the St Luke's Lindfield choir for the 8 a.m. Sung Eucharist. She made no secret of the fact that young families taking over the 10 a.m. service, and insisting on modern music, had blown a hole in her Sabbath.

Throughout the day, Abi made pleas to stay home. They could get pizza. They could watch whatever he wanted on DVD. Something with explosions. But Stu was unmoved, and as evening approached, Abi accepted her fate and went to wash her face.

At precisely 5.58 p.m., she heard the distinctive sewing-machine whir of the Daihatsu engine in the driveway. While Stu showered, she carried Jude down and buckled him into the back seat, heavy-hearted, then passed his little overnight bag and a cooler that contained her entire archive of frozen milk through the passenger window.

Elaine kept both hands on the wheel. 'Well, happy birthday then, Abi,' she said, to move proceedings along. 'Many happy returns. We'll be off now because I'd rather not have to take the Northbridge way at this time of day.'

Abi leaned into the back seat a final time and kissed Jude's forehead, hoping to feel a temperature – mild but sufficient to warrant calling off the sleepover. His skin was smooth and cool. 'I will see you tomorrow, Jude. Mummy loves you so much.'

'You wonder how much babies really understand of what we say, don't you?' Elaine said, shifting the car into drive.

Abi watched the Daihatsu turn out of the driveway with a swift seven-point turn then walked back upstairs alone.

Stu was standing in the living room, wet-haired, with two cans of beer already open. 'What you need, birthday girl, is to get properly munted.'

'I don't think I do,' Abi said. She felt miserable. 'I'm not supposed to drink anyway. It says in *First Year with* …'

'*First Year with Baby* can go fuck itself. You need to have some fun and the contents of that cooler should last him until he starts school. Just bin the next lot. Come on, get your gear on. I'm taking you into town.'

Reluctantly, Abi changed and found her only lipstick. There was a dead mosquito stuck to the end and she applied a dash of Jude's Vaseline to her lips instead. Stu wandered into the bedroom, still holding the beers, now with a small wrapped gift tucked under one arm. He let it drop onto the mattress and Abi scooped it up.

'It's nothing. It's dumb,' he said, sheepishly. 'You don't have to like it or anything.'

Inside two layers of creamy tissue paper, Abi found a small cardboard sleeve with the words 'Precious Prints' written in silver cursive. Glancing at Stu, she peeled back the tab and found inside a thin chain with a silver disc, stamped with a small fingerprint.

'It's Jude's,' he said. 'It's Jude's thumb. We did it once when you were at uni. You send away for a kit and do it in plaster and then you mail it back to them and they make it up and then you get it back again.'

Abi turned it over and over between her fingers. 'Thank you so much, Stu. I really love it. Thank you. Some of the mothers at that playgroup I went to had these. The real mums.'

'Great. Cool.'

Abi put the necklace on and pressed the disc to her sternum. They smiled at each other awkwardly until Abi couldn't stand it anymore. 'Stu, what is happening? What are we doing?'

'Just … I don't know. I've missed you and Jude so much but I just thought, I don't know. You seem like you know what you're doing with Jude and don't really need my help. I feel like an idiot whenever I try to get involved. And then uni is so full-on, and I thought I needed a break but going home was so weird and boring and Mum's on my case the entire time. And then when you turned up at work last night, I felt like, I don't know, maybe you did need me.'

Abi bit her lip. Had he really not known that? Did he really think she preferred to be entirely on her own?

'I guess I have to figure it out. Anyway, take this.' He passed her one of the beers and she held the frosty can with both hands. 'I'll get us a drink for the bus,' he said as he jogged off towards the kitchen where, Abi knew, he would empty two more cans into a sports drink bottle, a nod to economy she had first experienced on a bus from Kingston to Clapham High Road. He was back in a moment. They were going out.

62.

My hands is very sticky

After they boarded an express to Wynyard that had been idling outside the ferry terminal, Stu handed her the bottle and she drank. 'There's a girl,' he said. 'Nice long sip.' Abi made a squeak of protest as he lifted the end higher and higher with a finger. 'There we go. That's better.'

Abi wiped her chin and handed it back, resting her head on his shoulder as the bus charged along the expressway.

'Right. This is us.'

There was a pub, already loud and full, a short way up. Stu steered her through the crowd inside, holding her by the back of her arms and speaking into the back of her hair, a long, continuous monologue she couldn't really hear although the vibration of his voice and the warmth of his breath made her shiver. At the bar he paid for schooners and tequila shots, and they found a standing table in a corner.

'Oh my gosh, I don't know,' Abi said, watching Stu drop the shots into the beer. 'I'm someone's mother now. What if Jude goes mental again and I have to go and get him from your parents, drunk? That wouldn't look good on an embroidered pillow. "Home is where your son's girlfriend turns up trolleyed from her night out."'

Stu laughed. It was clear he'd never consciously registered the collected wisdom of Elaine's soft furnishing and could locate it now in the recesses of his mind. 'I made Mum promise to ring if Jude looks like he's going to lose it. But I know from experience you can get yourself from shitfaced to convincingly sober in the time it takes to train it from the city to downtown Gordon. You'll be fine.'

Abi raised the beer to her mouth and drank for as long as he did, watching him over the rim. They were both panting when their glasses hit the table with a dull crack.

'I guess I still have it,' Abi said.

'I never lost it. How cute was Jude this afternoon though? I think he could be gifted.'

Abi kept a straight face. 'Do you *really*?'

'Yeah, genuinely. I do. He said "na" while I was wiping his face and I turned around and he was looking smack at a banana.'

Abi laid her hand over Stu's and gave it a little pat. 'How about we have a night off the Jude talk.'

'Oh yeah. Sorry about that,' Stu winced. 'Sorry that I can be a … sub-optimal boyfriend sometimes.'

'It's okay, I'm sorry for being … whatever.'

'Mega-ly intense. But who cares, babe.'

They picked up their glasses and knocked them together, beer sloshing over the edges.

After two more rounds, a pleasant numbness was spreading through Abi's limbs and everything became excessively funny.

Stu looked at her lovingly and stifled a burp. 'You may be shit at birth control but otherwise you are … very sweet.'

'Birth control is something it's good to be good at, though. My tongue feels so … tonguey.'

Stu reached out and took her hand, managing on the second attempt. 'You can't be good at everything, Abi. No one can't be good at everything. For example I am a good architect student but I am bad at not moving out when I feel like I want to. Move out.'

Something told Abi she should follow up the point but at that moment, she was fully occupied with licking tequila from between her fingers. 'My hand is very sticky. Stu. Do you know that?'

When they stepped outside some time later, the whole of York Street developed an unmanageable gradient. They leaned shoulder to shoulder, staggering towards no particular destination. It was like trying to come down a hill in very high heels, Abi thought, before breaking into a hard cackle for no particular reason.

'Woss-so funny?' Stu asked, taking a misstep and putting his hand out for a lamp post.

'Stu, stop, stop. I have to tell you something.' Abi put both hands on his face, feeling around like a blind person learning a new acquaintance. 'I can't remember.'

'I want to buy you some wedges. Abi, I do. You are so beautiful, I want to get you some wedges. Or a potato scallop.' He stabbed his own chest with a finger to emphasise the truth of it. 'I do.'

'I don't eat fish. I love potatoes though.'

'I love potatoes as well.'

'I do too. I love them.'

'Stu?'

'Yes?'

'My hands is very sticky.'

Stu nodded and with supreme concentration, led on to a takeaway that glowed from the mouth of the train station. The pavement continued to undulate like a hellish tilt-a-whirl and their progress was slow.

'Stu, Stu, Stu. I don't have any money,' Abi spoke in a loud whisper as they approached the counter.

'I got money, babe.' Stu plunged a fist into each jeans pocket and pulled out two crumpled handfuls of fives and tens. 'Look, I got all this, Abi. I got all this. Take it. Take this. I want you to have it.' He pressed the notes on her and she tried to catch them up in cradled arms. 'You deserve it so much.'

'You're so amazing to me, Stu.'

'What'll it be?' A man in a greying apron frowned at them from the other side of the counter.

'Wedges, large please. We are no seafoods people,' Abi said, sounding quite business-like in her own mind. 'How much? I've got all this.' She released all the money onto the counter.

The man picked up a five-dollar note and pointed towards a bank of fridges. 'This'll do. But I'd think about a soft drink too if I were you. Wait over there.'

When the order came, they walked towards Hyde Park, weaving through crowds and taking turns to forage in the oily bag. Abi waited on the footpath while Stu ran into a bottle shop for two more longnecks. She tried to save the last wedge for him, but couldn't. Soon they were lying side by side on their backs on the cool grass of the park. Stu opened the beers by screwing the lids into the skin of his forearm, and they drank without sitting up so that beer ran down their necks.

Fairy lights in the Moreton Bay figs glowed like a string of pearls in Abi's peripheral vision and she thought how nice it would be if she could just stay here, except for Jude who she loved so much even when he cried and went psycho and made her go psycho because he could be so psycho. 'I could sleep here for a hunjid years. This is the best birthday Stu, ever. The best. When I turned ten my mum said let's not bother about presents anymore eh love? And all my birthdays have been shit since then. True. I have never liked any birthday, except, have you seen *Cool Runnings*? I saw that on my birthday once, I don't know when.'

'That's the best movie,' Stu said with total passion. 'That team never gave up Abi even though ... they had no snow!' Stu rolled onto his side as though they were home on the mattress. Their faces were inches apart. 'I love you and shit Abi. I always have. I just forgot and now I've remembered. And I love Jude so much. I'm so glad we had him even though it wasn't on purpose and we only found out like, whoa you're having a baby tomorrow basically.'

Because Stu was suddenly kissing her on and all around her mouth, Abi was sure she wasn't speaking her thoughts aloud. It was not until Stu pulled away from her and struggled to his feet, knocking both longnecks over, that she realised she had.

'What do you mean? What?' Stu was shouting.

'What?'

'You said, that's why you didn't tell me *what*?'

Abi raised herself onto all fours but the ground lurched again. She grabbed two fistfuls of grass to ride it out, and tried to think. 'I mean, I knew you would love him when you saw him, so you just had to see him first. And that's … might be why I didn't tell you and because the right moment didn't come up.'

Stu reached down and dragged her to standing by one arm. 'Did you know?' He was too close, she turned away from his reeking breath. 'Did you know you were pregnant and keep it from me until it was too late?'

'What? No. I mean, yes. But only – ow, Stu you are hurting me. I just waited for a bit, but the right moment …'

'Did you get pregnant on purpose?'

'No! I promise. I was really careful. Mostly.'

'Mostly! Fuck!' He shook her like a child. 'When did you find out? How soon did you know?'

'Um, three weeks? Or a bit less maybe?'

'Why would you do that? How could you do this to me?'

'Because, you mighted – you might take him.' No that wasn't right, she closed her eyes and tried to sober up. 'I had to have him, Stu. I had to. You might have said no. Please let me go, please.

But he was the first nice thing that had ever happened to me and I didn't want you to take my best thing. But it doesn't matter because you love him now! Don't you? Don't you?'

'You lied to me. All this time, you've been lying to me. I don't believe this.'

Abruptly, Stu released her, so she pitched backwards. He began jogging towards Elizabeth Street. Abi tried to keep pace, with a slurry of alcohol and potato churning in her stomach, until he strode into traffic and stopped a slow-moving cab by slamming two hands down on the bonnet. While the driver cursed him out the window, Stu yanked the door open and roughly helped Abi inside. She pawed her way across the back seat expecting him to follow but when she turned, the door slammed. With her hands pressed to the greasy window, she watched Stu jog unsteadily towards the train.

The next thing she knew the taxi was stopped outside the flats. 'Miss,' the driver said. 'Miss, time you get out.'

63.

More than you ever will

Hard sunlight shining into her eyes woke Abi the next morning. She was still wearing her clothes from the night before and as she forced herself to roll off the pull-out, she saw that her knees were stained with dirt and grass. With her arms crossed over her engorged chest, she stumbled to the bathroom and relieved each hard, throbbing breast into the sink. A fine needle-spray of clear white milk shot into the basin and beaded around the plughole. The sight of her milk draining away made her ache for Jude. As she drank water from the tap, blood temperature, tasting of rust, she tried to think how to get herself to Gordon. Stu would be there, but as pieces of their drunken exchange came back to her, she knew it was over now. He would not talk to her. He would never forgive her. She told the truth and now it was all broken. How could she have explained to Stu how much she needed to have the baby? From the moment she found out, she was always going to keep him. There would be no more loss, no more missing people, no more ghosts.

Abi looked at herself in the mirror. Her face was streaked with dirt and there was a smear of dried blood in the corner of her mouth. As she tried to clean it off with a clod of toilet paper, there was a brisk rap on the door. Stu. Abi ran through, ignoring the pounding in her temples that accompanied each step. She flung open the door and there in the hallway was Elaine, holding Jude and his small bag of things and an empty cooler.

Although she was neatly dressed, her eyes had the swollen quality of recent tears. Abi lunged for the baby and Elaine relinquished him without struggle. 'Stuart has told us the truth about how all this came to be.' Her tone was venomous and Abi hid her face against Jude's.

'You must understand that Stuart is *my* son. My legitimate son and I love him more than you ever will. If, in fact, you ever did.'

Bowels turning to water, Abi found herself closing the door against Elaine and turning inside and standing with her back against the door. Elaine's voice continued from the other side. 'We will come and collect him on Saturday mornings and return him on Sunday evenings, until a permanent arrangement is made. We ask that you do not attempt to contact Stuart. He will not have his life derailed by any further machinations of a ... of ...'

Loudly, Abi began to sing to drown out the sound of the voice – wild, careening nursery rhyme-like things. 'I love you, Jude, I love you. My little boy, my little boy.'

Eventually, Elaine's shrieking died away, and minutes later, Abi heard the angry crunching of Daihatsu gears from below. When she was sure they were safe, Abi ran all the way to the big house, with Jude held tightly against her chest.

64.

Let us climb up the rockery

Phil was shocked by Abi's appearance at the back door. Her pounding on the leadlight sent Domenica into a fit of yelping and forced Phil to cast aside the Target Word and hurry through the kitchen, expecting flood or fire.

'Good Lord, Abigail. Whatever's happened?'

But the girl couldn't speak. Phil stepped aside to let her in, and seeing then that she was shaking, conveyed her upstairs, just as she had after the demise of one of Brigitta's high school love affairs or dramatic friendship implosions.

She chose Brigitta's room and lifted Jude out of his mother's arms as Abi sank onto the bed. 'Go to sleep,' Phil said, pulling the cover up with her free hand, 'and when you wake up, I think you'll find the world is still turning.'

Abi closed her eyes and Phil watched over her for a moment. As it was, Phil found herself in the mood for motherly ministrations after a brief, frustrating conversation earlier with Polly, who never seemed to require any. She closed the door behind her and carried Jude downstairs, sitting him on the soft carpet of the front room. He amused himself by pulling tissues from a box, and as Phil sat watching she recalled Freddie at much the same age, playing in the very spot. Sitting up but not yet crawling, always a favourite stage –

utterly engaging but too young yet to tug at her skirt, hover at her elbow, wanting to know if she'd rather have no head or no legs – a phase she found infinitely more taxing. Phil felt herself edging towards nostalgia and was relieved when it seemed Jude needed something by way of morning tea. In the kitchen, she prepared triangles of bread and Vegemite, which he ate one after another sitting on her lap.

There must have been a denouement between his parents. Abi's expectations had been rising vis-à-vis the return of Stuart and Phil felt an uncomfortable twinge of liability. Perhaps she'd encouraged her to overegg the pudding because, of course, they were so young and who was to say they even suited? Although surely, Phil thought, it isn't wrong to meddle when the object is ultimately noble – a united family, a solid home for the babe.

Brigitta so often accused her of trying to arrange the affairs of others, but in this case assistance had been required. And once or twice she had spotted Stuart out with Jude, the direct result of her working in the wings, which delivered a measure of private triumph. He seemed like a fairly solid if unspectacular young man who'd simply lost his way and needed shepherding back to the fold.

'Oh well,' Phil said out loud. She'd have the full story when Abi woke up, and in the meantime, there was Jude to tend to. 'Now,' she said, as the final triangle disappeared into his little mouth, 'what do you say to a story?'

* * *

Abi knew that she would not sleep but waited for Phil to close the door before sitting up and looking around the small, dim bedroom. She had only seen it through a crack in the door, and now she was able to run her hand over the wallpaper, pale green, printed with birds and gold bamboo. There was a faded pink slipper chair in the corner and rows of aging children's novels on a bookshelf beside it. As she lay, feeling the warm, starched bedsheets against her skin, the room seemed to contract around her. Abi felt she was a miniature figure tucked away in the attic of a rich child's doll house. She burrowed back under the covers and hid her face with a feather pillow. Stu was gone. Stu did not love her. He had once, but he would not again.

She could not bear to lie there with her thoughts. From the bookshelf by the bed, she chose a worn copy of *Anne of Avonlea*. Inside, 'Polly Woolnough' had been messily crossed out and replaced with 'PROPITY OF BRIGITTA WOOLNOUGH DO NOT TOUCH OR ELSS!!!'

Abi began to read, but her mind ranged over the events of the night before as she tried to put together a version that she could give to Phil. Telling the whole, exact truth only made things worse.

Soon, the sound of Jude's unhappy squawking rose from downstairs and Abi forced herself to get up. As she reached the bottom of the stairs, she heard Phil chatting merrily. 'All right, shall we have another? Goodness me, you're a reader like your mother.' There was the sound of movement across the room, followed by some rearrangement on the sofa. Abi pressed her back against the wall, out of view.

'All right,' Phil said. '*The Tale of Tom Kitten*. This *is* a favourite Jude, even if Beatrix Potter did go in for such a lot of smacking. Whose was this?' Abi heard the turning of pages. 'Ah, it doesn't say. Well, anyway. I expect it was Poll's.'

Abi's phone was in the pocket of her skirt and she drew it out, scrolling quickly until she found the recorder. She pressed it on just as Phil began reading in a voice rich enough for radio. 'Once upon a time there were three little kittens, and their names were Mittens, Tom Kitten, and Moppet. They had dear little fur coats of their own ...'

Abi could picture Jude nestled against Phil's side and she longed to be able to tuck in at Phil's other side.

'Let us climb up the rockery, and sit on the garden wall ...'

Phil paused. 'Perhaps we'll stop there, Jude. I forgot quite how long this one is.' After that, she sounded at a loss and Abi slipped the phone back in her pocket and signalled her coming with a cough. The scene was just as she'd pictured it, except Phil had her feet up, and Jude was curled in her lap. 'Abigail, you're awake. Come and sit, dear. You've had some sort of episode, I see.'

Abi sat opposite and slowly began. The swimming lesson, the endless crying, her flight to the pub, the terrible night out. Phil listened attentively, letting Jude play with her beads until he tried to reach them into his mouth and she peeled his fingers off and tucked them away in her blouse. 'Dear oh dear, Abigail. But why did you agree to a night out after all you'd been through?'

'I didn't even want to go but he was so keen. I said yes but I didn't realise he'd get so drunk.' A thought dropped whole into her mind and Abi heard herself continue, driven by the prize of being allowed back up to Brigitta's bedroom and not sent home. 'And then he got really angry for no reason.'

Phil's expression of concern compelled her to continue. 'He started to shake me, I didn't know what to do. So I ran.'

Phil gasped. 'Oh Abigail. I didn't think him capable of such wickedness.'

'Only when he drinks, which is a lot I suppose.' The lie had been told and now it was demanding reinforcement.

'Indeed? Well, I can only apologise. I've misjudged him.' Phil looked rattled as she stood and gave Jude to his mother.

Abi's cheeks burned, but it had been her only choice. This or returning alone to the flat. This or going back to Highside.

'Elaine brought Jude back this morning but she shouted at me as well,' Abi said. 'She said Stu was finished with me and they're going to take Jude on weekends.'

'This is all a scandal, Abigail. But we'll see about the weekend business.' Phil sounded more certain than she looked. 'And in the meantime, you'll stay here. Keep Briggy's room and do me a list of what you need from home. I'll get Noel to fetch it all down for you.'

'All right,' Abi said, gnawing on her thumbnail. 'Okay.'

65.

Eggs and soldiers

That evening, Phil prepared a supper of eggs and soldiers and set two places at the corner of the kitchen table. Jude was asleep on Freddie's cadet camp stretcher, set up in the corner of Brigitta's room and modified for safety with a rolled up quilt along each side. Phil had bathed him in the kitchen sink as Noel made trips in and out with essentials. Abi had hung around watching, uselessly checking her phone, and feeling increasingly peripheral each time Phil moved her out of the way to get to a drawer or locate a suitable towel. But each time she opened her mouth, the spectre of returning to Highside Circuit forced it shut again.

'Nursery supper, I thought, was in order,' Phil said, as she put Abi's meal down in front of her. Abi was sitting so low in her chair, her rounded shoulders were barely visible above the table. There was none of the usual spirit in Phil's voice. Abi stared down at the pretty egg cups, knowing she was the one who'd drained Phil of her energy. She looked up with wide, wet eyes. 'Phil, about Stu. We were having a row and I don't think he meant to ... he didn't. When I said he ...'

Phil raised a palm. 'I think I'm better out of specifics. There are always two sides to these things, but I'd rather have neither if you don't mind. Needless to say, you'll be here as long as you need.'

She dabbed the corner of her mouth with a napkin. 'I'm quite done in suddenly, I think I'll have to retire. You stay here, finish that, and things will feel much brighter in the morning.'

She patted Abi's shoulder as she passed by and left Abi alone in the desolate silence of the kitchen. All around her, the framed photographs, the mail pile, the Dutch Masters calendar. Once the prospect of being alone in here and able to study each piece one by one would have thrilled her, but now the sense of her own intrusion made her wish, for the first time, that she was back at Highside watching *Strictly* with Rae while Pat got up to light another Parliament off the gas hob. After lingering at the table for a time, Abi scraped her eggs into the bin. She'd eaten nothing since the oily wedges and her stomach was twisted with hunger. As she crept upstairs, she wondered if Rae felt like this all the time, hollow, emptied out. And whether you could come to like it.

* * *

Phil lay in bed swatting away each charge as it came. Entanglements. A magnet for strays. Brigitta had once accused her, in jest, of confusing people with projects and the unkind jibe repeated itself now. She could only imagine what they'd have to say about her giving refuge to the victim of a domestic knocking about. People's lives. People's awful, complicated lives.

Although in the past she had often picked up waifs and strays, they tended to be latchkey friends of her own children whose parents were off somewhere, too busy with their important jobs to be home buttering pikelets. Those who were truly down on their uppers were dispatched with a generous cheque in the Red Shield bucket and did not impinge upon her actual existence. Abi was a decent girl, clever and kind, who'd been dealt a heavy handful. But no matter how much Phil had enjoyed her company until now, the simple fact was it was all becoming too much. She heard Frederick's voice so clearly that she turned her face to his side of the bed. 'This isn't Pygmalion on the Point, Phyllida my love. I believe it's time to draw a line.'

Phil sat up and dug a pill out of her bureau. After sloshing it down with the dregs of last night's water, she picked up the phone and dialled Brigitta, feeling an urgent need for confession. To her shock, Brigitta picked up at the first ring.

'Oh,' Phil stuttered. She had no idea why she'd chosen to answer now after such ongoing resistance. 'Hello darling. I didn't expect to catch you. What time is it there? I'm so sorry, I didn't check.'

'Hello Mum. I don't know. Nine probably? There's a racket going on downstairs, but I'm hiding from Polly. Don't tell her, will you. She's working at home today and if I go down she'll have me rationalising her plastics drawer in a second. I've been lying here trying to send Toby *very* strong tea and toast messages with my mind, but he's clearly not receiving.'

As Brigitta spoke, Phil settled back into her pillow. That wonderful voice cascading out of the receiver, its pace and cackles and whispers made it clear Brigitta had no intention of wading into old hurts from her side, and things could simply start again from here if Phil so chose. What a good, good girl. Brigitta was really one of her own, Phil thought with an onrush on love. 'Oh darling, I *know*. Polly can be such a commandant. I'm reminded every time I'm forced to stoop over one of Domenica's revolting heaps and clutch it up in a polythene bag.'

'I'm sorry I haven't called, Mum. I know it's been far too long.'

'Briggy, not a word about it. I imagine you've been putting one foot in front of the other all these weeks, and I applaud you for it, darling. I'm just sorry you've had such a rotten time and that I couldn't be any help. Life can be a bugger and sometimes one can only wait it out.'

For a minute Phil considered redoubling her offer of asylum but decided against it and then, with a jerk, remembered Abigail somewhere downstairs. 'Meanwhile,' she went on, 'your mother's got herself into a frightful spot.'

'Have you? Well that makes me feel better. Go on.' Phil heard the rustle of Brigitta's bedclothes. She was settling in. 'You'll remember my little neighbour.'

'Abi, yes. With the baby and the cucumber soup.'

'Yes, well, I became rather involved, too involved one might say, in brokering a reunion between her and the boyfriend who had tried to bolt. It's ended badly and now I've accidentally, I think, possibly, let her move in.'

'What do you mean, possibly?'

'Insofar as I have, darling.'

Brigitta let out a torrent of laughter.

'It isn't funny, Briggy. I can't bear to be wounding, but I worry she's already very settled. I can only imagine what your father would say. The boyfriend may or may not be a bad egg, I can't quite get a handle on it.'

'Oh Mum.' Brigitta laughed again, although lovingly to Phil's ear. 'You were only being sweet. And don't you remember? Dad was such a hypocrite about your strays.'

'Pardon darling?' Brigitta was offering a recollection and Phil was hungry for it. She swapped the receiver to the other ear.

'Don't you remember when we kept getting the school magazine from Barker, and none of us went there? And when you phoned about it, it turned out Daddy was paying for Sharon's son to go through.'

'Oh yes, I'd forgotten. That sweet paralegal with the malingering husband. Goodness. People's lives, darling.'

'Mum, I can hear Polly. Do you mind if I hang up? I need her to think I'm asleep.'

'All right darling, of course. But while I think of it, perhaps we won't tell her about my current bind. Best not to give her another thing to tizz about, wouldn't you say?'

'Not a word. Although you will owe me.'

'I can't think how I'd ever repay you, darling. Goodbye.' Phil made a kiss into the receiver and hung up feeling infinitely restored.

66.

It won't be nice cold

Stu said he didn't want any but Elaine could not let his plate pass without spooning out a measure of mixed veg. She'd done three steam-in bags and even if he wasn't going to touch them, she'd be blessed if on top of everything else, they were going to eat from plates that lacked colour interest. All because of Abi.

'Mum, seriously.' Stu's elbows were planted on the table and his head was in his hands. It had been a job to get him off the loveseat after the terrible revelations that morning, when Elaine had come through in her dressing gown and found him lying with his knees drawn up to his chest, unresponsive. But it had all come out eventually, the sordid truth, and Elaine had used up half a roll of paper towel mopping her anguished tears.

Afterwards, he had disappeared into his room and stayed there all day, but now Elaine felt tea at the table would be an important stake in the ground. The Kellett family way would not be undone by Abi's machinations ... Gosh, it is a good word, she thought in spite of herself as she set down the Pyrex of veg and began tonging out the sausages. It had been Word of the Day on the subscription email a fortnight ago, and here she was, having used it twice in a single day. 'Roger, you'll be for a sausage. They're devilled.'

Obediently, Roger moved his plate towards the oven dish, but Stu refused to raise his head or lean back to accommodate the tongs as Elaine held a sausage towards him. 'Mum, I'm not hungry,' he said, which couldn't be true because he had always had a good appetite, even as a small baby. It had been a point of pride.

Elaine sighed and tried to insert the sausage through the narrow gap between his bowed chin and his plate. She could see he'd been crying and the sight of his swollen eyes was a dagger through her heart. If she could do nothing else, she could nourish his being with a low-sodium sausage from the Coles Own range.

'Fucksakes, Mum!'

Elaine gasped, and shot a look at Roger, who cleared his throat and said softly, 'Son.'

She glowered at him, tongs held out like a weapon, and Roger tried again. 'We know you're upset, but keep a watch on the language, eh chief?'

Stu lifted his face and conceded to a dollop of cheat's potato dauphinoise. No one ever guessed that the potatoes were microwaved first and simply sliced into a half cream–half sour cream mixture and given a light grilling. Satisfied for the time being, Elaine recovered the dish with foil and picked up her cutlery. 'Your father and I –'

'Mum, please don't.'

'We simply feel –'

Stu leaped up and fixed her with a look so hateful, her undercarriage actually spasmed in shock. The private sensation forced her to cover her mouth.

'How about we talk it out later, Laine,' Roger suggested anxiously. 'I think he just needs some time to think, for now.' He looked up at Stu. 'Mum is only trying to help, son.'

Stu slapped the table with an open hand, causing the cutlery to bounce noisily. 'No, Dad. She's not. She isn't. She never gave Abi a chance, even though she's actually a good person. Abi is,

I mean. She's a really decent girl and I loved her. But I've had Mum's drip-drip-drip fricking poison since the second she got here. What if I still love her? What if we're meant to be ...' Stu's face reddened and he left the thought to hang.

Elaine stabbed her sausage and began slicing it into rings with hands trembling. But as soon as she put the first meaty disc in her mouth, she realised Stu's accusation could not be left to lie. She was not a poison dripper! Elaine pressed a fingertip to her lips so neither of them would speak until she had swallowed. The truth had to be told.

'All I would say is that you are very young and if you made the decision ...' Elaine chose her words carefully '... if the decision was *made* that it was best to just move on, knowing as we now do that she can't be trusted ...'

Stu's eyes were growing wider and wider until Elaine felt he actually looked quite menacing. Bravely she persisted. 'I think you would find it's easier than you think to sever the ties and get back to your own life.' She set her cutlery down and, with her wrists resting on the edge of the table, held up two hands in surrender. 'There. That's all. I've said my piece.' No one spoke. 'You might even meet a lovely –'

'So, are you saying I should just move on from Abi, or forget Jude as well? Yeah, forget him. Let's forget him. He's only my son. Good thinking, Mum.'

Elaine looked at her husband balefully.

'What your mother means is ...' Roger began, before turning unexpectedly to Elaine. 'Love, I don't know. I don't know if it's as easy as all that.'

She listened aghast. They were ganging up on her! This is why women need daughters, Elaine thought. To always take their mother's side. She fiddled with the small pendant at her neck and stared at Roger in dumb fury, unsure whether she was about to scream or cry.

'Excuse me.' Stu stormed out of the room before she'd had a chance to do either. 'This is rooted. This is all totally rooted.'

A second later, they heard his bedroom door slam, rattling the glass-fronted china cabinet which sat just outside it. Elaine made a note to check *a-s-a-p* that none of the Lladro inside had been damaged.

'Well,' she said, when it was clear Roger wasn't going to be the one to break the unhappy silence. 'That was very upsetting.'

Although her appetite had faded, she slid her fork through the small mound of mixed veg and managed it into her mouth, chewing in silence as she waited for Roger to see sense. Abi had shown herself to be a calculating, premeditating ... Elaine couldn't think of a word in her vocabulary that could do it justice, whilst also being savoury. Anyway, she had shown her true self and Elaine only required an acknowledgement of that fact from either Stuart or Roger who, for no reason she could understand, was still not obliging her.

'He's had quite a shock,' he said finally. 'He's bound to be a bit emotional.'

'Of course. But it's our duty as his parents to help him keep going and begin to rebuild his life.'

Roger stroked his cheek. 'But you wouldn't want to lose contact with the little tacker, would you? Your only grandson.'

'Of course not,' Elaine said sourly. But if it came down to it, if she was made to choose between Stu and her grandson ... she terminated the thought. 'Of course not, but our first priority must be Stuart. He's our son, Roger. *He* is our son.'

'I suppose so. But still.'

'Will you eat this last sausage?' she said, lifting the tongs.

'I've done well, thanks dear.'

'I'll only have to put it in the bin if you don't. It won't be nice cold.'

'All right then.' Roger held out his plate.

'I hate waste.'

'I know, love,' he said, gamely beginning on the last sausage. 'I know you do.'

67.

Owing to my prostate

Phil found the days that followed Abigail's arrival severely testing. She clearly had no intention of leaving and having served her an open-ended invitation, Phil now found herself unable to broach the subject of future plans. Spring was usually her favourite time of the year, but a cloud overhung it.

The poor girl seemed content to spend entire days padding noiselessly about the house or playing half-heartedly with Jude in the garden. Occasionally she made efforts to be helpful around the house, inexplicably Hoovering only the stairs, or offering to make dinner if Phil could tell her what to cook. But being made to think was so much more enervating than scrambling an egg and being done with it.

In the evenings after Jude went to bed, Abigail would sit in the front room with her knees drawn up inside of her enormous jumper, sleeves hiding her hands, and stare at the garden barely visible beyond the dark windows. Although Phil was sorry to see her in such a state, her presence there also ruled out the prospect of anyone else watching *Q&A* with a glass of something. Even when Abigail took Jude out for a walk, Phil found that going about the little customs she had built into her own long days made her feel self-consciousness in her own home. And although she hated to be petty, there was also the fact that Jude was a much busier boy than before, now at that pulling up stage that means every cup of tea's got to be on a high shelf. As closely as Abigail supervised him, he had still managed to reach her lovely hand of coral off the coffee table and pull it onto the floor, breaking off the loveliest spines.

Eventually the question of Abigail's finances would also need to be addressed but Phil found herself putting the subject off, unable to decide whether giving her a little lump sum, or a temporary stipend, was a necessary kindness or an overstepping of things.

Yet, as unpleasant as it was to have a truly untethered human soul at one's own breakfast table, as much as she might have wanted to employ an entrenching tool, Phil found herself unable to give Abigail even the gentlest prod towards action.

The simple fact was that in all this time, not a single person had rung the mobile that never left Abigail's hand. Phil knew she was not hard enough to overlook the awful fact that, at this moment, Abigail had no one besides her. She spoke to no one and only very occasionally pecked out the odd text message, which Phil hoped was to a friend back home, but was more likely connected with the transfer of custody that now took place on weekends.

It began as threatened shortly after Abigail moved in, and although Phil wasn't party to handings-over, which took place on the neutral ground of the kiosk, it was awful to see Abigail return red-eyed and go straight up to Brigitta's room, where she stayed, doing goodness knew what, until Jude was given back on Sunday evenings. Phil felt hostage to it all, depressed and irritated, but until such a time as she felt able to bring about a resolution to the unsustainable arrangement, she could only up her quotient of outings, starting with much earlier jaunts to the kiosk when Abigail was reliably occupied with the baby's breakfast. The really vexing thing, Phil realised, was that she still somehow missed the prospect of running into Abigail there – the old order of things, another of her little compass points, had been lost. Now she could only depend on the presence of Noel and his newspaper.

After so many shared mornings together, he and Phil fell into a quiet rhythm of light conversation, followed by amiable silence as he read the obituaries in his paper, and she did all of the Quick and as much as she could be bothered of the Cryptic in hers.

Phil always hoped that by the time she got back, Abigail would have dragged herself out with the pram and Phil could enjoy an hour of proper solitude, even if it was overhung by the prospect of her return.

'Noel,' Phil said, one particularly warm October morning. She was restless and needed a fresh occupation. 'I'll tell you what. Let's make it a race of today's crozzie. Five minutes on the clock, and we'll see who fills in the most.' She bit the end of her pen – feeling oddly girlish – and started scanning the clues for Across.

Noel demurred with a polite laugh. 'Oh, I don't think so, Phil. I'm not a wordsmith like you.'

Irritated, Phil moistened a fingertip and turned to the stock prices.

'B-b-but, I had another funny thought,' Noel stammered. 'What would you say to getting a bit of dinner out one night? You and I. We could give that new one up at the junction a test run. I understand it's Asian fusion.' He looked at her helplessly for a moment, and then as her face set in an expression of concentrated neutrality, he dived for his coffee with such unusual vigour, Phil was forced to lean back to avoid him.

'Ah. Indeed.'

'I only thought, I've lost my Wilma and you've lost your Frederick and it can't hurt us to give each other company. Or, even *companionship*.'

Phil felt ill. 'Noel, you'll forgive me, but Frederick's passing was rather more recent and I would hate to … because there could be no question of any … perhaps it's best not to set out on that road.'

'Well, no, you're probably right,' Noel said, looking very hard at a near-passing skiff. 'You're right and I couldn't be any use to you in a, ah, connubial sense,' his eyes fell to his lap, 'owing to my prostate.'

Phi's flat white threatened to repeat on her and she pressed her fingertips to her lips. 'No, well, none of us are quite the specimens we once were. Oh look, is that really the time? I'm so sorry Noel, forgive me, I must get back to my charges.'

Noel rose as Phil did and for a split second, she feared he was planning a more intimate farewell.

'All right, well, good morning,' she said, scuttling up the ramp towards her home.

It was too much. How was one meant to move elegantly and privately through one's own grief journey when others kept inserting themselves into it? All the way home, Phil tried to force the distressing episode into an anecdote at least. She could recount it to Abigail, if they became short of talk at their next table supper. Phil could picture her though so clearly, it shocked when she looked ahead and saw Abigail running towards her from the other direction, clutching Jude who wore only a nappy.

68.

Brigga's Box of Sad Things

Abi tried her hardest not to get in Phil's way or knock into the skirtings with the Hoover, eat too much from Phil's cupboards, or let Jude cry. The pressure to be invisible was exhausting but better than the prospect of returning to the flat. And anyway, Abi told herself, she was good at waiting. Most of her life had been waiting although it was more difficult with nothing specific to wait for. Perhaps only the vague and unlikely possibility that someone would tell her what she was supposed to do next.

She learned every inch of Brigitta's room like an inmate learns his cell. One day while Jude napped on his stretcher, Abi looked through the contents of the wardrobe. Folded winter blankets, tennis racquets, a carton of old school blazers and then at the very back of the top shelf, she found a small Clarks shoebox with a square of paper sticky-taped to the lid. BRIGGA'S BOX OF SAD THINGS. DEFFINATELY NO LOOKING. There was nothing inside except an ancient tube of eczema cream with its lid crusted on. Abi held the box in her hands, feeling she could fill it without effort. Beginning with the small tragedy, which passed unnoticed by anyone except her and Jude, of having to stop feeding him because her supply failed after his first weekend away. Thawed milk administered by Elaine would be the last he ever had. Abi couldn't even turn to *First Year with Baby* for condolence. It hadn't made it into Noel's delivery of essentials, although she could recall the section on weaning that described it as the end of a unique symbiotic relationship, which could also bring late-onset PND and for further information turn to Chapter 12.

Next in would go the fact that Stu never called her or replied to any of her text messages. Elaine was her only point of contact with the family now. Abi had also discovered, almost immediately after arriving at the big house, that Stu had suspended the weekly payment he had been making to her bank account since his first retreat to Gordon. Did Elaine and Roger know that their son had cut her off? Worse, had they encouraged him in it? Either way, it seemed nobody at Gordon was giving concentrated thought to what she and Jude might be living on.

She had said nothing about it to Phil, but just as her balance sank into single figures, Phil emerged one morning from Frederick's study with a cheque and pressed it into her reluctant hand.

'I'm sure you know I don't go in for money talk,' Phil said before Abi could speak. 'However, I assume Stuart and his blasted parents are no longer of help to you fiscally. Let this tide you over until all the mess is cleared up. Although Abigail,' she added sternly, 'I can't promise funds of an ongoing nature.' With no other choice, Abi accepted it, waiting three days to push the pram up to the bank and deposit the inconceivable sum of one thousand dollars.

There would be no more university study, of course, now that Phil was housing her, feeding her and funding her. Accepting another round of fees would be unthinkable, if it was even offered, and she could not spend her own scant funds on anything indulgent. Besides which, Abi knew Elaine would no longer be willing to look after Jude.

As she sat cross-legged on the carpet beside Jude's stretcher, stroking his head and listening to his gentle breathing, Abi imagined pressing it all into the Box of Sad Things and closing the lid.

* * *

Phil went out a lot and it was only then that Abi let herself wander more freely through the house, sometimes taking Jude out to the garden, sometimes standing in front of the fridge and shovelling in as many spoonfuls of cold leftovers as she could without making a visible dent in the container's contents. Occasionally the phone would ring. Phil did not have an answering machine because she believed they were apt to encourage waffling, and Abi would stand rooted to the spot until it rang out.

One morning, after she heard Phil leave, she took Jude and his plastic bowl of breakfast out to the garden. A feeling of reprieve came with feeding him on grass rather than over Phil's floor.

It was warmer that day than it had been in months, and the new tropical scent that filled the air carried her back to her first days in Sydney. So as not to prevail on Phil's top loader, Abi removed his little T-shirt and shorts and began spooning Weetabix and banana into his open mouth.

Jude held his arms above his head and bounced excitedly up and down between mouthfuls. Abi knew she should talk to him, but cheerful commentary was beyond her at the minute. Instead she sang a few tuneless bars of something made up. There was the pool, she thought idly, as she waited for Jude to receive the next mouthful. But without the prospect of finding Phil there, the effort involved did not seem worth it. As she scraped around the edges of the bowl, she heard the phone ring from the kitchen. After a time, the ringing ceased but seconds later began again. The pattern repeated itself again and again. 'Should we get that,

Jude? Do you think?' She stroked his thickening mop of hair out of his eyes.

When another cycle began, Abi got up and walked slowly to the back door, hoping she would miss it. But as she entered the dark kitchen, the cordless was still vibrating in its cradle and warily, she picked it up. 'Hello? Um. Woolnough residence?'

'Who's this?' said a woman whose voice hovered on the edge of hysteria. 'Where is Phil?'

'It's Abi. From next door? She isn't here. Can I take a message?' Abi shifted Jude to her other side and began looking around for a pen.

'Where is she? This is her daughter. I need her right away. It's an emergency.'

'Oh, is that you Brigitta?' There was a red ballpoint in the fruit bowl, and Abi yanked the lid off with her teeth.

'What? No, it's Polly. It's extremely urgent. Extremely urgent!'

Abi spat the lid out. 'I think she might be on a walk. I could go and find her for you and she could ring back.'

'There's been an accident,' Polly said with an emphasis that seemed to imply Abi was being purposely obstructive. 'A bad accident. *Go*. Go and find her, now please. Get her to call me straight away. *Now*.'

Abi said a hasty goodbye, threw the phone on the table and ran as fast as she could in the direction of the kiosk, Jude bouncing on her hip.

As she came around a bend, she saw Phil ambling beneath a tree that had exploded with purple blooms and rained its petals down on her, so that she appeared like some sort of religious vision. Abi quickened her pace until she was within hearing and started calling out, 'Phil, Phil! Something's happened.'

'Settle down, I can't understand a word you're saying.' It was obvious Phil was expecting an emergency in the order of mashed banana on one of her Persians.

'There's been an accident, Phil. The phone kept ringing and I answered it and it was Polly. She sounded a bit hysterical.'

'What is it? What did she say?'

'She didn't. She just said you have to phone her straight away.'

Phil hastened towards the house, basket battering her side. She puffed and heaved and demanded details from Abi, who ran beside her, crab-wise, struggling with Jude and insisting she knew nothing.

As soon as they were inside, Phil snatched up the phone and Abi found herself dithering by the back door, unsure whether to pass through or stay or disappear back out it, as Phil began a frantic exchange with her daughter. Abi could hear rapid speech on the other end, and watched confusion and fear and horror and pain pass across Phil's face.

'Oh,' she said at one point, staggering backwards towards a kitchen chair. As fast as she could, Abi set Jude down where she stood and dashed over to steady the chair.

'Oh Polly. Polly, no,' Phil could barely breathe. 'Polly, no. What do they say, what are the doctors saying? How soon until someone can get there?'

For a second, Abi considered putting a hand on Phil's shoulder, but she didn't dare. Instead, she picked Jude up off the floor and retreated upstairs. The pitch of Phil's voice could be heard from below, and Abi listened for any clue as she arranged Jude on the camp stretcher for an early sleep, patting him until his eyelids drooped and he let his face turn to the side.

In the absence of detail, Abi's imagination threw up one terrible scenario after another. One of the grandchildren had been killed. Brigitta had been hit by a black cab. They were all dead and only Polly was left. Even as she worried for Phil, a small, terrible part of her sensed opportunity, and she punished herself for the thought with a painful bite down on her thumb.

When the voice below died away, Abi snuck downstairs and found Phil still in the kitchen chair, with the cordless in one hand and a disintegrating tissue in the other. Somehow, the top button of her blouse had come undone, exposing a wedge of flesh-coloured lace, and one side of her hair was standing up. 'What's happened?'

Phil did not turn to look at her but explained in a wavering voice that Freddie had been in a motorbike accident. 'He's in Goa. The hospital only just tracked us down and he is already in surgery.'

Abi couldn't think where Goa was. The last envelope she had posted on Phil's behalf was addressed to some sort of hostel in Laos.

'No one is able to say if he was riding it or got hit by it. Briggy's trying to get a flight out but she's a day away at the very least. Polly is demanding I stay put until we know more. She's got Mark phoning the hospital but no one is giving proper information. He was responsive when they brought him in,' Phil's voice shredded, 'but what does that mean, Abigail? I must know what that means!'

Abruptly, she got up, and before leaving the room with phone in hand, she fixed Abi with a fierce stare. 'I will not lose another child, Abigail. Do you understand that? I will not.'

* * *

The phone continued to ring throughout the day, and Abi heard Phil speaking as she went about minding Jude, tidying up a bit and letting Domenica in and out. Occasionally Phil would appear in the doorway, looking anxious or grave, and share whatever new piece of information she had received.

'He's coming around from the anaesthetic, but we won't know the outcome of the surgery for hours more. But he is talking. Apparently,' Phil wrapped a hand around her throat. 'It's impossible to get good information.'

'Well that's good,' Abi said, weakly. 'I mean, not good about the information. But good he's out of the operation. Can I get you anything? To eat, or anything?'

'No, I don't think so.' Phil disappeared to the front room but called out again after a moment. 'Actually Abigail, two of the fizzy aspirin, would you please.'

Abi found them in the knife drawer and dissolved two in a big glass of tap water.

'Oh,' Phil said, accepting the heavy tumbler. 'You've made quite a summer drink out of it.' And then more kindly, 'I realise I'm glad not to be alone at this moment, Abigail. Brigitta will be on the ground by the morning and then I shall make preparations to fly out as soon as I can.'

69.

Is she a wreck?

Phil spent the next day in a whirl of useless activity, willing the phone to ring and waiting to hear if Brigitta had landed. By late afternoon, her inability to sit even for a moment had worn her out and she took herself upstairs for a rest. 'Afterwards, I will start packing. You must come and fetch me if the phone rings.'

Abi set Jude up on the kitchen floor with a set of plastic measuring cups and sat with him while he put them all in a bowl and tipped them out again. When the phone rang, she leaped up to answer it.

'Is that you, Abi? It's Brigitta. Can you put Mum on?' There was an echo on the line and Abi could hear her own voice come back with a delay.

'She's just gone upstairs for a rest. Do you want me to go and get her?'

'No, don't. Let her kip. Is she a wreck?'

'Um, she's quite restless. She really wants to get her ticket booked.'

'I'm sure. But, Abi, listen, it's not a good idea. I've just arrived and Freddie's out of danger, apparently, but he looks incredibly rough, and I don't think we should let her put herself through it. Not this soon after Dad. He's got a tonne of stitches and this hospital is incredibly hectic. Not the cleanest you've ever seen either. She'd hate it, and if she goes to bits, which let's be honest is a fairly sure thing, her being here won't help Freddie at all.'

Brigitta went on to explain that now that his internal injuries had been seen to, the shattered leg would be dealt to with an assortment rods and pins. 'And they haven't fixed his front teeth yet,' she added as an afterthought. Abi heard a heavy sigh. 'He'll be all right,' Brigitta went on, 'but for now he's a mess. Not to put you on the spot or anything, but since you're the one with her, it would be great if you steered her away from the idea of coming. To reinforce what Polly and I will tell her.'

'Yes, I can try, definitely.'

'You're such a good one, Abi. Mum can be bloody hard work. We Woolnoughs are lucky to have you on the team.'

Without wanting to sound pleased, Abi thanked her and hung up, writing down the key pieces of information on a notepad. If Phil was cross she hadn't been woken as asked, Abi would say Brigitta told her not to.

In the week that followed, Abi began to feel indispensable. She made up trays and took them through to the front room where Phil had set up her headquarters. She removed untouched cups of tea, plumped sofas, spritzed the cymbidiums in the courtyard, minding not to wet the leaves as per instructions.

Whenever it came up, Abi tried to temper any talk of Phil's flying out to see Freddie, until Phil frogmarched her to Frederick's study and stood behind her while she looked up flights. Feeling it would be what Brigitta wanted, Abi said the system wouldn't accept her booking. 'Well then, I will have to get Mark to arrange it with an old-fashioned travel agent. It's maddening, Abigail! I feel as though I'm losing my mind.'

When the weekend came, Abi walked Jude to the kiosk and dutifully handed him off to Elaine, who was waiting at the top of

the ramp. On the way back, as always, Abi let herself weep for
the loss of him until she got to the sandstone escarpment that
signalled halfway, then wiped her eyes and walked more briskly to
the house. As she let herself in the side gate, she saw Phil standing
outside the kitchen door, shaking so violently that the phone she'd
been holding had dropped to the ground and lay there now with its
batteries scattered across the brickwork.

70.

A dead-set waste of time

There was nothing to do with a baby in Gordon. The one playground within walking distance was a depressing seventies situation with a tin slide that you could fry an egg on by 10 a.m.

Summer wasn't even in full swing, but whenever Stu tried to take Jude for a walk in the crappy pram Elaine had been thrilled to find at Bubs on a Budget behind Turramurra station, he would forget the hat and suncream and within minutes, Jude would start to look a bit scorched and they'd have to turn back.

Stu struggled with it being just the two of them. Elaine handled the bulk of the baby care for the fortnight after he moved back to Gordon for good, having been fucked over by the girl he thought he loved. At the time, it was hard enough just getting out of bed. There was no reason to once he'd resigned from the pub via text message and Roger had taken it onto himself to phone the Dean of Architecture and arrange compassionate leave. Stu didn't care about uni anymore. Sitting around drawing a bunch of buildings that would never get built felt like a dead-set waste of time now, all things considered.

And all the time Elaine shadowed him around the house, checking, suggesting, trying to press devon sandwiches upon him. Even when she wasn't home, Stu felt her presence in every rearrangement of his Lynx bottles and appearance of a pamphlet about a local counselling service on his desk, even though until then, he'd been led to believe Kelletts didn't go in for 'new age mumbo jumbo'.

Then as the first shock of discovering Abi had hid her pregnancy began to subside, Stu noticed that Jude would reach for Elaine instead of him whenever he had the choice. Against every instinct to go back to bed for the rest of his life, he decided to raise his game.

So far, though, the abortive walks were all he could think of to do with a baby. There was never anyone else out walking in the wide suburban backstreets. The only signs of life were the wet driveways recently hosed clear of leaves, and enormous wheelie bins that appeared at certain times of the week, as if by magic.

Every week that he had spent back at Gordon since Abi let him go the first time, every night he'd gone to sleep in his childhood bedroom, had made him feel like even more of a coward, an even worse father, and so, so lonely. Lonelier than he'd ever been in his life. Now that he was back for good, Stu began to despise the suburbs. All those stupid Klugers, the mums doing a big shop in their tennis gear, the teenager who turfed the *North Shore Times* over the fence as he rode past on his bike. Whenever he saw a copy crisping up on the grass, there'd be a fat schoolkid on the cover holding a certificate. Elaine still had his, framed and hung in her sewing corner. *Stuart Kellett, Year Eight, Gordon Boys High School. Bronze Duke of Edinburgh*. Fuck the leafy upper North Shore and the postie bike it rode in on. Fuck it all.

Stu wanted to go home. But home wasn't here. It wasn't the flat. It was Abi. Even when he wasn't trying, he could see her kneeling on the bathroom floor swishing Jude in two inches of warm water and cooing at him. Curled up asleep on the pull out, all the busy, nervy energy wrung out of her by a long day. Perched in the corner of the kitchen bench in undies and one of his T-shirts, dropping her lit fag out the window the moment he walked in, saying with a hoarse laugh, 'Shit. Sorry. That was my last one, definitely.' One day she'd be responsible for Cremorne Point's first bushfire.

Still, no matter how pretty or funny she was, how much of a nice mum who never lost her rag with Jude and made lasagnes with eight creamy layers, no matter that she'd seemed so sweet at the start, it turned out she was a player and he'd been had. Yet, every night before he switched off the light, Stu took a drawing block and pencil out of his bag and tried to sketch Abi, from memory.

'Draw me like one of your Croydon girls.' He'd watched *Titanic* since then. A bit long, but he liked it, mostly because of her.

And now, another featureless Saturday afternoon. Stu returned from an eight-minute walk and registered with relief that the Daihatsu wasn't in the drive. He left the pram outside the conservatory doors and carried Jude inside. Roger was sitting at the table, trying to fix the garage door opener with a delicate screwdriver. He set it down when he saw them enter and gave them a warm nod.

'Hey,' Stu said.

'I'm just trying to fix this doodackie,' Roger said. 'How are you, Stuart?'

'Did Mum make you ask?' Stu asked, regretting it as soon as he saw embarrassment pass across Roger's face. His father was not his enemy. 'Sorry, Dad. Yeah, I'm all right. Bored shitless, but all right. Wait one sec, Jude needs to go down and I'll be back.'

Stu changed Jude's heavy nappy on his bed and laid him down in a travel cot that Elaine had originally set up in her sewing corner and Stu had since relocated to his own room. If Jude cried in the night, Stu wanted to be the one who heard him. What if he was missing his mum and couldn't say so? When the thought first occurred to him, Stu felt so overcome with sadness for Jude that he considered chucking the whole weekend set-up and letting Abi keep him all the time. She had a way with him and Stu knew in his gut that the constant separation would be killing her.

Stu wiped the dummy Jude liked for sleeping on his jeans and plugged it into his mouth. Jude's wide, dark eyes fixed on Stu and he smiled. The dummy fell out. Stu put it back in. Jude giggled and let it go again. It was a brilliant game, and Stu played along until he felt like that would probably be enough for the time being. Some of the baby stuff was really boring. He patted Jude lightly on the head, and left the room.

Roger was screwing the casing back on the garage door opener, looking pleased.

'Want a drink, Dad?' Stu asked

'No thanks, chief. I'm as right as rain.'

Stu took a Solo from a section of the fridge that was now continuously stocked with the food and beverages he'd liked most as a child and was meant to find irresistible still. Kraft singles, cabanossi, Wagon Wheels. And Grandma Jenny's Microwaveable Self-Saucing Puddings, Flavour Selection. Elaine must have seen them at the flat although they were actually Abi's favourite. And she'd been right about them, Stu thought. One in four always was a dry one.

* * *

Roger watched his son cross the kitchen and crack open his fizzy drink. Theirs wasn't a relationship built on sharing per se, but Roger longed to ease his son's anguish in anyway he could. 'But hey listen,' he said, 'you're welcome to come and sit with your dad and shoot the breeze.'

Stu looked sceptical. 'Yeah, I don't know. Are you sure Mum didn't put you up to it?'

Roger felt the sting of humiliation. It was true, Elaine had asked him more than once to try and 'engage with Stuart', but the offer now was his own idea, with no express motive.

'No, no. Just father and son. And not everything has to get back to your mum, if I can say that with love.'

Stu plonked himself in a chair, finished his can and threw it towards the sink. It missed, but it was very close. 'Want to know the most fucked up bit, Dad?'

Roger winced. He did, if not in those terms.

'The most fucked up bit is I miss her. I can't stop thinking about her, even though she's been lying to me from the get-go.'

Privately, Roger was upset by the assumption that a termination would have been the unquestioned course of action had he known about the pregnancy sooner. Even Elaine had echoed the sentiment once and Roger had been so disturbed he'd had to go outside and vacuum both cars.

But Stu was opening up and Roger held his tongue. 'All that, and here I am still constantly thinking, maybe it will be okay somehow. Maybe we can fix it.' Stu's hand formed a fist, and with genuine force, he thumped himself in the side of the head.

'Don't do that, love. It's all right. It's okay. I understand!'

Stu looked at his father with so much pain in his eyes Roger needed to grip the fabric of his trouser legs under the table. 'The thing is, Dad, I would never have made her have an abortion anyway. Never. But she'll never know that now, will she? Her life's been sad enough already, with her dad and that.'

'You're a good man, Stuart.' The admission so elated him, he was able to let his trousers go. 'And for what it's worth, even though obviously Abi has one or two issues around, ah, communication, she's a really great girl.' He glanced over at the loveseat, where their nice conversation about American toilets had taken place many months before. 'None of us can say why people do the things they do, until we've walked a mile in their shoes.' Roger cleared his throat. 'And perhaps I wouldn't necessarily say this to Mum as yet, but it doesn't *have* to be over. Not if you don't want it to be.'

Stu was listening. Scowling yes, but listening, and Roger started to feel audacious. 'Have a scratch around, Stu. There might be other reasons for what she's done. I don't think malice was one of them. Just, don't rule out giving her another chance. Even if it's just for Jude's sake.'

Stu dropped his head into his hands. 'Maybe. I dunno. Maybe.'

'Keep an open mind. That's all I'm saying.'

From the other room, they heard Jude announce the end of his short nap with a series of happy screams.

'I'll go and get him, son. You stay there. We're good mates, Jude and I.' In his mind, Roger was planning on being called 'Pa-pa.'

71.

You've been such a trooper

As was now the norm, Brigitta had phoned Mark, who notified Polly, who called Phil, now standing in the courtyard stunned. Abi crouched to gather up the phone batteries. 'Briggy says police have been to the hospital, questioning Freddie. Apparently there was also a girl on the back of the bike who had a number of illicit substances in her system. Her father is some sort of diplomat and he's decided to go after Freddie. Mark is on his way out to relieve Briggy, who I hope will come here. Or Polly will. Or I may go there. Certainly I will go there.'

Abi suggested they go inside and have a cup of tea and then she'd be more able to think. Too agitated to sit, Phil paced the kitchen with her hands on her head, as if she was going mad.

When Phil ran out of catastrophic scenarios, all of which she believed were sure things, her attention returned to Abi. 'Either way, dear, grateful as I am for your recent ministrations, when my children arrive every bed will be needed. And at such a time as this, they will expect it to be family only. Of course you understand. You've been such a trooper, Abigail. I'm sure I'd have starved myself to death were it not for your saving trays!'

It was already settled, Abi knew, and she made no move to protest.

'I wonder, in fact, if I haven't overworked you,' Phil carried on. 'You look awfully tired. A few days back in your own home ought to be just the ticket.'

It was clear to Abi then that Phil had forgotten the reason she had first come, so that cushion plumping and having her stairs Hoovered no longer seemed like sufficient reason to have her there.

'I'll just get our things,' Abi said as evenly as she could. 'And I'll be going. Thank you for having us.' Only because it was true, she added, 'It was like a bit of holiday for me.'

'Oh, I didn't mean this *instant*,' Phil said, but she did not move to put Abi off.

'That's okay. It won't take a minute,' Abi said as she turned and scurried upstairs.

* * *

When Abi came back down with their things hastily packed, Phil was sitting on the edge of the sofa with her glasses on and a thick leather contacts book open on her lap. She glanced to where Abi hovered on the threshold. 'You're off then. It's not goodbye of course, dear, as you'll only be up there after all. Thanks again for so many kindnesses.'

With a silly saluting gesture she would regret all afternoon, Abi slipped out of the room.

Although half expecting to find the locks changed, Abi's key turned in the door.

The flat hummed with its own emptiness. The hot, stale air suggested neither Stu nor Elaine had let themselves in during her many days away.

Someone had shoved old mail under the door, and as she knelt down to sort it, her eyes fell on an envelope with a British stamp. She tugged it out. It was addressed to her but had been on a journey of redirection, the postcode missing and the flat number unreadable. Inside was a single page of airmail paper, lightly scented with Parliament smoke.

Abi love, I know I said I'd always be around to keep an eye on your Mum but I've not been well – chesty – so I'm moving in with my son owing to the leg – he's in Leicester – I've sold my house to a very nice family of Islamics – she wears the scarf – I'm very sorry but I know you'll understand – Although, Abi love – truth be told – I have got my worries about our Rae – we both know what she's like – hanging onto a bit of tat and the like – I think she misses you more than she'd be letting on – so perhaps you'll think about coming back at some point – I've put meals up in the freezer but I'm sorry to say the ones you left for her were still in there and I had to throw them out – sorry Abi love – I would have phoned you but Rae couldn't put her hand on your number – all the best – Your friend always, Pat.

It was dated from a fortnight ago. Abi read it through again, found her plastic lighter and let it burn in the kitchen sink. There was no need to write back. Rae was going to hang on forever, and whenever Abi returned she knew what she would find.

72.

And crisps

Polly told the driver to wait while she ran into the school's after-care centre. They had less than an hour to get to Heathrow, which at this time of day was almost guaranteed to take much longer.

Mark had touched down in India twenty-four hours ago, and by calling in a lifetime of favours, pulling strings by the handful and roping in every imaginable crony and high-up, was beginning to make strides towards shutting down the threat of a civil suit, now that the police charges had been dropped. Freddie's blood wasn't taken on the scene, and there was no way, Mark was sure, that a test could be done retrospectively.

According to one or two questionable witness statements, Freddie had not been driving erratically but had hit a dog, and the impact had thrown the girl off the motorcycle. She had been wearing a helmet and walked away better off than Freddie although a laceration on her right cheek would mean she might not work again since she was – Polly learned without surprise – a model.

As soon as the accident happened, Polly started handing off as many cases as she could to colleagues. All of them, she knew, had followed her sister's scandal in the paper, although none were game to admit it. But now the senior partners were starting to make noises about her 'eventful' family life. They'd been lenient after her father's unexpected death almost a year ago. But now a request for unpaid leave to attend to another unspecified drama? Another absence was granted but there would be no more talk of partnership.

Polly felt her innards clench as she punched in the centre's entry code and stepped into the lobby, which was plastered with children's artwork. Immediately inside, she saw Max and Toby sitting obediently on a bench, wearing their schoolbags and holding each other's hands. She wanted to scoop them up, one in each arm, and weep into their hot little heads, but instead she scrawled her name in the sign-out book and dragged them towards the waiting cab, without pausing when Toby dropped his packet of cards.

'Come on, leave them,' she said in a cross voice he clearly considered her usual tone. 'Please, darling,' she said more softly. 'Could you please be sweet and come, and I'll buy you some more at the airport. Any sort you like. If you'll just hurry.'

He followed in scampering half-steps and dived into the car after his brother. 'And crisps. You can even have crisps,' Polly added as an afterthought, in case a bag of Cheesy Wotsits from Smiths could make her a fun mother.

She had a change of clothes for each of them in her carry-on and had planned to shower them in the Qantas lounge, but at this rate, they'd be flying twenty-six hours around the world in their junior school sports uniforms.

Mark would follow her once all the loose ends were tied off. Thank God he could work from anywhere in the world, Polly thought not for the first time, or the Woolnough troubles would have ruined them twice over by now. Brigitta and Freddie were making their own way back, whether together or separately was yet to be decided, on the basis of his recovery.

And in the meantime, Polly would keep her mother company and bring an end to the business of the girl from the flats who had, according to Brigitta, insinuated herself nicely into their mother's life.

Polly's jaw tightened, and she checked her bag for the half pill she'd put in for the night portion of the flight. As the car joined the traffic grinding along the Talgarth Road, she handed the boys a Nintendo each and rested her head against the window, watching the rows of dilapidated terrace houses, blackened with exhaust, pass by outside. Polly could not let herself think about the long flight ahead – the exhausting change of planes, the tangle of legs and headphone cables, knocked-over cups and the need to shepherd a suddenly-busting child out of their seat without waking a suddenly-sleeping one. For a moment, she felt like crying. But tears were a luxury of the weak, and somebody needed to be the strong one.

73.

Hosing the green bin

'It was all comings and goings outside Phil's this morning,' Noel said brightly, as he put a coffee in front of Abi and sat down. Under a cloudy sky, the harbour was flat and unshifting. Foamy scum had gathered around the pylons of the wharf. There was no breeze. 'I was hosing the green bin and saw her oldest girl arrive with two little ones. That'll be nice for Phil, after everything she's been through.'

'It will,' Abi said quietly. 'It will be so nice.' She had witnessed the same scene from her bedroom window. The drawing up of a huge airport car, Phil appearing at the side door and dashing out to enfold a woman who must've been Polly, and then two boys, in a long embrace on the nature strip. The two women walked back in with arms linked, leaving the driver to unload four matching black cases. From the kitchen, Abi had watched the boys run outside and onto the grass, wrestling and spinning and falling over in fits of laughter, until Polly appeared to call them inside.

Abi came down to the kiosk after that, hoping for company that would help her through to the moment of Jude's return late in the afternoon. Elaine had requested to have him for the day, his attendance being required at the St Luke's Nans and Tots Tea.

Noel was the only one still there, Valentina now off speedwalking, he said, and Barb and Sandy on their way to an exhibition of gouache paintings from the original Kama Sutra. Thinking about how much Phil would have enjoyed a nugget like that made Abi feel freshly miserable.

'There's nothing like having the kids home,' Noel said. 'I expect they'll go up to Palmy, stay through to the weekend.'

'Right, yeah,' Abi said. 'What's Palmy actually?'

'Palm Beach, love. The Woolnoughs have a house up there. Lovely spot actually. Wilma and I used to take the boat up whenever we got the chance.'

Abi's attention drifted as Noel told a lengthy anecdote about having to call the coastguard one Australia Day because of a dicky rudder. 'What about you, Abi love? Busy one, is it?'

'Definitely,' Abi said. 'Mega-ly busy.'

'Well, I suppose we ought to push off,' Noel said, draining his cup. 'The knees give me grief when I sit for too long.'

They walked companionably along the path until Noel peeled off and Abi walked the rest of the way alone.

Noel's hunch was correct. Later in the afternoon, Abi witnessed Polly packing the Volvo. Phil appeared outside in a white shirt dress, holding the hand of each boy. Abi watched them get in, one by one, Polly in the driver's seat. A moment later, the car backed out and the house relaxed into stillness. Now, in her mind, Abi could wander through the empty rooms, recalling every detail. Freely she'd walk by the window seat, study the clustered paintings, every framed photo and vase on a sill, the plumped cusions of the velvet sofa.

Abi checked the time. Nearly an hour before Jude would be brought back. With nothing else to do, she thought about how nice it would be to slip in the side gate and pass the time in Phil's garden. Or, with a book from Phil's shelves, take the carpeted stairs up to Brigitta's room and read it between the starched sheets. But no, she thought, that's mad. She'd never do that, even as into her mind came the picture of the key in the planter so clear and exact, it made her hands tingle with the sensation of feeling around for it.

* * *

The Volvo was passing through Avalon when Toby realised that the one-eared Garfield he needed for sleeping was next to the basin in Granny's upstairs bathroom. Polly tightened her hands around the steering wheel. 'Well we can't turn around for it now, Toby. We're nearly there. You'll have to be brave and go to bed without it.'

'I can't!' Toby pleaded. 'Mum, I can't! I'm not brave!'

Max snickered, sending his brother into floods and causing Phil to whip around from the passenger seat. 'I heard that, Max. Don't be cruel.' Turning back to Polly, she said, 'Pidge, really, why don't you dump us at the house and whiz back for it? The boys and I will have a lovely time and you'll have a moment to decompress, darling. Call Mark, have a bath, you'll still be back by teatime.'

And so it was that very late in the afternoon, Polly returned to Milson Road.

74.

Up and down the
highway like a yo-yo

'I've been wondering if it isn't time to sell the unit,' Elaine said, receiving a cup of tea from Roger. She had just managed to get Jude down in the travel cot, after a successful morning tea at St Luke's, during which she'd managed to deflect three pointed inquiries about the imminence of wedding bells, per Stuart and Abi.

'What? You mean Milson Road?'

Elaine pursed her lips, by way of confirmation. 'It's the drive. It will be the end of me, Roger. I'm up and down the highway like a yo-yo. And then the handovers themselves are so draining. Jude gets very unsettled and of course it falls to me to soothe him.'

'I don't mind doing the run up and back with the little man. I thought you said you preferred to though. And we've never talked about selling the unit before.'

Elaine took a careful sip of tea and returned her cup noiselessly to the saucer. 'We'd get a fortune for it. I know that much. We could buy a wonderful investment property nearer here, and rent it to a nice family. We'd get four or five bedrooms for the same money.'

Roger felt as though he was being presented with a riddle. 'But what about Abi, in the meantime?'

'I haven't thought about that yet,' Elaine said. 'Well, I have. But not for hours *and hours*. I just don't think we're duty-bound to house her for all eternity now that she's finished with Stuart. I think three months' notice would be perfectly reasonable, given everything.'

Roger loved his wife. He loved her very much. But sometimes he felt that he must be misunderstanding her because surely she'd never suggest they put Abi out of the flat?

But more and more of late, she was saying things that could actually be taken as quite unkind.

He'd been so sure that by now she would have come around to Abi. He loved having a daughter in his life all of a sudden and Elaine had so often said 'I never got my girl, Roger, I never got my girl,' he'd assumed she'd be the same. Ever since Stuart had gone off to kindy and they'd officially decided to stop 'trying' and just be happy, it had been her reason for never actually being happy. Roger had accepted it, but now here Abi was, alive and kicking, and everything had stopped making sense.

75.

You don't look Korean

Automatically, Polly reached into the planter for the door key. When her hand didn't find it, she used the one on the Volvo key ring. There was a pair of worn-out ballet flats by the back door, which looked far too small for her mother's famously broad feet, Polly thought as she worked the lock and stepped inside. It was dark and quiet except for the low hum of the fridge and the tick, tick of a dripping tap. She picked up the cordless and dialled Mark's hotel.

While she waited for an answer, Polly made a loop of the front room in case Garfield wasn't where Toby had said. Her mother's deep velvet sofa stretched out invitingly. Although it was so large, Polly was reminded of what a nice house it was to be in alone, wandering through the rooms as you liked, popping upstairs to nose through a cupboard or two. Polly turned up a few cushions. No Garfield.

'Hello, Poll,' said Mark's faraway voice. 'Really good timing. I've been on all night with a guy at the High Commission and we could have all the docs together by next week. Then as soon as we get sign-off from the orthopod, he'll be clear to fly out. It'll have to be first class because of the knee, but that's no surprise somehow.'

'Put it on the tab,' they said in unison.

'You sound tired, Polly. How is Phil?'

'She's all right,' Polly said, mounting the stairs.

Mark started to explain a new detail of the settlement he was arranging with the father of the injured girl, but as Polly reached the landing, she heard a muffled thud from the far end of the hall. Like something knocking against glass, or a drawer closing.

'Hang on, Mark, I think a bird might have got inside.'

She held the phone away from her ear and took quiet steps down the hall. The sun was low in the sky, and through the dormer window, a shaft of yellow light caught the motes of dust.

As Polly opened the door to Brigitta's room, the sound came again. Clearer this time. Polly realised it was coming from further along the hall.

'Mark,' she whispered, 'There's someone here. Stay on, would you?'

She heard him say something about leaving right away and ringing the police, but Polly's hand was already wrapped around the handle of her mother's door. It opened with a faint click. Polly put one eye to the gap, then threw it open so sharply the handle on the other side slammed against the wall with a crack.

'Who the fuck are you?'

'Darling? Darling?' said Mark's distant voice from the phone.

She'd never laid eyes on the girl who was standing barefoot in the middle of the carpet, with a strand of amber beads in her hands. But now Polly realised she knew exactly who the girl was, from a description Brigitta had once given. The sparrow shoulders, the unusually luminous skin. Thin legs that, just then, seemed to be knocking together.

As Polly strode into the room, the girl backed away towards Phil's tall dresser, where she dropped the beads into an open drawer.

Polly's voice came out as a snarl. 'What are you doing up here?'

'I'm the cleaner,' the girl stammered. 'I'm just the cleaner.'

'My mother's cleaner is a Korean man. You don't look Korean to me. Would you like to try again?' Then into the phone, she said, 'Mark, are you hearing this? Are you getting this, Mark?'

'I'm sorry, I'm sorry,' the girl cried. 'I thought your mum might have gone away and I wanted to make sure someone was coming over to feed Domenica. And then I heard the door and … I'm sorry.'

'Who the fuck is Domenica?'

'Phil's dog?'

'My mother's dog is called Sophie,' Polly said very slowly. 'And I would love to know why you know so much about *Phil* when she has never, ever mentioned you.' That part wasn't true, but Polly felt herself on a roll.

'Yes, no, she just calls her Domenica Regina because she has a regal bearing and …' The girl looked wretched and abandoned her attempt to clarify.

'You will leave now. And I will make absolutely sure, I will make it my *job* to ensure that you never see or speak to my mother again. This family is in crisis and the last thing we need is the involvement of *outsiders*. You are not welcome here, whatever you've been led to believe, and if you are ever caught in here again, I will take the matter to the police.'

Polly stood to one side. Obediently, the girl passed by her towards the stairs. Polly marched behind her and could not resist making a few legal-sounding comments to Mark in the girl's hearing.

At the back door, Polly grabbed her by the wrist. 'Hang on a minute. How did you even get inside?'

The girl looked ready to bolt, but when Polly let her go she reached into her pocket and took out the key that would no longer, Polly decided then and there, be kept in the planter.

* * *

Abi ran straight to the kiosk, realising all of a sudden that Elaine was due back with Jude any moment. As she stumbled down the ramp, face streaked with tears, she saw the crew standing up to leave as the man behind the counter rolled down the grill and padlocked it.

Valentina saw her first. 'Abigail, what happen to you? You look like the ghost.'

'You do, Abi. You're as white as a sheet,' Barb said. 'Isn't she Sandy?'

Noel motioned for her to sit down, but adrenalin was still coursing through her veins. 'Actually I'm not staying. I've actually decided to go home. Back to England, and I've just come to say goodbye.'

'You're really going home just like that?' Barb asked.

'You no lucky in love?' Valentina was forlorn.

'We'll miss you both, love,' Noel said. 'When are you off?'

'I'm not quite sure yet.'

'You've been a real cheer germ, Abi. All the very best to you.'

When he reached out to pat her shoulder, Abi threw herself into his arms.

'Oh that's nice,' Noel said, sounding unsure of the protocol in a situation such as this. As Abi remained with her face buried in his golf shirt, she realised she would not tell anyone else she was leaving. This would be her only farewell and she tightened her grip around Noel's waist. 'Just mind the hernia, love.'

It was only when Abi heard the distinctive whir of the Daihatsu that she let go and turned to see Elaine nosing into a parking space for small cars only.

76.

We're not exactly badly off

Phil felt that Polly was overreacting. As soon as her daughter had arrived back at the beach house and found them all sitting at the outdoor table eating an eggy tea, she'd sent the boys inside and began pouring out the entire story of finding Abi upstairs in the big house. She refused to sit down as she went over and over her shock at discovering that Abi knew where the spare key was kept, that she had the gall to let herself in and seemed to know her way around the house so well. That she'd clearly been riffling through Phil's drawers and had the audacity to pretend she was the cleaner.

'Well,' said Phil, trying to wave it off, although truthfully, the drawer aspect was on the nose. 'She's had a rough trot, Poll. I wouldn't put too much store by the whole thing. She's perfectly benign, only somewhat needy. And anyway, I'm sure you will have put the mockers on any future comings and goings. You'll have scared her witless.' The boys' abandoned dinner plates were starting to attract insects, and Phil tossed a napkin over them.

'You never should have let her come and go at all. You're a widow living alone. You must be sensible.'

'Oh Polly, please darling. You make it sound like I'm ready for a shower chair. Anyhow, she wasn't living with me. I merely let her stay for a time. And she was really quite helpful after Freddie.

I actually feel rather guilty for turfing her out.' Phil slapped at a mosquito that was trying to needle through the fabric of her sleeve.

'Oh my God, mother!' Polly said, stunned. 'You didn't tell me she was living with you! I thought she just visited! Oh my God! What else do I need to know? Tell me right now! What else?'

Phil was beginning to resent the inquisition. 'You're overstepping the line, Polly. It's really none of your business.'

'What else?'

Phil's nostrils flared as she turned away from her daughter. 'I did give her a little leg up with her university fees. Just to get her started. And there might have been a one-off sum to get her through after things went truly pear-shaped. I really can't recall.'

Polly was duly outraged.

'Oh settle down Polly, please, we're not exactly badly off.' Phil waved towards the expanse of darkness stretching beyond the veranda, the moonlit curve of sand leading towards a lighthouse. Its light blinked in the distance. 'And don't forget darling, that it's my money, to do with as I choose.'

Polly sighed and finally flopped into a chair. 'What you don't understand is that every time you choose to mother a stray, someone still has to mother your actual children. And guess who that turns out to be. Guess! Do you know Mark and I are sixty thousand in on Freddie's accident so far? Not counting the first class flight he's about to take here, and rehab or whatever he's going to need.'

Phil looked away again, embarrassed. She'd not thought as far ahead as bills, consumed as she was by Freddie's recovery and legal issues. Historically, Frederick would have attended to that side of things and it was unfortunate that her mind hadn't yet run in that direction. She regretted bringing the question of money into it in the first place and opened her mouth to apologise, but Polly was still going.

'And of course Brigitta enjoyed three months' free room and board –'

'I don't think *enjoyed* is the right word, darling.'

'Either way! I should be in London working to pay for all this and probably trying to save my career at the same time, but guess where I am? That's right! Here!' Polly's voice splintered, and for the first time in Phil's recent memory, angry tears began coursing down her cheeks.

'And in the meantime,' her daughter went on, 'you're buying treats for all the neighbourhood ring-ins and getting to feel brilliant for being so lovely and generous. It's not fair. *It's not fair!*' She rested her forehead on the table and her shoulders started to heave. 'Nobody ever thanks me!' Oh dear, Phil thought, Polly never was a pretty crier.

Still, she felt she ought to comfort her daughter in some way, even though Polly was such a notorious hater of touching. 'Is it possible you really are quite tired, darling?' Phil asked, giving her back the merest suggestion of a pat.

77.

Love-rat director given boot by radio star wife!

That Mark had not been able to book her on the same flight out as him came as an immense relief to Brigitta. There was so much for him to tie off before leaving India, and Freddie was yet to announce when he would return to Sydney, but he had been deemed fit to fly alone, which freed Brigitta to make her own plans.

The day of her departure, goodbyes were said in the hotel lobby and Brigitta tried to mask her elation at the prospect of being finally alone, with the hospital, the miserable hotel, and all India behind her.

At the airport newsagent, she bought chocolate, an air-freight *Vogue*, two British newspapers and at the last minute a week-old *Heat*. After boarding, she collapsed into her window seat, buzzed the stewardess for two bottles of red, and used them to wash down a sleeping pill. Minutes later, she let the magazines slide off her lap as she relaxed into a heavy sleep.

After a brief stopover, the second leg from Mumbai passed slowly but eventually Brigitta felt the beginning of their descent. She pressed her forehead against the window and watched as Sydney appeared beneath her. The blue fingers of the harbour, the orange rooftops, and the backyard swimming pools scattered like little blue jewels. As the plane banked sharply to one side, she made out the Cremorne Peninsula bathed in early sun.

In no time at all, family would all converge on the big house and remain there for some yet-unspecified period. A plan needed to be made for Freddie, Phil had said. Polly felt Brigitta needed to regroup. Freddie thought Phil could do with some company. Mark said he planned to put his thinking cap on and come up with a new career path for Brigitta. He was wondering about PR.

Although Polly had offered to come down from Palm Beach to meet Brigitta at the airport on Sunday morning, she'd declined, wanting to savour her last precious hours by herself. Warm air, salt and jet-fuel enveloped her as she stepped out of the terminal. The sky was ablaze with cloud, streaked pink and orange and family groups milled around outside with a distinct lack of the freneticism that she never got used to in India.

Brigitta found a taxi and slid into the back seat.

'Where are you heading?' the driver asked without turning around.

'Cremorne – actually, no. Bronte, the pool there. Do you know it?'

Growing up, Brigitta's family never really did the eastern beaches – not counting Shark Beach, because as Phil liked to point out, Vaucluse was technically nearer to Mosman than anywhere and really, someone ought to put a bridge between the two. In high school, Brigitta and her friends had started bussing themselves to Bronte, so they could smoke and sunbathe with their bikini tops almost off without fear of being spotted by anyone's mother.

When the taxi deposited her near the stairs down to the ocean pool, Brigitta stood for a moment to take in the enormous waves pounding the beach and turning the entire bay white and fizzy. One solitary figure was walking a dog along the sand. She managed her suitcase down the stairs and sat down on a painted bench, weary and dirty and almost home.

Early-morning swimmers made even laps of the turquoise water and Brigitta watched for a minute, before drawing the *Heat* magazine out of her bag. Leafing backwards through its pages, she came to a picture of Guy, smiling brazenly at the camera.

> **Sylvie to Guy: It's over! Love-rat director given boot by radio star wife!**
> *Embattled West-End personality Guy Kidd has moved out of the £4m North London home he shares with wife Sylvie, after a rumoured affair with a seventeen-year-old model–actress who starred in his most recent production, according to sources close to the couple. A bitter custody battle over the couple's son Ludo and newborn daughter Thea is expected to follow.*

Brigitta rested the magazine open on her lap, and looked up again at the squalling ocean beyond the pool. Her name appeared at the bottom of the story, as a sort of after note put in by a journalist who needed another 200 words. 'It is not Kidd's first indiscretion. Earlier this year …'

In India, there had been hardly any time to think about Guy, the scandal, the probable end of her career. Only occasionally, lying awake in her hot hotel room did she dare to consider that if there was one upside to Freddie's disaster, it was that no one in her family was talking about hers anymore.

The thought made her sick with guilt, but then her family had a knack for moving on when it suited them, and it always fell to her to remind them of stories and things and people they'd forgotten or become bored by. In this instance, Brigitta was happy to leave them to it.

And already, her time with Guy was starting to feel like something she'd imagined, distant and unreal. The only thing that shamed her still, as she looked at the pictures, was the fact that one day, those lovely children would read about what their father had done and his pretty wife would be forced to explain.

Brigitta rolled up the magazine and stuffed it into a nearby rubbish bin.

With few people about, she stripped off her jeans and shirt and walked down the rough stone steps into the ice cold water of the pool. A breath caught in her chest as she lowered herself in, but she needed to be cleansed. Standing against the wall, up to her waist, she lifted her feet off the ground and then with two fierce kicks, she forced herself forwards through the deep, eyes wide open.

78.

The doghouse

Abi offered local pick-up only. She scheduled collections for Saturday afternoons when Jude was with Stu and the Cremorne Point Benevolent Society could be relied upon to be kipping in their quiet houses. She could not bear the idea of them seeing one of their donations carted away by a stranger. Every sale was accompanied by a prick of guilt, and only the increasing thickness of the envelope hidden underneath the mattress made it bearable. She had made $544 dollars so far, boosted by a surprise bidding war that broke out over Sandy's retro-kitsch cutlery tree. Counting two more fortnightly child benefit payments to her UK bank account – she never had quite managed to cut them off – she hoped to have enough money to leave before Christmas. Each small withdrawal she made to buy nappies and noodles seemed to push her departure back by another hour. She let her phone credit run out, and her contact with Rae ceased.

To keep moving forward, she packed her suitcase and began living out of it, although it was only just November. 'I feel as though I'm living out an ending. The fag end to be sure,' Phil had once said, and now Abi knew what she meant. She spent each slow-moving day trying to occupy Jude in the flat and watching eBay. Occasionally, very early in the mornings or just as it was getting dark she would hurry Jude out for a swing, hoping to slip into the playground. Whenever she heard a noise from Phil's garden, she covered her ears, and so that she would not look down, she hung sheets over the windows. They cast a flat, white light across the room. No one came up except her, Jude, and a trickle of successful bidders.

'Thank you, bye,' Abi said, closing the door on a Chinese lady who left with Barb's stackable mixing bowls. She had only got $7.80 for them, but she added it to the envelope. As she sat on the mattress counting it out again, a trickle of sweat ran down her chest.

On a humid Saturday evening, Jude removed to Gordon, Abi sat refolding the contents of her suitcase. There was nothing else to do. Folded beneath her underwear was her swimsuit. She pulled it out, feeling the familiar fabric, and thought.

Jude would not be back until the following morning. And so for the first time this new summer, she snuck down to the pool. The lights in the towers on the other side of the water were flickering on, and ferries chugged past, brightly lit from inside. The sky was ribboned with pink and yellow above a sinking sun. Abi opened the gate. An earlier party had left behind a plastic garden chair and pool lounger, and after looking around to make sure she was on her own, Abi lay down on the lounger. It would all be gone by the next day. A resident would ring the council. She closed her eyes against every memory that lived within the pickets. Phil on that bench. Phil holding Jude over her forearm and shouting, 'Kick, Abigail, for Lord's sake!' Newborn Jude sleeping under a tree with the soles of his bare feet pressed together. She pressed the tips of her fingers against each eyelid. A single gasp of pain came out with her breath. For the shortest time, she had had it all. Stu. Phil. Jude. Everything she had ever wanted.

At some point, the gate rattled and she sat up, squinting through the dusk. A figure with a lopsided way of walking entered and came slowly towards her. As he got closer, Abi saw that he was leaning on a walking stick. Then, as he came and stood right in front of her, she noticed a thick red scar raised along one cheek and another one, more jagged, down the centre of his forehead.

'May I?' he asked, gesturing towards the empty plastic chair, where he tossed the striped towel that had been draped around his neck.

'Okay,' Abi said. She rotated her stiff shoulders and gave a smile that died unseen in the dusk.

He lowered himself into the plastic chair, and let the stick fall away. His head dropped back and he closed his eyes.

'You're Freddie aren't you?'

Lazily, he cocked his head towards her. The corner of his mouth lifted into a half grin. 'So sorry, I can't remember where we've met,' he said, in the precise Woolnough accent.

'We haven't. I know your mum. I used to.'

He sat up and studied her. 'You wouldn't be the girl from the flats, would you? The one with a habit of popping in when no one's home. My sisters have been bringing me up to speed.'

Abi said nothing.

'So we're both in the doghouse, are we? I'm grateful to you – Annie is it?'

'Abi.'

'That's right, Abi. The only time my sister gets off my back is to give my mother a go about you. Apparently you're a menace to society, although looking at you, I'm struggling to see it.'

As he looked her up and down, Abi pulled her knees up to her chest and wrapped her arms around them. 'You look like one of those tiny gymnasts. Very useful on the parallel bars.'

Abi felt the back of her neck tingle.

'You look like you'd really stick your landing,' he said, miming a final flourish to the judges. 'Perfect ten.'

Abi could not help laughing. 'You look so much like your mum.'

Freddie pretended to be offended. 'A much manlier version, I hope. Are you swimming then, Jim?'

It took Abi a second to figure out why he'd called her that. 'I don't think so.'

'Go on. Don't make me swim by myself. I'm infirm, you know,' Freddie said.

'Your mum taught me to swim in this pool,' Abi said, staring at the flat surface, as black as the empty sky.

'Well that makes two of us. Are you any good? There's a very real chance I'll require rescue.'

He stood up and hopped towards the edge, leaving the stick where it was. 'Come on then, Jim,' he called after easing himself in. 'It's lovely once you lose feeling in your legs.'

79.

Infamous Abi

'So where's this baby of yours? And your husband for that matter?'

Freddie was swimming around her in lazy circles, kicking sporadically with one leg, forcing her to spin as she trod water in the deepest part of the pool.

'He isn't my husband. He has the baby at his parents' house. We had a row and haven't spoken since. His parents hate me. Well, his mum definitely does. I'm going home soon anyway.'

Freddie raised an eyebrow. He looked amused.

'It isn't funny. Why are you laughing?'

'I'm not laughing, Jim. It sounds like a fucking nightmare to me. But if I was your chap I'd be in no rush to leave you, no matter how naughty you'd been. You could end up swimming in the middle of the night with an unbelievably good-looking stranger.'

The words gave Abi a pulse, so mortifying in its intensity she had to press her hand between her legs, unseen in the deep. She couldn't think how to reply. For what felt like an eternity, she hadn't spoken to anyone who wasn't angry at her, disappointed, confused or in a hurry to get her pretty pine desk into their van. She felt undone by Freddie's attentions, his care. She let herself sink all the way to the bottom and lingered there for as long as she could, stroking her arms slowly back and forth. When she opened her eyes, there was nothing in front of her except darkness.

Freddie dropped under and pulled her back up by her wrist. 'God, Jim. I thought I'd lost you there for a moment.'

'We should probably get out.'

'Where are we going?'

'What? Nowhere. Home. To our own homes. Separate homes.' The idea of him leaving her and being allowed to walk into the big house made her long for Phil. Only to be able to see her, to have a chance to explain.

'Well, the only thing I've got to look forward to at home is a fresh bollocking from Poll. What about you? Why are you in such a hurry to get home?'

Abi thought for a moment. 'A whites wash.'

Freddie let out a rich laugh.

'It's in the common machines,' Abi said. 'It will have finished and someone might take it.'

'Jim, the only person who's interested in your whites wash around here is me. And I promise I won't touch a thing. Don't go just yet.' He moved nearer to her. 'If you're cold we'll get out and dry off. But really, you're easily the loveliest person I've spoken to in some time, not counting one rather sweet little nurse back in India. Don't deprive me of company. Not in my condition.' He was so near her now, the water between their bodies felt warmer than the water at their backs.

'Gosh,' Abi said, gathering herself. 'You're getting loads of mileage out of your sore knee.'

'I've got nothing else going for me, if you ask any Woolnough. Let's get out, but really, stay for a bit. If I'm late back, it will give Polly something else to be worked up about. You'd be doing her a favour really.'

'Okay, well. Maybe ten minutes. But if my washing gets taken, you owe me a whole load of smalls.' She went up the ladder, sensing Freddie waiting below her, watching.

'Smalls?' he said. 'You sound like a Victorian housemaid.'

'What do you call them then?' She paused, hanging off the handles.

'I don't, Jim.'

Abi dashed dripping to the lounger and felt around for the bath mat she'd brought with her to dry off. Before she could find it, Freddie threw his in her direction.

'Here,' he said. 'This'll be better than that sad little flannel.'

'It's a bath mat actually.' Abi pressed his towel to her face and inhaled a deep draught of Phil's eucalyptus laundry liquid.

'We don't want you catching your death.'

Abi wrapped herself up. 'Your mum always says that.'

'Bugger, she does, doesn't she?' Freddie took his chair and draped Abi's bath mat across his shoulders like a tennis player on a water break. 'Here I am, trying to be charming and instead I remind you of a middle-aged woman.'

'How is she? Your mum?' Abi asked quietly.

'She's all right, Jim. But it's almost a year since my father died. That's why we're all hanging around. She's been pretty wobbly. A lot on her plate. Partly my fault of course.' The lightness in his voice fell away.

'Could you tell her I'm sorry?'

'I'll try, Abi.' He touched the scar on his cheek. 'But I'd say, don't get your hopes up.' Abi did not think she could feel worse than she already did, but Freddie's sympathetic face lowered her even further.

After a moment he stood up and, with one deft movement, kicked his stick upwards and caught the handle. 'Now come on, Jim. Show me to this common laundry and we'll see what's left of your smalls.'

The five-minute walk back to the flats took half an hour. Freddie demanded frequent rests on account of his knee whenever they came to a low section of wall. All along the way, around every bend and through every thicket, he pointed out a personal landmark.

'Ah, now. That bench, Jim, is where I spent the night after a particularly blistering Year 12 formal. It really ought to have a plaque commemorating my heroic recovery from Long Island Ice Tea poisoning. I seem to remember my father docking me for a new tux.'

Further along, a tree root snagged the end of Freddie's stick and he slung his arm around Abi's shoulders to steady himself. He did not seem in a hurry to let go. Music and laughter wafted down from houses above, and from the other side of the harbour came the dull pop-pop of fireworks.

'Jude and I have lunch on that grassy bit sometimes.'

'Who's she?'

'No, Jude. My son.'

'Right, the baby. I'd forgotten already. Forgive me. Blame the recent concussion. Well, next time you bring him here, you can tell him about the great Freddie Woolnough whose alcohol tolerance remains the stuff of legend to certain-age Loreto girls.'

'I probably won't.'

'No. But it's enough to know you'll be thinking of me next time you eat your sandwiches.' He put his mouth so close to her as he spoke, his warm breath filled her ear.

At the last curve before the flats, she slipped out from under his arm and took a few quick steps ahead. He prodded her with the end of his stick as she broke away. 'Are you actually in a hurry, Jim, or have you forgotten I'm the walking wounded?'

'I haven't. This is me, though.'

'You really are right next door. How convenient.'

'It was nice to meet you.' Abi tightened her towel. Perhaps he would forget to take it back. 'I am sorry, about everything. I didn't mean to make trouble.'

'You can stop being so miserable, Jim. I couldn't give a fuck what you've done. Now listen, are you sure you don't need a hand up with that washing?'

'From a man with one working leg?'

'You shouldn't discriminate against the disabled. I meant in a purely supervisory capacity.'

'I think I'm all right, thank you for offering.'

'Fine. Goodnight then. It's been a pleasure to meet the infamous Abi from the flats.'

He grinned and lumbered off into the darkness. As Abi began to pick her way towards her block, Freddie's words came at her, again and again. Infamous Abi, infamous Abi, like a chanted chorus. Infamous Abi, infamous Abi. The blank glass door to the foyer gave back her reflection, as she stood with one hand stretched towards the handle. She barely recognised herself, skinnier still, cavernous hollows below her eyes. Infamous Abi.

When she caught her own eye, she spun on her heels and ran back the way she'd come. She reached Freddie just as he was about to lift the latch of Phil's gate.

'Freddie,' she whispered.

He turned around and threw his head back, supressing laughter.

The voices of the other Woolnoughs floated out of the open kitchen.

'I think I do actually need help with my smalls.'

'I knew it,' Freddie said. He stepped into her, so close, his breath picked up a strand of her hair and blew it into her eye.

She pushed it to one side. 'But in a purely supervisory capacity.'

'Well. If you insist. It sounds like they're getting on perfectly well without me in there.'

She took his hand and moments later, she was stumbled backwards up the flat stairs. Freddie had tucked the stick under his arm and had his hands on her hips, letting himself be led up. Her own recklessness was intoxicating. She had tried so hard to be good and look what had happened. What else was there to lose? As she struggled with the front door, he kissed the side of her neck and slid the straps of her damp swimsuit off both shoulders.

She held it up as they stumbled in, and although she tried to apologise for the state of the living room, Freddie began kissing her with such unyielding force the words came out in a mumble. 'It's usually much tidier up here.'

They found the bedroom and she let him tug off her swimsuit and fling it towards the window. His neck smelt of pool salt, more faintly of soap or honey. Abi felt a surge of pure love as they fell onto the mattress and Freddie climbed on top of her. She grabbed for the body above her, clutched it and pawed it. This time she would not let go.

She fell into a sort of trance as the dark bedroom shrank in around them. Everything became hollows and spaces, warmth and wetness.

'Do you have a thing, Jim?'

Abi could not bear to get up and dig one out of Stu's shelf of the medicine cabinet. 'No, sorry.'

'Well, I'm as clean as a pin so if you're all right I'll just,' he whistled two short notes, '*whip out* when the time comes.'

Abi murmured assent but after that something shifted. Their rhythm was lost. Everything she did seemed to cause him pain in some unseen place and he'd say 'Fuck, Jim, that's not going to work.' She tried to think of something else from her slender repertoire but felt self-conscious, and then came the slow creep of shame.

Freddie suggested they concentrate on her for a bit, but when he flipped her to his other side, her eyes fell on Jude's empty crib in the near dark. She looked at Freddie, whose face was set in laboured concentration, and saw Stu. Regret flooded every cell in her body as Freddie finally hit his mark. A minute later it was over.

Abi dashed to the bathroom, sat on the toilet seat and wept into a scented baby wipe. When she eventually stood up, she knew immediately that Freddie had mistimed his exit.

She was desperate for a shower, but needing to expedite Freddie's departure, she pulled on some dirty clothes that lay on the floor. The realisation that she had just made another, even worse, mistake gripped her chest.

When she emerged, Freddie was hopping back from the kitchen with a jar of water.

'It's a tad sparse up here, isn't it, Jim? You're not a big one for furniture.'

He was still naked and Abi lifted her eyes to the ceiling. 'It's temporary.'

'I'd hope so. That sofa looks like it was dragged up on Hard Rubbish day.'

Freddie ambled back to the bedroom, and with mounting terror, Abi realised he was intending to stay over.

'Oh,' Abi said. 'You're not going to pop home then?'

'What, were you just going to use me for your pleasure and then boot me out?' Freddie pulled the sheet to his waist and put his hands behind his head, exposing tufts of underarm hair.

'No. I just thought since you're only next door, you'd prefer to sleep in your own bed.'

'I'm a gentleman, Jim. And I'm tired. Bloody hell. Did my Mum paint that?' He gestured towards the small frame Abi had moved from the living room to the floor beside the mattress.

'She gave it to me.'

'I'm sure she did. Odd seeing it here. It used to be in the laundry loo. Anyway, I'm spent. Night-night, Jim.'

80.

A slave to your wash cycle

Abi lay rigid on her side of the mattress until it was light enough to get up and reasonably start making tea. Freddie had slept deeply all night, resisting every telepathic request Abi had made for him to wake up and go. Elaine was bringing Jude back straight after the St Luke's 8 a.m. service, owing to the Newcomers Lunch she had agreed to host afterwards, 'but only as a one off'. Abi desperately needed Freddie to leave so she could strip the bed and take the sheets to the laundry.

Freddie did not wake up even as she moved noisily around the flat, and with no other option, she knelt by the mattress and began trying to roll the fitted bottom sheet off each corner and slide it out from under him as he slept.

'What *are* you doing?' Freddie sat up and ran his hand through his hair.

'It's wash day. Sorry. Do you mind? I always do sheets on a Sunday.'

'You're really a slave to your wash cycle, aren't you? Fine, I'll get up. Is that for me?' He nodded towards a plate of toast Abi had put on the floor beside the mattress, then got up slowly and found his swimming trunks.

'Take the toast with you if you like. You don't have to eat it here.' Abi went to the living room to find the laundry key. When

Freddie appeared, with toast between his teeth, he was wearing one of the T-shirts that Stu had left behind. 'Your baby-daddy won't mind, will he? I can hardly go home in my trunks.'

Abi felt as though air was suctioned out of her body, leaving her weightless, floating. Stu.

'What's with the curtains, Jim? Do you grow a lot of weed up here?'

'No,' she said defensively, yanking one of the window sheets down and rolling it into her pile. 'They're for privacy.'

Freddie came up behind her and looked out the window. 'Ha, look at that. Breakfast *al fresco* for the Woolnoughs. How do you open this window? Let's give them a little shock.' In the instant it took Abi to shove him away from the glass, she saw Phil at the table, leaning back in her chair so that Brigitta could refresh her coffee. Polly sat at the other end, leafing through the newspaper. Mark was kicking a ball with the boys, as Domenica ran excited circles around them.

'What are you doing?' Abi cried. 'They can see up here.'

'Ow, fuck, careful,' he said, as he stumbled back and gave her a hard stare. They were strangers again.

As much as Abi wanted to stand guard at the window and keep him from taking a second look, she tore herself away to hunt for the laundry key, overturning sofa cushions, rifling through kitchen drawers and tipping out her neatly folded suitcase. Freddie began to wander behind her from room to room, either bored or amused, Abi could not tell. As her hand found the key under one side of the mattress, powerful knocking sounded from outside the front door.

'Expecting anyone?' Freddie said, ambling out as though he intended to answer it.

'Freddie, open up!' came a disembodied voice. 'Are you in there? It's Mark. Come on, pal. We saw you from downstairs.' Abi balled the dirty sheets up in her arms and, unable to think what else to do, followed Freddie towards the door. Between each appeal, she could hear Mark take another jagged breath, as though he'd run all the way.

'The jig's up then,' said Freddie. 'Mark's come up to claim me.' He appeared to find the idea amusing, even as Abi tried desperately to stuff the sheets under the sofa.

'Hurry up, Freddo,' Mark said, pleading now. 'Come on, your sister's on her way up.'

'Fancy meeting you here,' Freddie said, as he threw open the door to reveal Mark mid-knock. 'You're a friend of Abi's as well, are you?'

'Don't be a twat, Freddie. Polly's behind me. You've really gone too far now, mate. Too far. She's ropable.'

Abi had backed herself into the farthest corner of the living room and watched as Polly tore up the stairs, knocking Mark into the doorframe as she flew at Freddie, pummelling his chest with her fists. 'You bastard. You fucking shit. What were you thinking? What is wrong with you?'

'Ow, Polly, stop it.' When the pummelling did not cease, Freddie grabbed his sister's wrists. Even then she continued to flap her hands uselessly in front of his face, and delivered a strong kick to his injured leg.

'Fuck, Polly. You're insane.' Freddie's face turned grey as he clutched his lower leg, releasing his sister so suddenly it looked like she was going to fall over.

'Okay, that's enough.' Mark put his arm around Polly and tried to steer her towards the door. 'Come on, he's got the message.'

Polly threw off his arm. 'Has he, Mark? Has he? Because it seems like we all abandoned our own homes and jobs to help him stay out of a third-world prison and five minutes later, he's getting his end away with the girl from next door.'

'Easy, Pidge. Is it possible you're overreacting?'

Polly spun around as though she was intending to come at Freddie with fresh blows, but as she turned, she saw Abi for the first time pressed into the corner. Expecting Polly to come at her next, Abi put her hands over her ears. Instead, Polly looked straight through her as though she was nothing.

'Stop calling me Pidge!' Polly said as she locked back on Freddie. 'I am trying to keep this family together and you just stand there making stupid jokes. You are tearing this family to shreds and you don't even care.'

The three of them fell into a mad tussle, and Abi looked on in horror.

'What are you all doing up here?' Another voice came full-force from the threshold and everyone turned to see Phil, who had come up the stairs unnoticed. 'Freddie, I need very much to understand what has happened. I do hope it's not the sordid business it looks like.' Next, Brigitta appeared beside her and immediately burst into tears.

'Mum, it's nothing, honestly,' Freddie said, sounding like a boy who'd been caught in the pantry. He was panting, and gave Mark a small backwards shove. 'Polly has got the wrong end of the stick.'

Everybody began speaking at once and Abi tried to shrink further and further into the corner, with her hands still covering her ears.

In the middle of the roar, Phil turned and looked at her. A moment of perfect stillness passed between them, all the noise seeming to die away as their eyes met. As Phil's features slackened, Abi saw the depths of her disappointment. Phil turned back to her own children.

Abi was trapped. As the Woolnoughs raged on, she glanced towards the open door, contemplating escape. But as her mind tried to map out a route between the shouting people, the sofa cushions she'd cast onto the floor during her hunt for the laundry key and the boxes of kitchenware stacked and waiting collection by the door, she saw Stu appear in the dark stairwell, with their son sitting high on his shoulders and a bunch of bright pink tiger lilies under his arm.

'Hey, what's going on? Who are all of you?' Confusion spread across his face as he slid Jude off his shoulder and looked at the five strangers, in various states of torment and weeping, standing around in his flat. Next his eyes were drawn to the packed boxes. Polly's gaze followed his, and instantly she recognised one of her mother's platters.

'Is this ours? This is ours! Mum, why does she have all your stuff?' Polly lunged at the boxes and began pulling out piece after piece and loading it into Mark's arms.

'Are you leaving, Abi?' Stu's voice cracked. 'Where are you going?'

'Nowhere,' Abi said. One of her legs had started to shake violently and she tried to press her knees together to stop it.

'No, you're going. Are you going home? Are you going back to live with your mum?'

The floor dropped away beneath Abi and she felt herself lean against the wall. Phil let out a gasp. 'Do you have a mother, Abigail? Do you have a mother, alive and well?'

Polly dropped a serving dish, which exploded into a thousand tiny pieces.

Abi did not speak.

'Ah. Well. I see I've been wrong about you on every possible count.' Phil turned towards the others and in her most commanding tone ordered them out.

The Woolnoughs formed a straggling line and moved towards the hallway, passing by Brigitta, who was still in the doorway weeping. They looked like teenagers being marched out of a party that had got out of hand. As Freddie came to Stu, standing to let them past, he paused and peeled off the T-shirt he had taken. When

Stu made no move to reclaim it, Freddie let it fall from his hand onto the carpet.

Brigitta stayed where she was until the others had disappeared into the stairwell. She raised her hand as high as her shoulder and gave Abi the smallest wave. 'I'm so sorry,' she croaked. 'But don't worry. It'll be all right.'

Before she could wave back, Stu cut in between them and held Jude towards Abi so that his little legs dangled in mid-air. The flowers fell to the ground with the soft crunch of cellophane.

'Weird to think I came to sort everything out.' His freckled face turned red and tears rose in his eyes, clinging to his blond lashes. 'But it seems like you've been busy. You can go home if you want, I thought you probably would.'

He placed Jude in her arms but kept a hand wrapped around the baby's foot. 'I never thought you'd leave without letting me say goodbye.'

81.

We are awful

The family trooped through the back door of the big house one behind the other, heads bowed. Although it was clear each of them wished to continue upstairs and shut themselves away in a quiet room, they all remained there, as though trapped by a force outside themselves.

Polly could hear the muted babble of cartoons coming from upstairs but had no energy to check the boys were all right. Not fifteen minutes ago, she had herded them in from the garden, with a firm injunction against moving, after Freddie had been spotted peering down on them from a top floor window of the flats.

By chance, Toby had arced the ball high into the air and Mark had looked up to watch it sail over the fence to the flats, only to catch his brother-in-law smiling down at them all from on high, bare chested and very possibly naked below the waist-high window sill. When the boys began shouting for Mark's attention, Polly had looked over to see what had distracted him, following her husband's gaze towards the top floor where Freddie could still be seen, taking a few stumbling steps backwards, grin still in place. Mark was already taking great strides towards the gate, urging Polly to stay where she was, but after grabbing the children and shunting them through the French doors, she followed him out, shrieking her brother's name.

Now Mark was the first to take a seat at the pine table, scraping a chair noisily over the flagstones and causing Phil to tense even further. As though taking a punt on his closest ally, Freddie took the place beside Mark and sat with his eyes downcast and hands folded in his lap, a posture of uncharacteristic apology.

Polly helped Phil into a chair at the other end, where she sat ashen-faced. Once or twice she reached up for Polly's hand.

Brigitta leaned against the sink with her face buried in her hands.

Nobody spoke.

After some minutes, Mark's phone rang and he reached into his pocket to silence it. The sound seemed to rouse Polly and she squared her shoulders. 'The first thing will be to call …'

'We are awful. We are awful, terrible people.' The table turned towards Brigitta, who had started shouting over her sister. 'We should go back up there and apologise to that poor girl for how we have treated her. I can't believe what just happened. I can't believe what we just did.'

'Why on *earth* would we do that?' Polly could not believe what she was hearing. 'She's a total fantasist, Brigitta! You heard, this entire time she let Mum think she's a dear little orphan when all the time she's had her own family back in the UK. Seeing the lengths she's willing to go to to ingratiate herself into this family, I think we've had a lucky escape.' Polly shot a furious look at Freddie. 'She may actually be some kind of sociopath. We ought to report her, actually. For the break-in at least.'

Polly looked to Mark for support but his expression was dubious. 'I don't know, darling,' he said, pawing his chin. 'Really? She seems pretty harmless to me.'

'She is totally harmless!' Brigitta cried. 'She is just lonely and lost. But we were all happy to use her anyway.' She looked past Freddie and tried to catch her mother's eye but Phil angled her face away. 'Nobody seemed that worried about her mental state when she was being useful, but now that she's become a bit problematic, we'll just chuck her. I am so ashamed!'

Brigitta looked furiously at each of her family members, but no one moved to respond. Even Polly felt too exhausted at that moment to contest Brigitta's accusations.

'Why won't anyone think about her for a minute? Can you imagine being stuck up in that flat with a tiny baby and a rubbish boyfriend who bails on you and no friends obviously, except Mum.' Again Brigitta looked at Phil, still refusing to be drawn in.

'She just wanted to be your friend, Mum, that's all. Everyone does and you know it! Everyone gets charmed by you. The poor girl didn't stand a chance if you think about it.' Brigitta blushed deeply then, but forced herself on. 'And really, how is she any different from us? We all just want your attention! Why else are we all here? Abi was the only one brave enough to show it.' Brigitta's arms were rigid at her sides and her hands formed tight fists. 'I don't see why it even matters if she's got her own mother. She just wanted someone here to be kind to her. That doesn't make her a sociopath.' Brigitta drew a deep breath before slumping against the edge of the counter. 'We all just need to grow up.'

Slowly, Freddie got up and went and stood beside his sister, who had buried her face in the crook of her elbow. He put an arm around her shoulders and she gave him a sharp jab in his ribs before letting herself sag against him. 'Fucker,' she said. 'You're a fucker, Freddie.'

'Right,' Polly said, massaging both her temples. Somebody needed to take command. 'We know what you think now, Brigitta. Thank you for that. Still, our first priority has to be getting her out of that flat so Mum can get back to some sort of normal.' Unusually, Polly was struggling to order her thoughts. 'Mum, you won't need to see her again. Mark and I will handle everything.'

'But you *should* see her, Mum,' Brigitta interrupted again. Polly was losing patience, but there was no break in her sister's impassioned appeal. 'You should, Mum. Go and talk to her. You know you ought to. You are *friends*. It could all be quite easily fixed if you'd just bloody try.'

Polly could stand no more. 'Brigitta, don't tell her what to do. You've got yourself totally wound up. You're not thinking clearly. Mark, which estate agents do we know?'

'Actually Polly, I must stop you there.' Phil lifted her daughter's hand off her shoulder and craned around to where Polly loomed above her, 'I suspect Briggy is right on this score.'

Brigitta looked shocked. She cast around the table to see if the others had heard it. But all eyes were on Phil as she stood up and tucked in her chair. She turned towards Brigitta. 'Although I expect I won't, darling. Rather, I can't. I really am terribly sorry.' And then to them all, 'Did we all remember your father died a year today?'

82.

Looking a gift horse
in the mouth

Elaine did not make another journey down the highway after Stuart had returned from dropping off the baby, that very strange Sunday a month ago, and announced with tears in his eyes that there would be no more weekend visitations.

Maddeningly, he had refused to provide any detail as to why, before shutting himself in his room, where he mostly remained. Whenever Elaine rapped on the door and demanded he pass out the dirty dishes, and the waste basket overflowing with Gatorade bottles and torn-up drawing paper, the bodily smell that wafted out of the room made her gorge rise.

She could not let herself think about his degree in tatters, his tarnished future, the fact that she would be forced forever more to use common-sounding phrases like 'from a previous relationship' and 'my son's ex'. The only upside was that Abi had lost her final toehold in Kellett family life, and Christmas would be spent pleasantly, just the three of them again. As it had always been. Only Roger was granted admittance to Stuart's gamey-smelling chamber and would spend entire evenings in there talking with his son. But the substance of their conversations remained a mystery, coming only like a low, bass-ish rumbling through the wall to which Elaine pressed her ear.

Elaine did not like mysteries, unless she was the mastermind, and in the matter of selling Milson Road she was certainly that. In one of life's heavenly coincidences, not long after she'd had the idea of putting the flat on the market she had received a telephone call from a high-end estate agent with offices on the best side of Neutral Bay.

Apparently, the agent explained, another resident in the building had plans to 'push through', which was why their offering price was so extraordinarily above market. Quietly, Elaine had accepted the offer and gone about the preparation of deeds and contracts in the inviolable privacy of her sewing room, knowing that when the time came, Roger could be pressed into signing. 'We'd be mad not to,' was going to be her line. 'We'd be looking a gift horse in the mouth.'

With the proceeds, she planned to help Stuart towards a nice three-bedroom, one-point-five-bathroom townhouse with ample parking and a level garden that would one day be suitable for a growing family. On that front, she'd also begun forming a shortlist of candidates from among the single daughters of her choir friends, and although she sensed it was a touch on the early side to bring it up – bearing in mind Stuart had apparently given up showering for the time being – Elaine hoped Christmas would provide opportunity for some gently orchestrated meetings.

Occasionally, it was true, she experienced an involuntary wave of longing for Jude. Usually when one of his toys turned up behind a cushion, or someone at choir practice delayed the start of vocal warm-ups with a long and joyous anecdote about something their grandchild had said or done. Despite the circumstances of his birth, Jude had grown up to be quite nice, and the days Elaine had minded him on her own while Abi was at university were some of the most pleasurable of her life. Although she would never admit it, because the very plain fact was, to indulge her own desire for ongoing contact with Jude would only prevent Stuart's wound from healing over. She needed to be stoic, for the sake of her own son.

83.

Such an arse

'Mum!' Brigitta shouted the moment Phil stepped into the crowded kitchen. 'Somebody finished all the normal tea!' Brigitta was holding an empty foil bag upside down, raining black dust onto the flagstones and waiting, apparently, for her mother to magic up some more.

Toby and Max sat at the table making nasty-looking robot figurines fight with each other in a way that was putting obvious dents in the pine. Polly, in running gear, stood at the sink filling a water bottle and ignoring them. Somebody had changed the radio to a commercial station, which filled the kitchen with the infuriating babble of advertisements, and from the next room Mark's baritone boomed about offshore something and regulatory something else. Only Freddie was absent from the scene, asleep upstairs no doubt, blissfully unconscious and bathed in the morning sunshine that poured in through his window.

Tensions simmered on in the big house, lifting to a hard boil over idiotic things like the washing up. After her violent disquisition at the kitchen table, Brigitta had continued to lobby her mother to go across to the flats, but Phil had dug in with Polly on her side, and the campaign was gradually abandoned.

Without the tea she'd come down to make, Phil left the room and walked straight back upstairs, returning to her unmade bed.

She wanted her house back. Having longed for the companionship of her children all year, she now wished only for space.

Polly had annexed Frederick's study, working well into the night to keep with London time. Mark preferred to take calls directly below Phil's bedroom window, the single advantage of which was that she was learning a great deal about capital markets. Freddie and Brigitta had set up camp in the front room, both of them yet to announce where they were going after Christmas, and in the meantime, picking up their adolescent personae with gusto. Brigitta lazing endlessly in any patch of sunshine like a house cat and traipsing wet footprints through the house after a swim, coming obviously bra-less to the dinner table; Freddie constantly needling them all, teasing, coming and going as he pleased.

When Polly finally took over the kitchen as well, Phil resolved to come downstairs as seldom as she could. 'Why are you letting Freddie act like such an arse?' Polly had screeched at her some nights before, when a risotto she'd asked him to watch caught the bottom of the pan and had to be turfed out. *Letting!* Phil thought as she evacuated. As though her powers of letting and prohibiting, where Freddie was concerned, hadn't ebbed away years ago!

But it was true, Freddie was such an arse. Never had Phil wanted so much to throttle him, bodily, as when she'd first seen him in Abigail's grotty flat, grinning like a rat-trap, as though it was all a terrific joke.

She'd barely been able to speak a word to him since, even though he'd dialled up his charm by a good few notches. As a boy he would push his luck too far, then deploy his full magnetism to win Phil's quick forgiveness so he could feel golden again. Bulletproof. Nothing had changed.

Brigitta, Phil could see, was slowly being won over by her brother's efforts, their constant bickering gradually replaced by giggling and private jokes. Surely nothing was properly resolved, but at least their cessation of hostilities was kinder to the ear.

After the anniversary of Frederick's passing came and went, it was somehow settled they would all stay on for Christmas. Phil could not remember being consulted about any of it and was forced to accept as kindness what had come to feel like a continual invasion. There was no quiet, no opportunity to think properly about Abigail and the awfulness that had transpired between them. Half-formed thoughts came and went, between rushes of anger, moments of true wistfulness, and the constant low hum of wanting to know why. Why had Abigail done everything she'd done? Was she malicious or foolish? Cruel, or merely as lonely as Brigitta supposed.

In the sanctuary of her bedroom, Phil straightened the covers and reached for the le Carré. A hundred pages in now and she'd simply stopped worrying about who anybody was and why they were all pointing guns at each other. She let her mind wander as the lines passed in front of her eyes.

'Have I uncovered a passion? Are we both readers?' Phil remembered asking the first time she noticed Abi throwing hungry looks at last year's Booker on her lap. Was it their first ever appointment at the kiosk? How long ago that felt, although as clear as anything Phil could see the smile that spread across Abigail's face as she'd received a 400-page stinker like the most wonderful gift.

Such a trifle. The word repeated itself. Is that all their friendship had been? A trifle. A pleasant diversion from real life, in which Phil got to be kind and generous, was amused and amusing, with none of the ancient grievances and hurts and wrongs dragged up daily by her children to pollute simple companionship?

Nothing was ever entirely forgiven, let alone forgotten, in the layers and layers of family history, so that your only chance for a morning passed peacefully at a pool or in your own garden was with a total stranger. Someone else's daughter.

The idea brought Phil up short. She tossed the book away and it landed with a soft thud on the carpet. Abigail was a stranger – possibly even a fantasist. That had been Polly's word for it, one of the more repeatable ones. She'd had a mother tucked away the entire time and must have lied and edited and skirted around the fact constantly, every day they had spent together. Why had Phil not caught her in the lie? It was true, she had no memory of Abigail expressly *saying* her mother was dead. Only that there'd been an accident with the father and sister. But, as she found herself combing through scraps of conversation – 'I expect there wasn't anyone to teach you,' 'I'm used to being on my own a lot but it's a different sort of alone when you've got a child' – it was clear she'd never owned to her mother being alive either. Phil sighed. Was there a father stashed away too? Was the dead sister merely an invention? The sudden appearance of doubt on that front refreshed Phil's melancholy. Eventually she forced herself to get up and run a bath.

But as she flung on the hot water and sat waiting for it to fill, Phil felt a sting of accusation. Because neither was she entirely innocent in it. She had let herself come to rely on a girl who she'd known from the outset to be a pit of need. Was it any wonder that Abigail had become attached? In that, she'd been careless. Yes, that was her only crime, Phil thought in her own defence, carelessness. It was beside the point now. She'd never been playing with a full deck. Whenever she felt an unwanted twist of guilt, she would remind herself of that.

84.

There is one thing

'Are you sure you won't come, Stu?' Roger was standing outside his son's bedroom door with his wife's car keys in his hand and a large box wrapped in dinosaur paper under his arm.

Stu was leaning against the doorframe in nothing but boxer shorts, with his arms folded across his chest. His hair was sticking up in wadded clumps, and Roger sensed it could do with a shampoo. 'Nah. I don't think so, Dad.'

Roger lingered for a moment, hoping Stu would change his mind. Instead, Elaine appeared in the hallway with the clean, damp sponge recommended for the careful cleaning of Lladro. 'What's that?'

'It's a birthday present for the little fella.'

'I thought we said we would *post* something.' She spoke in the pointed tone Roger remembered her using to spell out l-o-l-l-y and b-e-d in front of Stu when he was a young boy.

'Did we Laine? I can't think why I'd have agreed to that. I want to see him on his special day. He was the best present I've ever had.' Before his nerve could fail, he hastened down the hallway and buckled himself into the Daihatsu like it was a tiny, fuel-efficient getaway car. All the way down the highway, Roger drove dangerously close to the speed limit and ran a series of orange lights through Chatswood. And all the time, his excitement grew until he was standing outside

Abi's door holding the present with both hands. He had missed Jude so much that he knocked much harder than he meant to. Abi opened it an inch and peered through the gap. She didn't look very well. Pale, and like she'd lost a great deal of weight. Roger felt quite upset to see her like that, but managed a smile as she let him in and he saw Jude crawling around the empty room.

The flat was completely packed. Most of the furniture was gone, including the pull-out. The only thing left was an open suitcase in the middle of the floor. Although Roger was happy to crouch in front of Jude and present him with the gift, it made him feel quite sad to see that Abi had managed to get the little fellow a bought cake and had put it down on a towel laid out like a picnic rug. They must have been about to have it when he arrived. She offered him a slice, which he accepted even though he knew there was a distinct chance he could ruin his dinner with so much icing.

'How have you been, Abi?' he asked. Abi seemed very anxious and Roger longed to set her at ease. 'Stu has told me a few bits and bobs about what's happened, but you're not to worry, Abi. I'm not the sort to throw stones, as they say.'

Abi looked relieved and sat beside him on the carpet. She undid one end of the present so that Jude would be able to tear the rest. After a period of concentrated effort, his patience began to wane and Abi helped him with the last bit.

'They're always more interested in the paper at this stage, aren't they?' Roger said modestly, although to his mind, Jude looked very taken with the high-quality digger he'd chosen from an overwhelming selection at Killara Toy Planet the previous day.

'Is there anything I could do for you though, Abi?' Roger glanced around the empty flat. 'I'd love to be helpful in some way.'

'There is one thing.' Abi stood up and held Jude's hands until he got himself up on two feet and then, to Roger's amazement, clambered up Abi's leg and onto her hip like a little monkey.

'Anything, truly love.' He got up and brushed off his trousers, keen to be put to work.

'Do you have $223 that I could borrow?'

His heart sank. Stu had told him the story of returning to the flat that day and finding Abi there surrounded by boxes, with a dicey fellow from next door, and Roger understood in theory that she had been planning to take Jude back to the UK. The point was, it was only now, seeing the empty flat for himself, that he truly realised Abi would not be around much longer. And neither would Jude. Roger wished, so powerfully at that moment, that she had asked him to look at a leaking tap.

As it happened, he'd withdrawn $300 that morning and although he hated to give it to her, knowing it would be put towards their tickets, Elaine's fruit and vege co-op money was burning a hole in his pocket. Abi wouldn't ask if she didn't truly need it. And she'd never do anything that would hurt little Jude. Roger took the notes from his wallet and began counting them into her palm, until eventually he closed her hand around all of it. 'And I can send you more, Abi. I will. I don't want you to worry about anything.'

'Thank you, Roger. You've always been so nice to me.'

Neither was game to look at the other. Instead, Abi carried Jude over to her suitcase, open in one corner of the room.

'Would you be able to give something to Stu as well?'

From the inside pocket, Abi took out a sealed envelope containing a thick, folded letter. Roger held it carefully.

'Well,' he said 'Well …' It seemed like there was nothing left to say. 'I suppose I'd better be getting on. Do you think I could –'

Before he was able to finish, Abi turned Jude towards him and Roger was simultaneously elated and destroyed when Jude reached out, wanting to be held. Abandoning all modesty, Roger held Jude close to his chest and kissed his warm, sticky cheek and smelt his lovely hair. With a stab of anguish, he gave the boy back to his mother and hurried towards the door.

Abi was behind him when he paused to look back.

'I love you, Roger,' she said, kissing his cheek.

Roger had never told anyone that he loved them except Elaine and Stuart, and as much as his heart longed to say the words, his mouth wouldn't form them. 'You'll always have a friend in me, Abi. You always will. Goodbye, little fella,' he said, taking Jude's face in his hands again. 'Don't forget your Pa-pa.'

85.

One adult and him

Before dawn, Abi readied them both as fast as she could, and when everything was done, lifted Jude into the carrier. Even facing outwards, the clips would barely fasten around him and he felt as heavy as a sandbag. At the last minute, she had decided the pram would be too cumbersome for her to manage on her own and had folded it away in a corner of the flat. Abi took a last look around, the nubbly carpet, the hard white walls, the windows slid shut against the stirring trees, black shadows against a black sky. She closed the door and slid her key back through the gap.

Her suitcase contained nothing but essentials, which slid around as she bounced it downstairs. In her pocket was a second letter, and as her taxi arrived, she darted over the grass verge and pushed it into Phil's letterbox. It was overgrown with a cloud of jasmine and she twisted off one of the fragrant tendrils and put it in the pocket of her tracksuit pants.

As the cab carried them away, Abi closed her eyes. She did not want to see the glinting harbour, the terracotta rooftops on the peninsula, and somewhere through the trees the mint-green pool that would be as flat as a mirror in the early morning. Jude babbled, sucked two fingers, held out a hand and promptly fell asleep in the cab's furry car seat. Abi envied his not knowing.

But she could not cry and performed each function – getting out, paying the driver, finding a trolley and the Air India desk – like an automaton.

'We're one adult and him,' she said, directing the clerk's attention to the oversized infant strapped to her front. 'To Heathrow please.'

The woman studied her crumpled documents with disapproval. 'You're too early. Your flight doesn't board until 5 p.m. I can't check you in for another seven hours. You should go home and come back later.'

Abi looked down at her suitcase. Slowly, she turned and began to walk away, with no idea where she was going. The straps of the baby carrier were already cutting into her shoulders.

'Actually,' the clerk called after her. 'Ma'am? Because you've got the little one I could probably make an exception. You don't want to have to drag that bag around all day, do you?'

Abi could only whisper her thanks. Moments later, she accepted their boarding passes and watched as her worldly possessions were spirited down the conveyor.

'Merry Christmas,' the clerk said, signalling the end of their interaction with a glance over Abi's shoulder to the next in line.

Passage through customs was mercifully swift and, revived by a cardboard tray of hotcakes, Abi wandered the departures floor to keep Jude amused. As the hours passed, the airport began to feel like a small town she had lived in all her life. They developed favourite places, learned which were the better toilets, and sat on the floor between rows at the newsagent and read every book in the children's section one by one, ignoring the shop attendants' repeated suggestion that she either buy something or leave.

By the time the flight was called, Abi had lost the sense they were even waiting for something. She joined the back of a long, slow-moving queue at the gate, deeply certain so many people could not fit on one plane. Again her world shrank, from the terminal to a single seat, 86F, the centre of the hot, back row. Jude had not slept since the ride to the airport and was passing through tiredness into something more ominous.

While the cabin filled, Jude wanted to stand on Abi's lap, treading his feet painfully up and down on the tops of her thighs. He threw his head back in a moment of wild, bent-backed mania, connected with Abi's forehead and let out a piercing cry. Refusing even then to sit down, he grasped the headrest in front with both hands and wrenched it back and forth with all the strength in his short arms. It became a game, him reaching out, Abi peeling his hands away. The man in front quietly switched places with his young daughter who, to Abi's untold relief, waved through the gap and began passing stickers back to Jude, who finally abandoned his tantrum to inspect the tiny farm animals adhered to the tips of his fingers.

By the time the violent juddering of take-off lifted them up and away, Jude was asleep, still clinging to a handful of hair.

Abi leaned forwards and craned towards a window on the other side of the aisle, permitting herself a final glimpse at the city spread out beneath them, shining under the setting sun. 'Thank you. Thank you for being such a nice place,' she whispered, then dropped back against her seat and closed her eyes.

The stewards began distributing meals. Abi declined a tray, sure that trying to peel off the scorching foil and scoop the contents into her mouth one-handed would wake Jude.

Sometime later trays were cleared, nylon blankets crackling with static were distributed and as the pinprick lights were turned down, the cabin's inmates sunk into an uncomfortable torpor.

To forget the angry buzz of her left hip, pinned against the metal armrest by Jude's sleeping body, Abi gazed at the flickering colours on her neighbour's screen. In the white noise of the back row, phrases of her letters played back in her mind. But it didn't matter anymore. Phil, and Polly, Stu and his parents, all of them would know the truth by now, and would soon be behind her, on the other side of the ocean she was passing over at a thousand miles an hour.

86.

All our mornings

In an effort to ease tensions at the big house, Polly had drawn up a duty roster. Freddie burst out laughing when he saw it stuck to the fridge, and asked if he could look forward to a cool robot sticker for taking the bins out every night for a week.

Polly had thrown a wet sponge at him but otherwise, Brigitta reflected, as she walked back from her job of piddling Domenica, the roster had actually improved things.

Everyone was being nicer to each other and the boys' excitement about today had diffused the sense of endless waiting.

A few days ago, Phil had dug out the box of ancient and deeply familiar decorations and they'd all sat around with flutes of fizz, watching Max and Toby clump them together on the lowest branch of a tree Mark had organised. They put it where they always put it, and a warm breeze through the French doors spread the smell of pine needles through the house. And now it was Christmas Day.

Brigitta still did not have a plan, beyond this walk. She and Freddie were supposed to prepare a cold luncheon, so it was really only taking a lot of lids off and tipping it out onto the platters that Polly had snatched back from Abi, that awful day. Brigitta still could not think about it without shuddering.

No one else was out in the midday heat and Brigitta wandered slowly past the other big houses along the path. Most looked closed up for the summer, but now and again a family out on their patio would wave or call out 'Merry Christmas'. As she passed the flats, she looked up at the third floor but there was no sign of life, and she walked on, resolving to be more grateful for her messy, demanding, spoilt family, as though doing so now could assuage their treatment of others. Notably, orphans. Of course Abi *did* have a mother after all, Brigitta thought, but to spend so much energy pretending otherwise surely meant there was something pretty wrong with her.

When she came around the front of the house and leant down to unclip Domenica, she noticed an envelope sticking out of the box. She tugged it out, expecting a Christmas card hand-delivered by a neighbour who had missed the last post, but when the envelope came free it appeared much too thick and soft, as though many pages were folded inside. Brigitta turned it over and saw her mother's name in the small, careful handwriting of a schoolgirl.

She slipped through the gate and went straight up to her room, perching on the edge of the bed with her back to the door as she unsealed the envelope and took out the folded wad of paper.

Dear Phil

I am so sorry for all the trouble I have caused. I never meant to lie to you about my mother. It was only a misunderstanding but then I couldn't bring myself to clear it up, because the truth is, ever since I met you, I have wished that you could be my mother instead. You probably knew that already, but it was the only reason I did all the things I did. You don't have to keep reading this but I know I won't see you again, so I want to tell you the real, true story about my mother. Her name is Rae.

Brigitta looked away from the page. It wasn't meant for her and reading on would be such an invasion, but she couldn't help herself. The poor girl, pouring it all out on paper now, as though things could still be set right.

As Abi began to describe the miserable facts of her life since an accident killed her father and sister, her writing became a scrawl, enormous messy letters making only three or four words to a line. Parts of it Brigitta could barely make out.

'Herding? No. Oh God ...' she said under her breath.

... my mother started keeping things. Hoarding them really. I was only 10 when it started, and I tried to ...

Brigitta turned the page.

... then started to lose lots of weight and I still feel bad because I didn't notice to begin with. She always wore ...

'Oh God.' The details that followed made Brigitta's stomach churn, and she scanned ahead until her eye fell on her own brother's name.

Brigitta laid a hand across her forehead. She couldn't bear to know the details of how Freddie had acted towards such a vulnerable girl, who had probably come away thinking it was all her fault. That knowledge would change their relationship for ever, Brigitta knew, and she turned to the last page.

Even though I feel so ashamed, I'm still grateful for everything you did for me. All our mornings at the pool, drinking coffee and talking about books and the funny things people do, they were the best mornings of my life. I've never been happier than I was then and I will always be glad I met you. I know that Jude won't remember

you, but one day when he's old enough, I will tell him all about
you and his first year in Sydney.

'Oh God,' Brigitta said for the final time. A hot tear rolled down
her cheek and dropped onto the page.

'Brigitta, where are you?' Polly's voice came from the bottom of
the stairs. Hurriedly she refolded the letter and noticed a postscript
that had been added to the outer page.

PS. My name isn't actually Abigail. Abi isn't short for anything. I want
to be truthful about that too, although I know it doesn't really matter.

'Briggy!' Polly was coming along the hall. 'We're all waiting to do
the presents.' She put her head around the door. Brigitta shoved the
whole lot under her leg and turned to see Polly looking around the
room suspiciously. 'Are you coming down? We want to get started.
Why are you sitting by yourself in semi-darkness?'

'Just having a moment to myself, Pidge.'

'All right, well, can you not because Toby's about to pass out
from waiting.'

Polly ducked out and Brigitta tried to decide what to do with
Abi's letter. If she gave it to her mother, it was bound to upset her.
If Polly got hold of it, she'd get rid of it before Phil ever saw it.

Dragging a chair to the wardrobe, Brigitta reached to the highest
shelf and slid it between two folded blankets. As she reached the
very back, her hand met something cardboard. She put the letter
between her teeth and yanked it out.

Written on the lid in her own childish script was, 'BRIGGA'S
BOX OF SAD THINGS. DEFFINATELY NO LOOKING'. The
only thing in it was some crusty tube of ointment, but seeing it for
the first time in so long made her feel homesick for a different time.
She put Abi's letter inside and hid it all back behind the blankets.

As Brigitta made her way downstairs, bracing herself for festivity, she could only think how useful the box would have been this year. Her father. Guy, her career, Kentish Town. Polly being so hard on everyone, Freddie being so Freddie, her mother's doing as she pleased between moments of mad denial. Even Abi and her sweet babe – in it would all go. But, she thought passing by the window seat, she'd have needed a much bigger box.

87.

Well, Merry Christmas then

Roger was not getting into the spirit of things and it was making Elaine tense. She had not been up since 6.30 a.m. brushing a half-ham with an expensive ready-made gourmet glaze at ten-minute intervals, so that he and Stuart could sit like a pair of sad sacks around the thoughtfully decorated conservatory table. Clearly, neither of them had paused to consider how difficult it was to make citrus pomanders from scratch.

Elaine shook the end of a Christmas cracker at him. 'Roger!'

'I've already done one, thanks Elaine,' he said, pointing at the pink paper Christmas hat pulled down as far as his woolly eyebrows. Stu had refused to put his on but at least, Elaine had decided, he'd deigned to come out of his room.

'Well, Merry Christmas then,' she said, grasping both ends and trying to apply opposing force. Because she had opted for the more expensive kind with better prizes, the thick foil would not yield and she lost her grip, toppling a glass.

Roger leapt up to avoid the tide of Sparkling Appletiser washing towards him and managed to spare his special occasion slacks. But as he stood dabbing the tablecloth with a napkin, he frowned, then his mouth fell open, as though in the grip of an idea. Elaine twitched. Generally, she preferred Roger not to have ideas.

'Stuart,' he began, voice quavering.

'What?' Stu was leaning back in his chair, staring into the middle distance. After two bites he had pushed his plate away, a criminal waste of glazed ham, but Elaine consoled herself with the knowledge that, because it had come out so unusually moist, it would do for sandwiches.

'Stuart, you can't let her go.' Roger pulled off his paper hat and screwed it into a ball.

Stu looked at him askance. 'What?'

'You mustn't let Abi go.'

Elaine could not remember the last time Roger issued a direct command and she was not enjoying the experience now.

'Newsflash, Dad. It's over,' Stu said, sounding emptied of emotion.

'Only if you let it be. Plenty of couples have got over more than this, just by setting their minds to it. You've got a son to think about. If you let her go, you can be sure you won't see him grow up. Have you thought of that, Stuart? Really thought about it? I don't like to be direct with you,' Roger's volume rose and rose, 'but I think you're making a damned huge mistake.'

'Roger!' Elaine snapped. 'Please don't curse on the day of our Lord's birth! We're in the middle of Christmas lunch. Sit down and finish your ham.'

Roger turned to his wife and, for the first time in their married life, looked at her with something approaching anger.

'I am very sorry,' Roger said, pushing in his chair as though he was finished with festivities. 'I think I need to go for a drive. So ... Elaine ... the ham will ... *have to keep!*'

She clutched her small bosom in shock. For a moment, nobody moved, until Elaine stood up and, defying every cell in her body, began scraping their plates at the table. 'This Christmas has just gone to hell in a handbasket, hasn't it!'

But Roger was right about one thing. Elaine could not deny it. Being so truly moist, the ham *would* keep.

88.

Mostly it's been torture

'Righto you lot. I'm done for. Merry Christmas all.' Mark stood up, looking distinctly wobbly, and crunched over the carpet of wrapping paper, plastic packaging and pine needles. Phil had retired with the boys, and now Polly and Freddie and Brigitta were alone in the front room, lit only by tree lights.

Freddie was lying on the floor, tooling vaguely through the Blackberry Mark had given him. Brigitta was curled up at the foot-end of Polly, who lay the length of the velvet sofa. All three were stuffed, woozy with drink and too tired to go to bed. The King's College Christmas CD was playing on repeat. It had been on all day; no one could be bothered to turn it off.

Brigitta yawned. 'I know we didn't plan this exactly, but I haven't minded being all together. Today, I mean. Not the whole time. Mostly it's been torture.'

'Me neither,' Freddie said, without looking away from the screen. 'Even though you are both fucking crackers.'

'*We* are fucking crackers?' Polly said, but her voice was warm and teasing, as if all the stress of her year had been dissolved in champagne or, Brigitta thought, relief that the day was over and at this moment, no one was having a crisis that required her intervention.

'I mean it as a compliment,' Freddie said.

'Obviously.' Polly moved onto her side and closed her eyes to sleep where she lay.

'I miss Dad,' Brigitta said into the soft silence. 'Do you realise this is actually our second Christmas without him? It feels like the first, don't you think?' She finished the warm dregs of champagne in a glass within reach and fished out the bloated strawberry at the bottom. It fizzed softly in her mouth.

'I feel like it's all been blur,' Polly said, eyes still closed. 'I think I've just been in survival mode for twelve months.'

Freddie tossed the Blackberry aside and stretched. 'God, I miss Jamie.'

Brigitta and Polly sat bolt upright and stared at their brother.

'What?' Brigitta said.

'*Do* you?' Polly asked. 'On special days do you mean, or all the time?'

Freddie turned his head lazily in their direction. 'All the time. What? Of course I do, don't you? I miss him every minute, you silly bitches. We shared a room every day of my life.'

Brigitta did not know what to say, and could see that Polly was struggling as well. The last time they'd discussed it between themselves, they'd both admitted to missing James in a vague, conceptual way. He had become such a distant figure, any lingering sadness had been replaced by the sharp ache they felt for their father. Brigitta realised then that she'd never thought Freddie would be any different.

Freddie propped himself up on both elbows. 'Why do you think I'm such a fuck-up? You've had each other this entire time, but I lost my only brother. I was nine for fuck's sake.'

Brigitta caught Polly's eye and felt guilt, remorse, understanding, love pass between them. We have, she thought. We have had each other this entire time. Polly looked away, visibly chastened.

Freddie picked up his phone again, moving on as Brigitta knew only Freddie could.

'Hey, Brig, do you remember Will Binney? My mate from school?'

'Mmm. Mum used to give him haircuts in the garden when he'd been docked for it touching his collar.' She stretched out and lay, top and tail, against Polly's side. 'Why?'

'He's in London now. In *the arts*, and he's just pinged me, asking for your details.'

'Will *Binney*,' Polly said. 'He had the biggest thing for you, Briggy.'

'Please. Will Binney is gay on a tray.'

'I've been on a sixteen-day rugby tour with Will Binney,' Freddie said, 'and I can confirm he's most definitely not gay. Anyway, he's doing that *Cloudstreet* thingo in London and they're basically driving around Shepherd's Bush at this point and pulling Australians into a van. Shall I flick him your wotsit?'

'Can you still remember how to do an Australian accent?' Polly asked. Brigitta gave her a swift kick.

'I don't know. I don't think so, Freddie. I've started to think I won't go back. Someone has to stay with Mum for a while and I'm not sure London's forgiven me yet.' Brigitta shot her sister a nervous glance, but for once, Polly let the moment go, focused as she was on picking an After Eight off the carpet with her foot.

'London couldn't give a fuck, Brig,' Freddie said. 'You're good and that's all. Besides, I don't think you fit behind Mum's drapes anymore.' He cast a glance at the tall curtains on either side of the French doors, which had once upon a time opened on Brigitta's many childhood plays, improvised over fourteen acts.

'And anyway,' Freddie went on. 'I've decided I'm going to stay, as penance. I'll mind Mum for a bit, or let her mind me, whichever she'd enjoy most.'

Polly threw the wrapper at him but Brigitta could see she was smiling. He was not forgiven, but Brigitta knew he would be.

'Right! Custom has it the Woolnough children sneak out for a dip on Christmas night once the parentals are asleep. Come on.' Freddie got himself standing without his stick and hopped towards the sofa.

'Freddie, no. Shouldn't we clean up a bit?' Brigitta said.

'And I'm too tired. I need to go to bed.'

'Too bad, Pidge. It's tradition. I'm going to need one on each arm, I'm an invalid after all.'

* * *

Phil heard Brigitta creep up the stairs sometime after midnight and after a short eternity in the shower, she tapped on the door.

Phil was sitting with a glass of whisky. 'Yes?'

'Are you all right? I saw the light under your door. I didn't realise you were awake.' Brigitta padded in, squeezing a river of water out of her hair directly onto the carpet.

'Your father and I would always wait up until you all got back from the plunge.'

'Ha. How did you know about that?'

'Only by the quantity of sodden towels that greeted me every Boxing Day for twenty-five years. I think we've all now learned nothing goes unnoticed in this house.'

Phil held the covers back and, as always, Brigitta climbed in. 'Mum, Freddie just told me that a school friend of his is looking for actors, in London, and I thought I might give it a go but only if it is all right with you.'

'Do you mean that Binney boy?'

'Yes. You used to cut his hair, remember?'

Although it could just as well be used against you, Brigitta really was the most reliable rememberer of family facts and Phil smiled at the memory. 'I always thought he was a bit keen on you, darling.' From somewhere distant, Phil recalled his regular appearances at the back door that always coincided, to the minute, with Brigitta getting in from tennis.

'What do you think?' Brigitta sucked her bottom lip.

'About what, darling?'

'About me going back?'

'Oh.' Phil put her whisky on the bedside table. 'Could you, darling? Please? It's been lovely, of course, but I'm beginning to feel quite murderous from all the rooming in.'

Brigitta clapped a hand to her forehead. 'You are actually, honestly, the most infuriating woman in the entire world. Can I sleep here?'

'Go on then.' Phil reached over and switched off her light.

As they settled into the darkness, she felt Brigitta reach for her hand. The large windows were open, and the breeze carried in the scent of gardenias. Laughter drifted in from a passing launch.

'Perhaps,' Phil whispered after a moment, 'once you're back you might look up Abigail. Not right away but you know, one day. Just to see that she got on. I see now she was something of a troublemaker but she was also my ballast this dreadful year, darling. For what it was worth.'

'I will. But her name's not Abigail though, Mummy. It's just Abi.'

'How do you know that?' Phil felt thrown. Would there be no end to the revelations?

'I don't know, I just do. Abi's not short for anything.'

Phil rolled away, and with the weight of Brigitta's arm across her middle she lay and thought about her, the girl. Just Abi. Her anger was spent and she offered up a vague prayer for her wellbeing, which petered out as she drifted gently into sleep.

89.

Lucky you

Abi had worked it out wrong. When they landed, it was still Christmas Day.

'You've come in from Australia,' explained the customs officer from behind his Perspex window. His pale face was the same dirty grey white as his shirt. Behind him, a sign reminded Abi that if she assaulted the staff or used obscene language, she was liable to be prosecuted. 'You gain a day. Get to have your Christmas twice.' He pushed their passports back under the glass. 'Lucky you.'

Abi thanked him and returned the passports to a waxed paper airsickness bag she had found in her seat pocket. On the back was a to-do list she'd written out somewhere over the Atlas Mountains.

Ring Tanya re job.
Sort nursery.
Some cleaning etc.

The long flight had left her nauseous. With Jude happy enough in the carrier for the time being, she lined up for an Egg McMuffin to settle her stomach. Someone had made a half-hearted attempt to decorate the food court with tinsel but it only added to the derelict feeling of the terminal, as though the building itself could not bear the weight of all the human experience that had taken place within its walls.

Egg McMuffins tasted much worse than Abi remembered, strangely metallic, and she tossed it into the bin on her way into the underground walkway that led to the London shuttles. The Tube wasn't running on Christmas Day, so there was no way to avoid the twelve pound fare.

She let herself be carried along by a tide of people surging beneath its low ceiling, until they were spat out at the other end. Her memory flared with the first lungful of cold morning air. The bus fumes and car exhausts, the smell of crowds pressed too close, steam rising off damp overcoats, the cigarette butts smouldering in overflowing bins, wet leaves and rain running in the gutters, it was in her bones. It was Croydon and Highside Circuit. It was Rae and Louise. It was long, lonely days in the Student Services office and the longer, lonelier trips home. All here, unchanged. London would absorb her back, just as it had let her go.

Needles of rain were coming down at an angle and Abi tried to find a place to stand under the glass shelter, but the travellers already huddled there did not move to admit her. She tried to shield Jude with one side of her hoodie but he was unhappy now and throwing his weight from side to side in the carrier. Abi had no energy left to rock him. Although icy wind cut through her clothing, sweat beaded on her upper lip. She did not feel well.

A shuttle came and went, fitting only half the waiting passengers. An electronic board tracking the next one flicked from eight minutes to fourteen. When it finally came, Abi was last on, missing out on a seat. She stood at the front, a leg each side of her suitcase, and one hand clutching a nearby headrest. Before the shuttle pulled away, a vagrant passed by the closing doors, which sucked in his stench. Abi breathed through her mouth, against another wave of nausea boiling up from her stomach to her throat.

Jude began to cry. Abi found her phone and scrolled through photos to distract him. 'Look Jude, there's Phil in her garden.' The green of the grass seemed to glow against the backdrop of grey faces and rain-slicked windows. She scrolled through each picture, whispering in his ear until his temporary misery subsided.

Slowly the shuttle wound its way out of Heathrow and joined the A-road. At a set of traffic lights, Abi looked out and saw a girl a few years younger than her, waiting to cross with a pram. She had a dozen gold rings of descending size in each ear and a curl stuck to her forehead with gel. She was wearing a pair of reindeer antlers, shiny leggings and ballet flats with the backs trodden down. Abi had almost forgotten about them, that kind of mum, and she looked away quickly in case the girl happened to look back and mistake Abi for one of her own.

The shuttle let off at Mitcham. She needed to find a taxi but as she turned to look along the road, fatigue and biting cold and the smell of the fried chicken being eaten out of a cardboard bucket by a yellow-faced teenager made her feel suddenly faint. As she shot her hand against a tree to stop herself from tumbling over, a thousand white stars burst in front of her eyes. Abi found the paper bag in her pocket, shook out their passports and threw up into her to-do list.

90

It is not a special day for us

It was not until Abi was standing at the peeling front door of Highside Circuit that she realised she didn't have a key. Or any key, to any door, anywhere. Without credit, Abi had not been able to text Rae to say she was coming home, but she knew her mother would be there to peer through the front nets and let her in.

Inside the carrier, Abi could feel Jude's nappy soaking through and into her T-shirt. She was so thirsty her tongue kept sticking to the roof of her mouth.

She stepped over the waterlogged cartons spilling newspapers and swollen piles of junk mail in front of the door and knocked. The bins spewed rubbish, and rain pooled in the lids upturned on the ground. A single weed, trying bravely to establish itself in a crack in the concrete, was the only note of green. Although it was mid-morning, the pewter-coloured sky above Croydon gave no sense of time. It only was.

Through a gap in the nets Abi saw the blue flicker of the television in the front room. The rain was beginning to soften. She knocked again, stamping her feet against the cold.

When no one came she rapped on the window, until Pat's front door opened and a young woman stepped out, draping a scarf around her head.

'Nobody is home,' she said in a softly accented voice. 'The lady isn't inside.'

'Where is she?' Abi asked, looking around as though Rae would be somewhere in the concrete courtyard. She hadn't been further than the Iceland on the corner with Merton Road since 1998. 'I'm her daughter.'

'My husband drives a car and yesterday she asked him to take her to the hospital.' The woman looked at her and then at Jude with concern. 'Please come inside. It is very, very cold.'

Not knowing what else to do, Abi stowed her suitcase behind a carton and stepped over the low dividing wall. Inside, the woman took off the headscarf and hung it on a peg. She had long, dark hair that fell around her shoulders like a slippery shawl. Pat's Axminster carpet was gone and the wallpaper that was designed to make the hallway look like a birch forest in spring had been painted out. Someone was trying to remove the mustardy tinge to the Artex ceiling, formed by three decades of Pat's smouldering Parliaments, but had only got halfway along so far. Abi followed the woman to the kitchen where four young children were sitting at the table, eating bread and Nutella. She gestured towards the only empty chair. Abi sat and finally released Jude from the carrier, feeling the weight of his wet nappy in her lap. One of the children, a girl of about six, slipped off her chair and found a coloured plastic ring. She wiped it on her sparkly L'il Princess T-shirt and handed it to Jude.

'Your mother is not healthy,' the woman said, as she put a glass of tea in front of Abi and stirred in three large teaspoons of sugar.

'I know.' It had been a secret, well kept for years, and all of a sudden it seemed everyone knew. 'Do you know why she went in? What for exactly?'

'We hear a lot of coughing, very bad, through the wall, night and day. But I am not sure where she go because she never come outside. I bring her food but she say no thank you.' She spoke cautiously, as though the news would come as a shock. 'I am sorry to tell you.'

'I already knew. Thank you though.'

'My name is Darya.'

'Sorry, I'm Abi. Thank you for this tea, it's really nice.'

'It is St Georges Hospital on the Blackshaw Road. I cannot come with you because my husband is working.'

Buses did not run on Christmas Day. Already low on money, Abi realised she would have to walk. 'I know the one. Thank you. I suppose I should get going,' she said, although the tea was spreading warmly through her insides like dye in water, and she did not want to leave the warmth of the kitchen, where the familiar ghost of Pat seemed to hover. Abi tried to rouse herself.

'Perhaps, you do not know me, but I am trustworthy,' Darya said hesitantly. 'If you must walk you can leave the baby with us.'

'I would, I totally would.' Abi was eager to acknowledge the unusual kindness. 'But I can't ask you to mind him on your Christmas Day.'

'It is not a special day for us. If you feel happy, I am happy. Outside is very cold.'

The children had been following the conversation as they sat eating and now the L'il Princess girl stood up, stuck her hip out and folded her arms. When she spoke, Abi had to cover her mouth against erupting laughter. 'We was gunna do *parp*cleaners, innit.'

Home again.

When it was settled, Abi accepted a Nutella sandwich for the walk and kissed Jude goodbye. He refused to leave the little girl's arms, mesmerised by her T-shirt and pierced ears. Darya apologised for not having a raincoat or umbrella to lend her.

'It's all right,' Abi said. 'I'll be fine. If you don't mind me asking, how old are you? You don't look old enough to have four kids.'

'I am twenty-three years old.'

'Oh right. Same here.'

'So we are both feeling old enough, then.' With that, Darya stepped in and hugged her and did not appear to mind when Abi cried, just for a moment, into her lovely hair.

91.

I am a fucking social worker

'Could you tell me where to find Raelene Egan?' Abi asked the receptionist. 'She's a patient but I don't know which ward she's on.'

It had taken over an hour to walk to the hospital, and Abi had done two full laps of the squat redbrick building before she found an entrance. Foil-like windows, tinged with green, stared at her blankly, unconcerned, as the rain soaked her to the bone.

'How'd you spell it?'

'E, G, A, N.'

'Bear with me a minute.'

Abi watched the receptionist depress each key with a marked lack of haste.

'Here we go. Egan, R. She's no visitors at this time.'

'I'm her daughter.'

'ID?'

Abi had her passport and showed her the photo page.

'Right. Hold a minute.' She spoke briefly into her headset, at the same time drawing circles on a photocopied map of the hospital.

'Third floor to High Dependence.'

As soon as the lift doors opened, a doctor stepped forward, as though he'd been waiting for her. 'You're Raelene Egan's daughter?'

Abi wiped wet hair off her face and nodded.

'I'm Jonathan. Head of the team looking after your mother. I take it you have not seen her in some time.' He flipped backwards through a folder of notes.

'That's right, yeah. I was in Australia. I got in just now. Well, this morning.' Abi wondered if she was allowed to call him Jonathan.

'Before I take you in, I have to warn you, she presented under five and a half stone. Thirty-five kilos. We've been unable to improve on that. The body is working too hard with the pneumonia. Little response to the antibiotics, but we're limited in terms of dosage owing to the current weight. I'm very sorry, Abi, but it's about keeping her comfortable at this stage.' He paused, waiting for a show of emotion. 'We've been attempting to contact you for the last twenty-four hours even though your mother requested that you weren't to be notified. I am very sorry.'

Abi studied the zip of her hoodie.

'So, this way then.' The doctor placed a hand on Abi's back and ushered her along the corridor. 'And I'll talk to a nurse about getting you some dry clothes.' It was only then that Abi worried she would cry. But she would not be shocked. Abi, who had lifted Rae naked and unconscious out of a shower run cold. Abi, who'd slept in her mother's bed on nights when Rae couldn't get warm. Abi, who had spent her life watching her mother die. The chemical dread that flooded her body as she walked beside the doctor was only a reflex, she told herself, her zero-setting from a long childhood.

The ward was divided into four by thick paper curtains. A narrow strip of windows looked out on a featureless carpark below a flat, white sky.

The doctor held the curtain back and excused himself as Abi stepped in and saw her mother for the first time in a year. Her shell of clothing was gone. The parka, the jumper upon jumper, the knee socks over loose leggings, the knit hat. Instead, two bare arms lay at her sides, like lengths of rope knotted at each bulbous elbow. Her face was turned away so that her neck was a mess of sharp tendons and deep hollows.

Sensing someone's presence, Rae looked over. Her face stretched into a smile, skin against cheekbone, eye sockets dug out with a spade. Abi realised she was going to be sick.

'My girl,' Rae said as she watched her daughter lunge for the wastebasket beside the bed. 'My darling. You've come home. I told them not to bother you. I'm sorry, lovey. I didn't want to be trouble for you.'

Abi stayed crouched over the bin and spat out a final acid mouthful.

'You right, my darling? Hold a minute, I can buzz us a nurse,' Rae said as she was overtaken by a wet, burbling bout of coughing. Abi hauled herself to standing and carried the heavy bin out to the corridor, looking for someone who could take it away.

No one came. Eventually, Abi put it down against the wall and walked back to her mother's bed.

'This is the best surprise of me life,' Rae said. 'You've made me day, you have. Made me year!' After each exclamation, they both waited for a fit of thick, mucousy coughing to pass. 'If I'd known you was coming, I would have done us a proper ex-mas lunch. Where is my grandson? Where's the little man?'

'I've left him with a friend,' Abi said.

'What about Stu, love? Has he come with you as well?'

Abi shook her head.

'Oh, Abi love.' Rae's rictus grin faded. She reached out a hand, tight and pink and shiny, and Abi made herself take it. 'I wish I'd known you was coming. I only came in here yesterday because if I'm honest, I've only come in here because I needed a bit of company. No you, and no Pat. I only didn't want to bother you.' She brightened. 'They'll let me out now. Now that you're home.

And we could have Christmas tomorrow, couldn't we? I'll tidy up a bit. All the puddings and that will be on sale at Marks.'

Rae closed her eyes. She had exhausted herself.

As Abi went to sit down, the doctor reappeared and invited her to a nearby treatment room.

'I thought perhaps you'd have some questions,' he said, shutting the door.

'When do you think she'll be able to go home?' Abi asked. 'I'm here now, so I can look after her again.'

The doctor shuffled his seat closer to hers. 'I'm terribly sorry. Perhaps I wasn't clear earlier. Your mother will remain here until – I should say, her heart has been weakened by the years of chronic malnutrition. It will only be a matter of weeks. At best.'

'No.'

'I wish there was more we could do.'

'No,' Abi said, voice rising.

'I really am terribly sorry. Although it's fortunate that you made it back in time. Often patients are able to hang on until loved ones return.'

Abi felt a long anguished cry rise from her belly.

The doctor waited. 'We are able to connect you with a social worker, who can ...'

'I am a fucking social worker!' Abi cried. Then, dropping her head to her hands, she whispered, 'Well, I almost was.'

92.

Run to the pain

Every car and lorry gave Abi a blast of the horn as it tore past her. It was getting dark and the footpath had run out some time ago, and now Abi was running along the edge of fast-moving traffic, trying to find a gap in the high concrete barrier. She had left the hospital by a different exit and, unable to orient herself, she'd taken a narrow alley to where she thought taxis would be waiting. She could ask the driver to take her £6 towards home. Instead, she found herself edged in by a thin, dirty canal. To rejoin the right road she climbed through a hole in a wire fence, wet again and shaking now all over. Her feet ached from the rising cold but she could not stop running. Now she was approaching an immense roundabout. Six lanes of traffic converged from multiple directions. She hovered at its edge in a circle of street lamp, waiting for a break in the streaming cars. A white van slowed as it passed. The driver wound down his window, 'Give us a smile darling. It might never happen.'

As he hared away, a gap formed and she ran towards the other side. Horns blasted, and she was doused by puddle water as a motorbike swerved to avoid her.

In her pocket she held onto the key for her mother's house, tied on a ratty piece of pink ribbon. She had found it in the metal locker beside Rae's bed, along with her plastic coin purse and a brown sandwich bag filled with pictures of Julia Roberts at Cannes.

Abi kept running. She thought of Jude. She was no longer frightened about going back to her mother's house; she only wanted to be inside somewhere.

When she reached the Merton Road, she weaved her way between bundled-up people who'd risked coming out. She passed the Superdrug where her waters had broken the year before. It was closed, but a Christmas carol piped out of wire-caged speakers. 'Joy to the World, the Lord is Come.'

Finally, she saw the streetlights of Highside Circuit and stumbled up Pat's brick path. Darya wanted her to come in and get dry and eat something. Abi declined as politely as she could and the little girl brought Jude over. They had been sandwiched all together on the sofa watching a repeat of the Queen's Speech. He smelled like baby shampoo and was wearing a warm pyjama suit that Darya said she could return later.

Abi carried him outside and stepped over the brick divide. The smell, as she pushed open the front door, made her stomach turn so violently that she gagged. She held Jude's face into her shoulder. Bulging polythene rubbish bags lined the hallway. The carpet of the front room was hidden by layers of shredded magazine pages, like the lining of a litter box. Wads of soiled bedding and clothes had been pushed into one corner, and the card table stood like a lame animal on three legs. The walls had been turned into a shrine to Rae's favourite stars, hundreds of pictures cut out and sticky-taped together in messy striations. Abi looked in horror as the muted television illuminated a vast montage of Kate Middleton on her wedding day.

Then, as fast as she could, she threw open the window. Wind swirled in and picked up the magazine pieces like snow. She wrenched down the mural, which came away in a single sheet.

The kitchen was a midden of Argos catalogues, plastic bags and full pint cartons of skim milk. One had already exploded, and spattered up the window like a bloodstain bleached of colour. The cork tiles stuck to Abi's ballet flats as she picked her way across the kitchen to open the back door. In the freezer, she found two months' worth of ready-meals that Pat had left there, labelled with days of the week, entombed in a rough white block of ice.

When, from the corner of her eye, Abi saw the rustling of something alive, she ran out of the house and found Darya still waiting on the doorstep. She opened her arms for the baby. 'When my husband is home, I come and help you,' she said, taking him inside.

Abi took a deep breath and braced herself to re-enter. Upstairs, she found her own bedroom almost as she had left it, the door sealed against the creep of Rae's madness. She pulled open one of her drawers, looking for something she could tie over her nose and mouth. There was nothing inside except a single baby sock and her ancient Discman, stuck all over with apple stickers. She opened it and saw the hypnobirthing CD she had meant to return to the library. Without knowing why, she put on the foamy headphones and pressed play.

'You're comfortable. In control,' said a gentle new-age voice, over a synthesised version of Pachelbel's *Canon*. Abi had once described the piece to Phil, claiming it was her favourite classical song, although she didn't know its name.

Phil guessed it in one and then said, 'No dear, that's like having Vivaldi's *Four Seasons* as your Desert Island Disc.' Then she made Abi sit down and listen to Bach's cello concertos from start to finish, snapping off the player at the end and saying, 'Do you see?'

'Relax,' the voice went on. 'Your body knows what to do. Let your muscles become very relaxed. Your delivery will be successful in every way.'

Now, beyond fatigue, beyond hunger, beyond everything, Abi removed her heavy hoodie, pressed it to her nose and mouth and walked downstairs.

'You are the source of life. You are the universal mother. Run to the pain.'

93.

Conversationally at
Southgate Centre

Abi worked through the night, ignoring her roiling nausea. She concentrated on the soothing voice of the CD in her ears and the task of bagging rubbish and dragging it outside. She didn't feel cold, although the windows remained open to the night air. She was afraid a heater would cause the liquefied rubbish already in bags to stew where it sat.

When social services opened again after Christmas, she would do what she already knew how to do. Call the benefits office, arrange an emergency loan, the single parent allowance, a waste collection. But in the meantime there was only filling the next plastic sack until it threatened to split.

She emptied the kitchen cupboards of dry goods sticky with weevils and used a dustpan to shovel refuse off the small square of bathroom floor. Darya knocked on the door early the next morning with a jam crumpet wrapped in kitchen paper, which Abi ate without letting it touch her skin or clothes.

For the week after that, Darya came over whenever she could with her own bucket of cleaning things. She chose a corner to start on without asking and sang quietly to herself as she worked.

When Abi visited Rae in the mornings, Darya looked after Jude, wheeling him up to the play park with the others in a huge double pram. Abi could not bring herself to take Jude along.

'What is it that you listen to in your player?' Darya asked one evening as they bagged up newspapers in the hallway. Abi fetched the Discman and, blushing, offered her the headphones.

Darya's eyes became enormous as she pressed the headphones to both ears.

'It is like my English lesson listening,' she said loudly. 'Only ...' She tugged one headphone away from her ear.

'You'd not want to use it conversationally at Southgate Centre,' Abi said.

'Excuse me, do you know the way to the station?' Darya laughed. 'My womanhood is opening like a flower.'

After that, whenever they passed on the stairs, hauling bags and buckets, they exchanged gentle encouragements.

'Your body knows what it must do, Abi.'

'You are a strong, capable woman. You are deserving of an uncomplicated birth.'

When all the rubbish was gone, Abi began carrying out the furniture.

One morning, as she tugged down the stained nets from the bay window, she watched a van stop in front of the mounting pile and a man get out to load Rae's chair into the back. Nobody wanted the cathode ray television, the thinning pink wedding towels, or the fly-speckled standard lamp. Eventually, on a bleak, blustery Monday early in the new year, a council truck rumbled up and consumed the entire kerbside monument that Abi had made to her mother's life. Only once in that time did Abi cry, and only because the bottle of hospital-grade disinfectant Darya bought for the floors filled each emptied room with the clean, sharp tang of eucalyptus. That night, like every other, Abi crept upstairs bone-tired and, after scrubbing herself in the shower, curled herself around Jude, already asleep on her single bed. She took out her old phone and closed her eyes. 'Once upon a time there were three little kittens,' Phil began in her rich radio voice. 'Mittens, Tom Kitten, and Moppet.'

94.

Hello Morris

Abi left the wardrobe in her mother's bedroom until last. She knew it was the repository of Rae's real treasures. In the years after the accident, Abi would sneak in to examine the photo albums and trinket boxes kept there before carefully putting everything back in its place. Now she was going to throw it all away. She was sick of it all. Sick of her own longing, sorrow and sadness and wanting. That's what had got her into so much trouble. If she had nothing and wanted nothing, she could be free. Holding an empty bin liner in one hand, she tried to pull open the door, which had warped against the frame.

After a sharp kick, the door gave and a waft of wet, musty air filled her nostrils. Inside, the shelves bowed under the weight of shoeboxes and bulging albums, but the arrangement was unusually orderly. No rubbish, no magazines. Abi drew out a thick, plastic-coated album. It made a cracking noise as she lifted its blue and white gingham print cover away from the first page. There, behind filmy plastic, was Abi. Missing her front teeth and wearing a red home-knitted jumper and tartan skirt, sitting beside Louise, who had one foot up on the brown sofa that Abi had recently dragged out to the curb. Louise was pretending to rest her elbow on her sister's head and grinning at the camera.

It hurt to breathe as Abi turned the page – another crack – and saw her family, all four of them, standing in front of the turnstiles at Regent's Park Zoo.

'We'll make a day of it.' Rae always used to say that. Louise had her fingers in her ears and was making faces at the stranger they must have asked to take the picture. The girls had on matching navy duffel coats and Abi was leaning in against Rae, wearing a tight mustard polo neck and denim skirt, hair freshly coloured red. She was smiling with her face upturned to the man in the cord jacket, head and shoulders taller than her, standing beside her with his arm around her back. He looked proudly down the lens.

'Hello Dad,' Abi said, putting the tip of her finger on her father's chest. 'Hello Morris.' She wiped her eyes on the back of her wrist, then faster and faster, she turned each page. Morris wearing a pair of narrow jeans and leaning against a car he was washing in the street outside Highside, brand new nets in the windows. Another one of them lined up for the Tower of London, Louise scowling because – Abi remembered – she'd wanted Mr Whippy and not got it. A series of empty pages followed and then, on the final page, under the bubbling plastic, was every picture of Jude that Abi had ever sent to Rae from her phone camera.

They were terrible pictures, grainy and blurry, a half-moon of pink thumb often covering the corner of the frame. Jude on the platform of the pool, Jude on the grass, Jude sitting in the bottom of the shower wearing Abi's goggles. Each one had been printed out on plain copy paper. Rae must have gone all the way to the library, more than a mile away, and paid 20p a page. They were trimmed with scissors and arranged in a neat grid, the corners held down with stickers, roses and rabbits and love hearts. At the top of the page, Rae had written 'GRANDMA'S LITTLE TREASURE!' in a shaky hand. Abi let the album slide off her lap and slumped forward until her forehead was pressed into the lumpy floor. It absorbed the sound of her crying each of their names. Rae, Louise, Morris. Jude, Stu. Kind, lovely Roger. Phil. She wanted them all.

95.

Let me go now

Abi had promised to bring Jude down to the hospital. For more than a fortnight, she had put it off, saying he was at nursery during the day, which was almost true although nursery meant Darya's house. As soon as Abi could get her old job back, she would sort out something more permanent. But compelled by what she had found in Rae's wardrobe, Abi took Jude to visit his grandmother. She understood now that Rae loved her as much as she could love anything from inside her windowless grief. Late into the evenings, Abi had peeled every photograph out of the album and wiped them clean. She had studied each lock of baby hair wrapped in tissue, each matchbox of milk teeth, every trophy and trinket of Egan family life, realising as she went that it hadn't always been a regime of quiet desperation. There had been birthday cakes and Christmas trees, holidays, a station wagon. As Abi put the best bits into a shoebox she would take to the hospital, to prove to Rae that she had been happy once, she thought fleetingly of Brigga's Box of Sad Things, probably still buried between blankets in the big house.

In the front row of the 44 bus, Abi held Jude on her lap. She had put the shoebox in a Sainsbury's bag along with her ragged copy of *First Year with Baby* and the hypnobirthing CD she was going to return on their way home. Jude had woken early and he rested his head against her chest, as they both stared bleary-eyed at the boarded-up shopfronts and chicken outlets along the high street before passing onto the A-road. In her back pocket was the best photograph from the zoo, which she was going to stick up beside Rae's bed.

When they arrived, Abi zipped off Jude's jacket and walked the familiar corridors to the High-Dependency Unit. She carried him through the ward, accustomed now to the pip-pip of machines and suppressed moans coming from each curtained cubicle. Rae was sleeping.

'Mum,' Abi said in a loud whisper. 'Rae!' she said again when her mother didn't stir. 'Guess who I've got with me? Rae.' Abi reached out and touched the ridge of her mother's thigh beneath the white blanket. 'Mum!'

Slowly, Rae stirred and turned her face towards Abi and Jude, who was burrowing into his mother's neck. Abi turned him around so Rae could see him.

'Oh love,' she said, barely audible. 'Abi my girl. Look at him, eh?'

As she spoke, a thin ribbon of saliva leaked out of the side of her mouth. Abi picked up a corner of the sheet and wiped it away.

'He's a big boy. Aren'tcha? What a big boy.' Rae tried to smile at him. 'Haven't you done well, eh …' she began, before pausing to get her breath back.

Abi put the supermarket bag on the floor and reached into her back pocket. 'I brought you some things to look at.' She held up the photograph so Rae could see it.

'Ah, look at that,' her mother said with a tight smile.

'It's nice, isn't it? It's to cheer you up. We were having fun, weren't we? Until I fell over, remember? I was going to put it up somewhere.' Abi looked around for a section of wall clear of cables and monitors, alarms and sockets.

'Take it home wi' you, love. I'll have a good look another day.'

'I could just put it in your drawer and you can look at it later.'

'Abi. I don't want it. I can't look at it. I want to go.' A gurgling sound followed from the back of her throat. For an instant, her eyes appeared to bulge in their deep sockets.

'What? Where do you want to go?' Abi moved Jude from one hip to the other. He was getting so heavy.

'Abi, I just want to go. It was Louise that made me a mum and I was never a mother one more day, after your dad's done what he's done.'

'What do you mean? Mum! What are you talking about?'

Rae's face appeared to cave in as she screwed her eyes closed. 'He's done it to himself, Abi. You know that. You know he has. He's gone and put the gas on.'

A dazzling aura lit up in Abi's peripheral vision, shifting and blurring at the edges. 'He wouldn't do that! Why would he do that?'

'If I knew that Abi ... if I knew that ...' Rae looked down at the outline of her ruined body under the blankets.

'You told me it was an accident.'

'Of course I did. You were just a titchy thing. What else was I going to tell you?'

'But what about Louise though? He would never do that to Louise.' Abi tightened her hold on Jude, as another flash of light burst at her temples.

'He didn't know she'd come back in, did he? I should never have let her run home.' Rae covered her face with her awful hands. Each fingernail was thickened and brown. 'I should have kept her with me. But look what I went and done, letting her run off. Why else would I do this to myself, Abi. Why would I?'

Rae could not show her face and Abi was consumed with pity. 'I was no mother to you, Abi. I'm sorry but that's how it was.'

Gently, Abi lowered herself onto the side of the bed and held Jude over her shoulder so he could look the other way. 'You could have told me once I got older, so I'd understand and then I might have been able to help you.'

'I were helping you. I took it all into myself so maybe you'd never have to know. That was the only thing I could do for you, Abi, my love. You don't need me now, do you? Let me go, would you love, eh? I'm that tired.' A long, low bronchial wheeze came out of her mouth, and as she expelled the breath, Abi smelt something like meat beginning to turn.

'Mum! It's all right. Don't talk. Mum!' Rae's entire body began to tremble beneath the blanket. Her lips curled back, exposing dark bottom teeth. Abi ran into the hall shouting. Nurses appeared from two different directions and rushed past her, surrounding the bed. They called instructions at each other, as Abi pressed Jude's head against her shoulder and tried to press into the circle. 'Mum! It's all right. Mum.' Jude began to cry and Abi's last memory, before her vision exploded into white and she fell backwards to the floor, was of a nurse turning and diving to catch him out of her flailing arms.

96.

You look a bit rough

The doctor was standing beside the plastic-sheeted bed in the treatment room reading notes on a clipboard, when Abi woke up. Dazed, she swallowed and tried to sit up but a throbbing pain at the base of her skull sent her back into the rubber pillow. 'Where's my baby? Where's Jude?'

'Ah. Hello there. You're awake.' The doctor looked grave.

'Where's my baby?'

'Abi, I'm very sorry to let you know, your mother has passed away. An hour or so ago. You fainted and had to be brought in here to have your head stitched. We gave you something to keep you under until it was cleaned up. Again, I'm terribly sorry to have to deliver the news this way.'

Abi barely heard him. In some way, she already knew.

'Where's my baby?' Abi tried to sit up again.

'He was taken down to the day nursery by a social worker. I'll get him sent up when you're ready, but for now, you do need to stay here.'

'Where is the nursery?' Abi struggled free of the sheet and put her feet on the floor. Her legs felt like water, and she fell heavily against the doctor.

'Abi,' he said, helping her back onto the bed. 'Your son is fine. If you would please stay lying down, I'll ring downstairs now.'

As he took up the internal phone outside the door, he signalled to a plump nurse in a tight green uniform passing along the corridor. They spoke briefly, and after a moment, she entered the treatment room with a bright orange ice-lolly in a plastic tube.

'Have a suck on that,' she said, sneakers squeaking against the lino tiles. 'That's a Pedialyte. It's meant to be for children, but you'll be feeling well dehydrated in your state.'

Abi let the ice-lolly be put in her hand as she lay back. Her entire consciousness was centred on the throbbing in her skull.

The nurse had begun rearranging the sheet, tucking it tightly under her legs. 'There we go, that's better.' She perched on the end of the bed and gave Abi's foot a gentle squeeze. 'You need your rest. It's no good for the baby, all this stress.'

'I hope he's too young to understand it.'

'Of course he won't! Or *she*. We don't know yet, d'we?'

Abi levered herself onto one elbow, then the other. 'Pardon? What?'

'I said, or *she*. You're going to find out then, are you?'

Abi's mouth fell open. She stared wide-eyed at the nurse, who was looking back at her, confused. 'I had to do your bloods. Did you not –'

Before Abi could answer, the doctor put his head around the door. 'Your son's being brought up now. His father arrived a short time ago, so he's been down there with him. They'll be here in a moment or two.'

Abi's mind blazed. She could not settle on a single thought.

'Well, congratulations,' the nurse said, squeaking out of the room.

'She's in here,' Abi heard her say from outside. 'That's right. She's still a bit addled so keep things light is my suggestion.'

'Yep, right. Thanks. Come on mate, let's go see Mum.' Stu had a hiking pack on his back and his son on his hip. Jude was holding a plastic spoon in each hand. A circle of dried yoghurt had dried around his mouth and down the front of his Aran jumper.

'Hey, babe,' Stu said. His freckled face drew into a pained smile. 'How are you going? You look a bit rough.'

The instant Abi had heard his loud voice in the hallway, her heart had begun tossing itself around inside her chest. Blood roared in her ears.

'What are you doing here?' The great waves of relief at seeing him, her need to be gathered up into his arms, was only tiredness or painkillers or shock, she told herself as Stu took the chair beside the bed and sat Jude on the floor to play with his spoons.

'Dad and I started talking quite a bit once I went back to Gordon, after seeing you that day in the flat, and it helped me understand some stuff. And I read your letter, and after that, I knew I was coming. It just took me a while to man up, I guess. Mum wasn't really into it, but Dad sort of stuck it to her a bit on Christmas Day. I wish you'd been there for that. It wasn't funny, but it actually was pretty funny.'

'How did you know where I was?'

'Your neighbour told me.' Stu leaned over and covered Jude's ears. 'Fuck, babe. That house. Your neighbour said that was *after* you'd hauled most of the crap out. I wanted to put a bulldozer through it.'

Abi felt a surge of shame. 'Did she give you a key?'

'Nah, I just had a look in the window and then came straight here. Hey,' he said, 'I'm really sorry about your mum. The doctor told me when I got here.'

'It's all right,' Abi said flatly. 'I always knew it was coming. It was the slowest suicide in history, really.'

Stu appeared acutely uncomfortable as Abi went on.

'I just didn't think it would be now, or not today anyway. She's been gone for so long, I think I forgot it hadn't actually happened. That doesn't make sense, does it? But it's true. It's true to me.' She could not bring herself to tell him the truth about Morris.

'I get it,' Stu said. 'I'm so sorry you had to deal with all that, your whole life. Makes me realise why you wouldn't want everyone knowing everything.' Stu took her hand. 'Hey, listen. I missed you.'

Abi tried to pull it away, but Stu held on with a soft grip. 'I missed you, and Jude. The point is, I've done a lot of thinking and even with everything that's happened I want to give this another go. And to be honest, I don't really want Jude growing up in that house, now that I've seen it.'

Perhaps it was the way Jude was playing so happily, oblivious to the chaos all around him. Perhaps it was the outfit he wore that like most of his clothes, Abi had struggled to provide for him herself. Perhaps it was all the work she had done to Rae's house, with the help of a neighbour she'd only just met, not Stu. Or the fact that he'd written it off in a single moment, without the faintest idea of what it was like before. But as incandescent rage coursed through her veins, Abi raised herself to sitting, twisted away at the waist as though winding herself up and, wheeling back around, slapped Stu hard across the face.

'You don't get to be with me!' she cried, delivering hit after hit. With every movement, her skull howled with pain but she could not stop. Even when Stu tried to shield his face, she didn't cease, instead striking the back of his hands. 'You don't get to! You left me! Every time it got too hard for you, you ran home to your mother. You don't get another chance with me. I'm finished with you.' When the palm of her hand began to sear she dropped to one side and, mustering all the strength in her small body, brought her leg around and delivered a hard kick. With Jude still between his ankles, Stu was trapped and Abi landed a series of hard blows to his side.

'I don't need you! I don't need you!'

Finally, she drew her leg inwards, knee bent like a loaded spring, and dispensed a final strike to his stomach that sent him reeling backwards in his chair.

'Abi, stop, stop.' The final blow had winded him and he breathed hard from the top of his lungs. 'You'll hurt yourself.'

Her fit of fury had blinded her, but now Abi looked down and saw Jude bouncing up and down on his rump, giggling as though it was a great game and, for the first time she had seen, clapped his hands, three times in succession.

As much as she longed to reach down for him, when she tried to lift her arm, bone-crushing fatigue forced her to roll onto her side, draw herself into a ball and close her eyes. The back of her head felt like it had split open but her hand would not move to check.

Stu picked up the baby instead, straightened his little jumper and smoothed his hair. 'Are you okay, Abi?'

She screwed her eyes more tightly closed and did not answer.

'You just lie there,' Stu said, covering her with the sheet. 'Have a little sleep. Jude and I will just be here.'

Abi had already drifted into something deeper than sleep and there, standing around her, were Morris and Louise and Rae, Phil and Brigitta and Roger. She felt Phil lay her warm hand on her forehead as though feeling for a temperature. Morris spoke. 'I am so proud of you, Abi. You are such a good, clever girl.' Louise was sucking a sweet and danced a funny jig that only Abi could see.

She willed them all to stay as they were, so she never had to return to the empty, bleach-smelling world of the treatment room, but as her mind led her from one face to the next, she realised that Jude was not there. She had to go back for him. She lifted her heavy eyelids and let the dream die away.

Stu leapt up and held Jude close to her. With both small hands, the baby reached for her face and pressed his round, open mouth to her cheek. The wettest possible kiss.

'I got you a juice,' Stu said. 'You should probably try and have some even though it's tropical, which I know you hate, but I panicked.'

'I'm glad you're here,' Abi said. She felt tears roll out of the corners of her eyes and run into her ears.

'Well, I'm not going anywhere. I know I said it before, Abi, but I really mean it.'

'I'm pregnant.'

Stu was quiet for a moment. 'Any chance I'm the –'

'No.'

Abi lay still, waiting for him to get up.

'Right. Well, I guess that changes things a bit.' But he did not move.

* * *

It was decided that Abi would stay in overnight, and the next morning, Stu returned with Jude and waited while Abi signed her mother's paperwork, then her own. The doctor took a final look at her sutured head, then wished her well. She seemed like a very brave person, he said, as she accepted the envelope containing her discharge notes and Rae's death certificate. 'You seem to have done well, in the worst of circumstances.' She thanked him and Stu held out his arm so she could walk to the lifts, supported.

Earlier, on his way up, Stu had looked at his blurred reflection in the lift's stainless interior. He was scared shitless. Jude, in his arms, was looking less like a baby and more like a little boy. Fuck. The doors slid open. Stu swung Jude onto his other side and stepped out. 'Right. Here we go, mate.' No more cock-ups.

On their way through the lobby, Abi stopped and pointed towards a small plastic Christmas tree. Its lights flicked on and off. 'This is where I had him. Just there. By that stained bit on the carpet.'

'I'm only a year late then,' Stu said. '*First Year with Baby*, eh? I guess that's not going back to the library any time soon. I've called us a mini-cab.'

97

Captain of the Hockey Thirds

'Hey, hi.'

Feeling a tap on her shoulder, Brigitta wheeled around. 'Will Binney, hello. Fancy running into you here. I've literally just got off a plane.'

He offered her a hand and she shook it and then, as though it were an afterthought, leaned in and kissed her on each cheek. 'Happy New Year and all that.'

'Weren't we going to meet tomorrow to talk about dates and things?' Brigitta asked, stepping back and trying to take in the grown-up version of a formerly unremarkable, often annoying teenage boy. 'Gosh, your skin's really cleared up, hasn't it?'

'And you've had your braces off,' Will said, as Brigitta continued to appraise him.

'Really, it's so funny to think it's the actual Will Binney. Ten-speed owner, shot glass collector, captain of the Hockey Thirds.'

'*Vice*-captain. I can't believe it's you either, Brigitta Woolnough, eye-roller, bra stuffer, crème de menthe connoisseur.'

Brigitta couldn't think what to say just then and was relieved when Will changed the subject without appearing to notice her heightened colour.

'I know we're meeting tomorrow, but I was on my way back from Bristol and that flight's such a bastard I thought I may as well meet you. Your brother gave up your flight number after very little probing.'

'Freddie loves being probed.'

'Do you know, I got that distinct sense while I was doing it.'

A grin spread across Brigitta's face. In spite of herself, she couldn't shift it. It was just so unexpectedly lovely to see someone she had known, really, all her life and to be talking in a funny, almost intimate way as the dreary masses inside Terminal Four surged all around them.

Also, she had not been looking forward to getting the Tube to Ladbroke Grove.

'Here, give me that,' he said, taking the handle of her case. 'Car's this way.'

After he'd loaded it into the boot of a battered Fiat, Will got into the driver's seat and hesitated before starting the car. He glanced across at her, momentarily sheepish. 'Listen, if we're going to be working together, I should probably tell you that I actually used to have quite a big crush on you.'

Brigitta put a hand on his leg. 'Will. Everyone on the North Shore knew that.' She meant the gesture to be condescending, but his thigh felt firmer and warmer through his trousers than she'd expected and the sensation threw her off.

'Right. Well obviously I don't anymore.'

'Obviously,' Brigitta said, although it was not until they joined the A4 that she thought to take her hand away.

98.

I'm three fingers

It was a hot, hazy weekday afternoon and the footpath where Abi stood waiting for Jude to get out of the car was slick with decomposing frangipani flowers. Other mothers passed by as she waited, pushing strollers and coaxing older children along in the heat.

With an explosion of energy, Jude pushed his door open and sprang out, clutching his soccer ball. He let it roll down the front of his skinny brown leg, which was smeared with green paint and covered all over with a dozen penny-sized bruises, the cause of which he could never say. It rolled well ahead and he chased after it at speed.

'Carry it until we're inside, please!' Abi called. 'Jude! Don't let it go on the road.'

Sadie pulled down on Abi's hand. 'He is making a bad choice, isn't he Mummy,' she said in her hoarse little voice that, according to Stu, made her sound as though she enjoyed the occasional cheeky fag with Mum.

She looked up at Abi, unblinking.

'He is, isn't he?' Abi gazed back at her daughter. She had dark eyes, milk-white skin and waves of copper hair that Elaine continued to insist beyond reason were 'all Kellett'.

Stu decided not to tell his parents until it was too late, and they already loved her too much to take issue with her exact parentage. Abi did not want to lie, but it wasn't lying, Stu said, it was just slow-release truth.

And it had worked. Somehow, it had all worked.

'He might have to have a *cons-ne-kwens*,' Sadie said joyfully.

'Yes, he might. Shall we catch him up?'

Hand in hand, they followed after him, keeping in the shadow of the high sandstone wall, above which loomed the Victorian mansions of Annandale, carved up for flats and private offices. At intervals, the wall turned in for a wrought iron gate, and Jude disappeared into each recess, lying in wait until Abi and Sadie approached.

'Rar!'

'Mind out for people, Jude.'

'I'm scaring you, Mum! You have to go aghh!'

'Okay, aghh. But please watch where you're going.'

He tore ahead again and Abi watched as he vanished into the next alcove. A second later, he stepped out backwards, chin turned up, staring.

He took another reverse step onto the footpath and an elderly lady came out after him, glancing both ways for a parent. She was holding a large medical envelope in one hand, the other shielded her face from the sun.

Abi rushed towards her, ready to apologise for Jude. As she neared, the woman turned towards her.

'Abigail.' The rich, lilting voice sent a thrill through Abi's body. She gripped Sadie's hot little hand. 'Abi, rather.'

'Hello Phil.'

'It's been quite an age, hasn't it?'

'It has.' Tears already filled Abi's eyes and she made no attempt to blink them away.

Phil wore a washed silk blouse in the palest pink and the same amber beads, but all the thickness had gone from her middle. Her hair, still smartly bobbed, was entirely white.

Voice thick with sorrow, Phil looked down and said, 'And this must be Sadie.'

Sadie stepped out from behind Abi's skirt and tried to curl her little thumb into her palm, until four short fingers stood in a row. 'I'm three fingers.'

Phil looked at her wistfully and then said in a low voice to Abi, 'Freddie told us. After she was born.' Her eyes crinkled at the edges and their misty blue centres began to shine. 'It was decided we would stay away and let you get on.' Phil looked back to Sadie, who was still struggling to make the unneeded finger sit down. 'I always wondered if you intended the name, perhaps, to be a little message.'

'I always loved Aunt Sadie.'

'So it was then.' Phil exhaled. 'I didn't like to assume.'

Jude had appeared at Phil's side and was studying her intently. Surely, Abi thought, he doesn't remember her. But there was something so concentrated about the way he was looking at her, Abi couldn't help wonder if somewhere, very deep down, he knew her.

'Excuse me,' he said.

Phil's eyes widened in anticipation. 'Mm?'

'I just love rocks so much.'

'Well of course. There's so much to love *about* them.' Abi saw her working against a smile. 'And are you four by any chance, Jude?'

'I will be five in nineteen sleeps,' he said, 'and I'm getting Lego Rescue Helicopter and all the Lego and Batman. *Batman*!' The force of the excitement made him stand on one leg.

'It's good to see you, Phil,' Abi said. 'I am so sorry.'

'No, truly,' Phil stopped her with a hand. 'There's simply too much to be said.'

'I don't suppose you have time for a cup of tea, do you? We live just up there. If you want to. You don't have to though.'

Jude picked up Phil's hand. 'I know where our house is. It's over there, by that bird.'

Phil turned and let herself be led.

Jude struggled to open the gate by himself but did not want help.

'I hoped I would run into you again one day,' Abi said as they waited behind him. 'But I didn't think it would be over this way.'

'Yes, well, rightly,' Phil said. 'I've always found the Inner West a touch alternative. But I've a specialist here, so I'm forced over the bridge with rather frightful regularity.'

When the gate finally opened, Jude put his hand back in Phil's and walked with her up the path.

'That's my bike.'

'It looks like a very fast one.'

'It is.' Jude nodded solemnly. 'Red are always the fastest ones.'

Abi slipped past them and unlocked the door. 'We left in a bit of a rush this morning, so ignore the mess. Come in, Phil.'

99.

Crowded with incident

The cool, narrow hallway led to a bright kitchen added to the back of the terrace. Glass doors looked out onto a small square of grass, and as soon as Abi slid them open, Jude and Sadie ran outside.

Abi wiped the table with her forearm and spirited two plastic cereal bowls into the sink.

'Sit anywhere. Wherever's not sticky.'

'Well, isn't this very nice?' Phil said. 'You'd never know from the street what's inside.'

'Stu designed this bit,' Abi said. She leaned against the kitchen bench and tried to see it with Phil's eyes. It was high-ceilinged and light, gently cluttered with the colourful accessories of childhood. 'He and his dad did all the building. While we were living here, which was a bit mental, with a baby and toddler. I don't really know why we did that, now I think about it.'

Abi opened the cupboard above the kettle. 'I've got normal, Lady Grey or some herbals.'

'Whichever, dear. Anything loose.'

They fell silent as the rising whistle of the kettle made it too difficult to hear, and while Abi ran hot water into the pot and set a tray, she saw Phil turning to watch the children. They had turned on the hose and shed their clothes. Their bodies shone as they ran in small circles, laughing as the hose flailed and sprayed the doors, making the sound of small stones tossed at the glass.

'I can't quite get used to seeing you,' Abi said, sitting down. She busied herself with cups and spoons so as not to be overcome by the fact of Phil, the real person of Phil, in her very own kitchen. After Stu taught Abi to drive, she had occasionally taken herself as far as Milson Road, but only to drive past the big house, never to park and knock.

And whenever she took the children on the ferry, she would stare at the long, thin line of green water low against the harbour's edge, and try and point out the pool. But they could never see it. 'It's only trees, Mummy. Silly.'

'I find my senses somewhat overwhelmed also,' Phil said, without taking her eyes off Jude and her granddaughter.

'How have things been?' Abi asked.

'Ah. Well.' Phil returned her attention to Abi. 'What's the lovely Lady Bracknell line? It's been "crowded with incident". Indeed. Age is a bugger. Very little to recommend it. I haven't been especially well but ... goodness, I sound like Noel!' Phil reached out and put a hand on Abi's arm. 'Who is fighting fit, you'll be pleased to know.'

'Noel! Oh gosh!'

'Barb and Sandy moved off the Point a while ago, to a sort of community in the Southern Highlands. Like-minded, you might say. They took Domenica Regina with them, at my behest. I imagine the poor animal's had to withstand another name change. Vita Sackville-West, the *bichon frise*.'

'And Valentina?'

'Ah yes, well, she became so disconsolate after her son moved out, she booked a cruise and never got off. Our Lady of the Perpetual P&O. You can't imagine how very quiet it's been, Abi.' Phil shifted in her seat. 'I should say, I found your letter dear. In a

cupboard I was doing out long after our *annus horribilis*. I did intend
to respond.'

She inspected the back of a liver-marked hand. 'Although of
course, I never did. We all look back on it as the most dreadful year
of our lives, Abi. But in many ways, you and Jude were the currant
in my cake. I apologise now, for every bit of awfulness. You were
much wronged. By all the Woolnoughs.'

Abi bit her lip. 'How is everyone?'

Phil looked again at Sadie, who was trying to do a forward roll
and listing sideways every time. 'Polly finally made partner, which
seemed to give her a measure of psychic relief. She talks of coming
home but I'm not stringing up the bunting quite yet. Mark remains
utterly unchanged, a rock, you know. The boys are giants. Toby has
lost his thistle and we continue to mourn it.' She smiled dolefully
and continued.

'Brigitta found a chap. They're having a baby after Christmas.'
Like Phil of always, her voice dropped to a whisper, warm and
conspiratorial, and she touched Abi's hand. 'Although not married
I might say. He's also in *the arts*, so I expect they'll lumber the poor
dot with some invention of a surname. They're still in London.
And –' It was clear that Phil would have chosen to stop there, but
she took a breath and plunged on. 'And Freddie is – Freddie is
very much still Freddie. He met a girl of some South American
extraction, shortly after … well, you know.'

Phil looked drawn. 'Abi, I did want him to do the right thing by
you. Or at least by Sadie, but of course, he's never had a vigorous
sense of duty and I let myself be talked out of it. Much too easily, I
can see now. I really believe I fell into some sort of fugue state after
losing Fred, but again, that's no excuse.'

In all the time that Abi had lived with her own singular guilt,
she'd never thought to consider whether Phil would carry a burden
of her own.

'It's all right,' Abi said. 'It's okay. It's better this way. For Sadie, and for Stu as well.'

'She is legally adopted as I understand it. Polly explained it all at the time, but I refused to be shown the papers. I have felt wretched about it every day since, Abi. Truly wretched.'

Phil's shoulders slumped. She was a hollowed-out version of herself, and Abi longed for the old Phil to come back.

'It was Stu's idea, Phil, the adoption. I was grateful that Freddie agreed to it. And Kelletts always do the right thing, so –'

'I'm glad someone has done right by you, Abi. We Woolnoughs all turned out to be so criminally disappointing.' She smiled wanly and let her eyes wander around the kitchen again. On one wall Abi had made an arrangement of family photographs and children's drawings. In the centre hung a study of nasturtiums.

'You've created rather an idyll.' An aeroplane passed low overhead and Phil paused until the noise died away. 'If rather an *urban* one.'

'After my mother died ...' Abi stopped short, the force of an old habit. But Phil had read the letter. She knew the whole story of Rae, yet here she was. 'She died a few days after I took Jude back to London. Which is a bit ironic, I suppose, but at the time it seemed so unfair.' Abi began fiddling with the tea things again. 'I think she would have been pleased that her house helped us get this.'

'Well, I'm very glad you've found your own corner of the world. Relieved in fact, after the way my lot put the mockers on your previous arrangement.'

Abi looked momentarily confused.

'Ah. I thought you would know about that. It was Polly and Mark, in fact, who offered Stuart's parents the really ludicrous sum for their flat.'

'Oh, right. No, they never told us.'

'Mark will have done it through a trust, so perhaps they themselves didn't know. It was sold on fairly quickly, at my behest, because looking up at your windows, well, you can imagine my chagrin.'

'That's okay,' Abi said as it all fitted together like the pieces of a broken plate. 'It doesn't matter. I couldn't have gone back there anyway, and Elaine was never happier. She got an even bigger conservatory out of it.'

'The dear *Brush*,' Phil said, clasping her hands together. The layered rings on her wedding finger dropped away from the atrophied knuckle with a faint clink. 'I'm sure it's rammed with Lladro, is it, or must it be kept out of direct sun?'

They laughed in mutual relief. There was always the Brush.

'And we're happier here anyway. Phil, I did an arts degree, would you believe? I turned into a finisher.' She stood up and took a thick folder out of a sliding cupboard.

'I did English, with a bit of creative writing. You gave me such a taste for it, with that Fictive Self, do you remember? I went back as soon as I could.' She slid the binder towards Phil, who opened it to the first page.

'This is a work of fiction, is it?'

'Well technically. I suppose. Although really I just changed all the names. My tutor said he'll put it up for an anthology if I do a bit more work on it, because it's still too sad in places.'

'Well, if you've told the truth, I expect that could have been the title.'

'*Too Sad in Places*, by Abi Egan. It was for you, of course. I wrote it for you, and my mum.'

Phil reached into her bag. And while Abi watched and the children hollered outside, and a twisting ribbon of steam rose from the teapot and coiled up towards the skylight, Phil drew out a pen and wrote at the very top of the page in her lovely looping script, 'P. Woolnough, Annandale, December 4th, 2015, having just found Abi.'

'Now,' she said, folding her hands on top of the typed pages, 'will we pour that tea before it stews?'

Abi turned the pot by its handle so it faced Phil.

'No, no,' Phil said, turning it back. 'You be mother.'

100.

It means we have made it

In the last months of Phil's life, Abi visited nearly every day and helped her out to the garden, where they sat side by side on the wicker chairs and watched Sadie play on the grass that sloped away to the harbour. Jude had started school and the little girl occupied herself by rolling down the hill until she was covered in grass clippings and too dizzy to stand up. Abi stayed at Phil's side, filling in the crossword or reading out loud all of that year's Booker. Set in a village, but no mango tree. 'Thank heavens for small mercies.'

'Gradually, then quickly,' Phil said of her decline. 'Like that ruddy Hemingway says a person loses their fortune, do you remember? Gradually, then quickly.'

Sometimes, Abi managed to get the three of them down to the pool, Sadie streaking ahead with her goggles already on like flying glasses, and Phil making her way carefully along the winding path, leaning on Abi's arm. 'All right, Mrs Woolnough? Mind your step,' Abi said once, to be swatted with a rolled *New Yorker*.

Phil never swam anymore, but she seemed happiest on those days, with her face shaded by the enormous sunhat and a breeze mussing up the harbour. 'Ferry!' Sadie shouted, every time she saw one. 'What one is it called, Mum?'

It was usually the *Friendship*.

Brigitta came out to show her mother the baby, a plump, black-haired boy they had called James, which pleased Phil immensely, both as a memorial and because she'd been bracing herself for something much more theatrical. 'Benvolio Binney-Woolnough would be *such* a cross to bear.'

Polly came and went as often as she could, but it was Brigitta who went upstairs to check on their mother when she didn't come down for breakfast one warm, clear September morning.

The family gathered for a private memorial in the Bible Garden at Palm Beach. Abi had not expected an invitation, but one duly came and when she arrived there on a blustery Friday morning, she was directed to a reserved seat in the front row. Polly had done the seating.

Freddie arrived halfway through 'It is Well with My Soul', forcing the hasty addition of a folding chair at the farthest end of the row, beside Mark. Abi looked towards the commotion and turned back quickly, still catching the look of deep resignation which passed between the sisters, as Mark handed Freddie an order of service already opened to the right page.

Abi stared resolutely ahead, listening to the words. 'When peace, like a river, attendeth my way, when sorrows like sea billows roll ...' She had no wish to talk to him, to have her presence there force him to an awkward apology. Worse, to see traces of her daughter's face in his, when Sadie's energy and mad passions, her intense if fleeting attentions, had come to seem so much like Stu's. She was a child entirely able to defy biology. 'Whatever my lot, Thou hast taught me to say, it is well, it is well with my soul.'

As soon as the service was over, Abi left without saying proper goodbyes, although Brigitta, then Polly, waved warmly from where they were cornered in conversation with Noel *et al.* 'A French exit, dear, is what that's called. The only sort in my book,' Phil had said once. 'Why must things be allowed to drag on?' Abi smiled to

herself as she paused at the bottom of the narrow rock staircase back
to the road to remove her heels. Then, from a short distance away,
she heard Freddie call out.

Abi squared her shoulders and turned as he took the final steps
towards her. He held out his hand. For once, no golden grin.

'I hope you are well,' he said, shaking, then holding onto, her
hand. 'And your children. I hope she ... *they*, I should say, I hope
they are very, very well.'

* * *

Brigitta stayed on in Sydney for some weeks, and together she
and Abi packed up the big house. The rugs were rolled away, the
pictures and china wrapped for storage. Polly and Mark had decided
to move back and take over the big house before the start of the
next school year. 'I will do Dad's wardrobe then,' she told Polly on
a late night call. It turned out Phil had never quite got around to it.
'She always was a terrific rester,' Brigitta said, reducing them both
to tears.

On her last day, Brigitta asked Abi to help with the books.

'You should take one of these,' she called down from the
stepladder, holding a faded paperback in each hand. 'What do you
prefer? *Pursuit of Love* or *Cold Climate*?'

Abi was stacking le Carrés into a box labelled 'Crime and Misc'.
'Whichever one you don't want. I don't mind.'

'Between you and me, I never finished either.' Brigitta tossed
one down. 'I expect I will now.'

* * *

After Brigitta had gone, Abi closed up the big house, locking
windows, drawing curtains and hiding the key for Polly. Before

bolting the French doors, Abi stepped out onto Phil's patio and breathed in the sweet honey-scent of wattle that hung in the air. She glanced up at her old window, and back at the harbour, violet under a darkening sky. 'That, Phil, is wattle. And it means we have made it. Or near enough.'

Acknowledgements

My thanks to Catherine Milne, James Kellow, Libby O'Donnell and the faithful team at HarperCollins. To Ceri David and Justine Irons, kindest first readers, and Anne Spackman and Tomaso Capuano, who gave me the best possible start as a writer. And to Federico Andornino, Virginia Woolstencroft, Lynsey Sutherland, Paul Stark, Kate Moreton, Claire Keep, Esther Waters and everyone at Weidenfeld & Nicolson, as well as Claire Conrad Paterson, Marya Spence, and Lucinda Prain.

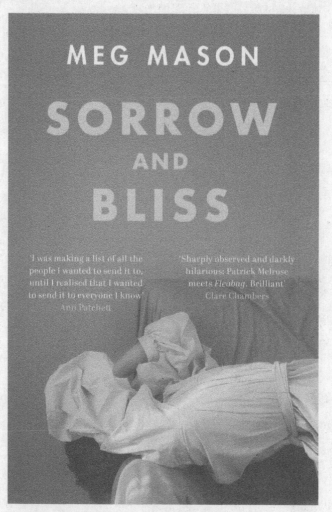

MEG MASON

SORROW

AND

BLISS

'I was making a list of all the
people I wanted to send it to,
until I realised that I wanted
to send it to everyone I know'
Ann Patchett

'Sharply observed and darkly
hilarious: Patrick Melrose
meets *Fleabag*. Brilliant'
Clare Chambers

'*Sorrow and Bliss* is a brilliantly faceted and extremely funny
book about depression that engulfed me in the way I'm always
hoping to be to be engulfed by novels. While I was reading
it, I was making a list of all the people I wanted to send it to,
until I realized that I wanted to send it to everyone I know'

Ann Patchett